THE
GRIEF
DOCTOR

THE GRIEF DOCTOR

JACK ANDERSON

RAVEN BOOKS

LONDON · OXFORD · NEW YORK · NEW DELHI · SYDNEY

RAVEN BOOKS
Bloomsbury Publishing Plc
50 Bedford Square, London, WC1B 3DP, UK
29 Earlsfort Terrace, Dublin 2, Ireland

BLOOMSBURY, RAVEN BOOKS and the Raven Books logo
are trademarks of Bloomsbury Publishing Plc

First published in Great Britain 2024

A catalogue record for this book is available from the British Library

ISBN: HB: 978-1-5266-6754-0; TPB: 978-1-5266-6752-6;
EBOOK: 978-1-5266-6750-2; EPDF: 978-1-5266-6753-3

2 4 6 8 10 9 7 5 3 1

Typeset by Integra Software Services Pvt. Ltd.
Printed and bound in Great Britain by CPI Group (UK) Ltd, Croydon CR0 4YY

To find out more about our authors and books visit www.bloomsbury.com
and sign up for our newsletters

To my parents, who set me on my path,
and to my wife, who walks beside me

I

Anyway, they asked me to write something.

Nothing ground-breaking, the doctor said, no need for poetry or intricate prose. Just an honest account of the day in question, summarised in my own words and, crucially, in my own time.

I told myself it would be simple, objective even. Settling down with a notepad and a ballpoint pen, I envisioned a dispassionate bullet-pointed list of events. An incident report, similar to those I conduct for work, requiring one sheet of paper and half an hour at most.

This document will constitute my seventh attempt. Three hours at my back, eight scrawl-covered pages on the floor beside me. I realise now I've picked a fight with something much bigger than myself, an entity I'd hoped had grown smaller over time, but which was actually just further away. Walking back to confront it once again, I've been rudely reminded of its true stature, each new attempt leaving me beaten, bewildered and with no one to blame but myself.

It was only a few minutes ago, on the brink of giving up entirely, that a new approach suddenly occurred to me. It came from nowhere, an unexpected glimmer of magic in a witch's brew of bafflement and desperation, hinting that one more ingredient might turn the concoction clear.

Even more unexpectedly, it seems to have worked, its effects emboldening and immediate.

I can already feel my pen gliding where it previously stumbled. A sense of cohesion and understanding, tracks rising up to meet the train.

The difference between this and my six failed entries? This is the only time I've written directly to you.

I hate talking about myself. Dull events relayed by an equally dull narrator. Yet whenever you would greet me in the evening, whenever you'd ask about my day, I'd watch you listen with this pure and gracious attention, as if I were somehow as intriguing to you as you always were to me. You made my emptiest days feel like a story, and somehow, through the sheer miracle of your presence, like a story worth telling.

I suppose it begins with a square of yellow paper.

You know the one.

It looks down at me, as the clock ticks round to midnight on 7 June, from the mantelpiece of our apartment. I sit beneath its strange gravity, as I do most evenings, shoulders hunched, breath rattling, eyes moist and red and upturned towards it.

I mustn't reach up, yet I can't bring myself to turn away; an ugly stalemate that leaves me pinned to our living room sofa, staring, resentful and alone.

I remain in this state until escape eventually finds me, drawing me onto the cool Italian leather and delivering me, gratefully, into the first overtures of sleep.

A moment later, I'm 500 miles away.

The air is crisp and cool. A light breeze sighs contentedly across my neck and forearms, the waters of Lake Annecy lapping against the hull of a small training boat. I'm gazing upward to a heavenly fresco of deep blue sky and majestic clouds. The white canvas of the mainsail flutters erratically, a hopeless romantic, sampling each fleeting gust on its search for something more long-term.

'Do you remember what you said?' a voice queries. 'When I told you I never learned how to sail?'

I let out a long breath and let my gaze fall, leaving the sky behind as I drift down the mast. My eyes finally meet yours, smirking back at me from the bow as you answer your own question.

'You said my parents *failed me*.'

'My god.' I half laugh, half cringe at my adolescent blunders. 'And that didn't make you run for the hills?'

'Oh no, it did the opposite. It put me on a *crusade* to educate you.'

'Interesting.' I laugh. 'And how did that go for you?'

'Oh, god knows.' You chuckle, shaking your head. 'Ask me when I'm done.'

I push the tiller as we tack gently starboard, turning through the wind until the sail finally catches. It had taken me weeks to get everything in place at work, just so I could negotiate these few precious days off. I'd slept at the office most nights, a drawer full of shirts and a calendar of 9 p.m. meetings, dreaming of the day when we would pack our bags and journey to the shores of Annecy together, the day it would all seem worth it.

'How was the farm?' I ask, as you turn back from the front sail to face me.

'Here?' You chuckle, gesturing to the scenery. 'That's what you want to talk about?'

'Yeah. What was your last day like?'

'Well ...' You begin tentatively. 'We had two schools in. We did pottery and painting with them. But some of them wanted to try beekeeping! I was floored – I mean, you'd think the kids would be scared of beehives, but I think half the time we project that onto them. They clearly find them fascinating. The colonies, the mini society. I said we should have a volunteer hive for under-fifteens. Carol shot it down of course ...'

'We don't like Carol, do we?'

'We hate Carol. Carol's the one who doesn't let her kid do gymnastics.'

'Yep, I remember now.'

'Anyway, that's by the by, the point is ...'

I settle in and watch you talk, basking in every idiosyncrasy. How you karate-chop your palm to punctuate your statements. How you advocate for people you've known for less than five minutes. The fractal blossoming of tangents upon tangents until the day's events form a rich and boundless tapestry.

Amid these moments, arriving without sadness or distress, a gentle reminder comes to me: we never made it to Annecy. We got too busy and pushed it back a year, turning calendar pages through days you'd never see.

As soon as this realisation arrives, I can feel myself starting to wake up.

In the last fleeting moments, I focus on you entirely. A living, breathing vision of that wry, victorious smile, that shock of untameable hair, the eyes so genuine and joyful that they do more than simply express happiness, but somehow feel like its very source.

I look at you, and I love you as much as I ever did.

Dawn breaks through the venetian blinds as I launch up from our living room sofa. Breathless, heart thudding, synaptic fireworks cascading beneath my skull, I cling with boundless gratitude to every facet of the dream, basking in a preoccupying swell of joy.

As I jump to my feet, my eyes pass over the square of yellow paper on the mantle, its edges measuring twelve inches on each side. I've practically lived beneath it for the past eight months, mournful and obsessive. Yet, as I relive the notes and phrases of our conversation, I scarcely feel the need to glance in its direction at all.

'Arthur?'

I hear my name, and realise I've been daydreaming.

I've been like this since I woke up. A happy, heady state that accompanied me as I showered, dressed and drove to my therapist's office. I feel the same even now, staring out her second-floor window, and across the copy/paste white houses of Belgravia.

I casually turn back towards the voice, considering whether I should have given today's appointment a miss.

'You're smiling,' Dr Dunn comments, noting the admittedly noteworthy.

'It was …' I clamour for the right words. 'I mean, it was amazing! I saw her, I talked to her, and it all felt real! I remember it so clearly. She felt like she was really …'

I stop talking, sensing a quiet caution behind my therapist's measured smile, as if my happiness were something she acknowledges but doesn't entirely share.

'This is a good thing, right?' I query, unsure how it could be anything else.

'No, it is.' Dr Dunn soothes tactfully, picking her words with the care and attention of someone navigating stepping stones. 'Seeing Julia again, it's a beautiful thing. I'm overjoyed for you. I just want to make sure we prepare ourselves. You're on a high right now, and that's wonderful. But our ultimate goal isn't height, it's level. This is a big, sudden shift and, well, I just don't want you to get overwhelmed.'

I stare at her from the sofa, non-plussed. I wonder how she can possibly say such a thing. After witnessing eight hollow months of unmitigated misery, to advocate temperance in the face of joy seems almost ludicrous.

'I'll be fine,' I comment, surprised at the sharpness that creeps into my tone.

'All right, well …' Dr Dunn continues diplomatically. 'Can I ask what you spoke about?'

I gladly sink back into the memory, eager at the chance to replay our conversation. Yet, despite it still being the same morning, I find myself grappling with the ephemeral dream more than I did previously. Aspects of our conversation slip through my fingers, some retrievable, some passing beyond the edges of my recollection.

'Nothing much.' I smile, warmly, over a sudden rush of terror. 'That wasn't the point.'

Two hours later, I'm scrawling into an office notebook, head down, shoulders hunched, compelled to record every word that passed between us, the timbre of our conversation, everything I saw and felt.

It's only got worse since the car picked me up from Dr Dunn's office and ferried me directly into work. I've spent the rest of my morning spinning operational plates while simultaneously fighting to keep our fleeting reunion in mind. A maddening feedback loop quickly developed: my tasks interrupted by thoughts of you, thoughts of you interrupted by the sound of smashing china.

I fight to get it all down on paper, all the while cursing my idiocy. Why didn't I write this down earlier? What did I think was going to happen?

'Arthur?'

I look up to find twenty people in suits staring back at me.

I'm in the afternoon meeting. A grey boardroom that smells of new carpet and whiteboard markers. A woman in a tailored blazer stands at the head of a long table, waiting for me to answer a question I never heard her ask.

I stammer pitifully, scouring the room for any possible clues, finding nothing more than a set of indecipherable charts and a justifiable flash of irritation.

'As I was saying,' the woman pointedly continues.

I shrink down in my chair, cheeks burning, averting my eyes towards the Canary Wharf skyline. A few faces flash my way, some compassionate, some contemptuous, the ratio between the two shifting to the latter with every passing week.

One of them glances down towards my notebook, and I instinctively draw it towards myself, looking down to observe the mad scrawls with shame and embarrassment. To my credit, I think I've done it, a comprehensive breakdown of our final conversation, yet, as I stare at each statement and reply, all I see are words on a page.

The evening closes in without my notice. Requisition forms, invoices and work orders pass across my desk with focussed regularity until there's nothing left of the day.

The dream remains, in some form or other – nostalgic embers steadily cooling in the cavern of my soul.

I wonder what it will be like, when its warmth is extinguished completely, and I am forced to reconcile our brief reunion with the open expanse of my inevitable future. I watch as my computer screen fades to black, searching for any reason to start it up again. When I discover I don't have one, an eerie calm comes over me, and I cease wondering entirely.

Night falls as I drift back home; a steady, comfortable walk that ends when I reach my mantle.

I stand before that square of yellow paper and, with steadier breath than I would have imagined, I take it from its place.

With incredible delicacy, I lift out a single vinyl LP. A central label, embellished with swirling black marker, displays the title: *A Song for Arthur.*

I lift the dusty lid from our automatic turntable and place the record on the spindle, a calm washing over me as I set the needle on the outside edge and hear the first soft crackles rise from the stereo.

Just when I was starting to forget your voice.

Hey honey! Ok you said you wanted it recorded so ... I've recorded it! Happy birthday! Don't show this to any music producers, Ok? Ok ...

The tentative strums of a ukulele echo from the speakers, building into the first unsteady chords of a song. I drink in the sound, turning up the dial until the melody washes across every corner of the room.

When a gunmetal sky's at your window,
And the dusk looks the same as the dawn,
And the far-reaching, heart-seeking tether that binds us together feels
*   weathered and torn*

I embrace a sense of calm resolution and push myself over to the kitchen cabinets, extracting a bottle of aged whisky and a glass tumbler. I twist off the cap and let the amber liquid fall freely into the glass, my hand shaking only slightly as the tumbler fills halfway.

> *When you feel like a shade of a shadow,*
> *And I feel like a voice on the phone,*
> *And life at its best is just test after test that you're destined to go*
>   *through alone.*

I rummage through our kitchen drawers, withdrawing an unopened box of pills, popping the blister pack until each capsule clatters onto the marble countertop.

I tell myself that it makes sense, that this is as close to you as I'll ever be.

You sing the chorus to me from across the room.

> *When the city's cold symmetry spans for infinity, you can call out*
>   *to me,*
> *I will find you and somehow remind you, we're seventy miles from*
>   *the sea,*
> *We're seventy miles from the sea, my love,*
> *Seventy miles from the—*

I wake up in the shower, sitting half-naked under a torrent of water, legs pulled up to my chest.

A huge chunk of the porcelain sink is broken off. A sterling silver salt grinder lies in two pieces, its cap dented, half its contents spilled out over the floor. A glass tumbler lies shattered in a pool of vomit and salt water.

A cordless landline phone rests on the toilet cistern, one missed call glaring at me.

I can just about hear your LP starting up again, muffled melodies from the living room as footsteps barrel up the stairway outside. I hear the front door splinter, people forcing their way into our home.

I manage to yelp that there's glass on the floor, before I sink to one side. My head rests against the edge of the shower, shoulders hunched, breath rattling, my eyes moist and red.

The water shuts off above me, the white noise cutting out, your voice reaching me through the dark, echoing apartment.

We're seventy miles from the sea, myyy love …
Seventy miles from the sea.

12th August

2

'So, what comes next? Well, environmental salvage was, of course, the matter of primary concern. Now that our legal obligations have largely been met, we've contracted an independent surveyor to assess the mid- to long-term requirements for the *Ardour's* eventual recovery. Next slide, please, Martin? Thank you.'

It's a slow business day in Meeting Room B as we discuss the ongoing salvage of the *Ardour*.

A frisson of animated whispers passed around the office when sensor data from a nearby oil rig indicated a 'rogue well' was responsible for the vessel's fate. Such phenomena are almost impossibly rare in the world of international shipping, with the *Ardour* being one of only a handful of ships to have had a confirmed encounter.

Where a rogue wave can reach upward of eighty feet in height, rogue wells constitute the exact opposite, taking the form of a sudden lurching drop, many times deeper than the wave crests they hide between. Almost invisible on a stormy sea, the well that took down the *Ardour* would have been practically indiscernible until the ship's bow suddenly lurched downward, the daylight closing up above the heads of its crew.

In my private moments, I find my thoughts lingering on those people, their bewilderment, the harrowing dread they must have felt. In a professional capacity, however, I'm more readily encouraged to mourn the cargo.

Projected slides of recent salvage wash over me, as a young woman in a tailored suit describes their contents in detail.

Myra Stewart-Mill stands at the head of the table, her hair tied up in a tight bun, gesturing to images of damaged freight with precise, confident movements. Despite being five years my junior at the company, it's no secret that she covets my position with an enthusiasm I only wish I possessed myself. She'd voluntarily covered my role while I was on leave and, in my more recent absence, was in talks to take on my duties full-time.

I must seem like a bad penny.

'Some consignments have been located on the ocean floor over fifty miles from the site itself,' Myra comments over a grainy aerial photograph. 'Which does indicate the need for an expanded search radius if we're to recover everything. However, on a positive note, early examinations indicate that most of these consignments are still intact, so it wouldn't be a wasted effort for us to—'

A perfunctory knock raps lightly against the meeting room's glass door. Without waiting for a response, an older woman tilts her head over the threshold.

Her hair is set in neatly styled salt and pepper waves, her calm expression underpinned by a set of piercing blue eyes, which lend a youthful intensity to a gracefully ageing face. She's dressed in an expensive blue coat, a leather handbag on her arm, as if our meeting were merely a brief stop on her way out of the building.

'I'm afraid I need to speak to Arthur.' She smiles, warmly but unapologetically, towards the room. 'Are you almost done?'

'Of course.' Myra shuffles her papers, understanding this is more an instruction than a query. If she's annoyed at the interruption, she hides it well.

'Just before we finish up.' A voice interjects, causing everyone's eyes to snap left. One of the department heads – a brash, overgrown Etonian, with the build of a rugby player and the accent of a Cambridge rowing captain – addresses me personally. 'I just wanted to say, Arthur, I know it's your first week back in the office and, well, I think I speak for all of us when I say welcome back and … well done, mate. Well done.'

He ventures into a booming clap, which falters quickly when no one else deigns to join in. The beats slowly taper off, the man lowering his hands back onto the desk.

'Ok, well,' Ms Stewart-Mill continues, 'I think we're going to need another meeting on this, but I realise people have places to be. Martin, will you send an email round and schedule something?'

A smattering of nods and availabilities flutter around the room, the woman in blue wandering inside as people make their staggered, respectful departures. She places herself by the floor-to-ceiling window, looking down on Canary Wharf as she waits for the space to empty behind her.

When the door finally closes, I stand up to join her.

'I haven't got long,' I remind her, tentatively approaching the window. 'I have Dr Dunn at one o'clock.'

'I'm so silly, you know,' she muses, ignoring my statement entirely. 'Why on earth didn't I get an office on *this* side of the building?'

'I'd have thought CEOs could switch offices whenever they want.'

'No. No, it would be vanity.' She waves the suggestion away. 'But I love that you can see our old building from here. Look there. Can you see it?'

She points against the glass, an invisible line which only really tracks from her perspective.

Fortunately, though I'd never set foot inside myself, Daubney House had been pointed out to me numerous times throughout my life, allowing me to easily discern the 1970s office block from its surroundings on the opposite bank of the Thames. Hunched between two larger, more recently renovated offices, Daubney House looks like a smoker's lung: the once red-brick frontage stained black by pollution, its windows an unseemly bile yellow.

'Your grandfather took us to visit it when I was … ooh, I would've been seven years old? We couldn't believe he owned the whole three-storey office. I remember playing on the roof, me and your uncle. We thought we were on top of the world.'

She turns away from Daubney House, taking in our current surroundings with renewed perspective.

'Look at us now.' She exalts the sight, eyes gleaming. 'Thirty-three storeys, middle of Canary Wharf, offices in six countries and another on the way. Seeing where we started helps me appreciate it, don't you agree?'

Her statement's a little misleading. We're still technically a three-storey office; the thirty floors below us belong to other FTSE 100 companies. I decide not to split hairs. In fact, as I look at the tempered glass before us, a different subject entirely comes to mind.

'Did you know they sealed my windows shut?'

She looks back towards Daubney House, somewhat more actively than she had a second ago.

'Mum ... my office windows, did you know that they—'

'Yes. They told me.'

'So ... what, were they worried if I could get them open, I'd—'

'It was just for safety, that's all. The board decided.' My mother marches briskly through the sentence, trying to move on from the topic as quickly as possible. She turns back to me, employing a practised smile to force a change of subject. 'I've booked us lunch at the Chantrey! It's been a while since we went there, hasn't it?'

'Oh wow, we've not been there in ... wait ...' My reflection and I both grimace. 'That's not why you cut the meeting short, is it?'

'That's right,' Mum remarks casually, her expression darkening when I let loose an exasperated sigh. 'Oh, what is it now?' She matches my frustration. 'I thought you loved the Chantrey.'

'No, I do ... I appreciate it but ...' I scramble for the words. 'Mum ... I'm trying to rebuild something with these people. Foster mutual respect. It doesn't help if the CEO's shutting down meetings to take her son out for lunch.'

'I'm taking the *Senior Director of Operations* out for lunch.' She states this matter-of-factly, reminding me of a title that I sometimes can't believe I still hold. 'It'll just be an hour or two. Anyway, the car's already outside.'

Mum begins to walk away from the window, considering the matter closed. I turn away from the city, my brow furrowing.

'You want us to go now? I can't. I have my session with Dr Dunn at one. I'm heading out in five minutes.'

'Oh, don't worry about that, I pushed it to six.' My mother holds the glass door open with unhurried nonchalance. 'You have plenty of time.'

For the past 160 years, the Chantrey has held residence in the southernmost edge of Regent Street, just as the thoroughfare branches off from Piccadilly and begins its languorous journey towards Oxford Circus.

The second-floor restaurant is easily recognisable by its famous demilune windows: semi-circles of ornate stained glass which overlook the street with the air of a doting grandfather.

The restaurant had managed to achieve that curious inflection point, having survived for so long that its age was suddenly an attraction in itself. Often referred to as a 'British institution', the Chantrey's continued survival had somehow become conflated with the preservation of classical Brittania, its ownership passing like a torch to some rich benefactor whenever it looked like its doors may close. Consequently, while similar establishments would rise and fall around it, the Chantrey had managed to outlive them all: simply too old to be allowed to die.

I do sometimes wonder how the Chantrey itself feels about this.

'Welcome back, Ms Mason! And Arthur! How are you today?' Carvel, the Chantrey's long-time manager, beams at our arrival, straightening up from behind an ornate wooden desk. 'Let's get you sat down, shall we?'

We're led through the ancient dining area, which smells like an old library and seems to have been constructed from three primary materials. The walls are a Victorian coat of white plaster. The support beams, floorboards and most of the furniture are constructed from the same lacquered wood. The final element is a dark green leather, the signature colour of the Chantrey, which upholsters the entire restaurant, from its seating to its dividers.

It hasn't changed at all since I was last here, which, for the clientele who can afford to dine here regularly, is undoubtedly the point. Change is a worrying spectre to those of good fortune; the Chantrey's consistency peddling a calming implication that some empires never truly fall.

'Everyone's so overjoyed to have you back.'

My mother's comment arrives out of the blue. For the past thirty minutes, our entire conversation has been work focussed – operational talk which, while not wholly unpleasant, doesn't feel like it warrants a high-end lunch to hammer out.

'Well, maybe not everyone,' I remark. 'I'm sure some people were hoping for a vacancy in Operations.'

'Oh, don't talk like that, of course they're happy to see you,' Mother scolds sharply.

We go back to our plates, lost in the liminal space between two conversations.

My mother has always wielded these moments effectively. There was often a beat of quiet before she spoke, as if the conversational tide had to recede before her own opinion could roll across the room.

I wait a moment, for some confident directive to finally arrive, then a moment more.

Almost a minute passes before I realise I may have misdiagnosed her silence.

She glances back down at her plate, focussed on a slab of pan-fried Cornish turbot, pressing the knife delicately as if fearing the blade might shatter.

It's only once she takes the first half-hearted bite that I realise what's happening. This meeting is about you, about the last two months. It's a subject my mother tiptoes around endlessly, out of fear for her son's fragile psyche.

I was half right, she's worried *something* will break if she pushes too hard, but it's not the cutlery.

'Well …' I offer a conversational branch, 'I'm just happy to get back to work.'

Mum nods quietly to herself, returning to her food.

'And how is Dr Dunn? Is she … all right?'

'Yeah, she's been great actually.'

'Well, just as long as she's doing what we pay her for,' Mum chides icily. 'You know Martha Fry-Martin sends her daughter there and that girl's still the biggest kleptomaniac this side of—'

'Mum.' I interrupt firmly, heading off the brewing storm of anti-Dunn rhetoric, a recent but already notable pastime of my mother's. 'Why are we here? There must be a reason beyond fried talbot and pheasant risotto, surely.'

A sea change occurs before me, my mother's features sinking in quiet consideration of the inevitable, a topic she can't avoid any longer.

'I want to show you something. Something important,' she asserts, the slightest ring of nervousness in her voice. 'I don't want you to dismiss it out of hand, I want you to give it proper consideration … for my sake … all right?'

I meet my mother's gaze: the concern written in the wrinkles of her brow, the glimmer of wounded hope in her cold blue eyes. It's the same expression I witnessed when I woke up in a hospital bed two months ago. It was, in fact, the very first thing I saw.

'All right.'

My mother pauses a moment, considering the sincerity of my response, before swinging into action.

She swoops down to the leather bag beside her chair, extracting a large A4 folder, a few shades off Chatsworth blue.

Straightening back up in her chair, my mother holds the document out to me, saying nothing at all as it hangs over our half-empty plates. The folder looks heavier in her hand than its meagre contents should allow. A palpable shudder of trepidation and excitement crosses the table, as if this were the climax to a process I had no idea was in motion.

I set down my knife and fork, reach out and take it from her.

19

There *is* a confident weight to it: heavy, silk cardstock with a matte laminate, professional but not ostentatious. Upon closer examination, the folder's dark blue colour is actually a photograph: a high-definition stretch of open ocean, its gentle waves taking up the entire front and back cover. Though I have no way of knowing for certain, something about the water looks decidedly British. Pleasant as it admittedly appears, it lacks the deep blue vibrancy of the Mediterranean; a sense of bracing cold radiates from its depths.

At the centre of the front cover, interrupting the calm seascape, is a single, almost perfectly circular island. A solitary green land-mass which just barely peaks above sea level, scarcely half a mile wide at any point.

At its southern edge, a large wooden boathouse stretches out into the ocean. From there, a thin footpath rises on a slight incline away from the shore, passing lush green lawns, through a curated circular garden, and finally terminating at the island's central building.

At least I think it's a building.

Viewed from above, the verdant greenery gives way to a vast, three-storey block of solid concrete. A perfect cube of obstinate grey cement. There are no visual clues as to the grim structure's purpose. Instead, the answer to its function lies in the final detail on the cover – a title, written in clean, modern font:

The Elizabeth Codelle Institute – Therapeutic Rehabilitation Centre
A Place Free of Judgement ... For a Life Free of Pain

3

I glance up at my mother to find her examining my expression with rapt attention.

'What is this?' I ask neutrally, peeling at an adhesive seal that holds the brochure closed.

'It was passed on to me by Sang-Min Han – he was at Ascot, and he heard about your … well, about Julia, and he got in touch with my office about it.' Mum smiles awkwardly, nervous about misstepping. 'This Codelle woman, she's a psychiatrist—'

'I already have a psychiatrist.'

Mum bites her tongue, suppressing the urge to criticise Dr Dunn any further.

'Well … I can assure you. This "Dr Codelle" is … she's extraordinary. I mean, truly *extraordinary*.' Mum shakes her head, as if in total disbelief. 'Youngest ever graduate from the Karolinska Institute in Stockholm. Lectured at Oxford before she was twenty-five. She ran a leading psychiatric practice in LA where she was given the John Bright Fellow Award! Usually, it's only bestowed following *a lifetime of significant contribution to the field of psychology*. She's only thirty-six!'

'So you're looking to adopt her?'

'Don't be silly.' Mum stares at me pointedly. 'The fact is, Arthur, she's considered a revelation in the psychiatric world. Far and away the best that they've ever seen, and a few years ago she opened an independent practice in the UK.'

The adhesive seal pulls away, the brochure falling open to reveal a set of promotional materials. Photographs of the strange building's interior, and one taken from the gardens: grass, sea, a warm sun rising over a distant mainland.

'So, the hospital's on an island?'

'It's a private wellness retreat,' my mother corrects me. 'But yes, it's off the coast of Wales … it's meant to be very relaxing.' She takes another sip of her wine, though I can feel her continuing to scan my expression with an almost intrusive intensity. In response, I escape deeper into the folder's various materials.

A four-page pamphlet illustrates a wide variety of high-end amenities. A swimming pool encased in a room of white marble, a gymnasium, a salt sauna, a games room complete with billiards, table tennis and darts.

'And I suppose she specialises in … what, grief counselling?'

'Exactly.' Mum beams. 'It's just *one* of her specialties. Of course, Sang-Min went to her for—'

'How much?'

I hear my mother's breath catch in her throat, prompting me to look up. Suddenly, I find myself reading *her* expression. She quickly collects herself, but her smile feels cosmetic, as if she's hoping to charm her way out of an answer.

'That's not for you to worry about.' She squirms.

'No. Mum. Seriously.' I stare across the table. 'You want me to visit this place, right? How much would it cost?'

The woman before me freezes, mouth half open, calculating every potential avenue for escape. When she finally relents, she answers from the side of her mouth, in a soft but lightning-fast flutter of words.

'It's … sevenhundredandfiftythousandpounds.'

'Seven hundred and fifty *thousand* pounds?!' I shut the folder and drop it at the corner of the table. 'For a wellness retreat?!'

'She only takes one patient at a time.' Mum's voice rises an octave, the first notes of desperation creeping in. 'It's an entirely bespoke service. She's … she's very in demand.'

'I don't care. We can't do this,' I exclaim, bewildered by the discussion itself.

'Why? You don't think we can afford it?'

'I know we … It's a *colossal* waste of money!'

'Well, comments like that are exactly why you need this!' Mum replies sharply. 'Your wellbeing is not a waste of money, and you're the only person who thinks it is! So many people are invested in you, *deeply* invested. If getting the help you need means—'

'I'm getting the help I need. Dr Dunn is helping—'

'Oh, that's nonsense,' my mother snipes, a sudden outburst of cold indignation. 'I'm sorry, but that's utter nonsense.'

'Mum—'

'You want to talk about wasting money?' Mum snaps. 'We'd already written her eight months' worth of cheques when you had your … and where was she when you ended up in the hospital? Leaving me to pick up the pieces following her negligence. You have no idea what it was like in that place.'

'Well, I think I have some idea.'

'You weren't there either,' my mother says darkly.

'What are you talking about, of course I—'

'No, you weren't! You weren't there!' Mum interrupts sharply, distress escaping like steam from a pressure cooker. 'You were in a bed on some ward, barely conscious. You weren't there for the consultations, having to talk about … about liver damage, about medications, about whether you'd wake up at all! You didn't have to call your father, while he gallivants around Europe with god knows who, saying he might need to say goodbye to you over the phone! You didn't have to sit, alone, in some freezing hallway thinking about your child's funeral! You weren't there for any of that and neither was she! I had to—'

Mum stops herself; whatever valve had burst within her has now shut off, normal service tentatively resuming. She picks up her knife and fork and, with hard-won composure, dissects the last of her turbot.

'Dunn had her chance,' she states coldly. 'I'm glad you're fond of her, but my confidence in her process is understandably shaken. Now, because of our family's success you have an opportunity for personal, one-on-one therapy with a world-leading psychiatrist. You can continue to resent that fact or learn to appreciate it for the privilege it is. Your choice. Personally, I recommend the latter.'

That brief outburst is the most she's ever spoken about that night. I knew it had been hard on her, but it's another thing entirely to glimpse the grim mechanics, the itinerary of her son's darkest hours. It lends a more defined shape to the spectre of guilt I've been harbouring these last two months.

For a moment, I sink inwards, slipping beneath the folds of my brain until I'm back there on that night. I'm struck by the memory of my phone, staring back at me from the toilet block as I waited for the ambulance to arrive. That one missed call. What it had done. What it had meant.

I wonder why I'd never told anyone about it, Dr Dunn included.

'Why does Sang-Min Han need a therapist anyway?'

'He doesn't. It was for his son,' Mum replies, her expression cooling. 'Remember your old schoolmate, Monty?'

I haven't heard that name in a few years, but it's enough to disarm the conversation slightly. I take a drink and consider the revelation.

'After Singapore?'

'Exactly. After Singapore.' Mum goes back to her turbot, skewering the final chunk of grey flesh with her fork.

'Therapy's not new for Monty Han though, is it? I remember him back in St Edmunds, he was in and out of rehab all of sixth form.'

'And he bounced around a few places after the incident as well.' Mum sighs. 'No psychiatrist could help him … or maybe they just didn't want to. Why cure someone when you can keep the golden goose alive?'

My mother's opinion of the psychiatric world had taken a decisive hit two months ago. In a single night, it fell from the prestigious company of other medical professionals to the lowest rung of her personal estimation. I will admit, however, given her newfound opinions of the industry, her veneration of this Codelle figure is undeniably intriguing.

'And so ...' I venture, reaching a thin olive branch across the table. 'Codelle says she helped Monty Han go cold turkey?'

Mum nods. She's quite aware Monty Han's affliction is vastly different to mine, but the parallel is clear. A shade of a man, lost to the most negative impulses of his own mind, reportedly conquering them, emerging whole on the other side, due to the action of a single doctor. I'm not sure I believe it, but the idea holds an understated gravity.

Regardless, I gain nothing by dismissing it out of hand.

'Would uh ... would Monty be ... willing to talk about his time there?'

My mother's pursed face blooms into a wide, energetic smile.

'You could talk to him today,' Mum blurts out, excitedly. 'I asked Charlotte to set up a provisional meeting with him, just in case you said yes.'

'I'm not *saying yes*.'

'I know, but still,' Mum continues. 'He said he'd be happy to talk with you about Codelle and her institute. Seemed overjoyed about it frankly. I can handle your responsibilities for the day and, of course, the company will cover your travel expenses.'

I tentatively pick up the Chatsworth-blue folder and, perhaps only to suggest due consideration, place it into my satchel.

'Wait ... travel expenses?' I look up, suddenly confused. 'He's not still in Canary Wharf?'

'What, at that grubby penthouse?' Mum scoffs sardonically. 'No. No. He's moved on from there ... thank heavens.'

4

Having worked alongside Dr Codelle the past three years, words truly can't describe my admiration for the woman being honoured here today. Which is bad news for me! I'm supposed to be making a whole speech about her!

However, luckily for me, Elizabeth's actions more than speak on her behalf. The fact that I'm accepting this prestigious award for her while she tends to the needs of her patients is a testament to the selflessness, dedication and care she has brought to our profession since day one.

That's the word I kept coming back to, as I wrote this last night. 'Care'. Care is so important, but it's something we all find difficult at times. Everyone in this room has struggled with apathy, fatigue, ego, sometimes forgetting why we practise medicine in the first place. But as I and everyone who knows her can attest, Dr Elizabeth Codelle can't help but care.

She is someone who'll stay at a patient's side long after her shift has ended, who embarks on the lecture circuit only when she has something important to say, whose ground-breaking research is conducted not for gain or recognition, but in the interest of advancing medical science, of saving as many lives as possible.

So, Elizabeth, though I know you're not watching, I am honoured to accept this award, on behalf of you and the practice you have revolutionised with your presence, on behalf of everyone you've saved and everyone you're yet to save.

Thank you for showing us what caring can look like.

The speech ends abruptly, the applause cutting out as the player for the John Bright Fellow Award video page cuts to black. I close my phone and sit up in my seat, examining the taxi's progress.

Monty Han used to live within a stone's throw of our office. In fact, if you were to walk from our atrium to his building's lobby, and then take the elevator up to his penthouse apartment, the vertical stretch would likely inch out the greater distance.

Han's father, the esteemed South Korean property magnate Sang-Min, had purchased the building for Monty to manage, hoping that a grand project would finally push his errant son to take responsibility. Rumour has it, as soon as the papers were signed, Monty delegated the building's management to a private company, moved himself into the penthouse, and set about converting the three-storey suite into the city's premium party destination.

From a business perspective, the operation was ludicrous: free entry, free bar, a bottomless pit into which Monty dumped millions.

However, by Monty's personal metrics – popularity, infamy and the capacity for scandal – the place was a categorical success.

From my colleagues' retellings, Monty Han's was lightning in a bottle; a Caligulan wonderland of expensive spirits, designer narcotics and uninhibited sexual exploration. I'd witness it myself when I worked late enough. The sky outside my office dancing with beams of light, shadow puppet silhouettes of countless bodies writhing in the windows, the bass thrumming through the London air like a rapidly beating heart.

It was only over time that the grim side of Monty Han's began to emerge, glimpsed only by the tenacious few who lasted an entire night.

These pioneering socialites would wake up, bloodshot and bleary-eyed, not in some party paradise, but in an empty shell of cold, unfurnished concrete. Stained mattresses, empty fridges, a lounge of strung-out bodies stepped around like furniture by a diligent cadre of cleaners.

At the centre of it all would be Monty himself. Up before everyone, or perhaps refusing sleep entirely. He would stumble over, attempting to pull his reluctant guests back into hollow celebration, trying desperately to keep the night alive, even with a window of cold daylight at his back.

My colleagues would politely make their exits and, in the long lift ride down, draw the same sobering realisation: that a man who chooses to live in a nightclub also has to live there when the lights come on.

A few years later, one of Monty Han's legendary benders led to him being thrown out of a Singapore night club. People had gleefully recorded the verbal altercation between Monty and the on-duty security. Those cameras were still rolling less than a minute later when Monty's SUV launched over the road, pinning the two-hundred-and-forty-pound bouncer between its crumpled hood and the nightclub wall, Monty screaming incoherently from the driver's seat.

When Monty woke up the next day, informed that his victim may never walk again, it was discovered he didn't remember the incident at all. Once the news reached London, my colleagues suffered a similar bout of amnesia, suddenly denying that they ever set foot in Monty Han's to begin with.

I'm glad the man is in a better place, even if that place takes three trains to get to.

Two changes and an hour-long commute to the southeast drops me in Staplehurst, where a private taxi carries me the rest of the way through the winding British countryside. Intermittent bus stops chart our journey into deeper and deeper obscurity, the number of services that frequent each stop dwindling with every turn. The final few shelters maintain only a single service, an example of which rattles past us on the narrow road as we drive beneath a crisp, blue sky.

You would have adored a day like today. I can picture you wanting to break out the walking boots to tread through these bright mulch-covered forests, breathing in the cold, clean air.

We didn't visit half as much as you wanted. For some reason, the countryside always seemed far away to me, as if merely travelling there and back would eat up half the day.

Nowadays, on the rare occasions I do find myself out here, I'm sickened by how close it all is.

'Here all right?'

'I'm sorry?' I look up to find the taxi driver watching me in silence. The tyres are still. An idyllic British village surrounds us, unmoving.

'I said we're here. This all right?' He gestures out the window, towards what the GPS confirms is Monty Han's home.

We're a very long way from Canary Wharf.

Before us stands the picture-book ideal of an English country cottage. A stout chimney sits like a melting candle on the moss-covered slate roof. The walls are authentic rubblework and lime mortar, inlaid with white sash windows and a holly red front door. The entire house rests at the centre of a luscious garden, bursting with life across its myriad beds and hedges.

You would have moved here in a heartbeat.

I thank the driver as I clamber out towards the house, the wrought-iron gate's latch shifting with a satisfying clunk. My shoes crackle over woodchip as I pass beneath wicker arches of cascading wisterias, bathing in the scent of honeysuckle, geraniums and wildflower bushes.

As I approach the red door, I feel my stomach start to turn over. I wasn't expecting to be nervous heading into this meeting, but I can't help but feel a strange and selfish anxiety. In the more arrogant corners of my consciousness, I'd looked down on Monty Han, judging him as a destructive, self-serving burnout, squandering his many privileges in the pursuit of an early grave. However, if my mother's comments – and his new residence – are any indication, the tables seem to have well and truly turned.

A hastily scrawled note hangs between the knocker and the door itself: 'If no answer, check out back'. Sure enough, after my few tentative taps entreat nothing but silence, I head towards the cottage's shady side passage.

The path leads onto a neat stone patio at the top of a long, gently sloping garden. The lawn begins with a neatly curated vegetable patch, continuing far downhill until it ends at a stone wall with a view of a farmer's field. The slope is framed on both sides by a wall of evergreen trees, lending a terrarium-like quality to the whole affair; enclosed from the cottages on either side, the verdant pines presumably immune to any particular season.

'Well, goodness fucking gracious! Arty, Arty! Over here! How the fuck are you?'

A face of brilliantly whitened teeth and gleaming brown eyes shoots up behind a veil of potato netting.

Monty Han looks practically unrecognisable. The wiry, sullen addict that I'd last seen being escorted into a Singaporean court-room is now gone. The unkempt mop of hair has been styled into a neat fade, his sunken jawline now defined, a slim-fit T-shirt revealing perfectly sculpted muscles that I'm sure were never there before.

All in all, he looks healthier than I've ever seen him.

I briefly wonder how I must look from his perspective. I haven't been to the gym in nearly a year, and though a distinct lack of appetite has prevented me from gaining weight, my clothes have started to hang unpleasantly loose, like sackcloth over a scarecrow's frame.

I suddenly find it difficult to look him in the eye, even though he seems overjoyed to see me.

'Hi Monty. It's good to see you.'

'So fucking good to see you too darling, seriously,' he says, genuinely enthused. 'I saw your father in Dubai just last month! I meant to congratulate him on the wedding but then I heard about, well, you know ...'

'The divorce?' I offer.

'Exactly!' Monty chuckles. 'Seems to have bounced back quickly though. Classic Malcolm! And how's Delilah? She's a gosh darn icon, that one, always thought that.'

'Yeah, Mum's good.'

'Good.' Monty grins, a moment of silence causing his demeanour to shift. He steps towards me, placing a hand on my shoulder with such force that I almost feel my legs buckle. 'And how are you doing? I heard about your wife. Julia, was it? Fucking bowled me over. And so sudden as well. Were you with her when she … actually, don't worry, how fucking rude of me.'

'It's ok. No … I wasn't there when it happened.'

'Well, I'm sorry at any rate. Look, let me finish up so we can talk properly.' Monty crouches back down and begins to fix the loose sections of netting onto a bamboo support. He doesn't look up, continuing the conversation over his work. 'This must be a strange sight for you. Eternal fuck-up Monty Han, party prince of Canary Wharf, pottering around a garden in fucking Kent of all places?'

'I might not be the best judge.' I shrug. 'Last time we spoke properly we were in school shorts and house blazers. You seem different to how you were back then though.'

'Hah! I was that same fucking child 'til about a year ago.' He chuckles, his fingers threading plastic ties through the delicate fabric. 'What, so you never came to the penthouse in its heyday?'

'Uh, no. Me and Julia were homebodies, I suppose. But you seemed to be having enough fun without us.'

'Hah yes … *fun.*' Monty lets the last word fall from his mouth. 'That's the order of the day, isn't it? Until you find yourself crawling into the same shit-stained bed you woke up in because you can't face the fucking daylight. Until you realise your friends only liked you when you were a raging alcoholic.'

His sardonic remarks hit with a strangely liberating effect, a refreshing bluntness after months of people tiptoeing around me. While Monty Han's inexhaustible lack of shame had got him in trouble in the past, right now it feels like a boon, like I can talk freely without any judgement.

'You say you *were* an alcoholic?'

'Dyed in the fucking wool, mate.'

'No, I mean … you don't consider yourself one now?'

Monty brushes the dirt from his hand and rises back up.

'It's fucking lovely to see you, you know.' He grins widely. 'Come with me.'

Monty marches us down the lawn towards the far end of the garden, nothing but the smell of pine needles and the quiet symphony of birdsong around us. We reach a windowless garden shed, nestled in the shadow of a fir tree at the very edge of his property. Monty removes a rattling keychain from his pocket, sorting through the candidates at a rural pace.

The lock turns, the malty, strangely sweet smell of fermentation passing over us as the door creaks open. The shed is packed to the rafters: a platoon of translucent, five-gallon barrels, each with a small protruding tap, sat across three levels of reinforced shelving. An amber-yellow liquid steeps in every barrel, in no hurry to be decanted.

Monty regards the shed's contents, radiating a sense of unabashed pride. He doesn't look away even when he starts to address me.

'There's this delicatessen just off the village green. I started brewing as a pastime, or maybe as a statement of sorts, I don't know, but for the past few months they've started bottling it and, well, it's gone out the door quite steadily to be honest. It's not the high stakes world of international real estate, of course, but it's enough for me. It's mead, by the way.'

Monty walks past me into the shed, retrieving a large dusty Tupperware. He opens the lid, extracting two clean glass tumblers.

'I'm getting my own beehives installed next week; currently I'm relying on a local apiary. We have vanilla, rosehip, chilli … you look like a bochet man to me, here.' Monty twists the valve on a dark amber concoction, filling both glasses and holding one in front of me.

I stare at the liquid. It seems strange to believe that such a simple substance could be the ruin of so many people, least of all the calm and collected man who currently stands before me. However, alcohol's effect on Monty Han is a matter of medical and historical record. Few could deny the destruction it wrought upon him, to those closest to him, even the unfortunate strangers who crossed his path.

I accept the glass with an awkward smile, but I can't help but feel unnerved as Monty holds his own drink aloft. I feel like I should step in, do something, swat it from his hand and remind him of the dangers it brought to his door.

'To sobriety.' Monty grins irreverently as he swallows it down.

5

Tentatively, party to an event that I'm not entirely sure should be happening, I follow suit.

The bochet tastes, not unpleasantly, like burnt treacle. The unmistakable alcoholic kick comes instantly, a sharpness on the tongue that radiates down the throat. As soon as I feel it, I instinctively look towards Monty, who chuckles.

'You seem uncomfortable,' he comments, looking like he'd mildly enjoy it if I was. 'During my darker years, my father threw all the booze out of my house. I'd still find ways to get it. I'd order it online to a neighbouring flat, get my friends to sneak it in. If I was within a ten-mile radius of any off-licence, it would be all I could think about. How far away it was, how I'd get there. I was powerless.'

He tilts the glass in a slow circle, manipulating the drink around the walls of the tumbler.

'I still do daily breathalysers for my father. Least I can do.' He pauses, fixing his eyes on me to ensure I get the full extent of his words. 'I have a fucking micro-brewery at the bottom of my garden, Arthur, and I haven't charted above a 0.1 blood-alcohol level for seven months. Most days it's zero.'

I try to read his expression, entirely unsure how seriously I'm supposed to be taking this whole affair.

'... How?'

Monty smiles.

'Well, that's why you're here, right?'

It all seems preposterous. From my mother's retelling, I thought this figure, Dr Codelle, had helped Monty quit drinking. But the man himself is suggesting something even more profound: that his toxic relationship with alcohol has been entirely resolved, allowing him to drink as casually as any person would. As far as I'm aware, such a transformation shouldn't be possible, yet it's difficult to deny the scene that's playing out in front of me.

'Let's take these up to the patio, shall we?' Monty smiles, gesturing to the drinks. 'We can talk more there. Anyway, mead's supposed to be kept in the dark.'

A few minutes later, Monty is reclining in a black wicker garden chair, drinking in the serene vista that lies beyond his property. His glass of mead rests barely touched on the table between us. I take another sip of the now slightly cloying bochet as I try to work my way into a new line of questioning.

'So ...' I ask, placing my glass on the wrought-iron patio table. 'It was this doctor, Elizabeth Codelle? You're saying she *cured* your alcoholism?'

'That's right.'

'What sort of treatment is it? Chemical? Hypnotherapy?'

'It's totally bespoke.' Monty Han leans back in his chair, waving his hands to indicate a wide array of options. 'For me? There was exercise, lots of cognitive behavioural therapy, medication. She examines the problem and creates a course of treatment that's tailored to your needs.'

'And you'd say she can achieve things that other therapists can't?'

Monty Han baulks at the understatement, then tilts his head inquisitively.

'We weren't friends, were we?' he queries. 'Back at St Edmunds?'

'I didn't really have many ... I kept to myself. We had English Literature together, that's about it.'

'I remember that! You always read the book!' Monty chuckles, growing contemplative. 'But we were quite alike, to be honest. So many people in that school were rich without

36

condition: musician's daughters, ninth in the royal line. No strings attached. We were born into dynasties … dynasties we were supposed to continue.'

'Least we could do.'

'Ah, good answer. That's why you have the corner office,' Monty muses. 'See, I hated that. I fought against it. I realise now my father's also an addict of sorts, but his addiction is one society values. I had that same itch, but I avoided anything productive like the plague. Education, work … if it felt worthwhile, then it felt an extension of my father's plans for me. So what did I have left to get addicted to? Leisure, escapism, drink, pills. By the time I realised what was happening, I was already lost. I was living in my own head, but off to one side. I was a passenger and something else was driving, or maybe nothing was. It's bizarre, isn't it, Arty? Fighting with your own fucking brain and somehow losing?'

He grows almost bewildered, recollecting the chaos that once controlled his life. After a moment, however, he begins to smile. He takes another sip of mead, and, when he speaks again, it's with the measured pace of a man who wants to be clearly understood.

'Dr Codelle. She gave me back control over my own mind. She dives into your grey matter, and she finds *you*, wherever you are, and she … she re-thrones you. She places you back where you're meant to be, at the centre, on top, with all the grubby shit below you.'

He almost shakes his head in disbelief. Every time Monty Han speaks that name, it's with nothing short of pure, unadulterated reverence. There's even a sense of nostalgia in his tone, as if his tenure at Codelle's institute were a treasured memory.

I have to admit, as much as I respect Dr Dunn, I've never left her office feeling quite so electrified.

'And you think she could help me?'

'She didn't *help* me, Arty. Seriously, love.' He casually waves my comment away, before searching around in the aether for a suitable analogy. 'Does a firefighter just "help" when they carry

37

you out of a burning building over their shoulder? No. She *saved* me … pulled me kicking and screaming out of the flames of my own mind and, yes, I think she can do the same for you. I mean, let me be clear, she's literally Da Vinci! A one-woman psychiatric renaissance. Decades ahead of her time. She could help anyone.'

'Well … I mean, that's certainly a glowing review.'

A knowing smile curves on one side of Monty's face.

'But you're still on the fence, aren't you?'

I mull over what to say next.

'You didn't feel guilty? All that money so you can be happy again. Did you ever feel like … you were getting on a life raft that no one else was allowed onto?'

From Monty's confused frown, I can tell he never so much as considered it. Regardless, his expression quickly melts into an attempt at understanding.

'Here's what I think, Arty. One thing Dr Codelle put into sharp focus is that we only have one life. You know? No do-overs. No sequels. This is it. Of course, I had my doubts going in because, I mean, fucking hell, I'd been to rehab countless times before this, sometimes staying for months, sometimes for hours. I thought, what's the point in going through it all again? In the end, I asked myself one question, and I think it's the same question you should ask yourself now …'

Monty drains his glass, clinking the empty tumbler back onto the table as he looks into my eyes with complete sincerity.

'Honestly. *Honestly*. If you were going to feel *exactly* how you feel today, for the rest of your life … how long do you expect that life would last?'

6

'Honestly, Arthur? I can't say I recommend it.'

I'd barely got back to London in time for my six o'clock session with Dr Dunn. With a dead phone battery and no time to grab a taxi, I dove into rush hour on the underground, changing onto the Piccadilly line and walking briskly from Hyde Park Corner until I found myself, breathless, at her door.

Monty's words hadn't sparked some profound, cosmic epiphany. They weren't ringing in my ears like some universal truth, making my course of action suddenly clear. However, when the taxi pulled away from his house, as he smiled and waved in the rear-view, Monty's words were undoubtedly travelling with me. As I sat on the train and the city of London slowly crept in around me, I could feel his final question going about its quiet work in the back of my mind: delicately turning dials, pulling levers in its favour.

'She's apparently quite accredited.' I venture from Dr Dunn's colourful sofa, a patchwork cushion clutched idly on my lap. 'I've heard she's one of the youngest graduates from the, um … Karolinska Institute.'

'I know who she is,' Dunn states blankly.

'And?'

Dr Dunn, stares out the window, clearly pondering how to approach the strange curveball her patient has brought her. I trust Dr Dunn's impartiality, and I greatly value her opinion as a psychiatric professional, but even so, it leaves a bitter taste in my mouth, forcing her to discuss the viability of her own potential replacement.

'Well, I mean, she's a genius. I don't deny that.' Dunn sighs. 'A once-in-a-generation mind. She started as a surgeon, revolutionised several aspects of the field. I heard she moved to psychiatry for the challenge of it, and her contribution has already been ... notable.'

'Exactly,' I stammer, trying to cause as little offence as possible. 'I mean ... I've only heard positive things.'

'I'm sure you have,' Dr Dunn comments from the corner of her mouth.

'What does that mean?'

Dr Dunn hesitates, realising she may have let her true feelings slip out. When she speaks again, it's in her usual measured tone, albeit with an undercurrent of creeping exasperation.

'Just that ... well, just that her definition of "private practice" is more private than most.'

'You think she's up to something over there?'

'I really don't know. That's my point.' Dr Dunn thinks for a moment. 'So, she covers grief counselling?'

'The brochure says she has a programme. There're some great testimonials.'

Dr Dunn picks up her open leather notebook from the desk, closes it and places it beside her. When she looks back at me, her posture has changed.

'I'm just going to come out and say it, Arthur. I think it's a bad idea to interrupt your treatment right now.'

'I understand, but it would only be two weeks, and ... when I spoke to a former patient of hers—'

'Monty Han, you said?'

'Yes, that's right. He says ... *everyone* says it's like nothing they've ever tried before.'

'I'd imagine so,' Dr Dunn comments. 'She's a revolutionary thinker.'

'But that's good, isn't it?'

'But you don't have a revolutionary problem, Arthur.' Dr Dunn speaks almost sadly. 'You have a problem that's as old as humanity itself. From the moment we learned to love each other, we learned to grieve. There are no shortcuts, no panaceas and, despite whatever Monty Han may say, some conditions don't have an absolute cure. Some things colour our existence, that's just how it is. I don't think it's wise, at this point in your recovery, to try and brute-force an outcome that simply ... shouldn't be.'

I nod weakly, and stare across the Regency housing of Belgravia, the lonely pedestrians passing down below. I can feel the tears pooling behind my eyes.

'If there was a treatment, though ...' I mutter, trying to keep my voice steady. 'If there *was* a treatment, and happiness was on the other side of it ... you'd want that for me, wouldn't you?'

I hear Dr Dunn lean back slowly in her chair as I force myself to face her. I suddenly feel exhausted, overwhelmed. A swell of fresh tears breaks behind my eyes, a few drops escaping down my cheeks.

'I want you to know that I'm ... I want to keep you on as my psychiatrist. We'll just be ... freezing my sessions for the time that I'm ... that I'm away ...'

'Arthur—'

'I really appreciate everything you've done for me.' I push through, worried about what might happen if I stop. 'I hope you know I, um ... I don't share any of the opinions that ... I really want to thank you, but I just ...'

'Arthur, please take a moment to think about—'

'– I just want it to *stop*.'

Dr Dunn stares at me, a defeat in her eyes that I've never seen before. I expected to see something like it when I returned from the hospital two months ago, but she'd had nothing but reassurance for me. Instead, it's this act that seems to have robbed her of hope, this act which seems to concern her more than anything else.

'I just want it to stop,' I repeat, quietly but decisively.

'Well.' Dunn collects herself, professional to the last. 'I'm certainly always here, I know you know that.'

'I do. Yes, thank you, I do.'

Dr Dunn checks the smartwatch on her wrist, the pale white screen reflecting off her glasses. When she looks back, she makes no attempt to ease my discomfort with her usual parting smile. She wears her thoughts on the matter openly, bearing my decision with a quiet integrity but not pretending to agree.

'We don't have long left; is there anything else you want to discuss?'

'I … no, I … thank you, Dr Dunn. My office will handle the scheduling, everything will be … back to normal soon, I'm sure.'

I remove the cushion from my lap, replacing it carefully on the sofa. In the final silence, I cross to the door.

'Arthur?'

My hand rests against the handle. For some strange reason, I find myself unable to look back towards her. Instead, I simply stand, a hunched, lonely shell of a man, waiting to bear her parting comment.

'I hope she's everything they say she is.'

I don't know if it was her intention, but those eight words follow me home, hidden in the sounds of London traffic, echoing behind my forehead as it rests against my apartment door. Earnest as her remark undoubtedly was, I find myself increasingly resentful of its subtle implication and, as I cross the threshold and shut the door behind me, I'm content to leave her comment outside.

I hang in space for a moment, as the cool silence of our empty apartment washes over me. I drift through an unlit hallway, my energy seeping away like air from some untraceable puncture, my hand reaching for the light switch, missing, and falling back to my side without making a second attempt.

I walk through the darkness and collapse onto the sofa of our living room, my cheek pressed into the cool leather. My right ear faces the ceiling, playing host to the distant sounds of London traffic. My left ear, smothered into the sofa cushion, refocusses inwards, amplifying the whooshing rush of blood around my body, the faintest undulations of a heartbeat.

'Strange day, beautiful,' I say, as I stare into the dark outline of the kitchen. 'Didn't get much work done.'

The kitchen glows amber as the orange screen of the cordless phone lights up, the electronic ringtone rudely piercing the silence. I glance at my watch, realising it's been three hours since I arrived home, wondering who'd be calling me this late in the evening.

I cross the room, reach out and pick up the receiver. The screen reads 'Mum', which nowadays is a bit misleading, since it was you who programmed the phone book. My own mother comes up as 'Delilah', adding a certain formality that I can't help but think she'd prefer.

'... Lorraine?'

For the first few seconds, I hear nothing but breathing, as if the person on the other side called me before they were prepared to speak. A few moments later, I hear a shuddering inward breath, a woman on the edge of tears, or perhaps just passing beyond them.

I stare at the hanging silhouette of our copper saucepans, waiting for her to speak.

'Are you free for a bit?' Lorraine's quivering voice hardly carries through the phone. 'I didn't know if you'd be working.'

My mother-in-law's voice used to be bright and breezy, a warm Northern accent, ringing with the benign grace of someone dedicated to kindness. Nowadays, her tone conjures images of a wounded deer: a creature that has harmed no one, diminished by forces it never sought to provoke.

'Hah. I managed to escape.' I wander away from the kitchen island, and start to pace, slowly and aimlessly, through my unlit apartment. 'How're you doing?'

I take in my surroundings as Lorraine collects her thoughts.

I remember when we'd moved in here, the spacious flat comprising an entire floor of a 1970s Bloomsbury townhouse. A large living room, an adjoining kitchen with a six-hob stove, a bathroom of white Italian tile. Coming from the first flat we ever shared, this new space had seemed intimidatingly grand, as if we might lose each other in the hallways.

We eased into the space eventually, only for it to grow again in more recent times. Hollow, sterile, too much for one person.

Now I get lost in the hallways all the time.

Lorraine speaks, trying to maintain a calm tone, her voice still breaking halfway through the sentence.

'I've been looking at our photo albums.' She shudders, steadying herself before continuing. 'Did she ever get a chance to show you?'

'No … afraid not.' I wander into the hallway, flicking on the light before reflecting sadly, 'We kept putting it off, I suppose.'

'She loved to go through them. Feels wrong to put them away,' Lorraine mutters. 'Sorry, I know I always call you in a state after. Are you goin' to bed soon?'

'No, well … I wasn't planning on it.' I attempt to reassure her, knowing that she'll never truly believe it. 'I probably should, but … where's the fun in that.'

I look towards the bathroom, tiles from the empty shower glinting in the moonlight.

I hear a heavy page slowly turn over, as Lorraine gently sighs. 'She was such a ray of sunshine, wasn't she?'

'She really was.' I begin to entertain the same well of sadness myself, turning back down the corridor, until something unsettling catches my eye.

An untidy pile of stacked envelopes teeters on the table in my hall. Ten months of neglected post that I've lacked the mental presence to either read or dispose of. There should be nothing significant about this mass of bills and takeaway menus, except for the single envelope that rests on the very top.

It's grey, sporting a logo of a medical caduceus: two snakes wrapped around a sceptre. The words Cambridge Medical Examiners Ltd stand above it in the top left corner.

My stomach turns as I stare down at it, a sickening cocktail of guilt, shame and nausea so potent that I feel myself wanting to throw up. This isn't a new communication. It's been nine months and five days since it first came through my door. In that time, I'd actively neglected it, covering it with piles of other letters, rejoicing months later when I accidentally knocked the whole pile and watched it slip down the gap between the table and the wall. It had stayed there for half a year, and I would have been greatly at ease to let it rest there forever.

Which begs the question, how did it end up not only back in place, but right on top of the—

'Arthur?'

'I'm sorry.' I snap back to the conversation, guiltily. 'I'm sorry, what did you say?'

'I was … Would you like to see them sometime? Maybe some time soon?'

'The pictures? Yes, yes, I'd love to … That would be good.'

I stare back down at the envelope, wondering if I'd simply replaced it and forgotten.

'Sorry, um … it'll need to be in a month or so.' I suddenly remember. 'I'm going to be away; my mum's booked me on this therapy retreat.'

'Oh?' I hear a weak smile cross Lorraine's face; she's always found my mother somewhat amusing. 'What's that when it's at home?'

'I don't know … you know my mum. She just wants to be sure I'm not … that I'm ok.'

I wait for a moment, wondering if Lorraine's going to try to talk me out of it. I don't know why she would. Perhaps I just feel guilty about abandoning her. When it comes to you, your life, your absence, we're each other's only confidants. For some reason, I feel like I'm boarding a one-way train and leaving Lorraine on the platform.

'Oh, well, that sounds good, love, I hope it all goes well for you.'

'Thank you. I appreciate it.'

A silence passes in the empty hallway: my mother-in-law, a photo album, an envelope and me. Sad people and our tokens.

'So …' Lorraine chimes quietly. 'When did you say you were going?'

18th August

7

Thank you for your email.

I am currently on annual leave and will be out of the office for two weeks until the 4th September, without access to email.
 I will respond to all messages upon my return.
 During this time, please forward your operational inquiries to Myra Stewart-Mill, who is overseeing the Operations department in my absence. Personal inquiries should be forwarded to my PA, Charlotte Ives.

All the best,
Arthur Mason
Senior Director of Operations

I shut my computer down, leaning back in my chair and drinking in the silence.

I stare out at the overcast sky, my stomach gripped by a strange cognitive dissonance – a fear that my absence might cause problems for the company, and an equal fear that it won't matter at all.

Beside my desk, a large leather duffle bag holds two weeks' worth of clothes, a down feather jacket laid over it. The bag's a little underfilled, Dr Codelle's brochure indicating that everything I could think to pack would be provided on arrival.

I believe the phrase 'home away from home' was used.

Two sets of footsteps approach along the carpeted corridor outside my office. The blurred figures of Delilah Mason and Myra Stewart-Mill pass across my translucent office wall, their polite laughter marking the final pleasantries of a productive two-hour meeting.

Mum opens my office door as she finishes the conversation.

'We'll take them somewhere on Thursday and introduce you; I'll have Michael set something up.'

'As long as it isn't seafood again, that'd be lovely,' Myra wryly returns.

Most likely without conscious thought, Myra's eyes scan briefly over my mother's shoulder, unintentionally meeting mine and lingering for a second too long. I return her gaze with a half-smile, hoping to convey some measure of good feeling through the prevailing awkwardness. In response, Myra turns away, as if she'd simply glanced around an empty room.

'Great, see you at the catch-up.' Mum relieves Myra, watching her disappear down the corridor a moment before turning around and switching gears. 'You weren't waiting on me, were you?'

'Oh, no,' I reply. 'There were some last-minute things to sort.'

'Always are,' my mother notes. 'The car's already outside, showed up at three on the dot.'

'Well, this *is* Dr Codelle we're talking about.'

Mum shoots me a sideways look, unamused.

We walk down the corridor in silence. Halfway along, a pall falls between us, and I suspect we've reached a similar conclusion at the exact same moment. That my time at Dr Codelle's represents a daunting moment of truth, a last great push towards positive change. I'll either be coming home better, or with little hope for recovery, a man so broken that three quarters of a million pounds couldn't buy him peace of mind.

Once we climb into the lift, a second supposition briefly occurs to me.

'Mum ... were you in my flat while I was away? The second time, I mean. When I was at the hospital.'

'No, why?'

'Someone sorted my post, well … not sorted. A letter dropped off the table a while ago, yesterday it was back.'

Mum turns towards me and frowns; it's admittedly a strange thing to fixate on in our final moments together.

'Maybe Charlotte went to get some clothes for you.' Mum turns back towards the metal doors, watching the floor numbers dwindle to zero. 'She's always been good, that one. Wish she was *my* PA.'

We exit into a lobby of white stone and lacquered wooden panelling, the doormen letting us out into the parking bay. For a moment, we do nothing but stare over the crowded mass of black cabs, on the nervous tipping point between idle small talk and a strangely momentous goodbye.

'I just want the best for you. You know that, don't you?' My mother exclaims, unprompted, a rare quiver to her voice.

There's a sadness in her eyes, the same sadness I've seen from across a graveyard, across the boardroom, across my hospital bed two months ago. I thought at first it was disappointment, or, at my most cynical, her observation of a squandered investment. I want to apologise for misjudging her, for putting her through so much, for dismissing her concerns for my safety even while I teetered on the edge of oblivion.

However, something tells me this isn't a time to project my own self-pity.

'Two weeks,' I assure her. 'I'll be back in two weeks, and we'll have dinner at the Chantrey.'

Mum recovers the stoic poise she holds so dear, yet with the hint of a smile at the corners of her mouth.

'I'll call Carvell tonight, sort us a table.' She nods. 'Come on now. We're both expected somewhere.'

My mother opens her arms tentatively, and we engage in a hug so awkward that it feels like it takes place in three distinct stages. There's something sweet about the effort, however, leaving me oddly emboldened as my mother disappears back through the revolving doors.

I take a deep breath and begin to walk.

The three o'clock crowd of half-drunk colleagues saunter past me, stumbling back from their business lunches as I move against the current. I wander to the edge of the parking bay, wondering if I'll be able to discern my own conveyance among the sea of corporate taxis.

I needn't have worried. As soon as I fix my eyes upon the car, I can tell it was Dr Codelle who sent it.

All the things I'd heard about her seem to be reflected in the vehicle. The sleek, grey 4x4 exudes a sensible balance of form and function, her documented regard of privacy expressed by the dark tinted windows. The lack of exhaust – the tell-tale sign of an electric vehicle – seems fitting for a 'one-woman renaissance', someone so dedicated to her medical career that 'do no harm' extends even to her carbon footprint.

I'd love to pretend I identified the car on these observations alone. In truth, the deductions are made in retrospect, after I notice my name on a printed sign held by one of the largest men I've ever seen.

Standing at six foot six, seemingly growing with every step I take towards him, Dr Codelle's driver has the chiselled, clean-shaven jawline of a Hollywood action hero. Though he must be in his mid-forties, he possesses the well-honed physical presence of someone much younger. The man is built like a statue, chin raised, chest out, feet planted a shoulder-width apart, dressed in an impeccably tailored black suit and a chauffeur's cap, the laminated sign that bears my name looking slightly too small in his hands.

If I were someone preoccupied with my own emasculation, I might request another driver.

'Good afternoon.' I venture as I draw towards him. 'I imagine you're from Dr Codelle's?'

The chauffeur smiles, nodding. He reaches a gloved hand out for my luggage, lifting it from my grasp with ease before opening the back door of the car for me. I shuffle into the beige leather interior, glancing around as I hear him place my luggage in the boot.

A set of calm footsteps carry him to the front of the car and he clambers somewhat uncomfortably inside. His cap brushes against the doorframe as he sits in the driver's seat, settling himself behind the wheel and straightening his driving gloves.

'God, it's north Wales, isn't it? Sorry you had to come all this way.'

The chauffeur smiles briefly, as if to wordlessly absolve me of guilt, before pressing a blue glowing ignition button with his thumb, a keyless entry fob presumably somewhere on his person.

The car hums softly to life, the subtle sound of the motor and the slow roll of tires against tarmac. The chauffeur's hands cross over on the wheel as we take a graceful arcing turn onto the main road.

Just like that, we're on our way.

It isn't an immediate departure. The building that houses Mason Industrial is tall enough to be seen from any point in central London. Rather than passing out of view in the first few turns, it follows me, hanging in the background even after we leave Canary Wharf. In the end, I make a conscious effort to turn away from it, putting my co-workers out of my mind, half hoping they'll do the same for me.

'So, how long have you been with Dr Codelle?' I lean into the middle of the car as we take the North Circular past Wanstead Park.

He continues to drive without answering, and I teeter slightly between a fear that I'm disturbing him, and an equal fear of being anti-social.

'Seems like an interesting place to work,' I postulate idly, resolved to let his response set the tone for the remainder of the journey.

Still no answer. Instead, he reaches across to the glovebox, retrieving what looks like a blank white business card between his thumb and forefinger.

Closing the compartment and centring himself back on the wheel, he holds the card over his shoulder for me to take. The first side of the card is empty. On the other side, printed in a black, typewritten font, is a block of text.

Your driver, Mr William Villner, is currently observing a period of Therapeutic Non-Vocal Reflection, electing to refrain from speech between the hours of 12 a.m. to 11 p.m. each day.

If urgent, your inquiries will be answered in writing at the next available stop.

Answers to frequently asked questions can be found in the seatback in front of you.

I glance up from the card towards Mr Villner, who smiles apologetically into the rear-view mirror.

The Chatsworth-blue folder in the front seat pouch does seem comprehensive, outlining a number of time-passing amenities for my travelling enjoyment. A screen in the front headrest, containing a wide selection of films and television shows. A tablet with a small library of books, magazines and music streaming apps. A set of noise-cancelling headphones, seemingly purchased on a client-by-client basis, folded in a central compartment beneath the middle seat.

Appreciative of the options, guilty at my lack of desire to engage with them, I instead rest my head against the window and let the world roll past me.

We drop off the M25, sweeping through a patchwork of open fields that take us past Kettering. Turning northwards on the outskirts of Birmingham, the M6 carries us towards Manchester, before arcing back west towards the England-Wales border.

True to his vow, Mr Villner doesn't utter a sound on the way. A brief bathroom stop, made at my own request, was acknowledged with a decisive nod and no further comment. In fact, when I returned through the service station entrance and approached the car once again, I found the man sitting with his hands on the wheel, staring quietly ahead, as if he hadn't moved a muscle in my absence. Much like the car he drives, Mr Villner seems a being of efficient function and understated calm.

'Croeso i Gymru', a sign flashes past at the side of the road. 'Welcome to Wales.'

A stylised red dragon heralds us onto the north Wales expressway. Small towns rise and fall around us as we push towards the coastline, a sharp left turn on the far end of Abergele situating the ocean on our right for the remainder of the journey, its hue the same deep blue as the brochure.

The next hour treats me to a series of seaside images: ice cream vans, windbreaks, grown-ups eyeing grey clouds as their children build castles from damp sand. There's something understatedly charming about the British beach holiday, of watching people sunbathe below a largely overcast sky. It comes with a wise implication – that I should try to make the best of what I've been given.

It's past eight when we reach the outskirts of Porthcoll: a sea-scarred sixteenth-century village. The pointed slate roofs make the granite houses look like a gaggle of old witches, huddling together for warmth amid the frigid coastal spray.

As the car inches through narrow cobble streets, flanked on either side by oppressive walls of pre-Victorian masonry, I see a few of the residents shuffling about their business. They watch the car with disinterest, quickly turning back to their own affairs.

Suddenly, on the far end of the village, the cobbles give way to an expansive dock of ageing concrete. A stone pier stretches out into the cold ocean, a scattered array of moored fishing boats rocking on the tide against it. Further along the dock, the concrete plateau tapers down into a steady slope, a jetty, descending under the lapping waves.

It's here, parked up against the algae-strewn slipway, that I catch my first glimpse of the *De Anima*.

8

Like a spacecraft from another world, a hundred-foot yacht rests
against the dock, its bow towards the open sea.

Dominating the meagre vessels on either side, the *De Anima*'s
highest point sits some twenty-five feet out of the water. Its hull
is a uniform cold blue, its deck topped by an immaculate white
cabin with panoramic windows. The name, some Graeco-Latin
phrase I'm not smart enough to translate, is printed on the bow
in clear, unadorned lettering, the rungs of a permanent ladder
engraved into the fibreglass just beyond it.

Villner rolls the car towards the slipway, taking a three-point
turn that puts us directly in line with the stern of the boat. His
hand reaches, once more, into the glovebox and returns clutching what looks like a sophisticated garage door opener.

A light click of the button yields an immediate, heavy clunk
from the *De Anima*. The stern opens out into a huge drawbridge,
supported by two metal pistons that extend with a constant
pneumatic hum. As the ramp lowers enough to expose the interior of the ship, a bare, matte-grey parking garage, large enough
to comfortably house a single vehicle, is revealed on the inside.

I glance to the rear-view mirror, for some reason interested in
Mr Villner's expression, as if he might be as shocked at the sight
as I am. His eyes, of course, remain utterly impassive, watching
the ramp make soft contact with the slipway as if it were the
most natural thing in the world.

As the tyres transfer from cracked, uneven cement to the
smooth grey fibreglass of the *De Anima*'s entrance ramp, I can't

help but consider the motives behind this incredible display of luxury. I'm certainly impressed, but I wonder what it's all for. Is Dr Codelle simply showing off? Is she trying to assure her more luxury-minded clients of the high standards they can expect? That they're getting their money's worth?

Part of me wonders if it's a statement of security, an assurance that everything has been thought of, that the hospitality of the Codelle Institute will be so all-encompassing that recovery should be my only focus.

The car rolls across into the belly of the huge vessel. As the ramp behind me closes once again, and the village of Porthcoll disappears behind a grey wall, I feel suddenly isolated, cut off from the rest of the world.

It takes some work to remind myself that that's the entire point.

Villner lets me out of the car, escorting me up from the stark, functional garage into a decadent lounge. My eyes travel over the wood panelling, leather upholstery, and the soft, warm lighting. When I look back to Villner, he's retrieved a drinks menu from a wooden bar at the corner of the room, offering it to me.

'I'm all right, thank you.'

Villner nods once again, placing the menu on the glass coffee table, smiling reassuringly before disappearing up a small set of carpeted steps towards the boat's helm.

Less than a minute later, I feel a lurch in my stomach as the *De Anima* pulls seamlessly away from the dock.

Fifteen idle minutes pass. With the engine thrumming, and the windows on either side displaying nothing but open water, I begin to wander around the edges of the cabin. Behind the small bar sits a chilled drinks cabinet containing spirits, wine, even champagne, though I can only assume it contained something different when Monty Han was onboard.

A shelf of ornate board games stands beside the bar, containing a chess board, a sealed pack of playing cards, and a mahogany case decorated with the tell-tale symbols of Mahjong. I presume that every conceivable pastime could be found in the inlaid drawers that surround the room, but once again, all this choice leaves me not knowing what to do with myself.

Instead, I pour myself a glass of water and sit on the beige leather sofa at the centre of the room. I glance to my right, looking up the steps into the boat's bridge. I can only make out the bottom of Villner's legs as they stand at the controls, still a shoulder's width apart.

Turning back to the coffee table, an object at its centre catches my attention. Dark blue leather, with the comfortable heft of an old ship's ledger, the words 'Guest Book' written across it. It's a stark contrast, a tasteful sliver of antiquity in my sleek modern surroundings.

I heave it towards me, letting it fall open on my lap.

Thank you so much, Dr Codelle!

I used to envy people who had their lives together. Now that's me! Dr Codelle, you are a genius!

Only the first five or six pages are filled in, some entries merely a few words long, others comprising multi-paragraph epics. Yet it's clear from even a cursory investigation that all of the comments are of a similar ilk: ranging from gratitude to an almost religious veneration for Dr Codelle and her operation. None of them are particularly informative, however. I almost close the book altogether, until I notice a small note in the bottom edge of page four, similar to the rest but strangely more impactful, perhaps due to the fact that it addresses me directly.

To someone starting this journey, from someone heading home. Know that it's all worth it. Every moment.

I stare at the quote for a long while, finding a kindred spirit in the ink. Though I have no idea who wrote the words, I hope to god they're telling me the truth. Who knows, in two weeks' time, when the *De Anima* is ferrying me back to Porthcoll, perhaps I'll be writing the same.

Thirty minutes pass before the *De Anima* finally slows, signalling our approach to the island dock. Seemingly out of nowhere, two walls of lateral wooden planks encroach across the windows, as a large boathouse swallows the *De Anima* whole.

The engine shuts off, Mr Villner wordlessly collecting my bag before opening a side door that leads out onto the deck. He disembarks confidently, lending a hand to help me onto the sturdy wooden pier.

The boathouse is long and surprisingly dark, the opaque walls blocking any glimpse of the outside world until we're right up against the large open entrance. I have to say, however, now that I see the island's central building up close, a few extra metres would have done nothing to prepare me.

Looming over us, as we trudge up a white chalk footpath, Codelle's institute is a perfect cube of seamless grey concrete. There are few features to speak of, but all of them are striking. A set of black double doors wait for us at the top of the gentle hill, and above them, a vast circular window looks out from the second floor, hanging at the exact centre of the building like a large, cyclopean eye.

A string of smaller windows wrap around the house, a row for each of the three storeys. Instead of standard rectangular panes, however, each window takes the form of various basic shapes, reminiscent of a child's stencil set: squares, circles, triangles, crescent moons, stars. The shapes repeat every so often, with no respect for any particular sequence, each one punched deep into the cement walls.

It doesn't look like it belongs here, though perhaps a remote island is the only place such a building *does* belong.

For the briefest moment, I think I see movement beyond the circular central window, a barely perceptible figure passing back into the unseen depths of the second floor. The window is just dark enough to cast doubt on my senses and, before I have a chance to look again, we've already passed beneath it, Villner pushing the double doors open and ushering me, politely, inside.

'Thank you,' I mutter, realising how little I've spoken in the last six hours.

My shoes dust the welcome mat with chalk as I step into an entrance corridor with a floor of chequerboard marble. The first few steps echo loudly, reverberating off a low ceiling.

As we shuffle along, a large, two-storey room steadily approaches ahead of us, the chequerboard floor expanding outwards into a wide, open space.

Sure enough, we pass out of the entrance corridor, finding ourselves in a vast square atrium. The room represents the cuboid epicentre of a perfectly cuboid house. The walls are pure white and, despite there being no windows, incredibly well lit. At the atrium's corners, identical white marble pedestals elevate single plant pots, leaves spilling down from within.

The middle of the atrium feels like the centre of a compass. The entrance corridor lies to the south behind us, with a single set of double doors on each of the north, east and west walls. Directly across from us, at the north side of the room, a spiral staircase of wrought black iron twists its way up to the second floor, melting into the intricate railing of an internal balcony.

Mr Villner waits silently behind me as I stare up at the strangest feature of this grand atrium. The painting of an abstract face stares down at me from the ceiling, measuring almost thirty by thirty feet in size, comprised of thick black lines that look like they were applied with a paint roller. It's incredibly simplistic: ovals for eyes, a lonely arc for the left brow, one swooping line to represent the nose and a larger one to form the outline of the head.

The standout feature, comparatively detailed among the minimalist linework, is a set of lips, with a distinct outline of the cupid's bow. A line bisects the top and bottom lip, curling upward on each side into the slightest hint of a smile.

Apparently, the house is no less eccentric on the inside. I start to wonder who could hope to find peace of mind in such a place, let alone live here.

'Mr Mason.' I look down from the ceiling to see a figure has arrived at the top of the spiral staircase. 'I have a feeling you don't like my house.'

9

I stare up at the figure on the balcony, her eyes resting quietly on mine.

I'd seen her before, of course; she featured prominently in the brochure and the bulk of my online research. Yet after all I've heard, after the sheer volume of conversations concerning this singular individual, an air of celebrity can't help but hang over our meeting.

For someone who has done so much with her life already, she's remarkably fresh-faced and youthful. Her large russet eyes, which blink so rarely that it seems more like a choice than a necessity, shimmer with bright optimism as well as a sense of sharp, perceptive intellect.

She wears a single-breasted blazer of pure, unblemished white, perfectly colour matched with a pair of cropped linen trousers and canvas pumps. The only thing resembling a pattern is a light silk blouse of vertical black and white stripes.

There is, in fact, a distinct sense of verticality to her entire posture. She stands neatly upright, her feet together, her hands on the rail in front of her. Even her charcoal hair is sculpted into a neat upward knot, ascending above her head, not a single follicle straying from its path.

At first glance, she is perhaps the most collected human being I have ever seen.

In stark contrast, I realise I've been standing with my mouth half open for the past eight seconds.

'I uh ...' I glance around the room as I remember her open-ing remark. 'It's lovely.'

'Oh, is that really how you want to start this?' Her playful accusation drifts down from the upper balcony. The brochure's modest biography had alluded to Codelle's family background, a mother from France and a father from Sweden. While there's no vocal trace of the latter, the faintest francophone lilt is detectable under an otherwise English accent, showing up and disappear-ing every fifth word or so.

She's entirely correct though, and I can't help but feel uncom-fortable at being called out.

'No, I ...' I begin to mumble reflexively. 'Sorry.'

'No need to apologise,' she replies, a relaxed confidence to her tone, as if everything she says is merely a calm statement of fact. 'There are few assurances in this world, but three things I can guarantee right now: while you're on this island, you'll never have to tell me you're sorry, you'll never need to lie and, most importantly, there's no need to smile until you mean it.'

The lattermost statement catches me off guard. I feel the façade of my smile give way, bringing an unexpected wave of relief.

'Now don't worry. It's not a test. It's not a mind game.' The woman gestures each concept away with her hands, before rest-ing both palms against the railing and leaning slightly forwards. 'What do you think of the place?'

'It's uh ... strange,' I mutter, still a little uncomfortable to be speaking so plainly on the subject. 'I mean ... I don't mind it, but it doesn't feel like it belongs here.'

She laughs: a warm, genuine chuckle.

'Well, that's quite astute. It doesn't.'

She speaks offhandedly as she descends towards the ground floor, her commentary scored by the soft clang of each step on the spiral staircase.

'In the 1960s, this was in Los Angeles, there was an archi-tect called John Prismall. He was a figure of ... unique vision. An artist. He was getting towards the end of a successful but *unfulfilling* career, when a famous musician came to him and said, "I want you to build me *your* perfect house. Unlimited budget. Full creative freedom. I've purchased a plot in the Hollywood Hills; consider it a canvas for your magnum opus." Well, Prismall was overjoyed, of course. He set to work on it immediately, poring over the blueprints day and night, barely eating, turning down all other work to focus on this one ... masterpiece.'

At the midpoint of her journey down the staircase, as the spiral turns her away from me, I glance briefly to my left, curious about what Mr Villner is up to during all of this. Unlike me, Mr Villner has his eyes fixed on our host, watching her descend with a smile on his face. I perceive in his features the same reverence that everyone seems to hold for this woman. At the very least she seems like a good employer.

'However, when he approached the musician with his completed vision, his *dream* house, the client got cold feet.' The white shoes turn down a final set of steps. 'They wanted something ... safer, with more resale value, more suitable for cocktail parties. Prismall was buried with notes, alterations, redrafts, until the finished product resembled the same modernist structures he'd been designing for decades. His magnum opus became a ... profound monument to compromise.'

She reaches the bottom of the stairs, stepping onto the chequerboard floor. It was difficult to discern from my view of her on the balcony, but now that we're on the same plane, she appears somewhat shorter than I imagined. Sculpted hair notwithstanding, the top of her head looks like it would barely reach my shoulder, placing her at no more than five foot three inches tall. Nevertheless, she radiates a sense of presence far beyond anything I can muster, her gaze never falling from mine as a steady smile curls at the edge of her mouth.

'You know what Prismall did?' she continues, clearly arriving at her favourite part of the story. 'He took his original blueprints, withdrew his fortune, bought an island off the coast of Wales and built this place. Prismall House. A perfect recreation of his original vision: brick for brick, every room, every fixture, every detail.'

She looks up at the face on the ceiling, her eyes lingering on its abstract smile before turning back.

'I had to court him for years to purchase it, and I could only move in after he died. As a somewhat unartistic person, I find the place utterly bizarre but, as someone who respects vision, tenacity, individuality, I wouldn't dream of redecorating.'

My host stands in silence for a moment, drinking in her surroundings, as if it were *her* who had just arrived here for the first time. I'm not sure if this was intentional, but her enthusiasm for this place is oddly infectious, forcing me to take in the walls with fresh eyes.

At the very least, I now understand why a psychiatrist would want to move here. Not only does the finished product represent a considerable victory over adversity, but given the deeply personal nature of its construction, the house must feel like the closest one can get to living in someone else's head.

I look back from the walls to find my host standing before me, a delicate hand outstretched.

'Dr Elizabeth Codelle,' she states warmly, a genuine smile across her face.

'Arthur Mason.' I accept her hand and shake it.

'I'm incredibly glad to have you with us, Mr Mason.' She beams, unblinking, before turning to the chauffeur. 'Villner, let's show Mr Mason to his room, shall we?'

Standing at the centre point of the house's grand atrium, I wonder for a moment which of the cardinal directions I will be taken in.

Villner eventually ushers us north, and we pass into a white-walled statuary corridor, underlit by LED lamps that shine like spotlights on a bare ceiling. A set of pedestals run along each wall, all of them presenting the white marble bust of some influential figure from the past millennium.

As we make our way along, I manage to recognise some of the figures from their head shape, hair and clothing. Though that's where the identifiable markers end, as it becomes immediately clear that each bust has had its facial features sanded down to a smooth, featureless surface.

'Kill your idols,' I comment quietly, as we pass a blank face with the frilled ruff and hair of William Shakespeare.

Dr Codelle chuckles.

'Yes, Prismall could be on the nose at times.'

The corridor ends at a set of double doors, presumably the house's northern exit, and corridors to the left and right. We turn towards the latter, facing us towards the north-eastern corner of Prismall House.

The hallway that awaits us is far tamer, but no less unique. This new stretch is lit by pale, white orbs, the wall on the north side lined with a set of external windows, moonlight now streaming through circle-, star-, triangle- and diamond-shaped shafts in the concrete wall. The opposite side is taken up by a vast artwork: a huge, flat slab of white marble intentionally shattered and reassembled with an inch's space between each fragment, an explosion frozen in time. A door lies at the end which, unlike its eccentric surroundings, is entirely featureless, not even a handle on its grey face.

'You're probably tired,' Codelle comments, her eyes on the approaching door. 'Our first session is at 11 a.m. tomorrow. It's going to be difficult. The first session always is.'

'That sounds a little ominous.' I glance sideways towards her.

'We'll get through it.' Codelle smiles, before gesturing to the remainder of the house. 'My point being you should make the most of your evening here. Plenty to do in your downtime, though of course if you'd rather just eat and sleep, I can have Mr Villner prepare you dinner.'

Impressed, I look ahead towards Villner, addressing the back of his head. 'You wear a lot of hats, Mr Villner. Driver. Chef—'

'As job titles go, he prefers the term aide-de-camp.' Codelle rolls her eyes affectionately. 'A little militaristic for my taste but you're right. He's invaluable.'

Mr Villner, reaching the featureless grey door, places his free hand against its surface. The contact of his palm elicits a slow, satisfying whoosh as the door recedes into the south wall. Villner crosses the threshold, and Codelle and I follow suit.

The suite is nestled into the north-eastern corner of the house, with the two external walls each bearing a single window, a triangle and crescent moon respectively. The room itself is composed entirely of what seems to be grey rock, every one of its features melting out of the walls, as if hewn from a single block of slate.

The furnishings are sparse: a chest of drawers built into the wall, a night table and a double bed. A second grey door stands at the south wall, leading to what I can only assume to be the bathroom.

'Double bed,' I comment quietly. 'Seems a bit ironic for a bereavement programme.'

Codelle laughs.

'Well, that's not the only service we offer, but I take the point. Would you prefer something smaller?'

I shake my head; Codelle smiles warmly.

'We'll give you the evening. The touchscreen on the wall will connect you to Villner's personal pager. No request is too small.'

'Thank you, I appreciate it.'

A silence passes between us, and it dawns on me that I'm truly, finally here. A sudden wave of doubt and separation overtakes me. Dr Codelle radiates a reassuring confidence, yet she also feels like an extension of this strange house: welcoming yet unfamiliar, entirely open yet oddly unknowable, a light on an island in a cold, cold ocean, with the capacity to be redemptive or utterly isolating.

Codelle's deep brown eyes find mine, a sympathetic but confident half-smile forming at the corner of her mouth.

'You look overwhelmed.'

'A little ... I ... it'll pass.'

'No. You'll overcome it. There's a difference,' Codelle says with quiet assuredness.

It's strange; ever since you passed away, everyone has been incredibly supportive, but they all live in palpable fear for my future – of whether I'll progress, of what I might do on some quiet, solitary evening. Even though she's practically a stranger, there's something compelling about Codelle's steadfast confidence that everything *will* be ok, not merely as a matter of optimism, but as a matter of fact.

Codelle crosses towards the corridor, turning back to me just before she reaches the doorway.

'You're going to be happy you came here, Mr Mason. I promise.'

10

Codelle's parting comment rings decisively in the air between us.

For the briefest moment, at least for as long as I remain in her eye line, I can't help but believe her. Codelle nods towards Villner, and they leave, disappearing behind the softly closing door, rendering me alone for the first time in almost eight hours.

Out of pure curiosity, I reach out and press my hand against a random section of the slate wall. Despite having the appearance of stone, it depresses slightly when pushed, a surface of foam padding, covered with an expertly textured sheet of PVC rubber. I wonder if this was a part of Prismall's original design, or whether it was devised by Dr Codelle as a layer of protection for her more self-destructive clients.

I turn towards the window and, minutes later, I've settled myself in the curvature of the crescent moon, looking out at the breaking waves.

'You know, I always fucking *hated* it when ...' I whisper absent-mindedly, after almost an hour of silence. 'I always hated it when ... people would tell me what you *would* have wanted. You know? "Oh, Julia would've wanted me to have those earrings", "Julia would want a church funeral", "Julia would want you to do this". I always thought, they can't just *use* you like that, you know? They can't ... cite you ... to back up their own opinions when you're not there to defend yourself. I mean, half of them barely hung out with you and suddenly they're the experts? Fuck, have some respect. Just admit it's what *you* want ...'

I pause for a moment. I can feel the dull, heavy swell of tears rushing up within me. I keep them held back and regulate my breath, each exhalation like the oars of a rowboat brushing through the surf.

'But I've got to … I've got to believe you would've wanted this for me, right? I mean, whatever this is, you'd want me to be here, you'd want me to be doing this.'

I wait for a response, for a sense of you somewhere behind me, the lightest feeling of arms wrapping around my chest, your chin on my shoulder, a whisper telling me everything will be ok.

Instead, I don't feel anything at all.

I end up skipping dinner, the next few hours passing in darkness. I've sunk down and pressed my back against the fake stone wall beneath the window, observing the projections of stencil-shaped moonlight on the walls of my bedroom.

I feel like a cliché, to have found myself wallowing alone in unlit rooms with such regularity. All I can say is, wherever I end up these days, the light switch always seems to be on the far side of the room.

Suddenly, in a moment so fleeting that it almost escapes my notice, a passing shadow interrupts the triangle of channelled moonlight, causing it to flicker against the south wall. As I sit up, paying closer attention, I watch as something moves outside, briefly passing by the crescent moon window.

Somebody's moving out there, walking around the northern, and now the eastern edges of the building, heading steadily south.

I clamber slowly to my feet, turning to look through the tempered glass. Nothing. Just shadowed hedgerows and a dark green lawn, a black sea lapping at its edge. I lean to one side of the window, hoping to gain a better view from a shallower angle, but the crescent-shaped shaft punched into the wall is several feet deep on either side of the glass, a thick tunnel cutting off any view of the periphery.

With the shadow now gone, the view outside my window as still as an oil painting; I turn my back to the glass and observe the perfectly made double bed. Now that circumstances have brought me to my feet, I consider crawling under the covers, leaving this strange day behind and arriving, well rested, to my first session with Dr Codelle.

I take five steps across the room, stare at the fluffed pillow, and place my palm against the surface of the grey bedroom door.

I pass through the beams of shaped moonlight – diamond, triangle, star, circle – taking a left turn down the now unlit statuary corridor. Almost absent-mindedly, I run my hand against a long-faced marble figure with wispy, balding hair, his sculpted garments forming a turn-of-the-century suit and tie, the temple tips of a pair of glasses still visible either side of his head before blending into the rest of the smoothed-down face.

I think this used to be Sigmund Freud. I'd hate to be wrong. He'd have a field day with something like that.

I pass across the windowless atrium, the bulbs still on, but dimmed. Though the light doesn't reach the ceiling, I can feel a set of abstract eyes looking down upon me as I pass into the entrance hallway and out into the island's grounds.

All around me, expertly pruned topiary bushes bob and rustle in a lifting wind. In the far distance, the boathouse's dark entrance looms like the mouth of a yawning sea monster. Between these two fixtures, halfway down the chalk footpath, a figure in a long black coat stands towards the rising waves, head upturned to the rolling grey sky.

He's shouting something, bellowing at the top of his lungs like King Lear, the sound waves buffeted by the tumultuous air, inaudible from where I'm currently standing.

I plant one foot into the chalk, taking slow, tentative steps away from the building. I make no attempt to crouch or hide, hoping that the wind, and the man's booming voice, will cover my approach.

I pass almost beyond the gardens when I can finally discern the figure, and the sounds emanating from him.

It's Mr Villner, that much is obvious – the short-cut hair, the broad shoulders, the notable height. Yet the man is not only

73

yelling into the night sky, but singing, joyously, rapturously and at the top of his lungs.

'Are you lonesome tonight? Do you miss me tonight? Are you sorry we drifted apart?'

Despite the storm's attempts to rob him of breath, a particularly strong gust forcing him to place a supporting foot behind him, Villner refuses to yield. Steeling himself, his slightly faux-American singing voice barrels against the gale.

'Does your memory stray, to a bright summer day, when I kissed you and called you sweetheart?'

Villner takes an exaggerated, arcing step, as he turns slowly on his left leg. The lumbering pirouette turns him towards Prismall House and, unavoidably, towards me.

His eyes lock on my own, his mouth open in a moment of surprise. We stand before one another as the wind whistles, each at a quiet loss as to how we navigate this strange encounter.

Villner makes the first move. He lifts his arm to head height, palm towards me. A wave hello. Without much of an idea what else to do, I raise my hand as well.

Villner grins.

'Do the chairs in your parlour,' he serenades, an unapologetic calm on his face, 'seem empty and bare?'

He pivots again, this time on his right leg, followed by his left, then his right; an understated dance across the moon-drenched lawn of the island grounds. He leaves me behind, both physically and mentally, as he continues his way towards the end of the song.

'Do you gaze at your doorstep, and picture me there?! Is your heart filled with pain? Shall I come back aaaaaaaa-gain? Tell me dear, are you lonesome—'

The wind drowns Villner out once more as he passes further across the lawn away from me. I can see him, however, still dancing, still calling out into the night. Recovering from the shock, I turn away from the disappearing figure, staring back at the grey façade of Prismall House, wondering what exactly I've got myself into.

19th August

11

I jolt unceremoniously back into the waking world.

I'm in my new bedroom, my back still propped up against the wall below my window, my legs splayed out across the heated carpet. I can't tell if I returned to this spot after my midnight concert with Mr Villner, or whether I simply dreamed the whole bizarre encounter. I'll admit, the ache in my back does seem to suggest the latter.

I rise and cross the lush, warm carpet towards the featureless bathroom door. It drifts aside to reveal a cavernous en suite, its sloping roof comprised of faux-rock formations in the same uniform grey as the rest of my suite.

The shower has no screen or curtain, its presence indicated by a drain, a series of pinholes set into the ceiling and a black touchscreen for temperature and pressure control. I end up not needing to use the panel at all, as merely standing beneath the shower elicits a rapturous volley of perfectly heated water.

Shower gel lathers luxuriantly, a eucalyptus sapling suspended within the bottle. When I step out, I notice an array of branded toiletries on the sink as well as a brand-new electric toothbrush.

I'm starting to feel like I needn't have packed at all.

I exit my room half an hour later, dressed for my first day in therapy: tan shoes, blue jeans, a charcoal jumper hiding a wrinkled white shirt. Dream or not, the corridor outside my room looks far more appealing in the daylight, and though the hall of statues remains equally disconcerting, I'm already starting to grow familiar with the company of blank faces.

The windowless central atrium glows with the same soft white lighting. Unsure what to do with myself, I decide to cross the south end of the room and step out into the grounds.

A wall of fresh August air rushes past me as I open the double doors, the bright, steeply rising sun sweeping across wind-tousled grass. I fill my lungs and stare down towards the boathouse, the direction in which I saw Mr Villner singing the night before. Surprisingly he's still part of the scene ahead of me, his presence now far less mysterious. The hulking man is down on one knee, clad in a green gardener's uniform of gloves, apron and work trousers, pruning the sculpted shrubs with uncompromising focus.

'Morning!' I call out into the gardens. He turns a moment, smiles, waves decisively and returns to his work.

I stare across to the distant mainland, the vaguest shadow of the Welsh coast on the horizon, until something enters the left edge of my vision. A fast-moving, pale shadow that soon takes on the shape of Dr Elizabeth Codelle. Clad in a white tank top and matching jogging bottoms, her hair knotted like thick rope behind her head, she arcs around the edge of the island in a steady, controlled run.

I find myself watching her, almost unconsciously, the only moving object in an otherwise perfectly still picture. Perhaps sensing my eyes on her, Codelle's attention flickers towards the house, before returning to the run. Her pace slows as she completes the island's final quadrant, before coming to a stop at the edge of the boathouse.

She places her hand against the lacquered wooden wall, stretching her calves, before turning to the house and walking purposefully back up the chalk path.

'Good morning!' Codelle calls, somewhat breathlessly, a glimmering sheen of sweat noticeable as she passes by Mr Villner. 'How did you sleep?'

'Uh ... very well, thank you.' I nod affirmingly. 'Looks like I'm the last one up.'

'Yes, we're early risers, though Villner puts me to shame most days.' Codelle smiles, her breath returning to normal. 'I do recommend you catch the sunrise at least once before you go home though. It's beautiful here.'

I stare across the Irish sea, which looks so still at this hour that I imagine I could walk across its surface. The sails of a few private vessels pass by on the horizon. Seeing this place in the daylight, it's immediately clear that there are far worse places to recover.

Codelle wipes her brow and looks at me.

'I assume you haven't had breakfast?'

At the mere mention of my developing hunger, Villner rises from his pruning and disappears inside. The doctor herself follows to get dressed. Sensing, perhaps, that I might find myself at a loose end, she turns back to me warmly, suggesting I take fifteen minutes to explore the various rooms of the house.

Knowing the atrium's north door leads into the familiar statuary corridor, I look instead towards the east and west walls. Choosing the former, I push through the doors into a bizarrely furnished games room.

A heavy blanket of stuffy heat hangs in the air, an artificial fireplace of faux coal and orange filament churning out the high temperature with thick consistency. The room displays the classic notes of the Regency period: chaise longues and writing desks, the floor covered in multiple Persian rugs stitched together in a bizarre patchwork.

More alarmingly, the room's multiple surfaces are littered with taxidermy, apparently dating from the 1960s. A grinning chimpanzee sits atop an antique, upright piano. A small flock of peacocks perch above the fireplace, each on their own shelf, ascending all the way up the southern wall.

It all hangs together, more or less. At the very least, no side of the room appears more peculiar than the other. Nevertheless, one can only feel so comfortable when surrounded by twenty sets of unblinking glass eyes.

To its credit, the games room is replete with all manner of distractions. Tables for foosball, billiards, and ping-pong, and an old pinball machine, all made from ornate polished wood.

A dartboard is fixed to the wall, the corresponding brass oche outlined in the floor.

It's only in small, scant details that Codelle's dedication to patient safety peeks out. Perspex instead of glass, fibreglass pool cues. When I wander over to the cabinet beside the dartboard, I'm not surprised to find the darts themselves ending in a blunt magnetic tip, adhering to the board without any need for sharp edges.

I step through a door on the opposite wall, welcomed by a bare concrete corridor and a set of descending stairs, carrying me to the previously unknown basement level of the house. At the bottom of these steps, a right-hand door leads to a well-stocked gymnasium, the left opening up into an underground swimming pool: an oblong room of pure white stone, a huge circle of soft light glowing down from the ceiling.

Somewhere nearby, I hear a light smattering of polite applause.

Curious, if a little perturbed, my eyes land on a secondary corridor, on the opposite side of the pool. I skirt the edge of the swimming pool and head down it. The applause stops, replaced by the rhythmic, percussive sound of a casual tennis game. Hit, bounce, hit, bounce, hit, bounce, bounce.

The applause starts up again as I find myself standing at the edge of a large, subterranean tennis court. The floor is astroturf. The entire wall is covered in a vast mural of sunlit bleachers and a bustling crowd of spectators. Like characters from a Donald McGill illustration, they stare with wide smiles and round, rosy faces, overjoyed to see me.

I place one foot over the threshold, and the background noise cuts out immediately.

Knock knock knock.

I startle as I turn to see Mr Villner's frame silhouetted at the end of the long corridor, his knuckles rapping on the wall.

Collecting myself, I happily leave the court behind.

We pass back to the atrium and take the western door, the only direction from this central room that I haven't yet explored.

The dining room is a long rectangle, dimly lit by three meagre chandeliers. The storm-cloud grey walls display countless artworks, from oil paintings to watercolours to sixties Pop Art, their frames ranging from gold to MDF, in rows and columns so far-reaching that the furthest pieces disappear into darkness.

Villner disappears through a door at the north end, a nearby chef's window offering a glimpse of a professional-looking kitchen.

I'm left to approach the room's standout feature: a long table fashioned from a single slab of wood, the thick, oaken legs engraved with intricate floral carvings, a wooden mouse nestled within its edging. There are no chairs along the sides – instead there's just one seat at each end, the two diners separated by an intimidating stretch of empty tabletop.

Codelle is already in her seat, browsing a tablet with her usual quiet focus. In front of her sits a teacup, saucer and silver strainer as well as a small plate of what looks like squares of dusted chocolate cake.

She catches me examining her breakfast, reacting with a half chuckle and a self-effacing grin.

'I used to eat this as a child; my father limited me to one piece a week. He worried I'd get hooked on the sugar. When I went to university, I realised I could eat as much as I wanted. Gained three kilos in a month.' Codelle picks up another piece and pops it into her mouth. 'You can ask Mr Villner for some; it's chocolate, coffee and coconut.'

'I'm ok, thank you.' I cross to my chair, the legs screeching loudly as I pull it out. 'Not that I'm against dessert for breakfast.'

Codelle chuckles, swallowing before speaking.

'Well, I suggest you eat something, I heard you skipped dinner.'

As if on cue, Mr Villner backs out through the kitchen, turning around to reveal a pair of tiered silver trays. He crosses the room and places the trays in front of me, returning soon after with a hand-thrown ceramic plate and assorted cutlery. The trays contain an array of breakfast foods – a tier of pastries; a tier of butter, jam and triangle-cut toast; and a bottom level containing a glass jar of yoghurt, with smaller glass ramekins of jams, currants and seeds to mix and match.

Villner steps back, waiting.

'Is there anything else Villner can get you?' Codelle chimes in.

'No, no thank you, that's, um … well, a cup of tea actually. Milk. No sugar.'

Villner disappears into the kitchen once again, quickly emerging with an entire tea set on an ornate silver tray. He unloads the set in front of me: cup, saucer, strainer and a final ceramic pot in a blue tea cosy. He takes my thanks as dismissal, nods once, and exits.

'I like this, um … ceramicware.'

'Thank you, I threw it myself. There's a pottery wheel upstairs if you want to try it.'

'Oh yeah, maybe.' I feign enthusiasm, wishing I really felt it. Admittedly, I'm a little curious how my work would stack up against Codelle's previous host of widowers.

We return to silence. I stare across at Codelle's crockery. Strangely enough, her own coffee mug and plate seem perfectly identical to my own, no variation, no flaws. One could argue that it's strange, to hand-make items with such perfect uniformity, but from what I've seen of Codelle, it makes sense. Self-sufficiency is the goal, not rustic charm.

'I, um …' I begin, looking back to Codelle, who places her tablet down and meets my gaze. 'I had a dream last night.'

'Oh really?' She raises an eyebrow in interest.

'I was in my room, and I saw someone pass by my window, so I went outside and …' I glance towards the kitchen, hoping to keep myself out of earshot as I push forward. 'I saw Mr Villner standing in the middle of a storm and he was … singing.'

Codelle holds back a laugh, nodding to herself.

'I see.' She grins. '"Are You Lonesome Tonight?"'

'So that, um … that really happened?'

'Yes, that really happened.' Codelle shakes her head. 'My goodness, on your first night as well. I'm sorry if it made you uncomfortable—'

'No. No, no.' I wave my hands to protest the notion. 'Don't know why I'm even mentioning it. Just … is it significant?'

'To him, yes.' Codelle nods, sipping her tea. 'It used to be quite a negative trigger for the man, hard for him to even listen to the song. To have him sing it out loud is … well, it's actually quite heart-warming.'

I stare at Codelle.

'Is … sorry … is Villner a *patient* here?'

'Was. A few years ago now.'

'Oh … right.'

I tip the teapot, watching sodden leaves slowly collect in the strainer. I'm not sure how to process this new information, that a former patient of Dr Codelle's now cooks her breakfast every morning. My opinion is still forming but, even in its primordial state, terms like 'responsibility' and 'undue influence' rise to the surface.

'Does that concern you?' Codelle comments.

I look up to find her eyes quietly fixed on mine.

'I uh—'

'It's all right. I understand,' Codelle continues. 'The subject of doctor-patient relationships whether romantic, platonic, professional, is always an ethical consideration. When Villner left this island, he'd made astounding progress. He'd recovered as well as any other patient and, like any other patient, I wasn't expecting to ever see him again. I heard things, of course. He'd flourished in the financial industry, gained a prestigious position, an apartment, relationships, hobbies, displayed every sign of independence. Then one day, two years after we last saw each other, he contacted the institute, said that our work here had struck a chord with him, that his own career, while successful, provided no moral benefit from his perspective. He wanted to enrich others, instead of just himself.'

Codelle picks up a final square of cake. It rests between her thumb and forefinger while she recalls the rest of the story.

'I had to weigh up his motives: was this man regressing to a place that represented safety? Or was this an independent, lucid human being who'd simply found his calling in life?'

'And you decided it was the latter?' I ask rhetorically.

'It was a judgement call – a difficult one – but yes, I did. Why, what would you have done?' Codelle asks, a genuine curiosity in her voice.

'I, um ...'

Codelle waits for me to speak, then, realising I don't have a response, smiles in understanding and bites into the final piece of cake. I'm something close to satisfied with her answer.

Codelle glances at her tablet.

'We have an appointment, Mr Mason. Fifteen-minute warning.' She wipes the crumbs from her fingers and stands up. 'Do eat though. We've got a long day ahead of us.'

12

Fifteen minutes later, I'm following Dr Codelle as she exits into the atrium, ascends the spiral staircase, and passes into the corridors of the second floor.

We walk in comfortable silence, skirting a western wall, moving through circle-, square- and star-shaped sunbeams as we approach the south side of the house. The final turn, and a short stretch of hallway, leads to a jet-black door: a cushioned surface of tufted leather, each of its padded dimples accented with a polished gold coin.

'Well then, Arthur' – Codelle smiles as she turns the large brass handle – 'step into my office.'

Codelle's office is a lesson in stark contrast. At a decent size of around thirty square metres, the walls of featureless grey encase a trove of ornate furniture. There's a Renaissance air about the place: high oaken bookshelves spanning the east and western walls, packed with non-fiction tomes from various centuries. An antique globe sits at the side of the room, long-defunct nations outlined on its stained wood surface. In the far corner, an oblong of white marble stands upright on a translucent plastic sheet, its upper half hewn into the rough form of a human figure, its lower half still entombed within the block.

At the south end of the room is a wooden desk so long and wide that I doubt Codelle could reach across it from the far side. Its neatly organised surface contains a high-end laptop, a 1980s landline phone, a classic notary lamp of green glass, and a brass sextant in a domed display case. The remainder of the desk is buried beneath piles of annotated paperwork, and a selection of medical textbooks.

Behind the desk: a vast circular window which fills the majority of the back wall. I recognise it immediately as the cyclopean eye that I had seen upon my arrival, its gaze centred on the boathouse, providing an elevated view of the distant Welsh shoreline. It's no surprise that Codelle chose this room as her office.

Codelle saunters around the desk and sits down, a vast halo of pale sunlight behind her. She levels her eyes on mine, and gestures to the opposite armchair, sorting through a final set of notes as I take my seat.

As the doctor collects herself, I take a second glance at the unfinished marble sculpture, a leather belt of stone-carving tools resting on the bookshelf beside it, the faintest layer of marble dust on the plastic sheet below.

'Is that … did you make that?'

Codelle looks up, briefly following my eye line before returning to her notes.

'Yes, a new venture of mine. I'm not very good yet but, well, just got to keep chipping away.'

I've never seen a marble sculpture in an unfinished state before. It leaves me almost anxious, as if the poor figure were trapped inside the layer of jagged rock. It also leaves me wondering what varied talents *I* could develop if I woke up at 5 each morning, though admittedly the notion passes quite quickly.

'What's it going to be, when you're done?'

'I'm not sure yet.' Codelle shrugs noncommittally. 'I'm discovering it as I go. Villner suggested I make it in his image, since he's the one who had to haul the stone up here.'

'You're going to need a bigger block.'

Codelle half chuckles and goes back to her papers. I shuffle in my seat, staring out towards the coastline before my eyes come to rest on the doctor's work.

'You've already made a lot of notes.'

'Most of these are Dr Dunn's,' Codelle remarks casually, finally tracking down the passage she was looking for. 'She was researching a diagnosis. Persistent Complex Bereavement Disorder.'

Codelle reads it off the notes, almost performatively, before looking up.

'It's a relatively new term,' Codelle continues. 'Describing people who have an overwhelming and continuing reaction to the loss of a loved one. How would you feel about being given that diagnosis?'

'I guess it makes sense.' I shrug. 'I mean ... it's accurate.'

'I didn't ask if it was *accurate*,' Codelle chides gently. 'How would you *feel* about receiving the diagnosis?'

'Well, I, um ...' I shift uncomfortably, avoiding her gaze. 'I don't really like the idea of being diagnosed with anything.'

'Why not?'

'Because I don't like the idea that ... my experience is somehow more significant than anyone else's.'

Silence follows. Codelle allows a slow pressure to build in the increasingly quiet room. After a while, I can't help but defuse it myself.

'I just feel like ... everyone goes through this at some point, right?' I wager, gingerly examining my own reasoning. 'Everyone loses someone, it's just a part of life. If I can't handle something so universal ... getting diagnosed feels like, I don't know ... an excuse.'

Codelle nods, the glint of a knowing smile at the corner of her mouth, before moving her notes to the side and interlocking her fingers.

'How did you meet Julia?'

'I'm sure most of it's in Dr Dunn's notes.'

'You're right, it is,' she confirms, waiting all the same.

'Ok, well, I, um ...' I stumble, unsure where exactly to begin, and let out a long breath. 'Well ... we were twelve years old. My father booked me on this sailing camp at Lake Windemere. He said it was to build character, make friends, though I've since learned he spent that weekend in Montenegro with his new girlfriend so ... that might've been part of it.'

Dr Codelle, sensing that I've found the humour in such reve-lations, matches my energy with a wry grin.

'Anyway, there was a campsite nearby. One night, they had this huge fire, and we were teenage boys, so we flocked to it like moths. It was a camping club social, lots of other kids. Suddenly I was alone, with all the social grace you'd expect from a student at an all-boys' school. I was nervous, just waiting for the fire to burn down, and she just … sat next to me … and it was effortless.'

I take a moment to appreciate the bizarre scenario, that we were once children, sitting by a campfire, barely able to think beyond the end of summer, but unknowingly laying the founda-tion for our entire adult lives. I have no earthly idea of what we spoke about, but the content wasn't important, the important thing was that we never really stopped.

'She was smart …' I continue, beginning to gush, 'and kind, and interesting and just … ridiculously funny. She had this streak of dark humour that you'd … you'd only get to see if she really felt comfortable around you. I mean … I couldn't talk to her enough, Dr Codelle. When we started texting, I'd fall asleep with the phone in my hand.'

Two dimples appear on the doctor's face as she smiles irre-pressibly at my recollection. I almost feel embarrassed, aware that I am coming across as a lovestruck simpleton, though not sure how to present as anything else.

'We were just friends for three years.' I push forward. 'I fancied her straight away, but she lived up north and I was in the south … also I was a huge coward. But the two groups stayed in touch and when we were fifteen, there was this camping trip. I had this romantic plan to tell her how I felt. I'd found this quiet spot by a lake. I asked her to take a walk there on our final day … but I got so nervous that I chickened out. I ended up blurting out my feelings at the coach station about a minute before she had to go back up north …'

'You were married before you were twenty, right?'

'Yes, I proposed when we were both eighteen; we got married later in the year.'

'A civil ceremony? I have "Southwark Registry Office" here.'

'Yeah. Mum was mortified,' I say, Codelle chuckling at the thought. 'My parents didn't come in the end. It was Julia's mother, six of Julia's friends, well ... they became both of our friends in time, but most of my friendships were introduced by Julia, she was the social one. Anyway, we could've planned this grand wedding and done it a year later but we just wanted to start our lives. We put our thirty-day booking in, paid for a photographer and a cake, wore our best clothes. It was about us, nothing else, just ... me and her.'

'Sounds incredibly romantic.' Codelle smiles. I nod.

'Some of those friends told us it was a mistake. The rest of them were thinking it as well, they told us so years later. Even Lorraine, Julia's mum, thought it was too fast. And I agree it was ... absolutely insane by any reasonable standard but ... God, it was just one of those few times when I knew *exactly* what I was doing ... and I was right, I mean, we were together for fourteen years after that. We were happy.'

I watch the journey of Codelle's expression. The warm smile, that optimistic gleam all consummate romantics get when they find evidence of love in the world. Slowly, however, in the silence that follows, a sadness creeps into her eyes, the joy washing from her face as she steps into the next topic of conversation.

'She died at home, didn't she?'

'Yes,' I say, matter-of-factly. 'In the living room.'

'You weren't there?'

'I was ... I was meant to be.' A dense, heavy welt forms in my throat. 'I had to stay late at the office. Her last text to me was asking when I was going to be home.'

'And how did it feel? The decision to take your own life?'

I wasn't expecting the sudden change in direction. It takes me a moment to shift perspectives.

'Like ... choosing between burning to death or drowning.'

'That's not an uncommon sentiment, the feeling of having no good choices,' Codelle concurs, and I quietly nod. She looks at me, almost reluctantly, as she presses further. 'Ultimately though, you chose to remain here. You called an ambulance, induced vomiting. One thing I can't find in these notes is … what made you change your mind?'

I take a deep breath, and let the silence linger for a while. I'd been asked this question before, in some form or another, but I'd always attempted to circumvent.

'It was a phone call. My mother-in-law. She's the only other person who … she phones me to talk about Julia. I don't know, suddenly I felt like I was abandoning her. I was worried she'd think maybe her call … was a catalyst or something … that she'd feel responsible. I couldn't do that to her.'

'Can I ask why it isn't in Dr Dunn's notes? Why your mother didn't mention it either?'

'I didn't tell them.'

'Why?'

'Because I wanted them to think that I changed my mind of my own accord, that I just decided against it.'

'But you didn't?'

'Lorraine called half an hour after I took the pills,' I confess, a strange feeling of shame washing over me. 'Before she called … I don't … you'd think it would be something I'd remember but I … I don't know if I would've turned back on my own.'

I feel tears build and break behind my eyes, quietly rolling down my cheeks.

'You're in the right place, Arthur.' Codelle speaks gently but with heartfelt conviction. 'When you take the *De Anima* home, you'll be on the other side of this. That's a promise.'

I look up to Codelle, my eyes brimming with tears, something resembling hope glowing dimly in my chest. As eccentric as this building may be, people in worse positions than myself have found salvation within these walls, under the patient gaze of Dr Elizabeth Codelle.

'We're going to pass into some troubled waters in the meantime, however,' Codelle admits, a sense of sincere regret in her voice. 'And occasionally I'll be responsible for steering us in that direction. Your opinion of me may change; some days I'll feel like an enemy, others an ally, or a detached medical professional, hopefully, at times, a friend. Regardless of how you feel about me, I want you to understand two things. One, I will never lie to you, and two, I will always have your best interests at heart. Do you understand?'

I nod, wiping the tears away from my eyes. Codelle pushes a box of tissues across the table.

'Unfortunately, our initial session will be more difficult than most,' she says with a despondent sigh. 'I'm afraid there's slightly more to your being here than you've previously been told.'

'What does that mean?' I examine Codelle's expression. There is a certain reluctance in her tone, as if this were a conversation she'd rather not be having, as if something or someone had forced her hand.

'This is a grief counselling retreat, Arthur, that's all it ever will be. But when I was conducting my background interviews, your mother raised a secondary concern, something she was planning to discuss with you, something that won't be easy for you to hear. On balance, I convinced her that it would be better to have the conversation somewhere safe, a place solely dedicated to your mental health, so that you have the time and space to process it however you wish.'

My sadness is replaced by an unpleasant confusion.

'So, my mother has news so devastating she wanted me on a private island in the care of a dedicated psychiatrist before I heard it?'

'The extra safeguards were my idea, but essentially, yes.'

'So … what … am I fired?'

Codelle gives me a look of sympathy, before rolling her leather chair back and pulling out a heavy drawer. She lifts a thick stack of A4 papers, bound together with a plastic spine and fronted by a cover of dark blue laminate. She places this dossier on the desk, still out of my reach, but facing pointedly in my direction.

'Three years ago,' Codelle begins, 'Mason Industrial undertook two contracts for military-aligned companies, one of which you were directly involved with.'

'I remember.'

'Then you'll recall that all higher-ups at the company were subject to extensive vetting: an audit of finances, political affiliation, friends, family. A full background check.'

'Yes … I passed. As far as I'm aware, everyone did.'

'That's correct. But some areas of concern were raised to the Mason Industrial CEO, your mother, and one was … troubling. Delilah Mason hired a private investigator to follow up on these concerns and she thought you deserved to know the results.'

A dispirited Codelle slides the bound document across the desk towards me. I take a final quizzical glance at her face before lifting the blank cover.

'This is …' I begin, before the words fall still in my throat.

I read through the scant text on the first few pages, my eyes darting from left to right, my mind jumping from amused disbelief, to confusion, to anger.

'Why would you show me this?' I say, my eyes still firmly fixed on the pages.

'Your mother's thinking, as far as I understand it, is that this was the truth. That you deserve to know, even if it's painful.'

'Do you agree?'

'I believe, if you were going to learn of this either way, I'd rather you be here.'

I stare back down at the crude and unsettling document. Phone records, a text conversation between two people, spanning a total of five years.

Aligned to the right-hand side of the page, a man known only as 078, his identity hidden behind a redacted phone number. The person on the left is easily identifiable by the name at the top of each message, as well as the recognisable rhythms of her prose.

Julia
When will I see you?

078-★★★★-★★★★
You tell me.

Julia
He's gone for the weekend. Come over, I miss you.

'This isn't real,' I whisper reflexively.

I flip through the pages, almost desperately, searching for the punchline, the disclaimer that tells me it's all some elaborate joke. Instead, I find exactly what the document appears to be: half a decade of correspondence between my late wife and an unknown man; flirting, planning, reminiscing about rendezvous I had no idea were taking place.

The more I read, the deeper it gets, every few pages mentioning some event that I vividly remember: a conference, a business trip. Responsibilities which carried me away from home for nights and weekends, each one serving as a window for their meetings, an entire sexual and emotional relationship filling the gaps I left for them.

I don't believe it. I can't. Despite everything in front of me, I refuse to entertain a solitary word. That is, until I reach a page barely an eighth of the way through the stack, a page which ends with a simple request.

Julia
His conference got cancelled, he's coming home. Promise not to forget about me?

078-★★★★-★★★★
Give me something to remember you by then.

A dull ache of defeat and sadness rushes over me, embarrassment rising in my cheeks.

There are no words on the next page. Instead, aligned across the left side are a series of three pictures. Clearly taken in our bedroom at the time. Julia is sitting demurely on the edge of the mattress, her bare skin lit by the light of the flash, smiling for the camera with a spark in her eyes I thought was reserved for me alone.

'Why are you showing me this?' I ask again, defeated and confused.

Dr Codelle doesn't answer.

Pages turn and turn and turn, crushing waves of betrayal barrelling into me and tossing me around like a rag doll with each successive discovery. I feel like I'm going to throw up. My lungs stop taking in air, my ears ring with static.

'She wouldn't do this. She wouldn't.'

Dr Codelle keeps her silence, a look of deep sympathy on her face.

'I … I don't … I might need some time,' I mutter, unable to look Codelle in the eyes.

'Of course.' Codelle's voice cuts through. 'This session ends whenever you want it to.'

I think that I nod. I think I say thank you. I think that I say I'll need some time.

I may not have done.

I barely remember leaving the room.

13

I start walking, without bearing, without consciousness, as a hundred hideous notions press against the confines of my skull.

Intrusive thoughts fester like some swelling organism, bloating itself on my pain and insecurity before splitting open, spilling its offspring across my exposed grey matter. Through the chaos, I hear the clang of my own footsteps on wrought iron, feel the walls of the entrance corridor penning me in until I'm finally struck by the cold rush of outdoor air.

I stand beneath a powder-blue sky, on the south shore of Prismall House, a storm of hot tears rolling down my cheeks.

The tapestry of my life suddenly feels like a grotesque jigsaw puzzle, pieces from an entirely different box forced into the scene until it becomes an ugly, disjointed mess.

Beyond everything else, I'm facing this heartbreak without any chance of clarification, or confrontation or closure. I could storm back to my London flat right now, but I'd find no one to question or rebuke or even forgive. Instead, all the rage I send out into the world simply crashes uselessly back upon me.

True to her word, Codelle gives me time by myself. Villner passes by occasionally, as I sit numbly on a bench in the gardens, but he makes no attempt at contact, meditatively combing the island grounds with a rotary mower.

Hours pass, and my gaze comes to rest on the distant horizon. It almost feels like you're out there, among the sailboats, on the vanishing point of the horizon. I feel I could let this version of you slip away, beyond that far meridian, allow myself to think less of you and, in time, to think of you less.

It would be as easy as sitting here and watching you go.

'I think I need to know what happened. All of it.'

I can see Codelle considering my request as I return, some time later, to her office. I stand before the ornate desk as she ticks through the implications, clearly balancing the psychological dangers against the potential benefits. Moments later, her judgement coalesces into a final nod.

I take the hefty document from her hands, and retreat to my bedroom in the north-east corner of Prismall House. One hundred and seventy-six bound pages thud onto my duvet as I stare down at it, unable to estimate the sheer density of heartache I might uncover inside.

Tossing my pillow onto the floor, sitting on the mattress with my back pressed against the wall, I take the document into my hands. I have no idea what I'm really looking for, no idea if it will bring me even a modicum of peace. I simply know it has to be done, and that it's going to hurt.

The affair my wife had been conducting over the last five years was passionate, elaborate and meticulously planned around my every conceivable absence. Moments of remorse shine through in a few rare passages, yet they're quickly snuffed out by an increasingly casual set of rationalisations: that I'm distant, that I'm cold, that the fact I didn't notice their activities proves just how neglectful I must be.

Pages arc from right to left just as the sun arcs through the sky beyond my window. Half a decade of messages pass before me, as lustful, rash behaviour slowly evolves into genuine proclamations of love. Short sentences give way to paragraphs, which give way to pictures; the contours of my wife's body playfully outlined beneath the sheets of our bed, the wry smile which seems more cruel with every page.

I stop dead.

A few lines from the top of page 143 catch my eye.

As my eyes slowly register the words before me, a series of separate images flash through my mind. A castle on a hill, a bright pair of eyes, a woman in a dark raincoat, a distant figure with salt and pepper hair, and finally, the calm, confident face of Dr Elizabeth Codelle.

I need to find her immediately.

I jump to my feet, barely registering that night has rolled in beyond my window. I snatch up the document and press my hand against the door, side-stepping through before it's even finished moving aside.

I pace back down the corridors, and into the grand atrium, turning through my options, from the second-floor balcony to the games room to the exit corridor and, finally, to the door to the dining room on the west side.

It's as good a place to start as any.

'Arthur, I wasn't sure if we'd be seeing you today.' Codelle looks up from the dining room table, stirring an earthenware bowl of glass noodles as the double doors swing closed behind me. 'I didn't think you'd be hungry.'

'You said my mother sent you this?' I utter sharply.

'That's right,' Codelle replies calmly. 'It was compiled by an investigator but, yes, I got it from her office.'

'On the fifteenth of November,' I begin, keeping myself in place despite the urge to pace. 'Two years ago, I was in Edinburgh as part of a two-day navtech conference. It took up all of Saturday and Sunday. I was walking through the Grassmarket and I remember having this thought ... what would Julia be saying right now if she was here? You know? Because I loved to travel with her, she had all these thoughts and opinions on things that never would have occurred to me. Travelling alone was like ... sightseeing with one eye closed.'

A warm, sad smile crosses Dr Codelle's face.

'I called her from the hotel that night, just to say that I was thinking of her, to hear about her day.' I struggle not to well up as I remember looking over Edinburgh Castle, calmed by her voice on the phone. 'From the looks of it, she was *with* him when she took my call. They spent that entire weekend together.'

Codelle bows her head slightly, as if sharing the weight of the revelation alongside me. When she looks back up, I see a look of radiating sympathy.

'It doesn't mean she didn't love you, Arthur,' Codelle begins, picking her words with slow, kind precision. 'She faltered, and from a cursory review of her correspondence, she wasn't free of guilt.'

'Then why didn't she tell me?'

'I'm sure she thought she was sparing you from … unnecessary pain. We can convince ourselves of so many things, even when we're just serving our own self-interest. She was a person, Arthur, a flawed human being, like we all are.'

I nod, letting Codelle's words pass over me.

'You know what happened next? After I called her?' I finally respond. 'There was a knock at my hotel room door. I thought maybe it was a work thing so …'

I force back a slow swell of tears, clenching and unclenching my fist.

'It was her,' I continue. 'It was Julia. She had a free weekend, and so she bought a train ticket to Scotland to surprise me. Outside my hotel room door, she asked me how it could be, that you could live with someone for so many years and still miss them when they're away for only two days. But I totally understood it. I felt *exactly* the same.'

I drop the heavy block of paper onto the dining room table.

'She wasn't with him that weekend, doctor. She was with me. The messages in that document from the fifteenth and sixteenth of November explicitly mention her being in London, with this … secret lover, but she was in an entirely different *country* and she didn't leave my side once. That entire section is made up … it's fiction. And if that section's a lie, then I think all of it could be. The entire document is just … it's a fucking fabrication.'

Codelle listens with calm, professional courtesy, the barest hint of a sigh when she finally speaks.

'I'm sure that's a comforting notion, Arthur, but a classic psychological reaction to news like this is—'

'No. This isn't denial,' I assert forcefully. 'This is *factually* impossible.'

'There are photographs, Arthur.'

'I know. They're perfect. A five-year affair, built around every conference, every time I wasn't home. If it wasn't for Edinburgh, I might have ... but it's not true. She loved me, I loved her, and after fourteen years, the *only* bad thing about our marriage is that it ended. But if my mother had this ... commissioned or ...'

Codelle remains silent, stone-faced. Her white-clad frame suddenly looks small against the heavy back of the mahogany chair, her effortless sense of calm authority drained away.

'It doesn't matter.' I raise my palms, letting go of the question, of this island, of everything. 'I'll take it up with her myself.'

'Arthur ...'

'I want to go back to Porthcoll tonight. If you can't spare your ... Mr Villner, I'll get a bus, a train, whatever takes me back to London.'

'Arthur, this is exactly why you came on this retreat.' Codelle's voice raises infinitesimally. 'To get away from parental influence, your job, the pressures of London. I don't believe it would be healing for you to turn ba—'

'I don't care.' The nervous energy suddenly falls away, my feet firm on the ground for the first time in a while. 'I came here because *my mother* asked it of me. After this, I can't trust her, and I can't trust you. I want to go home. Tonight.'

Dr Codelle stares at me. It feels like the air is alive with a hundred lines of argument, each being considered in turn by the woman in front of me. I can hear a stampede of stomping footsteps, a thousand doors slamming, as I storm out of the room in every conceivable scenario. A moment later, after what feels like much longer than the seconds it took, everything falls completely silent.

Dr Codelle places down her stone utensils, a switch flicking somewhere in the base of her skull.

'I am so, genuinely, sorry, Arthur.' She speaks slowly. 'This is, without a doubt, one of the most significant failings of my career. It's entirely my own fault, and I take full responsibility.'

I stay quiet for a long moment.

'Did my mother do this or was this—'

'It was me,' Codelle interrupts plainly. 'I fabricated the messages based on your text history, your schedule, your own conversations with Julia. The Edinburgh navtech conference was in your calendar, I confirmed your attendance, but I should have noticed Julia had followed you there.'

'And the pictures?'

'Synthetic media,' Codelle explains. 'Julia's face virtually imposed on a physical model in physical space.'

'*Physical space.* You had these taken in our apartment?'

Dr Codelle says nothing. She doesn't need to.

'Yesterday you said you'd never lie to me.'

'That was a lie,' Codelle admits, neither proud nor ashamed. 'The truth is, I will use every possible tool at my disposal, do everything in my power, in the pursuit of saving your life. I'll do anything to ensure that you leave here happy, healthy, and completely freed from the cycle of withdrawal and relapse that you've fallen into.'

'Withdrawal? What the fuck are you talking about? I'm not in *withdrawal.*'

'You are, Arthur,' Codelle responds. 'That is my contention. A contention validated through years of study, research and countless lives saved through its direct application to my work. It is my opinion that complex grief, and grief in general for that matter, more accurately presents as a form of Post-Bereavement Limerent Withdrawal and should be treated primarily as an addiction.'

'Post-Bereavement … what are you … this is insanity!'

'It's all the same, Arthur.' Codelle sighs. 'Alcohol, gambling, heroin, your late – and by all accounts lovely – wife Julia. Radically different stimuli, but when fed into the base neuro-chemistry of the brain, they elicit the same result. Heightened serotonin from a single regular source, growing over multiple years into a chemical dependency. Their removal precipitates oxytocin deficit, chemical imbalances, fixation, anhedonia, loss of function, self-destruction. From a clinical perspective, the symptoms are functionally identi—'

'— I'm not a fucking addict!'

'I'm afraid that is what most addicts say, in the beginning,' Codelle replies calmly. 'We'll talk about this more later. For now, all you need to know is that I am here for you, and that we will get through this together.'

I hear a door open and close behind me, footsteps arriving at my back before I can turn around. A heavy arm reaches across my body and draws tight, gripping me firmly in place.

A swell of panic rushes through me, my shoes thrashing and squeaking against the floor as I fight to break away. But the grip of William Villner proves as secure and unmoving as stone. Calmly, the man's free arm disappears into his jacket, before returning with a clear plastic syringe held between his index and middle finger.

My eyes widen in a wave of renewed horror as I battle wildly, desperately, against Villner's obstinate embrace.

'I'm so sorry, Arthur.' Codelle looks on, her eyes glassy with dismay. 'I am, I'm so sorry. That document was supposed to make things easier, an anaesthetic, ensuring the rest of our work was as painless as possible. I failed you and, in the interest of total honesty ... this is likely to become a much more challenging process.'

The needle slips beneath my skin. The compressor sinks down, unrushed, forcing a milky grey liquid into my veins. A dull yawn of lethargy rolls across my body, a gaping black hole opening in the back of my mind. My head lolls backward, my eyes scanning the ceiling as I collapse into a pair of waiting arms.

Before I fall entirely from consciousness, I hear Dr Codelle stand up from her chair, feel my heels begin to drag against the wooden floor. In the end, you're the very last thing I think of, your familiar silhouette outlined against the threshold of oblivion.

Eventually even you fall away, and the lights go out behind you.

Date Unknown

14

The first thing I'm aware of, as I'm pulled from a weightless slumber, are three new pressures being exerted upon my body.

The first is easy to comprehend. The supportive weight of a leather armchair pushing up against me, my back reclined, arms parallel, my heavy skull cradled against a luxurious padded headrest.

The second pressure is applied to the sides of my head: a set of noise-cancelling headphones cupping my ears, their airtight cushions trampling any external sound.

Finally, my weak limbs are held down by a set of restraints, hugging my wrists and ankles against the arms and legs of the chair.

From touch alone, I can tell these restraints are made from the same material as the armchair. The same cool leather, the same flat grain texture. Somehow, I'd feel more comfortable with zip ties around my wrists. At least then my captivity might feel like a panicked improvisation. Instead, I'm restrained in a chair clearly custom built for the purpose, exactly where my captors intend for me to be.

'Mr Mason.'

My eyelids finally eke open, cringing against the sudden rush of light.

I'm not in the dining room anymore. The cavernous hall has been replaced by a tiny room, scarcely ten feet in every direction. The walls are a matte black, smooth and windowless. The only light emanates from directly ahead: four fluorescent tubes framing the edges of the wall in front of me, forming a seamless square of light.

The room has the eerie feel of a private view gallery, its walls conspicuously blank.

'I'd wanted to do this face to face. It's the least you deserve.' Codelle's words invade my ears, her voice insidiously clear through the headphones. 'Unfortunately, your seeing me right now would muddy the process.'

'Wh thhh …' My tongue is like lead as I try to speak, unsure if our communication even goes two ways. 'What the … hell is this?'

'I want you to know that I take full responsibility for the error you discovered. It was a serious lapse in operational quality,' Codelle continues unabated. 'In the few days you've been resting, I have fully recalibrated your treatment plan to compensate, but such measures should never have been needed. I apologise.'

She sounds like she means it.

'If you can hear me …' I stumble through the words, a weak prayer to the disembodied voice. 'Let me … let me go. Just let me go.'

The doctor doesn't respond. I swallow with great effort and try once again.

'I can pay you. If it's the fee, I … I'll match it. I'll sign anything, just … let me leave.'

Silence rings in my ears, until suddenly:

clink. clink. clink. clink.

The four strips of light ahead of me blink out one by one. At the same time, a rectangle of grey light is projected against the wall, emanating from somewhere behind my chair.

It hangs empty for a moment, before the symbol of a white caduceus appears in the left half of the screen, a title card blinking in on the right.

Cambridge Medical Examiners Ltd
Drs Armisten & Goodknow Presiding
Clinical Examination Results for Julia Lynne Mason

An older man begins to speak in a calm voice.

*'Patient is a thirty-three-year-old female, pronounced dead on
the seventh of October—'*

The images scream out towards me. I shut my eyes tightly as the
first few frames claw towards my brain: a white room, a white
sheet, a mottled grey body beneath it.

clink. clink. clink. clink.

Over my gasping, rattled breaths, I hear the four lights turn back
on, their glow radiating through my eyelids.

As soon as the last one ignites, the sound of the video cuts out.

A cold horror rises from the depths of my soul, shredding
every nerve on its way to my panicked brain. I don't understand.
I don't understand what's happening. My ears ring in the silence,
my eyelids still pressed firmly shut.

'What is this? Why are you doing this?!'

There's no reply. Since the lights came back on, there's been
no sound at all through the irremovable headphones. Nothing
from Codelle. Nothing from the screen ahead of me.

Tentatively, my head faced down towards the floor, I let my
eyes creep open.

I stare at my feet in continued silence, my shoes bathed in the
pale glow of the four strip lights.

Slowly, reluctantly, testing the parameters of my situation, I
raise my head and fix it forwards, towards the square of four
lights, and the blank wall.

A return to darkness, a projection and a title card.

'Patient is a thirty-three-year-old female, pronounced—'

I jolt my head down from the horrific images.

clink. clink. clink. clink.

I press my eyes closed, retreating behind my eyelids while I try desperately to think.

The lights turn back on the moment I look away, a pattern steadily forming. All four of the bulbs turn off when I look forward, paving the way for the projection to begin. Then, if my eyes leave the screen, the lights illuminate again, signalling an automatic reset of the video, priming it to start over from the beginning.

There was a blue line at the bottom of the screen: a progress bar, detailing the time remaining on the video. It had moved quickly, meaning the video can't last more than two minutes at most. But the bar itself only confirms what I'm already coming to understand, something Codelle has patiently allowed me to realise for myself.

I'm not leaving here until I've watched this video through.

The process of understanding brings no comfort at all.

I keep my eyes shut, leaning back against the headrest, making a home in the darkness. Minutes pass, and I slowly begin to feel you behind me, your calming presence brushing over every hair on the back of my neck, your mere existence pushing back against the grey void ahead of me.

My back sore, my wrists and ankles aching against the restraints, I allow myself to drift into something close to sleep, losing myself in mind and memory until the room slips away entirely and I manage to achieve a gracious form of escape.

When I wake up, I briefly believe that I'm back home.

clink. clink. clink. clink.

'Patient is a thirty-three-year-old female, pronounced dead on the seventh of October, showing—'

My eyes scream open at the face before me. Mottled grey blotches, purple lips, dark coagulated veins running beneath the paper-thin skin of your cheeks. The unblinking eyes, pupils dilated under harsh overhead lights.

I tear my head away. Cruel afterimages burrowing into my grey matter. My lungs cast forth a gut-wrenching cry, overcome by the sheer hollowness, the emptiness of the shell I saw on the screen ahead.

clink. clink. clink. clink.

The lights flicker back on, and the video resets once more.

I don't know what to do.

I just don't know what to do.

The silence between each playthrough is sickeningly patient. From my brief interactions with Dr Codelle, I know she will have anticipated my initial refusal, that she would never have placed me in a position like this if she wasn't prepared to outlast me.

As the minutes pass, I settle on two conclusions. Firstly, I need to get off this island, which necessitates that I leave this room. My second conclusion, though it is perhaps more an act of wishful thinking, is that I must surely have seen the worst already.

It takes a few more minutes for me to lift my head and, unsure whether I'm being driven by courage or cowardice, to open my eyes.

The lights blink out.

clink. clink. clink. clink.

'Patient is a thirty-three-year-old female, pronounced dead by para-medics on the seventh of October, showing dilated pupils, no heart sounds, no pulse and no spontaneous respirations.'

I hang on through the onslaught of harrowing sights, pushing myself to keep going.

'The left lung contains multiple adherent emboli, completely occluding the bifurcation. In the absence of other issues, cause of death is determined to be acute pulmonary embolism, the effects of which would have been near instant.'

clink.

I blink, my eyes closing for a fraction of a second, opening again to see one of the fluorescent bulbs lit up.

I don't understand. Perhaps I don't have to. Perhaps I just need to keep going. But as a blade is drawn down a grey abdomen, I feel a swell of tears filling up my eyes. To keep the water from running down my cheeks, I blink another few times.

clink. clink. clink.

The square of light completes, and the video cuts out. After less than a second, the lights flicker off once again and the video restarts.

'Patient is a thirty-three-year-old female, pronounced dead by paramedics on the 7th of October, showing dilated pupils, no heart sounds, no pulse and no spontaneous—'

'I … I don't understand!' I speak into the darkness. 'I was watching! I didn't look away, why did you—'

Silence answers. I believed that if I watched the video, gave it my attention, that the lights wouldn't turn on. Now, the cause and effect seems so infuriatingly random, a grotesque Skinner box, punishing me for transgressions I don't know I'm making.

The doctor in the video restates the cause of death, knowledge I'd avoided for nine months, but which I've been forced to relive three times in just the last two minutes, as if the fateful prognosis were making up for lost time.

A medical blade carves a red fault line through bloodless skin. The tears return.

clink. clink. clink. clink.

'Patient is a thirty-three-year-old female, pronounced dead—'

I close my eyes as the video resets once more, a dull thud of understanding at the pit of my stomach.

The rules of this horrifying room were never communicated to me. Codelle withheld its mechanics, as if learning them for myself were part of the ordeal.

The four lights ahead of me are by no means random – if anything, they're governed by a technology more precise than I previously imagined, tracking so much as a blink and logging it as a strike against me. This footage requires more than my attention: it requires explicit, unbroken contact between my eyes and the screen. A staring competition with the most awful sights I've ever witnessed, repeated failure forcing me to watch it again, and again, and again, for as long as it takes.

I crumble in my chair, keeping my eyes shut tight for a moment longer. In the wake of the increasingly inevitable, I make a silent vow to the both of us: that whatever I see, it won't be my final memory of you. That as soon as I get back to my room, I will recover your photograph, an old Polaroid that I packed in my luggage, and stare at it every evening. Then, once I've returned to London, I'll find every album in our apartment and submerge myself in every page, every moment, until these awful visions are purged by happier images.

I slowly raise my head, and watch the lights flicker off one by one.

The video plays, every frame passing through my exposed retinas to the slick grey matter behind them. My eyes last scarcely five seconds before they begin to prickle and sting, the physical urge to close them raking at my resolve.

'We made a Y incision and removed the rib cage in order to examine the internal organs. The heart weighed—'

clink.

One blink. I force my eyes wider still, as the doctors dig into a hollow of glistening red.

I used to rest my ear against that chest, listening to your heart. Now meddling instruments cut and wrench at a lump of unbeating flesh, dropping it into a cold metal bowl.

clink. clink.

'Please, please, I can't—' I cry uselessly into the empty room, my eyes filling with tears, lungs being pulled from an open chest as I—

clink.

'Patient is a thirty-three-year-old female, pronounced dead by paramedics on the 7th of October—'

I see your heart being removed seven times more, your lungs following before I hit my limit, the four lights ahead stretching my will to previously unimaginable depths. Each time I'm thrown back to a world of pale grey, open eyes, incisions, excisions and back to the start all over again.

Yet with every new attempt, an unmistakable numbness draws over me. The expenditure of all emotion, the energy behind my panic and my horror draining away with each successive attempt. It's the tears that get me, stinging my eyes, forcing my lids to shut. But with every failed iteration, the tears slowly lessen.

Steeling myself, I surrender to the process, and open my eyes once again.

Grey skin. Open eyes. The scalpel's trail. The methodical removal of heart, lungs, kidneys and liver.

clink.

Just one blink, my eyes dry as I watch organs pass over a scale on a clean metal table.

clink.

*'The left lung contains multiple adherent emboli, completely
occluding the bifurcation. In the absence of other issues, cause of
death is determined to be acute pulmonary embolism, the effects
of which would have been near instant.'*

The words wash over me. Nine months avoiding the truth of
this moment, nine months looking away from the news on our
hall side table.

clink.

My eyes burn as the incision is sewn up, the camera capturing
the precise work of the two presiding doctors.

The video ends and I remain, staring at the three lights, as if
I'd never needed to blink in the first place.

A few seconds later, my eyelids descend, and I bow my head
from the front wall.

From somewhere behind me, I hear the projector being
switched off.

Sapped of all my strength, I squint passively, maybe even gratefully, as a transparent cannula is inserted into my arm. It fills with
a now familiar milky grey liquid, arcing and looping through the
tube and finally slipping its way into my veins.

I look up at the three lights, and the empty space between
them, until everything falls into an inky black darkness.

26th August

15

Ocean waves lap against the shores of my consciousness. I listen for a while, enjoying the peace of total dislocation, before my eyes gradually creep open.

I'm outside the institute, facing towards the open water, my limp body reclined in an adjustable deckchair. Predawn has drained all colour from the world, an overcast sky hanging above an equally greyscale ocean, the dark shadow of the Welsh coastline serving as the only demarcation between them.

I spend the next twenty minutes tentatively testing my motor functions, attempting to gradually flex my barely responsive fingers. During my efforts, the sun eventually heaves itself over the eastern horizon, burning away the cloud cover to reveal powder-blue skies, infusing deep green into the lawn as it sweeps across the island. Shortly after it rises in earnest, a long-absent warmth returns to my extremities, my fingers and toes slowly regaining feeling.

I can sense your presence behind me as my periphery expands. I can feel the light breeze streaming around your frame, trace notes of your perfume in the air, your calm sensibility radiating over me.

I can almost hear you getting closer, feet brushing gently towards me through the crisp grass.

'I thought I'd let you wake up in your own time.'

Dr Codelle appears over my shoulder, callously intruding. She places her hand on the wooden deckchair as she lowers herself to my side.

'I thought it was the least we could do, given the circumstances.'

'You're …' I attempt to speak, the words quickly collapsing under their own weight. 'You're a f …'

'Pardon?' Codelle glances towards me, leaning forward to watch my lips move.

'… You're a fucking monster.'

Codelle sits in silence. She nods minutely, before turning back towards the open sea.

'I've done many things that would be considered monstrous,' she comments offhandedly. 'I cut a man's heart out once.'

A strong breeze brushes through the grass in a quiet wave, sending up a cloud of chalk dust as it reaches the boathouse footpath.

'Of course, that only sounds monstrous if you ignore the context,' Codelle continues. 'That the heart was failing, that I was replacing it with a new one, a better one, one that would keep the man alive for many years to come. But yes, if someone with no concept of surgery were to stumble into that room, at that moment, I'm sure they'd have been horrified. Screamed at us to stop, called us sadists, wrestled the scalpel from my hand in the firm belief they were helping.'

Codelle turns to me, her voice plain, matter of fact.

'But we know that person would have been wrong, that what looked so obviously like harm was actually a truer version of help than they could conceive of. That their actions to prevent my work would have resulted in something much worse. The events of last night are not so different; a necessary incision to fix a much deeper problem.'

Codelle turns an object over in her hands. Rolling my head a few centimetres to the left, I can just make out the outline of another medical syringe, the liquid contained within this time a bright, clear amber. I watch Codelle remove the safety cap, the microscopic needle exposed to the open air.

'I'll … I can pay …' The words shuffle clumsily out of my mouth. 'I have six hundred … thousand pounds in my bank account … just let me go home.'

'I can't be bribed, Mr Mason.'

'It's not a … not a bribe, just … payment … restitution … buying out of the contract … it's business … please. *Please.*'

She places a hand on the back of my chair, rising to her feet. She gently turns my right arm until my palm is facing the sky. Looking down, I notice a circle of blue plastic pressed against my arm, sitting so seamlessly above my wrist that it might as well have been implanted into the skin itself.

In the seconds that pass, I realise that's exactly what's happened.

With a soft click, Dr Codelle lifts the plastic circle, revealing it to be some type of cover, shielding an injection port from the elements. Codelle presses the syringe through an imperceptible opening in the centre of the port, the needle entering my wrist as amber liquid rushes in.

'The recovery should work fairly quickly, and then your time is your own.' Codelle retracts the needle and closes the cap. 'Use it however you want.'

Codelle crosses back through the gardens and disappears into the house, leaving nothing but empty space behind her.

Her parting gift sets to work immediately. The chemically induced wakefulness of the amber 'recovery' combats the dull barbiturate haze with breakneck efficiency. A rolling storm of adrenaline rushes through my veins, my muscles tightening, pins and needles erupting across my arms and legs. In less than five minutes, I have full control of my faculties, albeit weakened and stiff from an unknown span of inactivity.

I push myself out of the deckchair, my knees thudding into the grass, using the wooden frame to raise myself onto my feet.

With no doubt in my mind as to my next destination, I stumble on unsteady legs back into the house. My feet drag across a chequerboard floor, the face on the ceiling smiling down at me as I pass through the atrium. Mr Villner is in the corner, balanced on a stepladder as he gently spritzes the potted greenery.

I force myself through the statuary corridor, stumble right and continue past the looming wall of fractured marble, until

I practically fall through the doorway of my room and towards my leather bag.

Please. Please, let it still be here.

My heart in my throat, I spend a few anxious moments searching through the various side pockets of my holdall until I pull out a monogrammed leather wallet. I dig through paper and plastic until I find what I'm looking for, retrieving a single Polaroid picture, letting the wallet itself drop to the ground.

I wanted to see you how you were, how I want to remember you. Strands of curled hair across your brow, your eyes lit up, your lips parted in laughter.

I stare at your smiling face, unblinking, drinking in this glowing, living version of you.

Yet, as the moments pass, the remnant ugliness of the previous night suddenly rushes through my body. Despite the beauty of the woman in front of me, my mind is drenched in a raging flood of mottled skin, burst blood vessels and stitched flesh.

I feel my mouth fill with saliva.

I barge through the door to the bathroom, collapsing against the toilet as I wretch into the clear water, your photograph clenched in a quivering fist by my side. I shiver, beads of sweat protruding from every pore in my face, before another wretch sends a glut of vomit into the basin.

Once I'm ready, I pick myself up and brush my teeth vigorously. In the absence of any sensible adhesive, I squirt a small bead of toothpaste onto the back of the photograph and fix the picture to the underside of my bed. Something tells me to keep this item close, and away from anybody else.

I take a good while to steady myself, drowning any remnants of vomit in complementary mouthwash, and sitting on the edge of my bed until my hands stop shaking.

When I feel they're suitably steady, I take a deep breath, and head back out into Prismall House.

'Where's Dr Codelle?'

Villner turns away from the last potted plant, spritzing the ferns a few times even as he stares in my direction. With very little expression on his face, he points upward, in the direction of Codelle's office.

Without another word, I march up the iron spiral staircase and pass into the corridors of the second floor.

The moment I leave the balcony behind, I hear a sharp set of footsteps cross the floor below me, followed by the clanking of boots on the staircase. I doubt Codelle's aide-de-camp is interested in what I have to say but, after the events of the previous night, I'm sure he's worried for his employer's safety.

I approach Codelle's office, locating a small buzzer beside the black leather door. Unsurprisingly, by the time the door unlocks, Villner is standing directly behind me.

Codelle's office looks exactly as it did the day before.

Emerging from the previous night, having been forced to stare into the ugly substructure of Prismall House, I half expected the rooms to have shed their pretence, to see dark corners and macabre intent in every shadow.

Instead, everything seems maddeningly normal, as if nothing untoward even happened; the sun rising in the east, Villner attending to his plants and Dr Elizabeth Codelle behind her desk, seemingly happy when she looks up to see me.

'Arthur. How can I help?'

16

I step into the centre of the room and plant my feet, bathed in light from the office's great window.

'I ... I need to understand.' I stumble over the words, suddenly nervous in Villner's presence. 'I want you to tell me what the fuck is going on here.'

'Of course. Where would you like to start?'

'Why ... why would you ...' Recalling the previous night drives a spike of jagged images through my mind: open chest, cracked ribs, slick red organs and black bile. I can still feel the sting in my eyes.

'It's called Conceptual Immortality,' Codelle begins, setting down her pen. 'You see, people with your condition—'

'Withdrawal. You said it was fucking withdrawal.'

'Post-Bereavement Limerent Withdrawal, or just Limerent Withdrawal. Yes,' Codelle states evenly, looking to me as if she truly wants me to understand. 'Those suffering as you do tend to idolise their lost loved ones, causing the deceased to take on an almost superhuman status in their minds.'

'You're judging me for idolising my dead wife?'

'Judging you? Of course not, it's commendable.' Codelle offers an affirming smile. 'Honestly, Julia was blessed to have a partner who held her in such high esteem. However, when someone who is so greatly elevated *dies,* that idealisation can become detrimental. Many alcoholics, for example, associate the drug with the best aspects of their lives: youth, social ease, risk-taking, sex, laughter. It's more than just a drink, it's salvation, it's freedom, it's a demon, it's a god.'

Codelle opens her hands out in a demonstrative plea to the heavens, her eyes flickering skyward for effect, before interlocking her fingers and resting her chin upon them, looking back towards me.

'They mythologise it, and that makes the addiction so much harder to break. They need to be taught to see it not as some powerful spectre, but merely as liquid in a glass. It's the same for you. The first step in our process is to break your own illusion, to dismantle that perfect version of Julia that you have in your mind.'

I stare with cold and venomous bewilderment at the figure seated in front of me. My mind flits back to the warmly lit hotel room in Edinburgh, the knock at the door, the glance through the peephole, the moment of disbelief as you stepped into my arms in your rain-soaked coat.

'You failed though,' I taunt proudly. 'You had to lie to defame her, which means you couldn't even find something wrong with her if you tried. All you've done is prove that she was everything I thought she was.'

'Well, yes and no.' Codelle concedes the point with unsettling grace. 'You're right, Julia wasn't unfaithful. As far as we could determine, she loved you as much as you loved her. Convincing you of her infidelity was the gentlest way to challenge that mythologisation. Failing that, our next step is to confront a more pervasive delusion.'

'And what delusion is that?'

'That she's still with you.' Codelle shrugs. 'That's what last night was about, Arthur. A short, sharp shock, forcing upon you the painful but necessary understanding that your wife is dead. She's not standing behind you in this room, she's not listening when you talk to her; she's dead, buried in the graveyard of Moorford's Church.'

A hot wave of rage swells across my forehead, my expression darkening. The accusation slaps me across the face – the idea that you're not there, that my comments to you are just delusion and denial, spoken into empty air.

'Dr Dunn encouraged me to talk to Julia,' I protest, shielding myself behind professional opinion. 'It made me feel better.'

'Dr Dunn's philosophy sent you to the edge of death,' Codelle replies pointedly. 'If it weren't for a chance phone call from your mother-in-law, you wouldn't even be here.'

'You think that justifies what you just did?'

'Of *course* it does,' Codelle says, self-assured. 'Yet another way that mainstream psychiatric practice is living in the dark ages. We do everything in our power to save someone with a ruptured liver, a failing heart, but a mind malfunctioning to the point of self-termination—'

'You're equating suicide with organ failure?'

'Suicide *is* organ failure,' she comments.

I stare at her, a profound silence spreading across the room.

'That's the stupidest thing I've ever … Are you insane?!'

'I'm quite in my own mind, Mr Mason,' Codelle states. 'I simply refuse to romanticise.'

'Well, I'm not surprised that romance offends you,' I snarl.

'Romance is beautiful, Mr Mason, romanticism is deadly,' Codelle retorts out of character. 'Good things don't need to be romanticised; its only function is to justify the unhealthy and the dangerous. Romanticism sends people to war thinking it will be glorious, drives victims back to their abusers by conflating violence with passion. Romanticism perpetuates the lie of the "poetic death". Swallowing poison over your paramour's grave, joining your partner in the great beyond, sacrificing yourself in the name of queen, country, principle. It's all the same.'

'You …' I shake my head, at a complete loss. 'It's *far* more complicated than that.'

'No, sometimes the correct conclusion is the simplest one, no matter how much the world attempts to complicate it,' Codelle argues, the slightest notes of irritation in her voice. 'I have the greatest sympathy for your plight, for the plight of anyone in your position, but as human animals with a natural drive towards survival, the act of self-termination is nothing more than the most ultimate failure of neurochemistry, and it is the duty of a medical professional to remedy that imbalance in any way possible. Modern psychiatry, modern *society*, may have misled you, but until such a time as someone convinces me otherwise, I will treat suicidal ideation in exactly the same way that I would treat a patient arresting on my operating table: doing everything I can to correct the symptoms of a failing organ until it returns to function, until my patient is healthy, happy and *alive*.'

I stare at Codelle for five long seconds. Her statements are impassioned but matter of fact; she is not arguing a position with the hope of persuading me but merely clarifying what she believes to be an inalienable truth. I look past her, through the giant window and across the ocean to the distant cliffs of Wales.

'That's why you're out here,' I comment, almost to myself. 'Off the coast, hiding from the world. If you were in a public medical organisation, if you had to hold these views up to scrutiny, they'd see you as the twisted fantasist that you are.'

Codelle half chuckles, half scoffs as she lets the barb wash over her. It's clear she has no real stake in this conversation. Continuing it is an elective aspect of her day, and taking my insults to heart is similarly optional.

She takes all the time she needs to formulate her response.

'There was a doctor called Ignaz Semmelweis,' she begins. 'A fellow surgeon, an obstetrician. He was seeing deaths on his ward due to a spread of postpartum infections. This was in the mid-eighteen-hundreds. In the interest of saving lives, and to reduce the infection rate, he proposed a revolutionary practice to the medical community. He was dismissed as a fantasist, a fool; he suffered a mental breakdown and was committed to an asylum by his colleagues where he eventually died. Do you know what his revolutionary idea was?'

I say nothing. Codelle continues regardless.

'He believed that doctors should wash their hands with chlorinated water between visits with each patient. It took twenty years for the medical community to agree that the now deceased Semmelweis was entirely correct. The application of my treatment has saved many lives. I don't want to die waiting for permission, waiting for an ineffectual medical community to catch up, and I refuse to let *you* die waiting for a cure I already have the power to administer.'

'A *cure* for grief,' I utter, my words grim and sarcastic.

'A cure for grief,' Codelle responds, clearly finding the descriptor reductive, but essentially accurate.

I take a moment to wrestle with what I've heard. I almost wish Dr Codelle's actions had been born of simple cruelty or corruption, that I could appeal to her greed and buy my way off this island. Instead, I realise I'm at the mercy of a figure who truly believes they're acting for my benefit. A figure who seems to genuinely care for my wellbeing.

Grief as addiction. My love for my wife merely a synaptic misfire. The lowest point of my life redressed as an anatomical malfunction. Any attempt to refute my problem would seem like the classic denial of the addict. Any attempt to leave, to get back to our flat, your pictures, your music, will be viewed by Dr Codelle as a relapse, a return to the destructive cycle of compulsion that she's been specifically employed to break.

'I don't want any part of it.' I force my words to remain steady. 'You are not allowed to keep me here.'

'You signed a contract.'

'No contract allows you to keep someone against their will!'

'Yes and no,' Codelle replies. 'The contract appoints the Codelle Institute as your approved professional mental health service. Under current legislation. if I believe you ought to be detained in the interests of your health or safety, then I can keep you here for a minimum of twenty-eight days to a maximum of six months. There are certain further stipulations, of course, second opinions, nothing that can't be addressed.'

'But ...' I stammer, feeling the situation slip out from under me. 'My ... my work is expecting me back on the fourth. My mother's the CEO of a multinational company, she's paying for this, you don't think she'll notice? You don't think she'll want answers?'

Without comment, Codellé turns quietly to her laptop, idly clicking through an unknown tree of branching folders. She hits a final decisive key and turns the laptop, an audio recording playing on her computer.

'Delilah, are you all right?'

'I ... Dr Codelle ...'

'Delilah, what's wrong?'

'We ... we checked ... oh god ... I'm sorry ... I'm sorry, it's just—'

'Take your time.'

'I went to the flat like you said, I checked around the ... the old places and ...'

'Was there something there?'

'There's ... it's pills! The same pills! I don't know what he's thinking ... I can't ... I don't ... please, I don't know what to ... I don't know what to do!'

'It's all right, it's all right, Delilah, please don't worry. Arthur's safe, he's ok ... this isn't unexpected, this is—'

Codelle stops the recording.

'You started buying them again, Arthur. Collecting them,' she comments. 'You weren't just worried you'd make a second attempt; you were building up to it, the same behaviour as before, even storing them in the same kitchen drawer.'

I'm struck into silence, my speech centres, unprepared for such a development. I hadn't expected anyone to know. I certainly hadn't told anyone. In a way, I hadn't even mentioned it to you.

It was just a coping mechanism. That's all it was. On my particularly bad days, I would buy a single pack and place it in the drawer, as if having the option somehow gave me control over the pain I was feeling. I suppose I never considered how many there might now be, viewed together.

Finally, the words arrive; late-notice appointments, shaking and unsteady.

'You'd only know that if you'd broken into my apartment.' I venture weakly. 'You can't use evidence you acquired illegally to—'

'Your mother, to whom you provided a key to your apartment, found them following my general suggestion of a welfare check,' Codelle continues, laying down one winning card after another. 'Given the new evidence, I'm authorised to keep you here for as long as I think is necessary, to personally oversee your recovery.'

I open my mouth one more time, but the river is dry. Dr Codelle has twisted the legal framework of involuntary admission to her favour, steered my loved ones into accepting the treatment without reservation, herded me into the centre of a gilded cage and locked the door, long before I noticed there was anything to escape from.

Worst of all, I doubt she found any of it particularly difficult.

'You were never going to let me go, were you?'

'Arthur, if I thought it was in your best interests, I'd let you sail away from this island today.'

'My best interests,' I say sarcastically.

'Of course. That's the *only* thing I care about,' Codelle states with total sincerity. 'I don't expect you to be civil, I don't expect us to be friends, but I promise you, as impossible as it might seem right now, I truly believe that you'll thank me when this process is all over, when you're cured.'

That word again. *Cured.* It was the term Monty Han had used to describe his own recovery. At the time, a cure for the dark, unending sorrow that ruled my days had seemed like a godsend. There's even a wounded part of me that still welcomes the idea. But if Dr Codelle considers Monty and I to have the same fundamental condition, necessitating the same fundamental remedy, then I can do nothing but fear, with every quivering nerve in my body, the version of me she intends to send back into the world.

I stare past Dr Elizabeth Codelle, beyond the cyclopean window, to the true horizon: the cliffs and valleys of the mainland coast, the known quantity of Porthcoll, the promise of winding roads leading me far away from this place.

The ember light of a long-lost resolve slowly rekindles in my chest. I promise myself, and I promise you, I will find a way to leave this place before Codelle's treatment can take its bizarre effect.

I let a tone of anger and defeat radiate in my voice, my head bowed in quiet acceptance as the lenses of my mind click into ever sharper focus. I stride towards the threshold of Codelle's office, opening the door to the rest of Prismall House before turning back one last time.

'I want some better fucking shoes.'

27th August

17

'One. Two. Three. Four. Five. Six. Seven. Eight. Nine. Ten. One. Two. Three. Four. Five. Six. Seven. Eight. Nine. Ten. One. Two. Three. Four. Five. Six. Seven. Eight—'

A quiet evening and a sleepless night have passed since I stepped out of Codelle's office, any chance of reasonable dialogue abandoned.

Dinner was eaten in silence, a yawning chasm spanning the table. Codelle seemed utterly unfazed by the day's events, occupying herself with the contents of her tablet as Villner busied himself in the kitchen behind her. I spent most of my time staring across at her, stirring a bamboo spoon through a bowl of chicken soup, wondering how she could seem so serene after the dark trials of the last twenty-four hours.

Every so often, a half-formed point, petition or plea would form in my head, and I'd briefly wonder if I could sharpen it into an argument Dr Codelle might actually listen to. But when I previewed each argument through the lens of the doctor's utterly alien perspective, I realised they sounded like the desperate deflections of an intransigent addict: hostile towards my saviours, pursuing relapse over recovery.

Once her bowl was empty, Codelle finally spoke, closing the cover of her tablet and rising to her feet.

'There'll be no sessions tomorrow.' She soothed warmly, an olive branch extended in her tone. 'Your time is your own; Villner will get you anything you need – within reason, of course.'

In the face of my continued silence, Codelle saw fit to add a final platitude.

'This is a place of healing, Mr Mason, of self-improvement, self-*discovery* – and it can be that for you too, if you let it.'

I returned to my bedroom to find a pair of white Velcro-fastened trainers on my bed, resting on a folded cream tracksuit.

Before I slept, I took the Polaroid of you out from under the bed, forcing myself to look for as long as I could, even as remnant waves of nausea washed through my brain.

'One. Two. Three. Four. Five. Six. Seven. Eight. Nine. Ten. One. Two. Three. Four. Five. Six. Seven. Eight. Nine. Ten. One. Two. Three. Four. Five. Six. Seven. Eight—'

A steady sun beats down through a clear August sky. My trainers trample through the chalk path that circles the island, overwriting the footprints of my previous lap. Sweat pours down my brow, the tracksuit clinging to my clammy skin, my atrophied muscles screaming from less than half an hour's exertion.

This is what we're looking at.

It takes 1,160 paces to circumnavigate the island's shoreline, 168 paces between the boathouse and the southern door of Prismall House and only 28 paces to walk along a single one of its walls.

I don't have any shoelaces or string, and it feels conspicuous to ask Villner for a tape measure. Luckily, you took me to that walking club in south London, where we learned everyone has their own personal gait, and that mine covers 100 metres in exactly 62 paces.

I make each journey several times over, allowing the pace count to develop a crude average. A practically circular island, 1,872 metres in circumference. A perfectly cuboid house with a length of 44 metres, and a 272-metre distance between the southern door and the *De Anima*.

After this I'll take myself downstairs to the immaculately stocked gymnasium to test my running speed on the treadmill. However, by my current estimation, if I had to make a break for it, I could cover the distance to the boathouse in 75 seconds.

If only to distract myself from my current circumstances, I'd spent the morning attempting to impress these numbers in my long-term memory, constructing the clearest mental picture I can of the island's layout, the resources available to me and, finally, how any of this information might coalesce into a means of escape.

There's no visible mainland other than the Welsh coast to the south, no secondary islands to speak of. After an hour of increasingly breathless reconnaissance, a few private and coastguard boats do peek over the horizon, but they seldom stray within signalling distance of the island itself.

As my long-neglected muscles begin to prickle with an uncomfortable heat, I turn my gaze inward, towards the residents of Prismall House. The pair seem to be going to great lengths to appear hands-off. I don't see Codelle at all during my run, and though the imposing silhouette of her housekeeper can be seen periodically among the hedges, his attention to me seems occasional, a brief welfare check undertaken between more pressing chores.

However, on my multiple tours of the island, a pattern does start to emerge. Villner always seems to be nearby whenever I close in on the island's boathouse, or whenever I approach the shoreline with any hint of intent. If anything, his duties within the island's garden seem secondary; idle busywork providing him with a clear view of my movements.

Arriving at the boathouse itself, I stumble to a halt and, as I catch my breath, glance into the gloomy interior. Thin sunbeams slip through the gaps in the roof slats, cast at irregular intervals like swords through a magician's basket, lighting up the hulking shadow of the *De Anima*.

After all the calculations, the most genuinely helpful scraps of information lie under the dark canopy of the boathouse. As far as I'm aware, the *De Anima* is the only independent means of leaving Prismall House behind. For all I know, its doors could be left unlocked, a satellite phone onboard just waiting for me to call the mainland, a spare set of keys resting in the bridge.

However, while my actions throughout the day so far could be interpreted as misdirected anger channelled into exercise, the act of entering the boathouse feels innately conspicuous. There's no way of spending any amount of time in there without my absence being noticed and without my intention to leave being immediately discernible to both Villner and Codelle.

I rest my hand on the exterior wall, paying down a heavy, wheezing oxygen debt. I briefly lock eyes with Villner, my gaze flickering up to view the vast circular window of Codelle's office.

As I feel myself being observed, a thought strikes me.

If I can't get onboard without them seeing ...

'You know what? Fuck this.'

Pushing sharply off the boathouse wall, I storm up the footpath as forcefully as my aching legs will carry me.

Building momentum, trampling chalk dust with each step, I call upon all the upper-class indignation I can muster as I approach Mr Villner.

'I want a G&T,' I bark, with the barest look towards the man. 'A double.'

To his credit, Villner reacts to my demand with immediate, mechanical compliance.

I march past, hearing him wipe his hands against his gardener's apron as I push through the double doors of Prismall House.

One hundred and sixty-seven paces. It's like clockwork.

I continue onward through the atrium, beyond the corridor of empty marble faces, and back towards my bedroom, where I immediately locate my leather holdall. It takes less than a minute to rip the drawers open, throw my clothes into the open bag and haul it onto my shoulder.

When I arrive back at the atrium, Villner's standing there with a highball glass of effervescent tonic. I snatch it, watching his eyes pass over my packed bag.

'What the fuck are you looking at?' I glower at Villner. 'Tell her I'm leaving. Go on.'

Villner regards me in controlled silence. The understanding that he could physically prevent my leaving at any time hangs openly in the air between us.

With a polite nod, Villner steps out of my way, and I pass back into the gardens.

Instead of seeking Dr Codelle, the man follows behind me, any hope that he might leave me alone for my trip down to the *De Anima* immediately dispelled. I see him fish in his pocket for what looks like a small pager, before pacing at his usual distance.

I down the gin and tonic, watching a fresh-cut lime slowly sink against the side of the glass, before casting the tumbler, somewhat dramatically, onto the ground behind me. I hear Villner stop to collect the glass as I cross the wide, open threshold into the boathouse.

The moment I step inside, the morning sun cuts out and the world shifts into medieval twilight. Each footstep taps on the wooden gangway, echoing off the sloped roof. Spanning the length of the structure is the shadowed, hulking mass of the *De Anima*, its spear-tip bow still pointed towards the house.

In the darkness, the ship suddenly feels oppressive, the gilded brig that conveyed me, with unparalleled comfort, into Codelle's strange custody.

And yet, if I want to leave this place without Codelle's blessing, the *De Anima* remains among a scant few options.

Carrying myself with a certain arrogant purpose, I haul myself onto the deck. I shamble through the darkness, running my fingers across the walls until I find a door. The handle turns but, unsurprisingly, doesn't give way, a single lock barring my entry to the central cabin.

Villner finally arrives behind me, striding down the jetty.

'I want this door unlocked right now. Toss me the key,' I order, raising my hands as Villner motions to board the ship. 'No! No. Stay there! I don't want you on here, toss me the key. Where's Codelle?'

A moment passes between us. Again, I'm acutely aware that if Villner chose to climb aboard, forcibly remove me from the deck and drag me back to the house, there would be nothing I could do to stop him. Wishing not to distress me, or perhaps simply recognising the futility of my protest, Villner backtracks onto the wooden gangway, distant footsteps on the chalk path signalling Codelle's approach.

I march around to the *De Anima*'s foredeck, tracing my eyes across the panoramic window of the boat's bridge. Having been on similar boats before, I know there's a chance that the *De Anima* doesn't even require an ignition key, that accessing the interior of the boat would be the only obstacle to commandeering it. However, the dark tempered glass of the windscreen provides only a meagre outline of the boat's control panel: no way to examine it closely from the outside.

'On your way home, I see?' Codelle's muted footsteps carry her across the gangway, her tone sickeningly non-judgemental.

I turn around to face her, letting my bag thud onto the foredeck.

'I am the heir to a multimillion-pound shipping empire!' I press my thumb and forefinger together as I punctuate each word. 'I am done running around this island. This is a farcical breach of UK medical practice and I want to go home NOW.'

'Mr Mason, what we're doing here is important.'

'It's illegal.'

'Legality and morality aren't always in alignment.' Codelle shrugs. 'If you go home and take your own life, do you think I'll sleep better knowing I towed the line of the GMC?'

'I don't care how you sleep. You know where I'll be sleeping? I'll be right here.' I point to the hard fibreglass surface of the foredeck. 'I'm not getting off this boat. At some point, you'll need to go back to the mainland – for supplies, for fuel, I don't care – and I will be here until you do. I'm not setting foot back in that house!'

I throw all my rage into the statement, the final syllable echoing off the boathouse walls.

From everything I've witnessed since I arrived on this island, I have to assume I'm always being watched by at least one of its two inhabitants. Pacing out the island's dimensions by foot was inconspicuous enough, but there was very little chance of me entering this boathouse, and examining important aspects of the *De Anima*, without my intentions being obvious to both of them.

In the end, the only remaining option was to do everything in plain sight: to march aboard the *De Anima* under the pretence of impotent protest, an ill-conceived bout of entitled indignation that one might expect of a shipping magnate's errant son. It's a role I've spent most of my life passively researching – every schoolmate who lambasted their parents for buying them the wrong make of car, every co-worker who scolded a waiter for opening their wine without the label facing outward.

In my experience, people who wore their emotions on their sleeve rarely had anything hidden up that same sleeve. As a consequence, under certain circumstances, blatant might just be the new sneaky.

Still, as I look into Codelle's eyes, I can only hope she believes it.

'We pride ourselves on providing a five-star experience for our patients,' Codelle begins, a sudden bluntness to her tone. 'That said, your recovery will always supersede your experience as a guest. I don't mind you processing your new situation in your own way, but if you attempt to sabotage your recovery by acting out, I'm afraid there will be a corresponding loss of privileges.'

I hold her stare, waiting for the hammer to fall.

Codelle sighs.

'Stay here if you want, enjoy the change of scenery. But if you're still here in three hours, you'll be subjected to increased observation while on the island's grounds and you'll be restricted to your room between eight in the evening and eight in the morning for the remainder of your stay. I hope we understand each other.'

With a nod to Villner, Codelle turns and heads back to the house. Villner remains, eternally wordless, his eyes fixed on the boat. In our shared silence, I take in the strange hill on which I've made my hopeless stand, pacing back and forth across the foredeck as if walking off my preoccupying rage.

I cross the bow and glance down the starboard walkway, its features blocked from the view of anyone standing on the jetty. It leads down the other side of the bridge, passing towards the stern, with another cabin door halfway along. There is one object I hadn't noticed earlier. Attached to one of the numerous metal rail posts, its red hue intentionally garish against the muted whites and blues of the *De Anima*: a vinyl bag with a large white cross on the front, emergency equipment for a ship or passenger in distress.

Worrying that I've lingered too long, I turn on my heels and march back to Villner.

'You have no fucking idea how much litigation I'm going to put you through, you bastards!' I yell towards him. 'My mother's going to bury this place!'

I brandish my arm, hoisting up my sleeve to reveal the plastic injection port.

'This? This'll land your fucking boss in jail! This is grievous! Bodily! Harm!' I punt each syllable in Villner's direction, my words bouncing off the man like a cricket bat striking an oak tree.

At the very least, in the face of such sustained and effortless disregard, I begin to feel a sense of genuine anger swell up to meet my own faux indignation.

'You don't give a damn, do you?' I mutter rhetorically. 'You don't care.'

Making it up as I go, I sweep my eyes over the hull of the *De Anima* and back to the bridge window.

'But you care about this.' I gesture to the *De Anima*. 'You care about this boat, right?'

Without another word, I stride over to the immaculately curved windscreen. Summoning the remainder of my physical strength, I raise my foot in the air and stamp it against the glass.

The shock jolts through my femur, a dull thud of reinforced glass, the vague outline of a chalk shoe print against the otherwise unaffected windshield.

It was worth a try.

I raise my foot again, striking my heel into it repeatedly, letting out a scream. Scowling at the statuesque Villner, I storm towards a light blue life ring that rests secured at the front of the boat, ripping it out of its placement and casting it off the starboard side.

I turn around, hearing the buoy splash into the dark water below.

'No? This doesn't pain you at all? You love everything neat and tidy, right?'

I continue my rampage down the starboard walkway, leaving Villner's eyeline as I march towards the red emergency bag.

I immediately tear open the Velcro as I hear Villner stepping onto the boat.

The next five seconds play out in a chaotic rush, barely long enough for me to track with conscious thought. I glimpse the contents of the pouch: bandages, water, emergency rations, whistle, pen knife, torch, matches.

No flares. No phone.

I look back to observe the deck at *De Anima*'s bow, the tip of Villner's boot visible, mere seconds away from turning the corner. In the precious final half second, I slip the torch out of the bag and fold it into my palm.

As I feel Villner cross the threshold of the starboard walkway, I raise the pack above my head and turn it in my hands, the contents spilling out into the water below, shaking the pack violently to fully disperse the contents into the dark, lapping waves.

I stare up at Villner, scowl, and launch the empty satchel in his direction. He catches it as the fabric harmlessly thuds against his chest.

I can see the slightest hint of pity across the lines of his brow, the insignificance of my actions in the reflection of his eyes.

Even so, I hold his gaze for as long as possible, hoping to keep his focus as the heavier elements of the pouch sink below the surface, hoping they'll assume that the torch sank too.

'Fuck you both.'

I march towards Mr Villner, and squeeze my way past to the bow of the ship, dropping down beside my luggage. I hear Mr Villner grab the rail behind me, assumedly looking over the side towards the objects in the water.

In that one quiet moment I have all to myself, I draw my bag open and slip the torch inside.

18

I avoid Villner's eye for the next two hours, festering in place, stewing in the charged, unpleasant silence of the boathouse.

'Two hours fifty-six minutes.' I look up to see Codelle on the jetty, silhouetted in the entranceway.

Creaking footsteps carry her further towards the *De Anima*, my eyes choosing not to follow her as she calmly continues. 'I'm not trying to aggravate you. Villner and I need to sleep eventually. Actions like this can only be accommodated to a point.'

I look ahead, examining the path that leads back to Prismall House. Even knowing there's nothing to be done on this boat, that I've gained everything I can from this place, the idea of wilfully returning to that building feels repulsive.

'Four minutes … three now,' Codelle comments. 'Extra supervision, curfew … don't make this more difficult than it needs to be.'

I allow myself a beat of silence, of performative consideration. Begrudgingly rising to my feet, throwing my bag over my shoulder, I trudge with a heavy, funereal pace out onto the jetty, avoiding eye contact with Codelle and Villner as I go.

Just as I'm about to take my leave, Codelle stops me, placing a gentle hand on my shoulder, her palm resting on the strap of my holdall. Her fingers slowly retract as she lifts the strap and frees me of its weight, our eyes locking as the bag is taken from me.

'I'm sorry to have to do this,' Codelle laments as she hands my satchel over to Villner.

I fight to keep my expression straight, even as a cold, throat-clenching dread consumes me. Villner's hand reaches over to the zip and passes beyond it, uncoupling the shoulder strap from its brass clip, a soft clink as he removes it from the bag entirely.

'So far I trusted you wouldn't do anything reckless,' Codelle comments. 'But it's standard procedure to remove straps, belts, shoelaces. I hope you understand.'

I look over to Villner, supporting my bag from the bottom, clearly prepared to carry it the rest of the journey. I reach out, snatch it from his open arms and march back up the path, neither of my guardians making any move to follow me.

It takes a long time for night to fall.

Once again, I find myself in the reclined curve of the crescent moon window, its shape punched through the thick cement wall. I'd spent a sleepless night waiting, in total darkness, until I could assume the other residents of this house had retired to their own bedrooms.

I turn the torch over in my hands, multiple LEDs packed in concentric circles behind the clear glass lens.

I'd told you once about reading ships' lights. I don't know if you listened.

Ships passing in the sea should carry a white lantern on their mast and on their stern, a green lantern on their starboard side and a red one at port. The combination of visible lights provides key information to an observer.

When the ship is perpendicular to the viewer, travelling past them, two white lights and a single coloured light can be seen. The port and starboard lanterns are also slightly forward facing, not visible from the back of the ship. Therefore, a ship heading directly towards the observer shows a white light and both coloured lights, whereas a ship moving away shows a white light and nothing else.

I think I remember why you stopped listening now.

My tired mind perks up as a twinkle of light passes in the distance: two white lights, one red, interspaced enough to indicate a sizeable ship, skirting the very edge of the horizon.

As I have done once or twice in the past hour, I take a deep breath, press the torch against the window and, with cautious optimism, begin to click the light on and off.

— — — ... — — —

Three long beams, three short flashes, three long beams. Amateur sailors aren't required to learn Morse code, but the simple SOS has long been introduced into popular culture to the point that anyone aboard a vessel would have encountered it at some point.

— — — ... — — —

The boat continues to sail past, no response from an onboard light, no acknowledgement at all that they've noticed my message. After almost a minute, the lights become more intermittent, the ship veering east, taking it below the horizon.

I rest my head against the padded wall, passing the torch impatiently between my hands. The idea that a ship would approach or even notice my signal on the first night is foolishly optimistic, but over the course of the next week or so, on multiple nights, multiple ships, there's at least a fighting chance that—

An uninterrupted green light passes across the pane. A ship, travelling somewhere from the north, 600, maybe 700 metres away based on the lanterns on the masthead and stern.

Wiping my sleep-filled eyes, I lift the torch again and begin my steady work.

— — — ... — — —
— — — ... — — —
— — — ... — — —

The ship passes the midpoint of my view, a formless vessel, cruising through the inky blackness with no apparent knowledge of my existence.

– – – ... – – –

– – – ...

Another light appears, a steady beam from the distant boat, a red light, of similar size to its green companion, sitting level with it out on the open sea.

The boat has turned; I'm staring down the barrel of the craft's bow.

– – – ... – – – / – – – ... – – – / – – – ... – – – / – – – ... – – –

My thumb rapidly clicks and unclicks the torch button, the difference between a dot and a dash growing increasingly meaningless. At first, I try to suppress my frenetic energy, the rush of summoning this distant vessel from the pitch-black nothingness and calling it to my aid. I soon find myself unable to temper my utter rapture, as the boat lights draw closer, the space between them widening as the boat carves through the water.

As the lights pass to within a hundred metres of the island, I stand up.

The light of my torch barely reaches the vessel. Just far enough to light up the white fibreglass bow and a familiar dark blue hull.

Before I can switch it off, the meagre beam of my handheld torch is obliterated by the stark, scouring ray of the *De Anima's* searchlight.

The crescent window of my room bursts into a stream of pure white as I throw my hands up to shield my eyes.

The vessel pulls to a stop and, with an ungodly sense of calm, a silhouette steps onto the foredeck, a dark female figure encircled by the searchlight. I can just make out Dr Codelle's arm as it rises to her mouth, as if preparing to speak into a handheld radio.

Moments later, the intercom softly cuts in behind me.

'I saw your signal, Mr Mason.' The disappointed tones of Dr Elizabeth Codelle float across the room, as she addresses me from the *De Anima's* bow. 'I suspected you might have taken something from the ship, but I wanted to give you the chance *not* to use it.'

A larger shadow falls between us, as Mr Villner crosses the beam outside, directly in front of my window. As my eyes adjust, his features come into ever sharper focus, a hint of melancholy in his hard, stoic face, a tin of paint hanging limply at his side.

'I told you. I told you,' Codelle laments, as if I've cruelly forced her hand. 'I told you, sabotaging the process would result in a loss of privileges. Firstly, the obvious …'

Villner wastes no time. From his right hand, a thick paintbrush plunges into the tin, drawing a glistening, viscous coating of cement-grey paint and slapping it against the glass of the crescent window. The paint splatters against the pane, blocking my view of Villner's face, opaque brush trails expanding out from the point of impact.

I step back, my breath catching as the *De Anima*'s searchlight is slowly reduced to a few disparate beams until, one by one, they're snuffed out by the broad strokes of Mr Villner's brush. The crescent window is now the same uniform grey as my bedroom walls – the grass, the ocean, the stars all redacted from my view.

I don't even look as Villner paints over the north-facing window, reducing my room to a dark, grey cell.

'Secondly,' Codelle continues. 'I *will* be imposing the curfew I spoke about earlier. Eight p.m. to eight a.m., excluding emergencies and necessary treatments, of course, until I am convinced you will use the time responsibly.'

I hear Villner's boots outside, brushing through the grass towards the northern entrance of Prismall House.

Panicked, I launch towards the doorway. I slam my flat palm against the surface, in a bid to get somewhere, anywhere, before Villner can reach me. The door doesn't respond, an immobilised slab of fibreglass, a sliding panel with no handle.

I'm trapped. For all I know, I've been trapped all night.

'Thirdly, I know I said the next few days would be your own …' As Codelle speaks, I hear Villner push into the house, turning sharply on his heels and marching down the corridor towards my room.

'… but if this is how you're going to spend your free time, I think it's better if we just push through.'

Desperate, I slam my hands repeatedly against the unmoving door.

It finally slides open, Villner's frame casting me in shadow as it fills the threshold.

'Stay back.' I shudder, my voice breaking as I shrink towards the darkened window. 'Stay back!'

Villner advances, unfazed, as I grip the blunt metal torch in my hand and steady myself for one good strike, one David-and-Goliath Hail Mary of ugly, blunt force.

My arm swings into an immovable object. Villner catches my wrist, his iron grip absorbing all momentum, the torch inches from his face.

Desperate, I press the torch up against his eye and hit the button with my thumb.

Villner snarls, recoiling, as a harsh burst of blinding light floods his vision. Leveraging half a moment of chaos, I try to pull away, sprinting towards the open bedroom door. I run into nothing more than a shoulder-wrenching jolt, as Villner recovers himself, grabs my wrist and yanks me back towards him.

The torch slips from my hand, my feet scraping against the carpet as Villner's free arm wraps around my waist and pulls me towards the corridor on his own terms.

As I'm dragged, struggling helplessly, along the hallway, I stare into the heart of the small metal torch, its beam reaching out to me from the carpet of my now windowless bedroom, growing more distant with each passing second.

A moment later, the bedroom door softly slides back into position, the torchlight cutting out behind it, as I'm carried into the unlit depths of Prismall House.

19

'Julia!'

Victoria Coach Station thrums around me, a glorious, unoiled machine, rumbling with the sound of engines, tannoys and shuffling travellers. The automatic doors close behind me, injecting a final gust of cold London air into the station's stuffy, over-crowded halls.

A sudden rush of delays and cancellations had caused the crowds to swell. The newly arrived and the should-have-been departed squeeze up against each other, carrying coffees and luggage through a corridor of errant elbows, piling around the departure board in search of an update.

It's among this assembly that I desperately duck and weave, trying to keep my courage as I sprint towards your coach. The only coach that seems to be leaving on time.

'Julia!'

Your head turns towards me, strands of curled hair cast across your forehead, a look of confusion blossoming into bemused surprise as your eyes meet mine. Your gaze barrels into me, blowing away the rest of my resolve. The single sentence, that I've been practising as I ran over, flutters away on the breeze.

'Hey.'

'Uh ... hey.'

In the interminable pause that follows, I look around for something talk about, anything except for what I actually came to discuss.

'Your coach takes *four* hours?' I comment unthinkingly. 'Isn't it quicker by train?'

You fix me with a look of sardonic disbelief.

'Of ... of course! Trains!' You exclaim with unbridled sarcasm. 'Why didn't I think of that?!'

'Ok, I ... It's because it's cheaper, right? That's why. You don't have to—'

'How'd you spell that? T R A Y N?'

'You know, I think it's this city.' I theorise, shaking my head. 'I didn't say anything stupid the whole trip, but as soon as we're back in London, I mess up.'

'Oh no, you said some pretty out-of-touch stuff on the trip as well, I just didn't tell you ...'

'Great.'

'I'm kidding.' You smile disarmingly. 'Though I think you could use someone to help you understand the common folk.'

'You mean like a governess?'

'Oh, fuck off.' You laugh, even as you roll your eyes. 'So, is that all you came back to say? That I should have got the train? If my coach crashes on the motorway, that's your sign-off?'

'Well, in that case, you really *should* have got the train.'

You roll your eyes again, this time perhaps a little more seriously. It's less about what I've said than what I'm clearly not saying.

Three years of idle banter, in-jokes and teasing, occasionally teetering on the brink of a meaningful conversation, constantly pulled to safety as I childishly run down the clock. The border between us had become paper-thin, but it was still paper; the act of crossing it threatening an obvious, irreparable tear in the fabric of our relationship, one that I'd constantly have to look back on if things went wrong.

The 568 service to York is now boarding. Please make your way to Bay 14.

People start to move, a steady parade that you keep pace alongside. My resolve is withering, some internal coward pleading with me to just bear out the next few yards in awkward silence, to accept the lesser of two embarrassments without putting anything significant at stake.

'Hey.' I let the short, sharp syllable hit the air, throwing my hat over the fence.

It's enough to stop you moving, enough to force me to engage.

'I … I really like you. Do you want to go out next time I'm in York?'

You look up at me, for what feels like an eternity.

Well, there we have it, I think to myself, I've just made the biggest mistake of my life. I've gambled my most treasured friendship on an outlandish bid for something more. I've attempted to fan the rare, brilliant spark between us, and instead blown it out entirely.

In retrospect, silence and denial had been a perfectly comfortable way to handle my feelings.

'Yeah … Yeah, I'd love to!'

For a moment, I feel nothing but dazed half understanding.

I can see in your eyes that same shy bewilderment, the vulnerable act of casting our true feelings out into the cold, blustery world to meet one another for the first time. For some reason, it makes me think of those cuckoo clocks that send wooden people out from separate little doors to kiss on the hour. I can only assume those figures spend the other fifty-nine minutes in terror that their partner won't show up.

'Ok … well,' I mutter, my brain still unable to absorb the enormity of your answer. 'Ok.'

Our moment is cut short by a final announcement. I try to negotiate an awkward hug, our arms lingering around each other for just a second more than normal. When we finally let go, and you turn away, your fingers brush down my arm, gently squeezing my hand for a fraction of a moment.

That fraction is enough. A floodgate of emotion bursts, an uproarious cascade of technicolour sparks rushing through my suddenly breathless chest. For once, the truth rises to meet the fantasy, clouds clearing on an entirely new world I'd feared was utterly imaginary.

I watch you board the bus, hoping you'll look back at least once. When you do, your look of excitement and joy meets my own and, once again, I feel like your gaze might throw me off my feet.

I can't get the smile off my face, and I don't want to. If I could, I'd live in this moment forever.

'Julia!' I hear someone call from over my shoulder.

I turn, confused, as I watch a figure approaching through the crowd, weaving towards us.

I look back and see you turn around, as confused as I am. The bus is empty again, the doors to the parking bay shut, the crowd returned to their previous positions with you back among them.

Before I can check again, the figure reaches us.

'Hey.'

'Hey.' You respond as the figure shuffles nervously before you.

I'm presented with a vision of my fifteen-year-old self, exactly as I was: the awkward baby face, facial hair like the crosshatching of a lazy sketch artist, the hunched, uncertain stance of someone who doesn't know how to fit into the space they now take up.

I take a step back, realising that I've become just another member of the crowd, an anonymous commuter in a space between spaces.

'Your coach takes *four* hours? Isn't it quicker by train?' The boy blurts out, glancing at the departure board.

'Of … of course. Trains!' the girl comments back. 'Why didn't I think of that?'

'Ok, I … It's because it's cheaper, right? That's why. You don't have to—'

'How'd you spell that? T R A Y N?'

I pull away, my eyes darting over the bustling crowd, searching for someone who finds this situation as bizarre as I do. But no one is looking, no one is listening. In fact, every single person is staring blankly at the departure board, their faces as cold and inanimate as storefront mannequins.

I watch my younger self pace alongside you, the huddled crowd drifting towards the coach bay without even seeming to walk.

'Yeah ... Yeah, I'd love to,' you comment, one foot on the concrete of the parking bay.

'Ok ... well. Ok.'

A hug, a hand squeeze, as two bodies separate from one another.

'Is he waking up?'

An unfamiliar voice echoes from every direction at once. A voice from outside this strange place, speaking with a confidence and understanding that utterly eludes me.

'Who is that?' I try to call out, staring up and around for any explanation.

'Julia!'

I snap back to the matter at hand. The hollow crowd parts mindlessly, creating a corridor for my younger self to pass through.

The scene plays out yet again.

'You mean like a governess?'

'Oh, fuck off.'

I feel suddenly claustrophobic, hemmed in by a horde of people.

I leave the two of us behind as I push back through the indifferent crowd. Bay 13, Bay 12, Bay 11, 10, 9. The automatic doors to the city open outward, the air moving in neither direction as I escape into a deserted crossroads, an empty street that roars with the sound of traffic.

Only one figure passes by me, sprinting desperately into the monolithic station.

'Julia!'

I'm back among the crowd once again, watching myself approach you in a room without temperature, without echo or warmth.

'He's starting to move.'

Unable to speak, unable to run, I feel my mouth open, my lungs compress, my windpipe fill. It takes all my strength, and every shred of oxygen in my body, to finally scream something into the open air.

My eyes jolt open as I wake in a hospital bed, my body thrown by the sudden change of orientation. The room is vast and dark, the ceiling composed of white vinyl tiles. An operating light illuminates me alone, distant shadows shuffling by at the periphery.

'He's awake.' The unfamiliar, barely discernible voice comments, the tone almost resembling alarm.

I try to sit up, only to feel the now familiar pressure of the medical restraints pinning me back against the mattress. A frenzy of useless struggle nets me nothing, save for the hollow satisfaction of having tried.

'Mr Mason, try to calm down.' Dr Codelle's seemingly worried voice emanates from over my head.

She rounds the corner, coming into view, staring down at me with obvious concern for my distress.

'Ah. It's not an adverse reaction,' she says, her sense of calm immediately returning. 'You're all right.'

'Where … where is—'

'You're in Prismall House. You're on the third floor.' Codelle speaks reassuringly, her hand pressed lightly against my shoulder. 'There's nothing taking place which isn't being overseen by a medical professional. This is simply momentary turbulence in an entirely safe and effective procedure.'

'What was that?'

'It was a dream, Mr Mason, a memory: guided hypnotherapy augmented by a selection of carefully chosen pharmaceuticals. It's all under—'

'What the fuck was that?!' I scream, jolting forward towards Codelle.

Codelle pauses and disappears into the dark reaches of the room. After a quiet moment, the top end of my cot begins to rise, bringing me upright. A moment more, and Dr Codelle returns, wheeling an office chair across the stone floor until she's able to seat herself at the foot of my bed.

She selects her words as Villner busies himself.

'This procedure is a proprietary treatment of the institute, a treatment that I've pioneered and perfected over many years, one which has helped countless people to *decouple* themselves from the source of their addiction.'

'Decouple?'

Codelle nods quietly. 'See, people have told you that addiction is a lifelong illness, that the closest thing to a cure is a lifetime of constant vigilance and abstinence.'

'How short-sighted of them,' I mutter, allowing contempt to pollute every word.

'Sarcasm aside, yes, it *is* short-sighted,' Codelle continues. 'It's settling for something lesser. You can go cold turkey, you can get clean until your brain chemistry rebalances, you can spend a lifetime watching yourself. But it's a plaster on a bullet wound, a half measure, something the entire psychiatric industry is guilty of. In a hundred years, we'll look back and wonder why we didn't actually *help* these people when we had the chance.'

'And I suppose they'll name a university after you.'

'I don't care about that. I care about now, about helping people.'

In the background, Mr Villner drops a bedsheet and my clothes into a plastic bin. I watch him seal and remove the bin bag within and carry it to the other end of the room.

'Back in America,' Codelle pulls my focus once again, 'I had a patient who was *obsessed* with his local barista. Dreams of her filled his nights, and, of course, caffeine filled his days, which didn't help. She consumed his thoughts entirely. Now, if I was treating his problem in the same way the medical community treats addiction, I would have told him that he'll *always* have these feelings, that the best he can do is get his coffee elsewhere, forever, to cross the street when he sees her. That's not good enough. I want him to be able to go where he pleases, to walk up to her counter and order his coffee without feeling anything. That's the best way to save his sanity and to ensure her personal safety: that's the definition of a cure.'

'Monty Han brewing mead in his back garden.'

'Exactly. *Exactly.*' Codelle stops for a moment, happy to see I'm comprehending her argument.

Villner reaches the other end of the room, and a metal panel in the wall. He pulls open some form of laundry chute, casting the bag down into the lower floors, closing it with a metallic clang before walking to the washbasin.

'I'm not going to let you erase her. You're not—'

'No one's trying to.' Codelle gently raises her hands, defending herself from the accusation. 'We're not erasing anything. Detachment Therapy as I've designed it is more … I like to say that your life with Julia is like a paint-by-numbers, coloured in with various emotions: fear, joy, anger, jealousy. That's what's misfiring in your brain, driving you to self-endangerment. Via this process, we dampen the colours that are too bright for their own good. At the end, some of the colours will be muted, some of them removed, but the memory, the outline of the picture will remain. You just won't fixate on it; you won't lose yourself to it anymore.'

My mind drifts listlessly backward. I remember listening, hopeful and naïve, as Monty Han described Codelle's methods across a patio table. He'd mentioned three personal examples: exercise, cognitive behavioural therapy and, almost as an afterthought, medication. I feel a dull ache of renewed betrayal, a hollow shriek of injustice in the face of such a titanic understatement.

'Then … how will I remember her?'

'You'll remember Julia as a treasured figure in a long, productive and *happy* existence.' Codelle shrugs her shoulders. 'That your time with her was a formative, beautiful chapter of your life but no longer the entirety of the book.'

Codelle's hopeful eyes sicken me to my core. I feel a fresh wave of cringing distress sweep over my limp body. Unable to move, I instead steel my mind against the creeping return of unconsciousness, fighting to stay awake as the fog rolls in on all sides.

'I'm not going back there,' I spit with desperate defiance. 'I'm not. You can't make me.'

'I can and I must,' Codelle assures gently. 'We can't stop now.'

'No. No. I'm awake. I know what you're doing now. It won't work.'

'Mr Mason, it already *is* working,' Codelle says sympathetically. 'I can assure you; you've been in this bed for quite a while.'

The medical bed thrums as it slowly levels out. I try to keep my head raised, but even the vaguest elevation strains my neck.

I start making desperate mental notes. An exercise to keep my brain alive. The laundry chute sits thirty-two ceiling tiles across the room from a star-shaped window on the third floor of Prismall House. Each ceiling tile can't be more fifty to sixty centimetres in width, plus a metre for the external wall which equates to—

'Julia!'

I barrel forwards, a blue merino wool blanket cast from my body as I launch up from a wooden deckchair. My knees thud into freshly mown grass, my eyes squinting against the sudden glare of the morning sun.

My pounding heart slows as I take in my surroundings, gasping breaths normalising as crisp, cool air feeds my lungs. I'm conscious again, that much is certain, kneeling on the island lawn in the same place I awoke two days ago. I assume this is Codelle's favourite spot for me to rouse myself: a peaceful garden, scenic views, positioned beneath her office window for extra oversight.

I return myself wearily to the canvas chair, taking stock. My body is well rested, yet my mind feels utterly ragged, as if the gruelling mental chaos of the night before had continued long after I was conscious of it.

I have no idea how many times I passed through that interchange, only that my brain feels like a spent muscle, each new thought pulling itself lazily together and barely maintaining cohesion.

Turning to my left, I find a small wooden stool, a metal tray atop it containing yoghurt, granola and assorted fruits. I leave it untouched, no desire to quell my growing hunger, as I wait for the disorientation to clear.

When I finally get up, almost an hour later, I find myself descending into the basement level of Prismall House. I stare across the cerulean blue of the swimming pool, slowly disrobe, and dive in.

I reach the other end and turn back the way I came. Head down, legs kicking, driven by the inescapable, troubling feeling that has followed me all morning.

From the moment I'd woken up in the deckchair, I had thought of nothing but our meeting in the coach station, the first time we realised our feelings for one another were mutual.

I can still see you turning through the crowd, the hair that fell across your face, the smile and the light in your eyes. But for the life of me, I can't remember feeling nervous. Like a favourite song played too many times, a worn VHS of a beloved film, the emotions I once felt are lesser now.

I remember you saying yes, I remember you squeezing my hand, I remember watching you leave, disappearing from London before my eyes. But, for the first time, I don't remember feeling anything at all.

30th August

20

For the next few days, I do nothing but walk.

I move purposefully through my morning routine, ensuring I'm showered and dressed in time for my room to unlock at 8 a.m.

I stare, on shifting feet, at the magnetic sensor at the top corner of my door. We have similar alarms at my office; a detector on the door itself resting against a metal strip set into the frame, a magnetic field shared between the two which, when broken, will set off an alarm in some other part of the building.

I'd barely noticed the sensor when I arrived, but now its red light glares like some vindictive warden, promising that, even if I could force the sliding door open, I would likely have thirty seconds before Villner came barrelling down the corridor.

I rush out as soon as it turns white.

I finish with a cold breakfast of fruit, yoghurt and grains by twenty past. Leaving my plates behind, I step out onto the freshly raked chalk of the island's coastal path, sporting a pair of breezy leather sandals, to begin my steady tour of the grounds. I march soulfully around and around until the cork soles are caked in white.

Crisp air invigorates my lungs, a sea of cold blue past my right shoulder, a green lawn and a slowly rotating cube of grey cement on my left. Apart from a few small features, the boathouse and the distant coast, the view from any point along this path is practically identical: an open expanse of perfect, cloudless symmetry.

To the figure in the western gardens, his eyes quietly tracking my every calm rotation, I hope to seem entirely aimless.

An idle saunter through hospital grounds, searching for calm in the regularity of quiet routine. In truth, with each round, I'm attempting to leave this place behind, to step across the calm ocean and back to the noisy streets of London.

And I do. After an hour or so, right under the man's nose, I manage to escape.

I can almost feel the carpet under my feet, the faintest electricity of your hand against mine as we pass down the aisle of the Southwark Registry Office. I travel further back, hearing the door close behind us as we carry boxes through the unfurnished corridor of our apartment. Further still and I see you hiking ahead of me, passing through sunbeams on the forest path near your hometown. I feel the ache in my calves, the weight of a ring box in my left jacket pocket.

I pass through each and every memory, finding them exactly as they were on my last visit. Each one conjures a familiar rush of tight-chested exhilaration, intermixed with a cold pulse of sorrow that punches through my ribs and twists at my stomach: joy and sadness in a fractious orbit.

Yet as I leave these memories behind and pass onto the linoleum floors of Victoria Coach Station, the waves fall still. My stomach untightens. I can still picture myself rushing towards you, stumbling over words, blurting my confession out into the open air. I can remember your reply as clearly as I ever have. But my sprinting footsteps no longer echo with the same desperation, the seismic spikes of nervous anxiety flattened to a smooth line, your acceptance, which once hit me like a freight train, now interchangeable with any other response from any number of casual conversations.

Codelle was true to her word. All the colour has been drained from that moment in time, the sadness and heartache they inspired gone, every other emotion sacrificed along with it.

I stop for the first time in hours, seeing my distant overseer tensing up in my periphery, pruning shears lowering to his side as he observes the sudden change in my behaviour.

Taking great pains to leave him unacknowledged, I walk back up the gardens and through the double doors into the still air of Prismall House. Villner's footsteps pace out behind me, grass to chalk to marble, as he returns from his duties on the front lawn.

I may as well admit to you, these walks have served an ulterior purpose.

A flaw of this institute, one of a slim few I've managed to discern, is its incredibly limited complement of staff. Codelle is clearly aware that her methods fly in the face of society at large, moving her practice to an island in the Irish sea to distance it from any regulatory body. I can only assume she had similar considerations when choosing her employees, a requirement for nought but true believers, whose silence could be relied upon in the outside world.

The echoing halls of Prismall House are a testament to how short that list must be.

While Codelle handles the institute's executive functions, spending a good allotment of the day in her second-floor office, the cooking, cleaning and clerical work is undertaken solely by Villner. The man seems to have an endless supply of appropriate tools, culinary ingredients, even a replacement pool filter which he sourced without leaving the island, yet I never see where he retrieves these items from.

After exploring the interior of the house, it's clear that I have access to only half of the basement level: the gym, the swimming pool, the subterranean tennis court and sauna. Somewhere behind those walls lies an entire section of Prismall House that I'm yet to explore, a section which Villner returns to every time he changes shifts.

His chores follow a seemingly random schedule, making it impossible to track his movements without following him the entire day. However, should I spend a prolonged amount of time outside, Villner seems duty-bound to keep a distant eye on me, dropping whatever he's doing and immediately undertaking the role of the island's gardener, pruning the bushes while making sure I don't wander into the sea.

His groundskeeping duties take no more than two hours on a normal day.

I've kept him from his other chores for an entire morning.

I drop quietly into the empty games room, a hundred taxidermy eyes watching me as I listen to Villner's movements through the door. He doesn't reach the atrium. In fact, he barely enters the building before I hear another door open and close behind him.

As soon as one steps into the entrance corridor of Prismall House, before you even approach the atrium itself, you are faced with two doors: one to the left, one to the right. I'd used them previously: each opens to a corridor running along the south side of the house, giving access to a few unimportant rooms.

It sounds like Villner has just entered one of them.

I slip my sandals off quickly, stumbling back through in hurried pursuit.

I pass under the painted smile on the atrium's ceiling, my bare feet so quiet in the usually echoing chamber that I almost begin to doubt my own presence. Hurrying back into the entrance corridor, I see the door on the east side still in the process of closing.

Before it has a chance, I manage to slip through.

A bare cement ceiling spans above me, a carpeted, dark blue floor at my feet. But in true Prismall House fashion, the walls of the south-eastern corridor are allowed no such mundanity.

Both sides are covered in a sea of overlapping mannequin's hands affixed to the walls, each one painted a different colour. The palms face the wall, the fingers of each hand covering the wrist of the one ahead, overlapping like opalescent fish scales in a winding mural of garish, technicolour plastic.

In my previous explorations of Prismall House, I'd regarded the piece to be quite striking, in an ugly, overbearing sort of way. But in all my wanderings, I'd repeatedly missed a critical feature of this corridor, now laid out for even the most casual observer to see.

A section of this strange wall is now intruding into the hallway, as if it has recently swung outwards: a hidden service door, less than ten metres away from me.

164

The plastic mannequin hands affixed to the door's surface are carefully severed at its edges. When it's set back into the door-frame, only the barest evidence of a seam must remain.

It won't be long until I see this for myself.

Villner's shadow is already passing under the frame, disappearing through the wall and into his own private section of Prismall House.

The door is already beginning to swing closed.

My steady footfalls become a desperate tiptoed sprint, the balls of my feet skimming the carpet as I lunge out for the closing door. The barest edges of my fingertips catch a red plastic wrist just before the door settles into the frame.

Holding my breath, I listen nervously as Villner's footsteps continue their descent, his stride purposeful and unbroken.

Craning my neck around the service door, I find myself staring down a steep stairway into the bowels of Prismall House.

Despite the architect's various, somewhat unsubtle artistic statements against class and consumerism, John Prismall spent very little time on the servants' quarters. Concrete walls follow concrete stairs towards a distant concrete floor, interrupted by pipes and pressure gauges: bare function without embellishment or ambition.

All the same, the corridor sparks an emotive response within me; a sudden shudder across the back of my neck, an internal plea to not walk down those steps, to consider what might happen if I am discovered. I can almost feel my fingertips twinge, testing the ease with which I could drop this door back into the frame and pretend I'd never seen it.

But as much as I fear the consequences of getting caught, of actively putting myself in harm's way, I remind myself that Codelle's treatments are going to continue regardless, that harm is coming whether I transgress or not.

I wedge one of my sandals into the doorframe and step onto the rough concrete.

The chill of unheated stone radiates through my bare feet as I creep down the stairs, my hands steadying myself on the rough-cut walls. Almost immediately, the sound of machinery shudders up to meet me, acerbic notes of chlorine and laundry detergent suffusing the air.

The stairs end at a sharp right turn, a peek around the corner revealing a twenty-metre corridor of smooth white-painted stone, terminating at the threshold of a vast, open-plan chamber.

The corridor is bare, with no doors or alcoves or even shadows along its featureless, well-lit span. It feels like I might as well be stepping down a gun barrel. I'm painfully aware that, if Villner were to pass through the large basement and merely glance down this corridor while I'm traversing it, I would be trapped inescapably in his sights.

But the man's business can only take so long. As much as stealth and patience seem to walk hand in hand, every second of hesitation increases the chance of Villner's return.

I bury my fear and slip into the corridor.

The narrow hallway seems to stretch further with every hurried step. I push forward, breath caught in my throat, the final fifteen metres, ten, five. Feeling the walls closing in around me, I brace myself as I approach the threshold of a cavernously large room.

I've almost crossed inside when the hulking profile of William Villner passes directly in front of me.

My eyes snap wide, my throat clenching to suppress a yelp of shock, balance straining as I bring myself to an immediate stop. He walks across the corridor's mouth, so close that his shadow passes over me. I can see the pale white at the corner of his left eye, painfully aware that, if a dark pupil were to roll in my direction, he'd find me immediately, a terrified portrait in a white stone frame.

But the man has already passed by, continuing towards his business on the left side of the chamber.

I realise I've forgotten how to breathe, replaying the half-second encounter in my head, with different permutations. What if Villner's head were turned a fraction more in my direction?

What if I had taken one more step across the border of his periphery?

I purge the useless hypotheticals from my mind. Instead, I listen as Villner continues on his own trajectory, until some unseen door opens and closes behind him.

For the moment, I have this place to myself.

The room is a vast, brightly lit expanse, rough-hewn walls painted immaculately white. The open chamber is almost entirely empty, its few features so scant and irregularly positioned that they almost feel like exhibits in a bizarre art gallery.

Ventilation shafts burst through the ceiling at random intervals. A block of eight washer-dryers rattle with activity, resembling the wall of a laundromat, yet completely free-standing in the middle of the room.

At another seemingly random point, a five-metre square of rubber matting signals the start of a spartan gym, with pull-up bars and a lifting rack composed of welded steel beams.

The most important feature is against the opposite wall: a set of storage shelves piled high with tools, sports gear, appliances and cleaning products.

Heart in my throat, borrowed time slowly disappearing, I pass swiftly through the cavernous room. At the midpoint, I duck behind the juddering bank of washing machines, preparing to make a break for the shelves, to scavenge a phone or a weapon or, perhaps, something suitably flammable to necessitate a call to the mainland.

However, once I reach the other side of the machines, two new features come starkly into view.

Firstly, descending from the ceiling almost directly above me is a square metal chute, its mouth hanging over a large, four-wheeled laundry basket. The laundry chute, which I had glimpsed during Codelle's treatments on the third floor, must open out on this level and, presumably, would be accessible from every floor of Prismall House.

Secondly, on a completely different side of the room than the one I entered by, I see yet another corridor, long and unlit.

Intriguingly, it seems to stretch beyond the boundaries of the house itself. Even in the gloom I see the beginnings of a set of metal stairs at its end, which must somehow lead up into the island grounds.

'Villner. Sorry to bother you.' Codelle's voice suddenly echoes through the room, relayed by some unseen intercom. 'I've got the phone working. Can you bring Mr Mason up to the office, please?'

21

I feel my remaining time ripped out from under me.

Washing machines thrumming to my side, I snap around to look back the way I just came.

It's only then that I see a row of hanging uniforms, each separated by wooden dividers, side by side, running along the wall directly beside my exit. Like outfits for a dress-up doll, each one represents a different function of Mr Villner: chauffer, chef, butler, nurse, handyman, gardener, each separated by cubby holes, relevant accessories and tools laid out within.

The significance of this open-air wardrobe doesn't truly strike me until a door on the right side of the room opens up and Villner steps briskly out towards it.

He emerged faster than I could possibly have crossed the room, my hesitation saving me from immediate discovery. But that same delay has placed me in an impossible position. Villner reaches the row of hanging uniforms, now standing less than ten feet from the basement's entrance, hanging up his gardener's apron as he proceeds towards his butler's uniform.

With him standing beside my exit, there's no chance that I can sneak past without being noticed. Yet, if I wait for him to finish dressing, I can only assume he'll proceed directly down that corridor, where he'll quickly discover my left sandal propping open the service door.

I'm trapped in this room, discovered if I leave, discovered if I stay, and I only have until the man dons his jacket, shirt and tie to fix it.

At least I have a second option.

Turning on my heels, I race into the dimly lit second corridor.

Instead of stone, this passage is lined by the glass doors of multiple refrigeration cabinets, their internal light barely straying into the corridor's gloom. Various syringes flash past on either side as I break for the iron steps at the far end. Launching myself up, I find a shadowed door, shaped like a submarine hatch and set into the ceiling.

Feeling the surface with shaking hands, I find a stiff handle, grinding the mechanism ninety degrees, as quickly and quietly as I can manage. Bracing my shoulder against the hatch, I push up the steps, urging it to open as I throw my entire body into the effort.

The hatch barely gives an inch before it stops dead, a scattering of dirt cascading down over the metal steps like sand through an hourglass. The hatch has been covered over, clearly trapped beneath the soil and turf of the island's artificial lawn.

Fuck. Fuck. FUCK.

I turn back down the hallway, sprinting past the fridges and through the open basement until I'm back behind the washing machines. I peer anxiously through the electrical wiring as I spy on Villner's progress.

He's half-naked, sporting nothing but black boxers as he carefully folds his gardener's uniform away. In ancient times he would have been a great hunter, a Spartan, a Goliath. The fact that I attempted to fight him a few days ago suddenly feels like utter lunacy.

Breathing in the quiet, cold air, I search my surroundings for any conceivable diversion, finding a loose floor chipping, about the size of my palm. Picking it up, weighing its insubstantial mass in my hands, I turn to the opposite side of the room and pelt it as far as I can.

It lands with a clatter, breaking into smaller pieces as it skitters across the floor. It isn't loud, but it's enough to be heard across the echoing basement, enough for Villner to stop his work immediately.

From my hiding place, I watch as Villner turns towards the centre of the room. I wait with bated breath and a pounding heart for the man to step away from my only exit.

He takes three steps forwards.

I rise up on my tiptoes, ready to make a fateful beeline across the basement floor.

Suddenly Villner stops and begins to scan the remainder of the room. His eyes glimmer with suspicion, mistrust, less interested by a random object than the mystery of what caused it.

Over the next few moments, he considers a number of directions, his eyes piercing the storage shelves, the ventilation shafts, a pointed glance towards the washing machines forcing me to shrink back into the shadows. Finally, just as I hope he might proceed towards the noise's source, he does exactly the last thing I want. He turns around, towards the stone exit corridor, passing into the very place I need to reach.

His footsteps carry him slowly down the corridor, towards the staircase with the propped-open door.

I feel like a rat in a trap. Nowhere to go, nowhere to hide, Villner's heavy footfall echoing, cruel and inevitable.

Predictably, in these seconds of wracking despair, my mind retreats to comforting thoughts of you. What would you do if you were here with me? You were always the right-side brain, balancing out my cold logic with lateral genius I could never comprehend. You were the person who unlocked our door latch with a selfie stick when we lost our keys. The person who de-escalated an angry drunk by convincing him she knew his mother. The person who, if she were here now, would tell me to calm down, look around, and consider the problem I'm facing.

I hear Villner's footsteps stop at the bottom of the stairs, and I run.

As silently as possible, I sprint across the room, passing the row of pristine uniforms. The short-sleeved gardening outfit is now draped from a hanger, shears and a leather belt in the cubbyhole beside it. A pure white chef's tunic and apron hang beside a set of stowed rubber clogs and a rewashable cap.

I can already hear Villner's steps returning.

Running on desperate instinct, I approach the crisp white shirt of Villner's domestic uniform, reach out for the sleeve, and run my hand downward, dirt from the exit hatch still on my fingers, leaving a faint but noticeable brown stain on the left arm.

As Villner returns back down the corridor, I move along the row of outfits, desperately looking for a space to hide myself.

It's when my eyes fall on the final unit, and the uniform hanging there, that time suddenly slows. In the last slot hangs Villner's black chauffer's uniform, the one he was wearing when he first met me in Canary Wharf.

The cubby holes beside it hold a chauffer's cap, a pair of driving gloves and, inexplicably, the keys to the *De Anima*.

I hear Villner round the corner, and I press myself against the wall beside the lightly swinging chauffer's jacket, a single wooden divider serving to block me from his view.

I barely allow my chest to rise, listening to every movement as Villner comes to a halt only two metres away.

A few firm steps, the rustling of fabric, the brief short buzz of a zip, the looping and buckling of a belt. His movements are ordered, routine, nothing suspected, nothing noticed. I hear the brief clatter of clothes leaving a hangar and then ... silence.

I stop breathing entirely, waiting to discover whether Villner has seen what I need him to see or, conversely, if he's finally sensed my presence.

After what feels like an interminable stretch of time, he turns on his heels and comes into view, his back to me as he marches towards the laundry section, the soiled shirt gripped at his side.

Wasting not a single moment, I snatch the keys for the *De Anima* and sprint to the exit corridor.

I hurtle back down the colossal gun barrel of a corridor, feeling the chamber spin behind me. I ascend the stairs two at a time, launching myself up and away from the basement.

My heart racing, my nerves torn to shreds, I ease myself out into the south-eastern corridor, removing my sandal and slipping it back onto my foot as the door closes behind me.

Unfollowed, seemingly unnoticed, my breath gradually grows calm: a slow dawning, cautious sense of victory.

The plastic hands on the doorframe meet their fingers on the adjacent wall, and, with a sound more satisfying than I could possibly have imagined, everything clicks quietly into place.

22

It takes less than a minute for Villner to locate me.

I'd hoped to get back to my room before I was taken up to Codelle's office, providing me with a chance to hide the keys for the *De Anima* safely away. But once I hear his brisk footsteps tapping across the central atrium, I'm forced to improvise, turning from my bedroom door to the wall-spanning artwork of exploded marble that runs across the hall.

Villner catches up mere moments after I tuck the keys behind one of the shattered blocks of debris, silently gesturing for me to follow him.

It's only once I fall in step with the man, leaving the incriminating tableau behind, that I realise I may have stumbled on a much better hiding place than my bedroom could have offered. With the changing of bedsheets, vacuuming, replenishment of the bathroom dispensers, there are very few areas of my private quarters that Villner doesn't regularly interfere with. I can only hope he pays less attention to the building's artwork than he does to me.

I doubt I possess the ability to read Mr Villner's mood to any degree of accuracy; still, as he leads me along the corridor to Codelle's office, there's no hint of disturbance across the lines of his face, certainly no indication that he's suspicious of the events in the basement.

Villner holds the black leather door open, allowing me to pass through into a familiar room of stark grey walls and wooden museum pieces. I mutter a brief thank you to the man, realising those are the first words I've spoken all day.

'Mr Mason.' Codelle looks up from behind her large wooden desk. 'How was your morning?'

'Quiet,' I mutter, as if annoyed to have been disturbed.

'Well, I hate to pull you away,' Codelle speaks, sounding like she truly means it. 'But we're moving forward, and that should be celebrated. Today's session will bring us another step closer.'

Codelle gestures to the opposite chair, which I can't help but regard with suspicion. After swiping the keys from among Villner's belongings, I'm arguably much closer to leaving than Codelle might imagine. Now it's just a matter of getting through the day without incurring suspicion or provoking any further limitation to my current freedoms.

Yet, despite every logical synapse telling me to play along with Codelle's treatments, the thought of wilfully participating makes me nauseous.

I sit down before her as she smiles gratefully, the afternoon sun casting light at a sharp angle through the window behind her.

'I see you've been taking walks; have you been thinking about Julia?'

I see no point in answering her question.

'I know it can be alarming,' Codelle continues. 'The sense of dissociation from the specific memories we target in our Detachment Sessions. Of course, by design, the more memories we detach you from, the less alarming it will become.'

'Is that supposed to make me feel better?'

'In the short term, perhaps not, but it will, I promise.' Codelle assures, almost comfortingly.

'I should never have come here.' I shake my head. 'Back home … I was—'

'Happier? Safer?' Codelle waves away my statement. 'We're both aware of your future intentions. Would you have even seen this morning's sunrise if you hadn't come here?'

'I would have rather died loving my wife than have to live as some zombie.'

'Ah, destructive romanticism strikes again.' Codelle sighs. 'Your mind is trying to harm you, Mr Mason, we mustn't let it.'

The doctor looks away from me, turning her attention to the desk between us. I can sense in these moments that she's saddened by the stilted nature of our relationship, that, every so often, she's reminded just how little I seem to understand her. Codelle collects up various papers, clearing a space, before reaching diagonally across and heaving the cream-coloured 1970s telephone to the centre of the table.

The doctor then searches below her desk and retrieves a black cable, a phone jack on its upper end. With a soft click, she connects it to the back of the landline, the rest of the cord disappearing off the edge of the table beside her.

Her setup completed, Codelle sits up in her chair.

'Did you ever meet Monty Han's entourage?'

'Some of them. The ones he had in school.' I focus on the bulky phone ahead of me; the only outside line on this island, the inanimate plastic urging me to snatch up the receiver.

'Monty Han excelled on this island. He undertook hobbies, sports, rediscovered his love of music,' Codelle comments matter-of-factly. 'The treatments were similarly successful. With his cooperation, we severed his emotional attachment to alcohol, developed new ways of thinking, set him up to entirely recover from his dependency—'

'Good for him,' I reply, tearing my gaze away from the phone and back towards the doctor.

'… but this island, it's not the real world,' Codelle continues. 'Back in London, there were significant, highly toxic influences in Mr Han's life; a friendship group who, by his own admission, enabled and encouraged his continued substance abuse, who would most likely attempt to drag him back into a life he'd battled to escape.'

'And what did you do? Murder them?'

Codelle can't help but sigh.

'We devised a short statement conveying his new goals and needs. He called around the more toxic members of his entourage one by one, and he explained that they were manifestations of a life he no longer wanted, that they would no longer be allowed to drive him back into addiction.'

'Well, I don't have an entourage so ...'

A moment of silence passes between us before Codelle reaches to her laptop and clicks the mouse.

'Mum keeps talking about redecorating, or selling my flat for somewhere in the City. She keeps saying it's about moving on.'

'Easier said than done, isn't it, love?'

'I ... I don't think she realises the effect that it has. This place was our home, this is where we built our lives together. Hell, it still feels like she's here sometimes.'

'Does she know that it's ... you know ... not the time for this sort of talk?'

'I don't know how I'd even tell her. I can see it just makes her so ... uncomfortable.'

'I have the same up here. Peter and Bridey used to tell me all about their Kelly – she's in business school now, down your way. But they don't update me anymore because they don't want me to feel—'

Codelle stops the recording, her point made.

'Your mother-in-law, Lorraine Darcy. You talk about Julia with her a lot.'

'You've been recording my phone calls?' I stammer, though the invasion of privacy feels the least of my troubles, as I sense Codelle building towards something at her usual unhurried pace.

'Only for the last two months, but I have the call logs from your home phone going back much further: inbound, outbound, frequency, duration.' Codelle checks the papers in front of her. 'Since Julia's passing, you've spent an average of twelve hours per week on the phone to her mother. Not much in the grand scheme of things, but considering your limited free time, and your general state of isolation, these calls seem to be your primary source of social interaction.'

The phone stands starkly on the table between us. The cream colour suddenly looks sour and sickly.

'She isn't a part of this.'

'She is undergoing a similar withdrawal.'

'From her *daughter*?'

'Yes. Her daughter. Your wife. People who share an addiction – to a substance, a behaviour, or to the afterimage of a personal relationship – they can either be a positive influence, providing mutual accountability and growth, or they can promote stagnation, fixation ...'

I scoff, thinking of my mother-in-law, the kind and welcoming soul who cared for you and me endlessly. To hear her being painted as some toxic, addictive influence feels like slander.

'We support each other.'

'You *enable* each other,' Codelle remarks, as if clarifying a simple misunderstanding. 'Before you knew that your condition had a cure, one could argue that she had some positive influence. Before you came here, your best option was pain management. But once you leave here, cured, any continued interaction will jeopardise your recovery – that is something we *need* to address before you leave.'

Codelle lifts the phone's receiver and holds it out towards me.

With her free hand, Codelle slides a piece of paper across the table; a set of evenly spaced, bullet-pointed talking points. There are four lines – calm, measured, crafted so diplomatically that they almost seem reasonable.

❖   I want to thank you for the support you've given me over the past ten months.

❖   I am now actively healing from the trauma of my wife's passing.

❖   However, as a part of this process, I believe it best that we end our relationship.

❖ In respect of my wishes, please cease all forms of
   contact with me in future.

I feel like my airway has closed. My mind flickers between this
moment and an imagined scene 200 miles east of here; a warm
but timid woman, inching by under the weight of her unspeakable loss, settling down for the lunch she's made herself, in a
house she no longer shares with anyone. A woman who never
takes more than three rings to reach the landline phone in her
kitchen, who's always so happy to hear from me.
   'No,' I mutter under my breath.
   Codelle doesn't put the receiver down, staring silently as I
continue.
   'She's lost everyone; this … this is just … unnecessary cruelty.'
   'It may seem cruel, Mr Mason, but it's not unnecess—'
   '– No!' I shout, my voice breaking as if surprised by my
outburst. 'This goes against everything you said you stand for!
You just said you wanted people to … to live, to "thrive", this
could *kill* her!'
   'In my judgement, the only person endangered from this
continuing correspondence is you.' Codelle speaks firmly.
'People who suffer from addiction exist on a scale – some
more vulnerable than others, some more prone to relapse. Yes,
she's in a dark place, but she can, in my judgement, overcome
it. You are already overcome by your condition, and the risk
of relapse, while minimised by your time here, is significantly
increased if you return to dangerous behaviours back on the
mainland.'
   The receiver continues its indifferent whine, cutting across
our conversation, begging to either be used or put down. I stare
at it, knowing what it represents, unable to reach out.
   The doctor notices.
   'You're in open ocean, swimming back to dry land.' Codelle
speaks softly, reassuringly. 'You can make the journey, but your
friend can hardly keep up. Suddenly, a boat arrives with one
available place. Would you begrudge your friend taking it?

Would you really be happy if they chose to stay with you out of misplaced solidarity, even if it killed them? Would you drag them back into the water, dooming them to drown, just to avoid swimming alone?'

I linger in silence for a moment as the doctor's words settle upon the room. A swell at the top of my throat, I snatch the receiver from Codelle's outstretched fingers.

Now empty, Codelle's hand drifts back to the phone itself and begins to dial.

I take a long breath. The soft nostalgic trill plays in my ear and I hope, beyond anything, that there's no one on the other side.

A second trill, and silence, before–

'Hello?'

23

I close my eyes as I hear my mother-in-law's voice, the now familiar sinking feeling of small, palpable defeats passing over me.

'Hi, Lorraine.' I sigh, choked up with regret, staring up at Dr Codelle's sickeningly neutral expression.

'Arthur? Oh, goodness, I ... I didn't expect to hear from you.'

'I ... I'm sorry if it's a bad time.'

'Oh no, the timing's perfect, I was just sitting down with a tea. Just a sec.'

Muffled steps, the sound of the radio falling silent, the tink of a spoon in a china cup. I breathe slowly in and out, on the edge of a grim threshold I don't want to approach.

'Well, tell me, how's the retreat going? I want to hear everything.' Lorraine settles herself down, an eager silence waiting to be filled between us.

'It's, um ... it's fine,' I mutter, my eyes on Codelle. 'Lots of bells and whistles.'

'How's everyone else there?'

'It's, um, just me actually.'

'Oh,' Lorraine muses impishly. 'Can't be very popular then.'

I chuckle, flickering up towards Codelle, who gestures towards the bullet points.

'Are you, um ... are you still doing the, um ... pottery classes?' I comment, struggling to even acknowledge the paper in front of me.

'Oh no, gave that up months ago, haven't got the hands for it.'

'Oh, you enjoyed it. You should go back,' I say, mustering encouragement in my voice. 'It was on the village green, right? Next to the post office?'

'... Oh,' Lorraine comments softly. 'Sorry, I'm not sure if, um ...'

'I'm just saying you should at least try,' I continue. 'You know, if only for me, you should—'

'– Hello?' Lorraine cuts across me quietly. 'Arthur, you've gone quiet. Might be me ... hang on.'

The line goes dead.

I look up to see Codelle's outstretched finger depressing the hook switch on the phone.

'What?' I say, confused.

Codelle turns to her computer and, without a word, begins to type a few keywords into an unseen application. Almost twenty seconds pass, the silence punctuated by only a few clicks of the keypad.

I feel my throat going dry.

'Your line has a two-second delay,' Codelle confirms, disappointment in her voice. She raises up the stretch of cable beside her, revealing that her other hand has been resting on a small black switch the entire time. 'A contingency, in case you deviated from the script. Your last comment to Lorraine would have sounded like static to her.'

Codelle turns the screen around, a panoramic street view of your mother's hometown. A building with the tell-tale red signage of a post office, standing on a narrow corner beside a building of tell-tale blue.

'I thought it sounded out of place.' Codelle sighs. 'Village green, next to the post office ... You were sending her to the police station.'

I press my lips together, my brow furrowing, exhaling through my nose as yet another desperate act is caught in mid-air and cast into the growing pool of festering failures.

I slam the receiver down indignantly, pushing the phone across the desk towards Codelle.

'Fuck it then. I'm not doing it.' I steel myself against Codelle's disappointed expression, crossing my arms as I sit obstinately in place.

'Mr Mason, please, this is a destructive relationship, your inability to see that is a classic symptom of your own—'

'You don't know a fucking thing! You don't know anything about actually loving someone or caring about them. You're trying to make me better, but your concept of what *better* is … it's …'

The low groan of wood against wood drowns out my stammering protest, as Codelle reaches into an unseen drawer. She retrieves a small, square object of orange and brown plastic, a garish handheld device not unlike one of my secondary school calculators.

She flicks out a little stand with her fingernail, placing the object on the table before turning it around. Not a calculator, a digital timer, with a liquid crystal screen and seven-segment display. Codelle presses a selection of buttons, and the screen comes to life, displaying three minutes, already counting down.

'Our session's going to end in three minutes,' she comments. 'If you're not prepared to cut toxic influences out of your life, then I will be forced to do it for you.'

'Do what you want,' I mutter, a low hiss of pure contempt. 'Can I go?'

Leaving my question unanswered, Codelle reaches for her laptop, as the timer quietly ticks down.

'Sorry, Arthur, you're saying she called you that evening?'
'Lorraine? Yes.'
'The day you were planning to take your own life?'
'… I wasn't planning on it.'

I hear my own voice coming from the speakers, perfectly edited digital audio, the words and phrases clipped from two months of phone calls. The disparate words are sutured perfectly together, the seamless notes of a conversation that never took place.

Codelle responds to my statements with the air of a concerned therapist, her own words presumably recorded at another time and place.

> *'Do you think that discussing Julia with Lorraine, dredging up those memories, contributed to your suicide attempt?'*
> *'I ... I don't think she realises the effect that it has. I don't know how to tell her.'*
> *'But do you think it contributed?'*
> *'... Yes.'*
> *'Would you like me to discuss this with her, on your behalf?'*
> *'Yes ... Yes ... That would be good.'*

The audio cuts out; Codelle turns back to me.

'How do you think she'll feel when she hears this?'

'This is ridiculous.' I baulk incredulously. 'It's a lie.'

'Yes,' Codelle comments flatly. 'But since you attempted to deceive me, the conditions of this session are going to change accordingly. In the next ... two and a half minutes, I want all of those talking points conveyed to Lorraine Darcy in full. I want her to say that she understands; only then will I accept that you've communicated it clearly.'

'... Please—'

'If you refuse to convey those talking points in the afore-mentioned timeframe, or if she fails to confirm her own understanding of your terms, I will phone her myself, on your behalf. I will tell her that you wish to cease contact, and I will play her that recording as evidence for your change of heart.'

'I don't give a fuck,' I spit venomously. 'Go ahead. When I get back to the mainland I'll just tell her it was fake.'

'Understandable. But let's consider your options, shall we?' Codelle comments patiently, time quite comfortably on her side. 'If you take our treatment on board, heal from your condition, you'll likely leave this island with no inclination to see Lorraine Darcy ever again, which means you are now choosing the tone of your final goodbye.'

My eyes shift reflexively to the plastic desk clock. Two minutes fifteen seconds.

Codelle continues.

'Now, if you successfully reject our treatment, if we somehow fail ...' Codelle gestures with the other hand. 'Then you'll be within your rights to contact her and explain everything ... but I'm empowered to keep you here for a good while, Mr Mason. How long do you want her to live with the guilt from that recording? A week? A month? Six months? Or do you want to do things gently, on your own terms? Ultimately, in either scenario, how does your refusal to pick up that phone benefit you *or* her?'

'You're bluffing. That recording would devastate her, even you wouldn't—'

'I don't expect I'll have to.' Codelle shrugs slightly. 'But it's important you understand that I'm prepared to.'

Without a sound, the display slowly drops below two minutes. The phone leaves its base again, the switch-hooks clicking softly, as my right hand grips the receiver and raises it reluctantly into the air.

Watching Codelle move towards the keypad, I instinctively reach out before she can press the first number, dragging the entire unit across the table and striking the redial button with a jab of my finger. I don't know what compels me, perhaps just a desire to act on my own terms, even if I'm beholden to her—

'Hello?'

One minute thirty seconds.

'Lorraine ...' I feel my voice on the cusp of breaking, collecting myself. 'It's Arthur again. I'm sorry we got cut off.'

'Oh, no worries, love, I'm sure it was on my end. You were saying it's going all right for ya?'

'The retreat?' I glance up at Codelle, her hand resting against the black switch. 'It's fine ... look, um ...'

'Do you know when you'll be back?'

'... No. Soon hopefully.'

'Ah that's fine, I'm just keeping those albums downstairs for ya. Don't wanna have to get the attic ladder down.'

My eyes track down to the paper in front of me.

'Arthur? You all right?'

'Uh … yes, sorry,' I stammer, realising I've become lost in the paper's scant few words. 'I'm ok, how are you?'

'I'm uh … I'm fine.' She seems almost embarrassed to admit it, mildly shocked to hear her own words as they pass through the phone. 'It's one of the better days really. I've got choir soon and then I've got to think about tea … but don't listen to me, it's going well then?'

One minute ten seconds.

I look past Dr Codelle, beyond the large window, into a painted blue sky of passing white clouds. The clouds drift east, in the direction of northern England, and in the momentary silence, it's easy to imagine how this same sky will pass over the house you grew up in. Flowers in the garden, clothes drying on the line.

'Lorraine,' I begin. 'I want to thank you for everything you've done over the past ten months, and everything you did for us while … while me and Julia were together.'

'Oh, love, we've helped each other! And you looked after her more than I did the past few years.'

'Yeah.' I swallow. 'I'm actually … I'm feeling much better recently. With the treatment with … I think I'm ready to move on. From Julia, from … and I think … I … I don't think we can talk anymore.'

'… Oh.' The soft surprise drifts through the receiver.

'I just … as part of the healing process, I don't think I can keep living in … I am not going to be discussing Julia anymore.'

'All right,' she mutters; notes of confusion fade from her voice, leaving only wounded defeat behind.

'I want to thank you for being in my life,' I continue. 'I want to thank you for raising a daughter who … But I would appreciate it if you … ceased all communication with me in future. I wish you the best.'

'Well, it's uh … that's … that's …' I feel her shuddered breathing, as I try to keep my own steady. 'I, um …'

I glance at Codelle, looking for acceptance that I've done enough. The beginnings of satisfaction dawning on her face seem to indicate that I have.

'Well, I …' Lorraine's voice ventures back into the conversation. 'If you ever want to talk, it's … You can always give me a call …'

Codelle's features flatten at the words, the faintest shake of her head.

Forty seconds.

'No. No.' I speak forcefully, desperation leaking into my voice. 'Lorraine, I'm sorry, I need you to understand, we can't talk again. I need you to know that. I wish you the best but you won't be hearing from me.'

'Oh I … ok, I understand, love, I'm just … I'm saying the door's open for ya, if you ever want to … you know, not about Julia, just … to check in—'

'No!' The volume of my voice surprising us both, the quickly diminishing timeframe tearing at my heels. 'No. I need you to tell me you understand. We won't be speaking anymore. This is goodbye. Thank you so much for everything, but you need to understand this is goodbye. Ok? I need to know you understand.'

The line goes quiet. My body tenses, shuddering, nothing but pure stringent desolation in every fibre of my body, my nerves screaming like violin strings, as I will a response from the interminable silence.

Twenty seconds.

Fifteen seconds.

Thirteen.

'I understand, Arthur.' Lorraine speaks, wounded, blameless, all joy robbed from the tones of her voice. 'I'm sorry I—'

Nine seconds.

'No. *I'm* sorry. Goodbye, Lorraine.'

'Oh … goodbye, Arthur. Sorry, I'm sounding all uh … Yeah, look after yourself, love.'

I rip the receiver from my ear and slam it down into the cradle.

I sit in wretched silence, shuddering quietly, hunched over and staring at the cold stone floor. When I finally look up at Codelle, I can barely feel any kind of anger inside me. Like an animal trapped in a fissure in the earth, realising that its flailing limbs will do nothing to ensure its escape, there is no emotion I can project outwards that will change the brutal reality of my situation.

'You'll delete that,' I stammer, my eyes resting blankly on Codelle's laptop.

Wordlessly, Codelle turns the laptop to face me, a screen overrun with audio mixers and samplers, a sound wave cutting through the centre. With a few deft clicks, the entire piece is erased.

'This was a substantial step forward.' She affirms soothingly. 'Pain relief has its purpose, until we heal the wound it was employed to treat. After that, its continued use is just a *reminder* of pain. A wound all of its own.'

My body shuts down; I'm barely breathing as my eyes stare into nothingness, my lips slightly parted. The only indication of any life within my slumped, utterly hopeless body is the steady drop of tears. They fall from my glassy, unresponsive eyes, pattering quietly against Codelle's desk.

Every time I enter this room, I tell myself with renewed resolution that I'm going to leave this place, but it's always been some hypothetical future event. It's never felt real. Now, like a patient on the cusp of a long-planned operation, I realise I've arrived at the eve of a long-awaited reckoning.

I need to leave this place tonight.

24

Grey linen billows in a bold upward swell, reaching towards the ceiling before collapsing back on itself.

Gripping two corners of a crisp, freshly laundered bedsheet, I watch the fabric cascade down and wait, with considerable dread, to see the face of the person on the opposite side.

As the linen drops, my eyes try to meet yours, only to find you looking off to some lonely point in space, attempting to parse the dark cloud of hurt and disappointment without looking it straight in the eye. By stark contrast, I can't look at anything but you. There's a dull, hollow feeling in my stomach, the wretched realisation that I've fucked up, that I've somehow managed to hurt the person whose feelings I hold above all others.

Our hands marry the corners, turning it onto its long edge, reluctantly moving closer to fold it into a neat square.

'I'll put it away,' I offer.

'It's fine,' you mutter, taking the folded bedsheet and placing it in our lowest bedroom drawer.

You pass into the corridor. I trail hesitantly behind, feeling like a piece of gum stuck to your shoe, an unwanted, foreign object that follows you with every step.

'I don't know what I was supposed to do.'

'Arthur, I have to pack.'

'I …'

'Arthur, seriously,' you warn. 'I just need some time, ok?'

I wait for a moment, and then a moment longer, before telling myself that the healthiest move would be to discuss this matter right now, to save ourselves from unnecessary hurt by resolving it quickly.

Sometime in the future, I'd realise these motives were purely selfish. I want to confront this issue because *I* can't stand the discomfort, because I just want to stop feeling like this as soon as possible.

'It's … it's chaos over there.'

'Seriously, Arthur.' You turn back, reluctant to enter the argument but quite willing to finish it. 'There's nothing to say. You have your work, that's fine. I understand it's stressful and changeable and a fucking madhouse at the best of times. But when you take annual leave, you take annual leave! I'm annoyed at them for calling you, they shouldn't put you in that position, but I'm just tired of …'

You throw your hands up, recognising the beats of an old, tired argument, unwilling to step any further into such a well-trodden dispute.

'It's fine.' You determine. 'This is the worst fucking time; you know I hate packing.'

You reach into a drawer, fishing a railcard from the depths and adding it to your purse.

I should admit that you're right, that I'm sorry. It's not pride that prevents me from doing so, but fear. I've told myself the life I'm living is sustainable, when really it's grown increasingly fraught, propped up by a creaking framework of stress and wilful ignorance.

If I apologise today, then I was wrong last month, and the time before that, and many times before that. Confronting each failure feels like a link in a chain reaction, spiralling down towards a horrifying truth: that I'm simply too weak to stand up to anyone, that, as the most forgiving person in my life, you're the person it's least consequential to disappoint.

'It's not just my work, it's … This is my family,' I argue, ten useless words when two would have solved everything.

You hold your hands up, utterly exasperated.

'*I'm* your family, my *mother's* your family. You made plans with *your family.*'

'Yes, but you don't *need* me. She *needs* me there tomorrow.'

'Well then … she's a being shitty boss, Arthur! Sorry, I know she's your mum, but she needs to keep her worlds apart.'

My mouth opens and closes silently, like a whirring factory with nothing of value to deliver. In the brief silence, I hear the joyful procession of Friday night partiers, laughing together on a warm summer night in Bloomsbury.

I wish we were out there with them.

'How can she …' I stammer. 'Julia, it's a *family* business.'

'No.' You throw a sundress into your overnight bag and look up at me. 'It's a business. Owned by your family, but still a *business*. They can't just call you in for overtime and say it's your fucking duty as their son to fix a PowerPoint.'

'That's not … it's not just a …' I dig even deeper. 'This is important.'

'Important?'

'Yes.'

'So important that no one else can do it? So important you have to break plans you made with people who are supposed to be important to you?'

'Oh come on, it's just a fucking barbecue!'

You grow quiet. A hardened, dull acceptance overtaking your expression.

I feel like I've waded into the ocean, only to look back and realise I've drifted hundreds of metres from where I left my towel. I don't know how I got this far from an apology, but it somehow feels impossible to reach from where I am now.

'You don't need to think that my family having a celebration is important, ok?' You state the facts bluntly, each syllable steady and controlled. 'That's fine. But I told you about this. Months and months ago, it was in the calendar. You said yes, you committed to it. I'm allowed to be disappointed that you cancelled the day before.'

'Well then, I … I …' I lose all composure. 'You know I don't want to do this! I don't want to do this, Julia! I keep trying to do right by everyone, I try to be responsible! But I don't know where the day goes! And I don't know why I'm defending my choice to do a job I hate as if it was my idea!'

'Then quit!' You shoot back. 'Quit, Arthur! Years and years you've … You will get a new job! I will help you! I will help you send off applications, I will move to another flat, another city. Just leave.'

'Yeah, well, we certainly couldn't live anywhere like this,' I point out darkly, wondering which member of my family I'm arguing on behalf of.

'FINE!' You throw your hands out, eyes wide and incredulous. 'I don't need to live in a building with a sauna and a cinema room and a fucking roof garden! We can move!'

In perhaps the most toxic of my subconscious reactions, I find myself resenting you, begrudging your unending support and wishes for my wellbeing. It places the ball thoroughly in my court, my continued unhappiness nobody's fault but my own.

And you're right. I know it. About everything.

I remember our student flat. The smallest place I ever lived. Smaller than some hotel rooms I used to visit in my youth. I remember that we could speak to each other from any room, without the need to even raise our voices. Conversations would carry on through doorways, across mornings and afternoons and evenings.

I loved us being in each other's way.

'If everything gets sorted early,' I venture, hating myself more with each passing second, 'I will get the next train up. I promise.'

The compromise hangs in the air between us, both of us knowing that there'll be no leaving early, that you'll likely return to our flat before I do.

'I'm going for a walk,' you comment.

'No, you stay, I'll go.'

'No, just … I love you, just let me walk.'

Like a lovesick shadow, I shuffle alongside you to the doorway.

194

I watch you put your shoes on, as the door to our flat opens. For the briefest moment, like the moon exerting pressure on the tides, you let all your hurt and discontent recede behind you, inexplicably managing to show sympathy for me, even now.

'I am so happy for what we have.' You affirm bittersweetly. 'You've worked so hard for us. But honestly, I would live in a place a quarter this size. I'd live *anywhere*, if it meant you could actually be happy.'

You step out and I'm left in silence, staring at the obstinate front door.

I remember my insides twisting around themselves, overcome with self-hatred, regret and shame. I remember worrying that the fracture I'd made today might slowly proliferate through our perfect relationship, that I'll someday be responsible for breaking us apart.

After a while, the memory changes.

I watch the bedsheet fall a hundred times, watch the door slam a hundred more, the worry subsiding with each iteration into a quiet sense of calm. Our argument begins to feel like it's behind a pane of glass, the events perfectly separated from the emotions they elicited. I feel myself growing numb to our words, to the pain I caused you, gradually freed from ill-feeling, freed of guilt.

I stare at my front door and I realise, with something close to relief, that I wouldn't mind if you never came back at all.

31st August

25

My body wretches, my back arching as the amber recovery ignites in my veins.

The walls of my London apartment splinter around me, crashing down as I find myself back in Prismall House. Villner crouches by my bedside, one hand on my wrist, the other withdrawing a voided syringe from the plastic port in my arm.

I force my sharp, juddery breaths into a flat line of controlled exhalation, resting myself back on the bed as the caffeine-like rush rolls through my body in waves.

The events of the past eight hours slowly return to me. My meeting with Codelle, the quaking voice of Lorraine Darcy, walking down the iron stairway, my legs heavy, my heart aching.

I remember Villner approaching me in the evening, the solemn understanding that a second round of Detachment Therapy had been pencilled in for the night. I remember numbly walking away across the grounds, staring out at the ocean before his inevitable force pulled me into darkness.

I remember the fight we had years ago and, though I know it's entirely artificial, I distinctly remember not caring about it in the slightest.

Villner rises from his knee, straightening his trousers as he does so. Without a word, he strolls to the bedroom door and leaves me in merciful solitude. Once he's gone, as the effects of the recovery begin to even out, I reach under the mattress for your Polaroid photograph.

I don't move a muscle for the next few hours, studying the contours of your face, my mind undulating between resolve and trepidation. Despite all the various tasks I'll have to complete in order to reach the outside world, the hardest step seems to be this one, the act of climbing out of this bed, of starting a process that, once in motion, cannot be stopped.

As the minutes tick by, I find myself returning to that argument we had, which I felt awful about for years, even after apologising and gaining your forgiveness. I have to admit, it does feel like an infinitesimal weight has been lifted off my shoulders. I start to see what Codelle is talking about when she implies that I'll leave this place with a markedly different mindset. It seems logical, that the more her process removes my sense of care, the less I'll ultimately care about her process.

But I have a long way to go before I don't care at all.

I jump to my feet, pacing back and forth until I regain coordination in my recently tranquilised limbs. Placing the Polaroid in my breast pocket, I reach under the mattress once again, my hand withdrawing a set of red and yellow magnetic darts from the games room.

Approaching the door, I stretch upward towards the magnetic sensor, its red light gleaming. I select one dart, running it across the surface of the sensor, until I feel it stick in place. One by one, I place the remaining darts against that same point, hoping that a significant amount of external magnetic force will trick the sensor into thinking the door is still closed.

But even that won't matter if I can't slide the thing open.

Placing my hands against the grey fibreglass, I press all my weight into my palms and slowly attempt to force it open. My feet slip backward across the carpet as they fail to gain purchase, the door utterly unyielding as I strain weakly against it.

Yet, after a few laboured attempts, the barest shift shudders through my palms, cool air drifting in through the slightest gap in the door.

My heart in my throat, I examine the sensor. The red light remains, indicating, at least for now, that I'm passing unnoticed.

Widening the gap, I squeeze through and creep barefooted into the unlit corridor, collecting the key for the *De Anima* from its hiding place as I go.

I pass down through the statuary corridor, through the atrium, into the long, windowless dining room.

Judging by the laundry chute's position on the third floor, it should descend directly through the kitchen. I rush past the long dining table and to the door beside the chef's window, attempting to turn the handle.

Locked.

I exhale, frustrated. It was never going to be that easy.

At least I have another floor to try.

It takes a minute for me to creep up the iron spiral staircase and along the second-floor corridor in the direction of Codelle's office. I make it halfway before I see a door to my right, positioned roughly above the kitchen. Slipping inside, I brush along the wall until I find a switch, closing the door behind me to avoid any light escaping into the hall.

It takes a few seconds to adjust to the light, and a few more to accept my new surroundings.

I've stepped into a child's playroom, yet with everything sized up by several orders of magnitude. I look over a stack of towering alphabet blocks, a rainbow-coloured xylophone as big as a keyboard, a toy car in the corner that I could easily clamber inside.

A mural depicting a crowded cartoon circus spans the entire wall. Smiling elephants, a ringmaster in red and gold, lions, trapezists, clowns and vast happy crowds.

And yet the laundry chute is nowhere to be seen.

With growing desperation, I hurry to the back wall and tap my knuckles against the plaster, testing for anything beneath its surface. After half a minute, rapping among a bandstand of circusgoers with open-mouthed smiles, the dull thud of my knuckles gives way to an almost imperceptible hollow echo.

Thud. Thud. Thud. Crack. CRACK.

The smiling faces splinter and break apart as a corner of heavy stone embeds into the playroom wall.

After scouring the space nearby for a blunt object, being faced with nothing but soft rubber and round edges, I was forced to undertake a desperate mental accounting of the institute's few resources.

Reaching a reluctant conclusion, swallowing down my anxiety, I had stepped back into the unlit halls of Prismall House and crept back down to the first floor.

Slipping nervously into the statuary corridor, I ran my hands across one of the marble busts, straining slightly to observe whether it was affixed to its pedestal. When the bust itself gave way, fairly easily, I hooked my arms underneath the figure's shoulders and took its weight.

Minutes later, with twenty kilograms of solid marble pressed against my chest, I had edged up the spiral staircase, one sideways step at a time. My forearms burned, my back straining, spurred on by the knowledge that, if I were to drop the heavy item now, the result would be an ungodly clanging of marble down iron steps, like a church bell ringing from the very centre of the house.

Keeping my resolve, I reached the second floor in silence and, though I had to resign myself to the noise it would cause, my effort quickly paid off.

I swing the defaced statue as far back as I can and throw my entire body into a final pendulous swing.

A golf-ball-sized section of the wall finally breaks inward, plaster and plywood like shattered teeth. I reach my fingers into the gap and prise away the plaster, cracks beginning to spread through the smiling crowd, inflexible Gypsum fracturing into fault lines across the drywall.

I breathe out, exhausted, as I observe the open breach I've dug out for myself. Like a stone tossed across the floor of an empty cathedral, the first reverberations of hope echo through my soul as I find myself facing the second-floor laundry chute.

Working the stiff, creaking mechanism open, a rush of cool air passes by me.

The perfectly square passage descends into utter darkness, the sides of the wall barely wider than my shoulders. Unpleasant as it may seem, this narrow passageway represents my only path to the outside world, even if it feels like I'm descending into the hungry gullet of Prismall House itself.

My hands underhooking the upper lip of the laundry chute, I step through until I'm sitting on the edge of the dark and narrow abyss, feeding myself into it inch by inch.

In my final moment, I twist myself around, staring into the eyes of a beaming lion as I drop away from the room entirely.

26

I gradually ease myself down, my body suspended above a long, dark void.

Urging myself not to panic, my fingers gradually slipping from the second-floor hatch, I raise my knees and push them into the wall in front of me, bracing my back behind me until I wedge myself in place.

Feeling my own hot breath against my face, I prepare to remove my hands and shift downward, aware that any miscalculation will send me plummeting into the darkness, or else jolt me into some immovable position, pinned in place by my own contorted limbs.

I loosen my grip, remaining mercifully in place.

Slowly, I push my palms against the wall and shift a quivering knee further down the chute. My heart pounding through the walls, I painstakingly lower one palm, then another. My entire body braces as I edge down into the darkness.

Minutes draw on tortuously as I shift my body deeper and deeper still. It feels like an hour before my hands find the outline of the kitchen's laundry hatch, only the midpoint of my descent. My head swims, my limbs screams, sweltering in an oven of my own body heat as sweat drips freely down my brow.

However, over the protracted minutes, my aching body begins to find a sense of pattern and regularity, a resolute progression carrying me, inch by inch, down the final few metres.

Thunk.

My foot stops abruptly, searching for the end of the chute, but instead finding only a rigid platform of uneven metal. Confused, I lower my other foot, until I find myself standing upright in the metal shaft.

Eyes wide, my neck craning downward, I glimpse the slotted surface of a thick iron grate closed entirely over the mouth of the chute. I press down with one foot, trying to force it open.

It doesn't move an inch.

Gulping down a rush of jagged breaths, I look back up. Twenty metres of smooth metal stretch upward. With the way down closed, all I've done is sink myself into a sweltering two-foot-wide tomb, shoulders crushed inward, limbs penned in, the dim light from the second floor unreachably distant.

A cry for help forms in the pit of my stomach. I keep my mouth shut and squeeze my eyes closed, battling to suppress the writhing panic inside me. I think about you, about our home, the memories that still brim with emotion, and perhaps more importantly, the memories that don't.

I stay silent, I look up, and I resolve to climb all the way back to the second-floor hatch.

I reassume the position, clammy palms and aching knees against the wall of the chute, bracing my back behind me. Immediately aware of my own exhaustion, of the lumbering weight of my own body, I push myself upward, clambering against sweat-slick walls, breathing sharply through gritted teeth as I climb away from the grate.

One hand higher, then another, then—

A slip, a jolt and a sudden, lurching drop slams me back down onto the grate. I grunt sharply, as the force of the landing shudders through my unbent knees, my entire skeleton quaking at the impact.

Yet, even through the pain, my mind acknowledges a second, enlivening sensation.

Something just gave way under foot.

The grate must be attached to some thick coiled spring, strong enough to hold my body weight without moving, but giving way when subjected to sufficient downward force.

A grim conclusion comes to me. My sudden fall shifted the grate only momentarily but, if I could drop from higher up, I could perhaps leverage it enough to open.

Though there's no guarantee that I won't bust my kneecaps in the attempt.

With a quivering breath, cringing from the promise of imminent pain, I plant my palms once again, and begin to crawl upward.

Half a metre. One metre. Two metres. Head-swimmingly high for what I'm about to do. Quick breaths streaming through gritted teeth, I look up to the distant light of the second-floor hatch. It doesn't seem as far now. Maybe I could reach it if I keep going, a return to captivity bringing its own freedoms – from fear and exertion and pain.

Instead I breath in, close my eyes and let go.

A split second of a whistling fall, followed by a slam, a metal screech and the sickening crack of bone. My legs pencil-dive into hard iron, forcing the grate open, carrying my shins and knees through, until my downward momentum no longer outweighs the iron plate's upward force. The grate springs back like a vice, trapping my lower thighs as an eruption of pain volleys from an undoubtedly broken left foot.

A pressure-cooker hiss bursting through my teeth, I twist and turn, working my body downward, battling through the jaws of the grate until I finally fall through into an empty laundry cart.

The grate snaps back into the closed position, sending a resounding metal clang through the open basement.

I lie on my back, cold air and the fumes of cedar laundry detergent rushing into my lungs as I gasp through the pain. The vent stares down at me, jaws closed, indifferent to the creature that has just escaped its clutches. Half my body screams at me to stay put, to not subject my aching, sweating, fractured limbs to any more punishment.

I dredge the depths of my very soul, scraping bedrock as I gather every last scrap of grit. With something close to surprise,

I watch my shaking arms reach up for the sides of the laundry basket and haul me to my feet.

I clamber onto the bare stone of the basement, testing my left foot to find it barely walkable, a pure, nerve-shattering pain radiating up my leg.

Holding my breath, I hobble across the open space in the direction of Villner's suit rack, fully conscious of how close I'm standing to what I assume are his living quarters. Limping with every step, I cross along the aisle of vacant suits until I find the ensemble of beige trousers and a green apron.

Reaching out, I recover a trowel from the tool belt.

It's only now, as I turn towards the distant tunnel that holds the unlocked exit hatch, that I hear movement behind Villner's door. The faintest rustling of covers, the creaking of bed springs and moments later, the steady rhythm of bare footprints on stone.

27

I plant my right foot and walk, struggling to balance haste, silence and destabilising pain as I limp frantically towards the tunnel.

Twenty-five metres. Twenty.

I can almost feel the fractured bones scraping against each other, as the unhurried bare footsteps from Mr Villner's room transition to the thud of boots.

Fifteen. Ten.

Five.

The door opens behind me as I duck into the tunnel, disappearing into its shadowed depths.

I listen as Villner moves steadily into the centre of the room, towards the laundry chute. I strive desperately towards the exit hatch at the corridor's end, knowing that I can't open it without making considerable noise and, once noticed, am in no position to fight back.

Keeping an ear on Villner's movements, I stare at the corridor's glass-lined walls. Refrigerated cabinets hold pre-packed syringes, a wall of labelled metal drawers below them boasting every type of medical implement.

Villner turns on his heels, his footsteps growing louder as he crosses the central room towards me.

As silently as possible, I draw a fridge door open, snatching up every syringe I can find. Opening the nearest drawers, my fingers close around the packaging of a disposable scalpel with a 5 cm blade.

I fumble with the pull tabs of the sterile packaging, backing into the darkness, crouching on the staircase beneath the hatch. I wait, with one hand now closed around a scalpel, the other gripping a chamber of grey tranquiliser, my thumb trigger-ready on the plunger.

I doubt I'll have more than one chance to use either.

A silhouette of grey pyjamas and dark shrouded features appears at the threshold. I can sense Villner's eyes peering down into the corridor, adjusting to the dark, searching for a foreign entity in the unlit tunnel.

For a harrowing few seconds his eyes seem to meet mine, before slowly continuing beyond me, turning away into some distant corner of the basement.

His oblivious frame passes back into the main room, towards his bedroom. I breathe the faintest sigh of relief, until I hear the man's steps continue into another hallway, towards the basement stairs.

He's planning to check up on me.

I snap around to the exit hatch, climbing the short metal staircase. Any pressure on my left foot sends excruciating waves across my body, tears brimming in my eyes as I collapse at the top. I force the handle into the unlocked position and push up with my back, the hatch budging barely an inch before struggling against soil.

I pocket the scalpel along with the tranquilisers I've collected. Taking a firm grip of the trowel, I reach up and drive it into the narrow gap.

Dirt cascades across my lap as I drag compacted soil into the corridor. My burning arms dig the trowel further and further into the gap, until my entire arm is able to pass through and clear the dirt above me. Huge chunks of earth burst over me as the space above hollows out inch by inch.

Forcing myself to stand, the hatch gives way enough for me to squeeze my body through into the small cavity I've excavated. Squinting up at the topsoil, I stab the trowel upward, the turf stretching as I push further and further up against it.

Finally, with a cathartic shower of dirt and mown grass, the surface tension breaks, the point of the trowel stabbing through the turf with my arm quickly following. Frantically I tear the topsoil away, clawing into the cold night air of the island grounds.

I pull myself up, spitting black saliva onto the ground, eyes scanning wildly to get my bearings. I'm at the north-eastern corner of Prismall House, the crescent moon window of my bedroom on the wall nearby, the distant shadow of the boathouse far to the south.

I turn towards it and run.

A cool ocean wind whirls around me. I inhale salt air with every second step, gasping sharply as something within my left leg rakes against itself. Whatever momentary adrenaline kept the pain at bay, it's quickly wearing off, the full gravity of the breakage quickly overtaking me.

I stumble into the corridor of topiary bushes, my feet kicking up chalk dust, the boathouse looming ever closer as I hear a growing commotion far behind me.

Suddenly, my ankle gives way beneath me. I slam into the earth, the wind knocked from my chest as the undergrowth before me scatters with loose syringes, the boathouse barely fifty metres away.

I hear the double doors of Prismall House fly open behind me.

I pick myself up and limp the final excruciating stretch. One foot in front of the other, passing into the dark, open mouth of the boathouse, the creak of wood quickly transitioning into rocking fibreglass. I pull the key from my pocket, hands shaking as I desperately try to force it into the lock.

I hear voices in the distance, torchlight streaming through the wall slats, growing ever closer.

The key slips inward, clicks, turns. I throw open the door and fall into the carpeted lounge of the *De Anima*, grasping a merciful banister as I take the weight off my foot and struggle up the stairs to the boat's bridge.

The piloting panel is mere metres ahead of me, torchlight from the chalk pathway dancing through the windscreen.

I put the key in the ignition, engage the starting mechanisms, and turn it sharply.

Nothing happens.

I turn the key again, looking out the window as two sets of feet appear beyond the front window, at the very top of the boathouse's opening.

Despair screams through my body as I analyse their movement. No wonder they didn't catch up with me as I limped to the boathouse. They're walking.

Turning away from the windscreen, I try the key again to total, deafening silence.

Horrified, I run my fingers across the bridge mechanisms, searching for something, anything that might allow me to leave.

My fingers make contact with a small panel on the underside of the console. I crouch down immediately, my heart in my throat, finding a black plastic cover that I slide open with quivering fingers.

I stare at a combination panel, a tactile keypad with an unknown code built into the console. My heart plummets, tumbling through the hull of the *De Anima* and into the dark waters below.

I can hardly feel the excruciating throb in my foot, hardly see the neat keypad right in front of me. I don't even hear anyone step onto the boat, until I finally rise to turn around.

Dr Codelle and Villner stand before me in patient silence.

'I understand why you did it. Still, doesn't this prove my point?' An upset Codelle gestures mournfully to my broken ankle. 'No one on this island has caused you harm, no one has threatened your life. You have. You're the greatest danger to your own well-being. And what was it all for? Where are you going, Arthur?'

Codelle seems at a loss.

'It's a genuine question,' she continues, her voice breaking slightly. 'Where are you going? You're escaping back to an empty apartment, back to solitude and suffering. Is that a victory? You struggle as if Julia's waiting for you on the mainland, but she isn't.'

Codelle looks at me, her eyes brimming with sadness and pity. She calmly speaks four pointed words, as if she wishes to imprint each individual syllable upon the fabric of my soul.

'Julia. Doesn't. Exist. Anymore.'

'Fuck you,' I mutter, tired and in so much pain. 'You're not a psychiatrist. You're a surgeon. You want the brain to be something you cut and fix, and you can't imagine that it's not. You brute-force people into happiness against their will, and you get away with it because they stop caring. Well, I don't want that. I don't want that.'

I fall to my knees, tears starting to flow, pooling at my chin and dropping onto the floor.

'Happiness is happiness, Arthur,' Codelle says, equally defeated by how little we understand each other. 'The fact that you reject it, that you're so eager to return to this desolate void – it just proves how much work we still have to do.'

Tap. Tap. Tap. Villner's boots softly cover the distance between us, a hand grasping my arm and lifting it high above my kneeling form.

I hear the cap of the syringe open, but nothing further.

24th September

28

I plunge like a stone through cool, blue water, leaving sound and sight and gravity behind me.

Sinking gently down, into a realm of silence and uniform pressure, I drift into my memories, seeking fragments of Julia Mason.

I find you in several places. Waiting on the Pennine Way for my panting, sweat-drenched body to catch up. Solving a jigsaw puzzle on our coffee table, abruptly asking 'Where the fuck are you?' to some elusive corner piece. Coming home to King's Cross station, your pace quickening suddenly as you notice me in the waiting crowd.

So many of these thoughts still exist, charged moments that flood my body with a rush of glowing adoration, that remind me how I feel about you.

But there are fewer to choose from than yesterday, and tomorrow there'll be even fewer still.

I rotate slowly and kick off the wall with my right foot.

I launch through the water with my breath held, cresting the surface and gasping for air before descending into a flurry of overarm strokes. Pale white light shines down on me from the large, circular fixture above Prismall House's underground pool before my head dips back into the chlorinated water.

After half a minute, I clumsily turn myself around and kick off in the other direction.

Of all the modes of exercise that can be undertaken with my damaged ankle, a daily swim is the only one that has truly stuck.

It's a relief to be free of the jolts of pain, the constant vigilance of putting any weight where it shouldn't be. Mostly, I simply crave freedom from the crutches Codelle has assigned to me.

Half an hour later, my muscles thrumming, I approach the aluminium ladder to find a hand already outstretched before me. Villner takes all my weight as I hop up onto the tiled poolside, handing me my crutches and a folded towel before letting me stand freely.

'Thank you,' I mutter, dabbing the cotton to my forehead.

My hair is still wet as I walk the island grounds, Villner consistently at my back. Dr Codelle suggested the walk, that I get used to the crutches for the time being, to minimise the risk of a fall.

I'd never truly noticed before, but all the various bushes and shrubs in this garden must be evergreen. They've retained the same verdant intensity throughout my stay, so much so that, if it hadn't been for the fading lavender and dead-headed roses, there would be no evidence that we had recently entered autumn.

Three weeks have passed since my ill-fated jaunt to the *De Anima*, a timeframe I've only been able to discern through a fastidious mental accounting of each passing day. I'd had my leg elevated in a wheelchair for the first week, Codelle's therapy sessions taking place, temporarily, on the first floor.

The Detachment Sessions have stayed on the upper level, however, moving ahead with increasing regularity.

Some days I would wake up, startled and straining against the unannounced appearance of the third-floor ceiling. Other days, as I assume was the original intention, I would simply wake up in my bed, somewhat unrested, with the dull residue of the grey tranquiliser in my muscles, as if the session itself had merely been a dream.

The morning passes, and I find myself watching the ships roll by through a rare heart-shaped window, breaching the horizon on a private jaunt between Dublin and the Isle of Man.

I discovered the Prismall House library in the last week or so, as the weather turned colder and my penchant for walks lessened.

The Renaissance-inspired space stretches between the first and second floors, joined by a staircase that runs up through the centre of the room. Wood panelling adorns every wall, interrupted by inlaid shelving that stretches up to the ceiling.

I wrap myself in one of the Codelle institute's branded fleeces, sip on the tea provided by Villner and read long into the afternoon, picking books from the shelves at random and losing myself in them: history, philosophy, the science of Olympic cycling.

I've actually started to learn a few things.

The ship passes beyond the window's view, and I drink my quickly cooling herbal tea down to the dregs, placing the cup beside me as I look to Villner.

'Do you have anything … stronger?'

I almost see the hint of a smile on Villner's face, as he rises from his armchair at the other end of the room.

'Or something unhealthy at least? Coke or something.'

Villner nods affirmatively, collecting my cup and saucer as I continue to plough through a book on Soviet photography.

Since the *De Anima*, Villner has been observing me far more closely; these brief errands are now the only times he leaves my sight.

The impact of his newfound priorities has started to become quite noticeable, as I draw a large amount of focus away from his role as Prismall House's primary carer. Running my finger across the underside of my nightstand yesterday evening, I was quite satisfied to discover an infinitesimal layer of dust.

I stare out the window as I wait for him to disappear down the corridor, before standing up, grabbing a single crutch and hurrying across the room.

A vast number of the old tomes in this room are entirely unmarked, meaning it takes trial and error to find a specific volume. I'd searched slowly as I waited for my ankle to heal, not wanting to bring too much attention, perusing a random set of books in Villner's presence to establish myself as a casual reader.

In truth, I have only one book in mind, and it was only yesterday that I finally located it.

I heave at an antique atlas. The tome could be described as a coffee table book, in the sense that it's roughly the size of a coffee table. I withdraw it from the shelving unit with some effort, my arms shuddering as I follow its momentum towards the nearest desk.

With a heavy thud, I set the book down.

After Villner's quick return yesterday, I'd left your Polaroid between the pages, a bookmark allowing me to get to work much faster. Sure enough, after just a few turns, the book practically falls open to display the photo, as well as a grand view of the Irish Sea and its myriad small islands. Despite the significant age of the atlas, its borders inked several centuries before the partition of Ireland, the village of Porthcoll stands exactly where it once did. A few inches to the north, the isle that now holds Prismall House lies unsettled in a faded sepia ocean.

Out of all the similar books in this library, this tome provides the most granular measurement of the north Wales coast. With only supervised access to pens and pencils, I make a few small tears in the Polaroid, using the scale bar as a reference to form a rudimentary ruler, before placing its edge in a straight line between the mainland and the island's shore.

Eight and a half kilometres.

Heavy footsteps echo from down the corridor, hard boots falling with military haste.

Maybe I should have asked for a more complicated drink.

With only seconds to spare, I kick the atlas under the nearest desk, tucking the Polaroid into my pocket.

Codelle's aide-de-camp slowly tours the room towards me, a carbonated drink with ice supported on an ostentatious silver tray.

I sip the drink while staring out the window into the turbulent Irish sea.

Eight and a half kilometres. Five miles of open water. One hundred and seventy laps of an Olympic swimming pool, with the added considerations of weather, tide and hypothermia to contend with.

I'm not that good a swimmer yet, but I'm comfortably better than I was three weeks ago. If I can play for time, it might be something close to possible.

A few hours later, Villner helps me down the library stairs to the quiet dining room and a dinner of spinach and ricotta tortellini.

After that, I return to my bedroom.

My mind still on the mechanics of the daunting swim, I clamber unsteadily onto my knees and slip the now regrettably torn Polaroid back under my bed.

My mental calculations suddenly hit a brick wall, as my fingers brush against an unknown object.

Confused, I reach further under the bed for a better sense of purchase. The object is thin, square, laminate and immediately familiar, not just because I've encountered it before, but because I'm already holding an identical object in my hand.

Slowly, almost reluctantly, I withdraw it from under the mattress, staring at a second Polaroid photograph.

One is marked with the various neat incisions I recently made, the other contains no such imperfections, yet both depict the exact same image: your smiling face, lit up to the brink of saturation by the flash of the camera. I'd taken that photograph myself at the loose party that we'd called our wedding reception.

I certainly don't remember taking it twice.

A now familiar wave of ill feeling overcomes me, like the shadow of a dark cloud covering the sun. I feel the punch-drunk sway of psychological imbalance, the foreboding recognition of Dr Codelle's hand moving pieces in the background for reasons as impenetrable to me as the walls of Prismall House itself.

Burying my unease, I stare sharply at the two pictures with renewed concentration. My eyes flit between them, examining every detail, attempting to understand why a replacement might have been left for me.

I don't know what I'm looking for but, after two minutes of constant focus, I manage to find it.

Even on my crutches, it takes half that time to locate Dr Codelle. 'What is this?'

Codelle looks up from an armchair in the games room. She notes her page and sets a book down on the table beside her. I drop the Polaroids next to it.

'Ah,' she comments quietly, before turning to Villner. 'Villner, leave us a moment, would you?'

Villner nods, making his way out of the room and disappearing into the atrium.

'They're different.' I accuse sharply. 'This new image, it's a different face, it looks like Julia but it's ... Who is this?'

'It's no one.'

'No one.' I chew the words and spit them back out, incredulous.

'Genuinely.' Codelle affirms calmly. 'The person in that photo doesn't exist, it's pulled from an image generator tasked with assembling a human face that's about 3–5% different to a chosen host picture.'

'You were trying to make me forget her.'

'Not forget,' Codelle assures once again. 'The aim is dissociation from the addictive source. That's all we're ever trying to do.'

'Ok.' I nod, ticking through the doctor's motives until I reach a satisfying conclusion. 'So, you thought I'd lost the original and you used it as an excuse to swap it with someone different. Is that what's happened here?'

Dr Codelle looks down to the table, considering her response for a moment, before looking up at me with sobering composure.

'No, Arthur. Neither of those photographs are of Julia.'

29

My brow furrows. Reflexively, my eyes flicker down to the two photographs, before returning back to Codelle, attempting to excavate meaning from her unyielding eyes.

'What?'

'We've been replacing that Polaroid every day since your treatment started,' Codelle explains. 'Subtle changes in the facial features, cumulatively resulting in a person who is similar but very much distinct from your wife.'

'No. No. This is just a fucking mind game.' I reason. 'This is the original, you're just trying to make me doubt it.'

'Are you sure?'

'I know what my wife looks like!'

'People are terrible eyewitnesses, Arthur. You'd be surprised at how much perception shifts when subject to gradual alteration.'

I feel all my muscles stiffen. Breathing sharply through my nose, I snatch the original Polaroid from the table.

I stare deep into the image, the world falling still around me. The curls of your hair, the easy smile, the silver earrings you picked out on a trip to Brighton.

'What colour were her eyes?'

The question penetrates like a splinter of broken glass, shattering an illusion I didn't know I was under. I was certain this was your face, the face of the woman I'd woken up next to for fourteen years.

Your eyes were a light, hazel brown, I'd sung Van Morrison to you on one of our drunken nights in. I remember staring into them, commenting that they looked like swirling nebula, the faintest emerald ring like a halo around each iris.

The person in this photo has green eyes, almost on the cusp of brown but undeniably distinct, the mouth curling into a slightly different smile, the eyebrows more symmetrical than the ones you always battled with. I realise now this person is a familiar stranger, perfectly constructed to usher me away from your true face without my notice.

My anger and indignation fall away, the legs kicked from under them, crumbling instead into a well of self-loathing. I feel like I've betrayed you, your memory. Every evening, when I had taken out that Polaroid and held it close, I had unknowingly been reinforcing your erasure, falling in love over and over again with a subtle chain of digital ghosts.

'You must have known I'd find out.' I place my index finger against the unmarked Polaroid. 'You left this under my bed, knowing that the old one was still out there. You must have suspected that I had it with me, that I'd eventually discover what you'd done.'

Codelle simply stares, not confirming or denying, leaving me to work out my own conclusions.

'You wanted me to notice.' The words barely pass through my lips, carried on a resigned sigh. 'What I'm feeling right now, you *wanted* me to feel it. Because there's no point in dissociation if I don't know it's happening.'

Codelle's silent look accepts every charge laid against her.

'I want the original,' I demand. 'It's my property; I want it back.'

Codelle sighs, observing my protest with a mixture of pity and disappointment. Her eyes meet mine, a look so controlled and calm, yet instilling within me a palpable dread.

'All right.'

I return to my bedroom soon after, just in time to pass Villner as he heads the other way. The two Polaroids held at my side, I place my hand against my bedroom door and allow it to slide open. Before the grey barrier moves aside, I briefly wonder what

Villner was doing here, why a man who's spent three weeks at my side had been sent away in the first place.

As soon as the door opens, I understand entirely.

Like autumn leaves, hundreds of loose Polaroids lie scattered across the floor. Of the pictures that lie face up, countless rows of smiling teeth gleam upward at the ceiling, thousands of eyes following me as I step despondently into the room.

I kneel down and select a few stray pictures, laying them out like playing cards in front of me. Three similar but distinct faces, variations on a theme, dancing around the essential features I'd fallen in love with before some irreconcilable aspect discounts them.

I put these stray photographs to the side and begin to gather the rest.

I tell myself I'm being lied to, that your photo is securely tucked away in a drawer in Codelle's office, that you're nowhere to be found among this pile of imposters. It would be the simplest thing for Codelle to omit your true face from this collection, forcing me to comb through every imitation until I conclude that I've failed to recognise you.

Yet the thought remains, metastasising as I sort through the first hundred, and the second, and the third, that the photograph containing your true face has already passed in front of me, that I discounted it, dismissed it, tossed it among the pile of facsimiles and buried it beneath countless more.

Hours pass. The last Polaroid quivers in my shaking hand before dropping onto the pile on my bedspread. Seven hundred and ninety-eight smiles.

Tears no longer fall from my expressionless face; I've already cried enough, passing through the storm and emerging utterly numb.

Three booming knocks echo through the door, more by way of announcement than permission. Looking up, I see Villner dominating the open threshold, waiting patiently for me to follow him.

I wipe my eyes on my sleeve and turn to face him.

'Please,' I lament exhaustedly. 'Come on, isn't this enough?'

Villner doesn't move. For the briefest moment, I can't help but marvel. How affirming it must be, for the implication of violence to loom so firmly in your own favour that force needn't even be applied. This must be how horses feel when their spirit is broken, the solemn understanding that all the branching choices you could make will inevitably be wrangled back into a single forced conclusion. That when all roads lead to your captor's chosen destination, the difference between rebellion and compliance is merely miles walked.

I pick up my crutch and follow behind him to the end of the hall and down the statuary corridor. Expecting to take the staircase to the second floor, I'm a little taken aback when Villner instead continues down across the atrium and through the entrance corridor, removing a set of keys from his jacket and unlocking the external door. With a heavy clunk, the metal bars draw back, the door swinging outward on well-oiled hinges, inviting in a gust of cold, autumnal air. Villner smiles, gesturing for me to step out into the grounds.

A brisk wind sweeps through the bushes, the cold air inflating my lungs and awakening my senses. Villner walks past me and continues down the path towards the edge of the gardens where a black sheet has been laid out on the ground ahead of us.

'Does she know you're doing this?' I ask.

Villner remains characteristically silent, stopping us at the edge of the sheet. I look down, my eyes adjusting to the darkness, to discover the tell-tale crossroads of red, gold and green tartan running across what appears to be a picnic blanket. Villner motions for me to sit, offering his arm to take the weight of my crutches.

I stare at him for a long while, before allowing myself to be awkwardly lowered onto the left side of the blanket, my injured leg rested in front of me, crutch dropped to my side.

He joins me as soon as I'm settled.

A gust of chill air whips past, both of us staring out at the sea beyond the boathouse, the distant twinkling lights of the shoreline and the drifting yellow beacons of the coastguard.

Villner stares casually down at his watch as I look back towards the house, tracing my eyes up to the vast window of Dr Codelle's office. I wonder if she's looking down at us right now, observing through that dark, ocular portal.

Part of me hopes that she is.

'She isn't up there,' a confident, low voice comments, the words carried on a Cymric lilt.

I slowly rotate my head back around to the man beside me, my jaw dropping open. He barely looks in my direction, staring out at the ocean as if he hadn't just addressed me directly for the first time.

'I thought we could talk,' Villner asserts calmly. 'Just us. Man to man.'

30

In the seconds that follow, I imagine my expression resembles that of a broken marionette: inanimate, wide-eyed, with a slack, unmoving jaw. Internally, a steady noise is beginning to crescendo through my skull, drowning everything out like the horn of a rapidly approaching train.

Shock, rebuke, curiosity and a hundred other reactions trample over each other, wedging themselves in the doorway of my mind. Stunned by the overwhelming cacophony of competing sentiments, all I can do is wait blankly to discover what I'm going say next.

'You're Welsh?'

Villner releases a warm, genuine chuckle, pulling a bottle from a cooler I hadn't noticed and striking the top against it until the cap topples into the grass.

'Oh, you thought I'd be English?' he replies, holding the opened beer towards me. 'Most English people do.'

I observe the chilled bottle, dewy condensation clinging to the glass. Though, in any other circumstances, a cold beer on a cool night in such a unique setting might be considered pleasant, the thought of accepting anything from this man makes my skin crawl. My imagination pictures him injecting poison through the bottle caps, blaming me for the recent brown spots on the atrium's potted ferns.

However, considering Dr Codelle's fastidious dedication to my wellbeing, and Villner's fastidious dedication to *her*, I can only assume the drink is safe to imbibe. Besides, if Villner wanted to poison me, he'd have very little trouble administering it directly.

I snatch the bottle from Villner's hands and drink.

'My mum told me you should say "thank you" when someone gives you something,' Villner chides.

'Oh fascinating,' I retort. 'What's her stance on kidnapping?'

Villner chuckles, rolling his eyes with bemused exasperation. As stoic as he appears in the undertaking of his duties, off-the-clock Villner seems incredibly good-humoured, reacting to my barb with a genuine and easy-flowing laugh.

'Snarky bastard.' Villner grins, shaking his head. 'You know, Arthur, I'm not being funny, but you've been nothin' short of a nightmare.'

He puts a bottle to his lips and tips his head back – a long, indulgent swig. I watch the liquid drain down the upturned glass, forming my first impressions of his speech and tone. Despite his fairly forthright admission, he doesn't sound angry; on the contrary, he sounds like he's winding down at the pub, reminiscing about a long shift at a job that he nevertheless adores.

He takes a break, rolling the half-empty bottle between his palms as he continues.

'That woman has been movin' heaven and earth to help you, and you've thrown it in her face.' He sighs. 'But you know what I remind myself every time you kick off?'

He waits, as if expecting genuine curiosity. I wonder if he understands the implicit power he wields over this situation. Perhaps he simply doesn't mind that his conversational partner is entirely beholden to his whims.

At the very least, I can choose to say nothing, a decision that Villner slowly accepts.

'I remind myself that you haven't seen what I've seen. People who wash up here broken: the junkies, the alcoholics …'

'The widows? The widowers?' I add incredulously, only for Villner to nod in agreement.

'Exactly! People who can't let go of the what's hurtin' them! Patients come to her without hope, because there's none to be found anywhere else, and she saves them. She pulls them from the edge, breathes life into their bones and sends them home with joy in their heart. She'd do it for free if she could; all she cares about is helpin' people. She's ... life's champion on earth.'

'You know what I see?' I mutter, before sipping my drink. 'I see someone who opened their mind to Dr Codelle and ended up her fucking butler. Seriously, she messes with people's heads for a living. You don't find it suspicious that you love her unconditionally?'

'Hah!' Villner booms into the air. 'Well, when you put it like that, it sounds right dodgy! But she doesn't care if people like her. All she wants to do is take away pain, heal people. You're like a wolf in a snare, Arthur, you really are, bitin' her hand while she's tryin' to free you. You'd see if you actually ...'

Villner sighs again, swallowing down the dregs of his beer, placing the empty bottle into the cooler as he immediately fetches a fresh one. He checks my own bottle, sees it's still unfinished, and proceeds to close the insulated lid.

'Can I tell you a story?' he asks. 'A story about someone like you, someone Codelle saved.'

'Do I have a choice?'

'Ugh, of course you do.' Villner rolls his eyes, annoyed but undiminished by my hostility, as if a child were repeatedly beating their fists against his chest. 'I ain't keepin' you out here, Arthur. I just thought you could use someone to talk to. If you'd rather get some sleep, I'm all about it.'

I turn back towards the house, no desire to engage with the man beside me, contemplating a prompt, defiant return to my quarters.

When I turn back, I see something just to my left. Glimmering in the moonlight, among the tangled roots of the hedgerow behind me.

Half buried in dirt, the transparent seal of a medical syringe, one of the many that spilled from my grasp when I attempted to escape three weeks ago. It lies, overlooked and forgotten, just at the edge of my reach.

My breath catches in my throat.

I've spent so much time trying to escape the locked doors of Prismall House, trying to come up with a plan to subvert its defences. Now Villner has brought me within a hundred metres of the *De Anima*, reportedly without Dr Codelle's knowledge, and with the means to subdue him close at hand.

There's every chance I could pull it off: surprise him with the anaesthetic, drag him to the *De Anima* and extract the ignition code from his dazed, compliant mind. I could sail away tonight and never look back.

All I need to do is pick my moment.

'Fine.' I relent, turning back to the man. 'What's the story?'

Villner smiles.

'There was once a child, a guilty little thing, bigger than most of his peers, but inside, he was as meek and mild as they come … three guesses who I'm talking about!' He chuckles at his own joke, as I quietly picture myself sticking a syringe into his neck. 'This kid didn't know what to do with his life, couldn't decide, didn't want to do wrong by anyone. His dad wasn't havin' it so he took his son to a career fair to get some *direction* in his life. Moment they walk through the door, his dad sees a booth for the British Army and suddenly he's *all* about it! Looks to his son and says, that'll be the thing to toughen you up, give you a bit of momentum, bit of discipline! You know what the kid said?'

'No,' I intone, my eyes cautiously returning to the buried syringe. 'Tell me.'

'He said, yes, Dad, whatever you want, Dad!' Villner shakes his head good-humouredly. 'His whole life, he'd lived with insides like bloody eels, guilty about everythin', scared of lettin' anyone down. God, you have no idea.'

I find it strange, how Villner recounts his somewhat unpleasant past with a kind of nostalgia. I steadily finish my drink, holding out the empty bottle for him to take, watching his fingers wrap around the neck.

I tense up, waiting for him to turn towards the cooler.

As soon as his head turns decisively to the right, I begin to steadily lean leftwards. Without a breath, moving my hand through the still air, I extend my outstretched fingers along the grass and over the dry, untilled soil.

I keep my eyes trained on Villner, the back of his buzz-cut head still preoccupied, as he places the empty bottle neatly away.

My hand brushes empty earth, forcing me to look away from the man.

Not far enough. I stretch out even further, straining every sinew for an extra few inches of arm span.

My fingertips tease the edge of the syringe, tantalisingly close as I hear the cooler lid shut once again.

I snap back to a seated position, burying my frustration, just in time for Villner to hand me a fresh beer.

'So suddenly, I'm eighteen and a thousand miles away. Just some big lug, forced to carry all the bags! Scrambling to find cover that'll, well, *cover* me!' Villner laughs again. 'But I did find somethin' there, a family I suppose, a bit of purpose. Again, I wanted to do right by them, like I always did.'

A light breeze passes by us, as a sea change suddenly over-takes Villner. I sip my beer and examine his expression, suddenly downbeat, thoughtful. When he speaks again, his tone feels like a funeral march, a dark conclusion foreshadowed with every word.

'We were clearing houses, one day,' he says, brow sunken. 'And I always say it's like London traffic – it's fast and urgent, and you've got to clear through in a certain amount of time, no muckin' about. And I'm movin' and shoutin' and checkin' corners, door after door after door. Then suddenly there's gunfire in the complex nearby, and it all kicks off, and we're pushin' through faster and faster and faster …'

Villner stops, and I sense something close to vulnerability in the colossus beside me.

'People don't realise they shouldn't yell, especially if they're not going to be understood … and they shouldn't hide things behind them, because it just means we don't see it. This old man was yellin', all aggressive-like, and I was panicked, and there were shots nearby, and music from this cassette player was drownin' out the orders and ...'

Villner lifts his bottle like a conductor's baton, punctuating two regretful shots.

'And he fell. I knew he was dead immediately, but I still heard gaspin' breaths. So I looked down, and right there, sandwiched between the man and the floor was this ... young girl ... ten at most, skull wide open, breathin' her last.'

Silence overtakes us; only the rustling grass, wind and waves can be heard. For the briefest moment, my attention is genuinely pulled from the half-buried syringe and towards the man's story. I wonder if this version of Villner could be appealed to, reasoned with, whether there might be a foundational flicker of humanity I could reach.

Villner looks at me, and I try to project an expression of sympathy and understanding, tentatively entertaining the hope that I might gain sympathy in return.

Instead, a set of percussive glottal stops resonates from Villner's throat, his mouth widening into an impish, cheery smile. His mouth opens, and the percussive sounds build into a bout of hearty laughter. He straightens up, a spark reigniting in his eyes as he shakes his head in good-natured incredulity.

'I never thought I'd see the day!' He practically doubles over. 'Pity from Arthur bloody Mason! Didn't think you had it in you!'

'What?' I ask reflexively. 'Wait, was that all some kind of joke?'

'What? No!' He smiles incredulously. 'Why would you ask somethin' like that?'

He looks at me, utterly bemused, until the hollow realisation strikes me. I search back through the last minute of conversation, the soulful pauses, the tinge of vulnerability beneath a weak smile, his seemingly diminished frame as he told his grim tale.

I realise that I had imagined all of it.

Villner had carried himself normally throughout the story and, expecting to see some guilt or remorse for the harrowing subject matter, I'd found glimmers of it in the canvas of his blank expression. Now I think about it, his tone remained the same, his voice perfectly level, his smile unfazed.

'You don't seem cut up about it.' I hypothesise, hoping he'll correct me.

'Oh, I was.' Villner chuckles, happily emphasising the past tense. 'I crumbled, shattered into pieces. You've killed a little girl, it's that simple, and now she's dead forever. And the guilt, Arthur, the guilt hurt *physically*. My brain felt like a fuckin' wasps' nest. I didn't eat, I didn't sleep. I'd bawl like a baby or else I'd stare at the walls like some zombie!'

Villner looks back on his old self and shakes his head disbelievingly.

In response, I quietly rest my hand on my crutch, preparing to lift it silently from the ground, to rake it over the soil and bring the syringe within reach as soon as I get another opening.

'But I was lucky, wasn't I?' Villner continues. 'Elizabeth was just startin' up here, lookin' for patients who could help hone the process.'

'You mean guinea pigs.'

'*Collaborators*,' Villner shoots back. 'We didn't even have to pay! Again, my dad pushed me into it. I didn't even want to leave the house!'

Villner smiles, lost in the memory.

'I was scared at first, when she put me in that chair and sent me back to that place. Blam blam. Blam blam. Blam blam. I took those two shots again and again, stared into that girl's eyes over and over. At some points I thought, this is what hell must be like!' Villner chuckles at how foolish he used to be. 'But when I came out the other side ... I still remembered every second of it, but it was a flat line, you know? Didn't feel good, didn't feel bad, it felt ... it just felt like something that happened. I was free, for the first time – no guilt, no self-hatred. It was a miracle.'

Villner breathes in the night air, a sense of true contentment radiating from him until I can almost feel it on my skin.

For the first time perhaps, I see the man clearly, understanding the ease with which he enacts the doctor's orders against me.

Not only has this man been pulled from the brink of ruin by Codelle, but he's been spared the experience of culpability. He doesn't feel bad for what he's done to me and, quite possibly, he couldn't feel so if he tried.

I down my drink, gulping the last few dregs before handing the bottle to Villner.

'You don't think,' I ask, as curious as I am disturbed, 'you don't think that … maybe you *should* feel guilty?'

Villner shakes his head good-humouredly, as if the question were almost funny to him.

'Why?! Why should I have to carry guilt for somethin' I can't apologise for, can't set right? How about you? How long should you avoid happiness to … to prove your love to a woman who isn't even *alive* anymore?'

He keeps talking as he turns to throw my beer away. I snap to my left, gently lift my crutch from the blanket, and reach out for the syringe once again.

The crutch surges forwards over roots and dirt, drawing back through empty soil, lightly tapping the syringe but failing to dislodge it from the earth.

'You'll see it soon, Arthur. Addiction, grief, unatonable guilt … they have no *use*. They're a one-way cul-de-sac. But once you're free of them … oh Arthur, it's pure happiness. You understand? I've seen it, and if you just give her a chance, you'll see it too.'

I hear the lid of the cooler begin to close. I rake the crutch back through the ground one last time, catching the syringe as it rolls into my outstretched fingers. I snatch it up and twist back towards Villner.

He's staring out at the stars, not even looking in my direction.

I breathe a steady sigh of relief, preparing myself for my one window of opportunity. A strike to the neck, a stab of the plunger, a steady fight to keep him quiet as he slowly loses consciousness. I cradle the syringe in my hand and look down through the transparent wrapping.

My face falls, as a dark amber liquid glints in the moonlight.

This isn't the sedative, it's the recovery, the chemical cocktail responsible for waking me up. This so-called weapon is totally useless, my desperate efforts towards escape, once again, rendered utterly futile.

'I …' I think for a moment, my options as sparse as the passing ships in the dark, distant sea. 'You really feel better, having let it go?'

'Oh, you have no idea!' Villner grins serenely. 'No idea at all. The freedom of acting without guilt, or pain, or sadness. It's a gift! I suppose that's why I brought you out here, you know? I want you to understand what she's offering you, maybe even help you to, I don't know … to accept it.'

I sit in silence. As I consider his words, a grim and unsettling course of action descends upon me through the night air.

I had spent so much time pushing against Dr Codelle and everything she believes in that it would be highly suspicious if I were to reverse my position now. However, in this moment, there's a chance I can convince Villner that his words have infinitesimally swayed me, opened me up to the possibility of compliance. If he can, in turn, convince Dr Codelle that I'm willing to participate in the treatment, then I might be able to feign progress, feign happiness, feign eventual recovery.

Eight and a half kilometres. Five miles of open water. One hundred and seventy laps of an Olympic swimming pool. Right now, I can cover only a fraction of that distance. Even if I throw everything I have into it, there's a chance Codelle's treatment will be complete by the time I can make the journey.

However, if I can convince Codelle that I'm better, gain her seal of approval and leave this island, a month, a week, a day sooner than anticipated, then I might reach the mainland with some aspect of our relationship still intact.

I say very little for the rest of Villner's hour, at which point he lifts himself to his feet, helps me up, hands me my crutch and proceeds to lead me back. True to his vow, once his hour is over, he remains entirely silent.

On the walk back to my bedroom, I try to appear introspective, as if I were turning Villner's words over, allowing them to take a steady effect on me.

It's easier than I'd like to admit. In truth, as I start to consider this act of false compliance, I begin to entertain the slightest sense of relief. For some part of me, the notion of giving in, even fraudulently, feels like finally lying down after months spent running in place.

For the first time since I got here, sleep comes easily, and it feels disturbingly peaceful.

Early November

31

Hi Mum,

Hope you're doing well.

I know you haven't heard from me for a while. I meant to write sooner but, well, time moves differently here.

You'd love this place, genuinely. The sky. The sea. The peace of mind that London so rarely offers.

It's beautiful.

I'd love to tell you I'm happy here, and for the most part, I am. But then, every so often, I remember how we left things and suddenly it feels like there's this shadow hanging over me. It was suggested, by someone much smarter than myself, that an apology letter could be a good next step.

I know I caused you pain. I understand that you're scared of losing me and that my recent actions gave you reason to believe that had happened. I know what I did was impulsive and selfish and that it would inevitably hurt you. Honestly, if I could wave a wand and make everything better between us, I would.

However, despite all that, this isn't an apology letter, and I'm afraid I have no intention of writing one.

My wife (as strange as that still sounds) is getting ready for an evening out. I'm writing this from our youth hostel. She's been laughing to herself for the past ten minutes, after she mentioned that we had our own room and I asked her what on earth the alternative would be.

Apparently, I don't know what youth hostels are.

Anyway, tonight we're going to a seafood restaurant, then we're going to get drinks and listen to Fado music in a seventeenth-century stable. Tomorrow we're taking surfing lessons (her idea) and, the day after that, whatever we want.

I know you wanted your only son's wedding to be something grander: more people, somewhere more auspicious than the Southwark Registry Office. I know you wanted us to wait until we were older. For the record, Julia was perfectly happy with waiting, she wanted to take your feelings seriously.

But I think we both know what you were actually waiting for.

I've heard a lot of 'some days' that turned out to mean 'never'. There've been times when you asked me to have patience, while secretly hoping that I would forget about some idea, or hobby or vocation. And you're so often completely right. Sometimes a few days were just what I needed to realise the object of my desire was a passing fancy, to help me realise I didn't care as much as I thought.

But if you'd taken the time to get to know Julia, really get to know her, you'd realise she's simply the most astounding person you've ever met in your life. It makes me genuinely optimistic to know the world can produce someone this intelligent and witty and kind. I feel like anybody who spent enough time with her would fall head over heels, that I was simply lucky enough to ask first.

I know this is all a bit more expressive than we're used to. I know there's this dream partner you wanted me to find – from a family like ours, who was raised to understand the burden of a dynasty as I was. I know you think that I'm just an impetuous eighteen-year-old who's made a decision he'll someday regret.

And while I agree my actions were impetuous, selfish and, regrettably, hurtful, I doubt I'll ever regret marrying this amazing, inspiring person. I didn't yesterday, I don't today, and if you ask me in ten, twenty, thirty years, I'm sure I'll say the very same.

If I'm wrong then you'll be getting one hell of an apology letter.

Your loving son,
Arthur

I press my index finger down against my name, checking my fingertip to find only the lightest imprint of ink, confident that the words have dried in the Mediterranean heat. I fold the letter and slip it into an envelope, its featherlike weight belying the personal gravity of its contents.

I let it fall onto the small desk and exit through the bright screen door onto the small balcony.

'Have we passed a post office at any point?'

'I've not been looking.' You scrunch up your face in recall. 'Put it in the bag, we'll post it if I see one.'

'Yeah, that's a good idea.' I stand beside you, as you guide a thin leather belt around your waist.

'What did you say?'

'Nothing, just smoothing things over … or just making things worse. Who knows.'

You chuckle, fastening the belt around a floral dress and gesturing for my opinion. I smile, taking your hand, before raising my arm over your head and turning you towards the balcony in a slow spin. I rest my chin on your shoulder, wrap my hands across your stomach and feel the warmth of your body as we look out on the view together: the wall of a nondescript office block.

'I will say,' I comment, only half serious. 'I'm used to better views than this.'

'Wowwww.' You draw the word out with a tone of mock offense. 'I should be the only view you need.'

You look back to me, our faces close together. Your response, sardonic as it was, serves as yet another reminder that all the things I was taught were so important – industry and endless acquisition, material pursuit and high living – don't matter as much as I was raised to believe.

'Do you think she'll want me there? At the company, I mean,' I ask. 'She was planning for me to come on board next year.'

'I'm sure she still will.' You soothe, before asking curiously, 'Do you *want* to work there?'

243

I think on the answer. Part of me wants us to leave everything and everyone behind, pack a bag and escape somewhere no one knows us. Part of me, despite my lack of apology, still feels like I've disappointed my family in some way, that whatever junior position my mother plans to give me might serve as a concession of sorts.

I choose not to tell you about this feeling, a decision which, in retrospect, would define the next decade of my life.

I gently nod against your shoulder.

'Ok,' you comment. 'That's good. Because I deserve better views than this.'

'Oh really.' I laugh.

'Definitely.' You grin evilly, turning back the balcony. 'I want to *really* look down on people, like they're ants.'

We fall into comfortable silence, resting together for a moment. No one watching, or commenting, or rushing us to be anywhere else. My arms wrap around you for what seems like an age, and I realise I've reached one of those transcendent states of human existence. Those moments that you can only achieve when you're not chasing them, where, for the briefest time, I exist in a world of pure, elysian contentment.

'I could teach you to sail someday, if you want.'

'I'd love that!' You turn towards me, your eyes twinkling at the idea, spellbound by the whispers of some new adventure. 'Next year?'

I smile as I look deeply into your eyes. For a brief moment, I can almost see it. Like the rippling heat distorting the Iberian coast, the impenetrable, intangible forcefield that's slowly creeping its way between us. When I pass through this memory again, the wall of chemically induced apathy will be that much stronger, freeing me from the burden of love and from the guilt of broken promises.

I take in your smile with sad affection, rest my forehead against yours, and close my eyes.

'So ... what did you see?'

I blink drowsily, the ceiling tiles of the third floor spread out above me, the sound of two figures working diligently just out of sight. I turn my head to see Codelle disconnecting the ECG, waiting for me to answer her question.

'Like you said ... the honeymoon.'

'*Like I said?*' Codelle muses on my answer, surprised. 'You heard me during the induction?'

I nod.

'I was always unconscious at the start of these treatments.' I reminisce. 'Maybe I'm just less medicated now or ... more willing to listen. I thought you were somehow chemically selecting specific memories.'

'Oh no.' Codelle gently retracts the cannula from my arm and closes the port. 'The process of selecting the memory itself is more of a guided meditation. We deliver the suggestion over audio with some subliminal visuals, but it's nothing more than a prompt for your mind to follow. In fact, the simpler the prompt, the better. The honeymoon. An argument. Ambiguity allows the patient to self-navigate to the strongest memory available and the stronger the memory, the greater the impact of the detachment.'

'So, you say honeymoon and I think of the memory that ... that I think represents the honeymoon most?'

'Essentially. The chemical aspect is nuanced but, yes.' Codelle flicks a bedside switch, and I feel the upper half of my bed slowly rise until I'm sitting upright.

When I first arrived, the third floor of Prismall House had been shrouded in secrecy. While it remains the most enigmatic of the house's four levels, its mystique had slowly fallen away over the last few weeks, as I started undergoing the procedures voluntarily, gaining the trust to enter and leave the space under my own steam.

Where the basement and ground floor had been given over to recreation and guest accommodations, and the second floor was seemingly devoted to conventional therapeutic practice, the third floor was a wide, open-plan space, vaguely reminiscent of an unused movie studio. A vast and hollow expanse, interrupted only by load-bearing pillars.

Crossing the space to my treatment area, I'd spotted a large square box with plasterboard walls residing in the shadows, held together by a neat scaffold. I've since realised this was the room in which I'd watched Julia's autopsy so many weeks ago.

Evidently, the top floor is the most versatile level of the house, with entire rooms constructed to meet a patient's individual needs.

Codelle administers the recovery and, after five relaxed minutes, I'm able to swing my legs from the bed, collect my crutch, and step freely across the cool tile floor.

Over the last few sessions, the dosage of the grey anaesthetic has been gradually reduced. My induction no longer feels like a sharp drop into a dark hole; instead, it feels like I'm being lowered softly into each memory, drifting through our time together with greater awareness and increased recall of each iteration.

I suppose this is what the treatment feels like when you don't struggle against it. I can see how those who undergo it voluntarily might even find it pleasant: the gentle sloughing of painful memories, coming out on the other side that bit lighter, that bit happier with every rotation.

I take an hour to eat breakfast of cereal, honey and granola. The supply of fresh fruit and vegetables seems to have dwindled, with Villner's increased responsibilities towards my care ruling out supply runs to the mainland.

It's a shame, I barely ate at all during my early days here. It's only now we've run out of fresh food that my appetite has seemed to recover.

Resting my spoon in an empty bowl, I make my way to the second floor, dropping in on Codelle's office with Villner close behind.

As I draw near to the black leather door, I hear the faintest sounds of conversation from within.

'Of course, I realise it's frustrating.' Codelle soberly placates some unknown caller, her tone contrite while still maintaining her innate sense of dignity. 'I will be postponing my upcoming lectures to accommodate you at the earliest opportunity.'

My hand stops on its way to the buzzer, listening at the door a little longer as Villner catches up behind me.

'Your frustration isn't unfounded, but my duty towards my current patient has to take preceden—' The caller clearly speaks over her, and Codelle waits patiently for them to stop talking. '… As soon as I know that, you'll be the first person I tell, and once you're here, you can expect the same level of—'

Villner arrives at my side, my loitering slowly becoming suspicious. Recovering myself, I press the buzzer, Codelle quickly finishing up her call before inviting me inside.

'Arthur.' She clears a desk that feels more paper-strewn than usual. 'How can I help?'

'I … I think I want to call my mother,' I muse, as if the idea had just come to me moments ago.

Codelle observes me quietly; I can feel her synapses clicking and calculating, considering every possible motive.

'I see.' Codelle examines the request as it bristles against her well-earned scepticism.

'I know.' I nod, realising I'm essentially asking to contact the mainland. 'This isn't some kind of … I just … Actually, don't worry about it … It's fine.'

I turn hesitantly towards the door, dropping the thread of my own accord, hoping the good doctor will pick it back up.

'I'm listening.' Codelle affirms gently.

'I … uh …' I pretend to search for the words, despite having rehearsed them exhaustively. 'For almost a year, I've been so lost in my own feelings that I didn't have time for anyone else's. But I just feel like a fog's clearing, and suddenly it's like … there are all these people I've neglected because I was so busy pitying myself.'

'There's nothing wrong with that.' Codelle nods. 'You were focussed inward because that's where the battlefront was. I'm sure your mother would say you were right to prioritise yourself.'

'No, I know … you're right,' I say, falling into contemplation once more.

My overarching plan is simple: to convince Dr Codelle that I've embraced her treatment, to exaggerate my progress and leave this place with some remainder of my love for you intact. The question of how to achieve it, of how to manipulate a person who I have never successfully deceived, had kept me up at night.

One evening, while resting on the lawn, it suddenly dawned on me that manipulation and deception were two different things. That if I was going to truly convince Codelle that I'd surrendered to her process, I would need to approach it as genuinely as possible, work towards progress, communicate my feelings honestly and openly.

I would need to embrace the steadily growing portion of my soul that genuinely feels the benefit of her treatment, and let it guide me. Making amends with my mother instinctively feels like the next step in my recovery and, if I can conduct myself sincerely enough, perhaps Codelle will see that.

'I just … I want to … I don't know.' I shrug, almost ashamed. 'I just want her to know that I'm getting better, you know? That I'm sorry.'

'I think that's very kind of you.' Codelle smiles warmly. 'Do you think it could wait until you return home?'

'That's true. I don't see why not,' I respond weakly. 'I suppose I just would have preferred your support.'

Codelle stares across the table at me. I return her quiet gaze with a meek, sad smile, resigned entirely to her judgement.

'I might have some *terms*.' Codelle delivers the disclaimer with a self-effacing smile. 'But if this is what you want, I'll have Villner hook up the phone.'

I nod quietly and leave the doctor to her work. Codelle may suspect that I'm playing her. She may think I'm genuinely engaging with her treatment. I find it both comforting and deeply unsettling that I'm not entirely sure myself.

32

One indication that Codelle is starting to accept my contrition is the steady increase in sessions taking place on the second floor. It's become clear that this level is reserved for more traditional therapeutic practices, anything more invasive taking place on the floor above.

I'm somewhat gratified, a few hours after my request at Codelle's office, when we climb the black iron staircase from the atrium and turn decisively away from the third-floor stairway.

My crutch taps against the carpeted floor as, two corridors later, we find ourselves at the north end of the house, the windows overlooking the open sea between Liverpool and Dublin.

Codelle reaches an unassuming door.

'You may want to take your shoes and socks off.' She advises cryptically, before gesturing for me to step through ahead of her.

I feel my bare feet against the carpet, brace myself, and lead us both into the room.

The space we step into is calm and surprisingly bright. Despite the room being windowless, a set of well-placed lights seem to perfectly mimic sunlight, the illusion complimented by the sky-blue walls and ceiling.

My crutch comes down and sinks slightly. There's a soft layer of sand covering the floor, neatly raked into swooping, curated swirls. Small plants and smooth rocks stand as ornamental pieces, spaced evenly throughout what seems to be an indoor garden, the sand curving around each object like swooping calligraphy.

At the room's centre, a circular platform of smooth black granite rises from the sand. On top stands a slightly alien-looking table of black and grey marble, a single curving base that melts into a flat tabletop.

The phone from Codelle's office sits on this table, the familiar black cord connected to it. Beside it stands an unknown device that vaguely resembles a printer.

Feet crunching against the cool sand, I walk through the garden, step up onto the platform and sink into an eggcup-shaped chair. I stare down at the items on the table, now able to see the mysterious device much more clearly.

I still have no clue what it is.

'It's called an aggregate psychometer. State of the art.' Codelle brushes through the sand and raises her small frame up onto the platform. 'When I was in America, a start-up in Silicon Valley made a few prototypes, not intended to be used medically but … well, I saw potential for the practice.'

'What does it do?'

'It absorbs various physical inputs: reaction time, eye dilation, perspiration, blood pressure, changes in voice and body temperature.' Codelle casually saunters through the list. 'Then it collates the signals algorithmically into a real-time depiction of a patient's emotional state.'

'So, it's a polygraph.' I stare with a newfound recognition at the device, an old instrument hiding behind a sleek, modern face. 'You know lie detectors aren't admissible in a courtroom.'

'Well, this isn't a courtroom, and that isn't a lie detector.' Codelle shakes her head. 'It's not here to show me what you're thinking, but there are some things it could show *you*.'

'Like what?'

'Your stresses, your sticking points,' Codelle outlines with quiet assuredness. 'I think this call is an opportunity for you to see how you feel about things.'

'Surely I already know how I feel.'

'Oh, gracious.' Codelle can't help but grin. 'If that were true, I'd be out of a job.'

I stare down at the grey plastic machine, an unassuming cube filled with cutting-edge technology. I wonder if I can trust what Codelle is telling me, or if I've merely sleepwalked into my own interrogation.

'You think this is just artifice.' Codelle observes me quietly. 'You think I'm trying to catch you out, that it's some kind of trick.'

I search for the words, unsure which foot to put forward.

'All right, then, let's make an agreement,' Codelle states, the slightest edge of emotion to her voice. 'You trust me, and I'll trust you.'

With calm resolution, Codelle reaches midway across the table, towards the phone. I watch as her fingers trace along the black wire of the interruption switch, the same switch she used to broadcast static during the call with my mother-in-law, the mechanism by which she'd interrupted my subterfuge before it could escape down the phone line.

With a soft click, Codelle withdraws the ethernet-like adapter from the phone. She looks at me plainly, though I sense a weight behind her eyes. She's removed the safety net from an outgoing call, allowing me free reign to say whatever I want.

'Do you still want me here for support? Or do you want to be alone?'

I watch the wire fall away and turn her question over in my mind.

The entire motivation behind this call was to demonstrate my loyalty to Codelle's process, to cement myself as a compliant patient, dedicated to her personal method of change. Yet, in a manner of which Elizabeth Codelle seems uniquely capable, the parameters of the situation have been warped and altered to such a degree that my old plan is now obsolete.

The removal of the interruption line means I can say anything I want, perhaps the greatest testament to Codelle's trust in me. With just a few words, I can convey the urgency of my situation to my mother, call every law enforcement agency down to this island.

Except that I have no way of knowing whether the line is truly free from Codelle's influence. For all I know, the doctor has a secondary failsafe: Villner standing in another room with a headphone to his ear and his hand on a switch. For all I know, my cries for help will be met with a sharp burst of static, netting me no benefit while communicating to Codelle, in no uncertain terms, that I'm still an enemy of the process.

Then again, if Codelle is truly investing her trust in me, if I can truly speak freely on this call, I would have to live with the fact that I stayed silent and played along through my single greatest opportunity for escape.

The waves of conflicting action batter and break against one another in my mind, until I find myself practically disembodied; no idea what course of action I'll choose, waiting for the words to leave my mouth before I find out what I want.

I tense up, staring down at the patient, opaque machine and back up to Dr Codelle, allowing the corners of my mouth to peak into a comfortable smile.

'I'd love you to stay.'

33

Codelle remains silent, but I can tell she's touched by the gesture. Her eyebrows raise in pleasant surprise, faint dimples appearing at the corners of her mouth, an irrepressible glimmer in her hazel eyes.

I wonder how she'll look when this call is done.

Under close instruction, I don the machine's various instruments: a blood pressure monitor and finger sensors. Codelle tells me not to think about my eyeline, that the machine's camera will track and monitor the dilation of my pupils on its own. In fact, by the time each implement is affixed, I hardly notice the presence of the machine at all.

I pick up the phone and rest it against my ear as Codelle dials my mother's personal number. A few trilling dial tones quickly give way to my mother's voice.

'Hello? Dr Codelle?'

'Hi Mum.'

A shuddering gasp echoes down the phone.

'Hel ... Hello, darling,' my mother croons quietly, her voice almost breaking on each word. 'Wow, it's ... it's been so long!'

'Yeah, well, you know ...' I mutter. 'Phoneless retreat.'

'No, I know, I know,' Mum comments meekly.

We fall into momentary silence, unsure quite how to continue. With a faint hum, a continuous stream of paper draws itself from the black machine, my emotional state condensed into an unbroken seismic graph, presently on baseline.

'I hope you're … doing well,' I offer awkwardly.

'Oh, it's all right here,' she replies, sounding as if she is keeping tears at bay. 'We're looking forward to having you back in the office.'

'Yeah. Me too,' I say, as the display in front of me suddenly arcs into wider, jagged lines. Despite Codelle's assurances that the machine before me isn't a lie detector, it seems tremendously fit for the purpose, the ache of despondency about my potential return to work writ plainly across the page.

'How can I …' Mum falters, before trying again. 'How can I help?'

'I just …' I begin. 'I suppose I wanted to say that … that I'm sorry. I'm sorry for what I put you through. I'm sorry for all the worry and the pain I've caused … What happened in June was … I don't know what I was thinking.'

I hear my mother's breath catch in her throat. I tell her what I know she wants to hear, statements I thought I believed myself. Yet when I stare up towards the polygraph, I see my comments ringing surprisingly false. Codelle observes it as well, fixing me with a steady, understanding look.

I'd come here to demonstrate my honest engagement with the process, yet I still find myself telling half-truths, barely able to imagine what a genuine statement would sound like if I spoke it. However, if I'm going to prove to Codelle that I care about my progression, I'll need to find out soon.

'Well,' my mother responds, 'I'm so happy to hear that you finally—'

'No, sorry, that's not right.' I interrupt. 'I did know what I was thinking, and I can't apologise for where I was. I was in a dark and horrifying place and I didn't have anyone to talk to and I couldn't climb out.'

The line drops down, my comments stabilising the quivering needle.

'You could have talked to me,' my mother says.

'You're right, I–' The polygraph shudders outwards once again as I feel Codelle's eyes flicker towards me.

Whatever calculations the instrument operates on, they're entirely correct. For a moment, I see what Codelle wanted to achieve from the application of this device. I wonder if I'd have told the truth at all on this call if I hadn't been forced into a bare accounting of my own lies.

'Arthur?'

'I couldn't talk to you,' I comment, the words tumbling from my subconscious. 'You hated her.'

There's a silence down the phone, shock and confusion evident, an almost flat line drawn across the polygraph.

'I'm sorry? Arthur, I don't know what …'

'She tried so hard to make you like her,' I continue, instantly bewildered as I recall the years of patient effort. 'She tried so hard, and I can't imagine how she didn't manage it, unless you were trying equally hard to … You never wanted to like her, otherwise she would've won you round …'

'Is Dr Codelle there?'

'Yes.'

'And she's recommending you say this?'

I glance across the table. Dr Codelle sits with her hands on her lap, her features at comfortable ease, the soft upward curve at the edges of her mouth conveying a sense of deferential support, perhaps even a quiet pride on my behalf.

'She's not recommending anything,' I confirm calmly.

The phone goes silent, yet I can guess what's happening on the other end. My mother has a small army of assistants, department heads and press officers on her payroll, each one employed to answer hard questions before they reach her desk. I'm sure she'd assumed Dr Codelle would serve a similar function, a psychological proxy, ensuring that the difficult conversations would never reach her door.

'I loved Julia,' Mum asserts with a quivering voice. 'Even if she wasn't the person I had in mind for you, I respected your choice. But she didn't respect things about you, Arthur. She *never* respected what you did, how hard you worked. And I can't pretend I didn't notice that, I can't pretend I didn't hear it in her voice, in every comment she made about you … reducing your responsibilities or … or leaving entirely! You gave her a life that few people could even dream of. It hurt, that someone would love you, and love the life you provided them, but have no respect for an entire part of your identity!'

'That wasn't her fault.'

'She was a grown woman, Arthur. You can't protect her from every—'

'I wanted to leave,' I say quietly.

The line on the machine is perfectly steady, and I start to feel similarly. In contrast, my mother can barely manage to breathe on the other end of the phone.

'I told myself I was just waiting for a good moment, for it to get less busy.' I chuckle darkly. 'Suddenly ten years had passed and I realised I was just a coward. I'd tell her I wanted to leave about twice a month. Over a decade, that's what, over two hundred complaints that I did nothing about? Fuck, it must've been miserable for her.'

Tears start to brim at the corners of my eyes, yet I still feel an intense sense of calm as I continue.

'She asked you those things on my behalf. I didn't ask her to. She did it because that's what I wanted. And I had a plan, I'd written my resignation. We were going to go sailing on Lake Annecy and at last, while we were there, I was finally going to—'

The line slowly shudders into a fractious arc, forcing me to accept the solemn and brutal truth: that I'd had that resignation in my file folder for over four years, that I had put off our trip to Annecy on countless occasions, intoxicated by the idea that I would be braver next year.

'I'm sorry, Arthur. I'm sorry you couldn't talk to me. I'm sorry you've felt this way for so long. If I'd known, I …' Mum shudders through her tears. 'Is that … Was that one of the reasons why you …'

'No. No,' I say firmly. 'I was just in a bad place.'

'And are you better now?'

I stare at the polygraph, wondering how far I should push it.

'No.' I relent, maintaining the stable line. 'No. Not yet.'

'But … is Dr Codelle … is she helping you?'

I breathe in, feeling Codelle's gaze, even as I take pains to avoid it. This is the question, the best chance I'll have to prove myself to Codelle. All I have to do is sell it. Believe it. The space behind my eyes swims as I deliberate between a damaging truth and a dangerous lie. I swallow back a heavy stone in my throat and calm myself, attempting to pass through the machine's glare with a steady mind.

'Yes.'

I lower my head, my eyes dropping down to the table, resigned to see the effect of my words on the scroll of paper below. I see nothing but a slim and simple line, my statement accepted as truth.

'Well … that's good.' My mother softens. 'We just want you happy, Arthur, we just want you home.'

'Yeah,' I comment, my eyes on the slow back and forth swing of the graphing arm. 'Well … that's what we're working towards. I'll see you soon, Mum.'

'I'll see you soon, darling. Love you.'

'Love you too.'

The phone lands against the connector, and the call cuts out.

'How did that feel?' Codelle smiles quietly.

'It uh …' I consider, while removing the various connectors. 'It felt good.'

Some hours later, my bedroom door closes behind me. I drift towards the greyed-out crescent window, and stare into my own vague reflection.

I'm a step further into Codelle's good graces, a step closer to going home. I even feel a momentary glimmer of pride at my unexpected victory against Codelle's polygraph.

Yet, as I stare at myself, as I reflect on the sharp, straight line the machine had drawn in front of me, a sudden realisation begins to overtake me.

'Oh, I don't know,' I whisper to no one in particular. 'I don't fucking know.'

I let out an involuntary snort of amusement, surprising even myself. It happens again, stronger this time, forcing my mouth open into tooth-bared smile, until my head starts to shudder in a wave of quivering laughter.

I empty and refill my lungs in a fit of total hysterics. Caught in a bizarre feedback loop, my reaction so unexpected, so absurd that it becomes something to laugh about on its own.

What an idiot, I think to myself. The sheer arrogance, to leave that room convinced that I had tricked the machine, that I had controlled every voluntary and involuntary response of my own body and passed through undetected.

Would it not be vastly more likely that I was simply telling the truth when I said those words? That I was starting to come around to Codelle's treatments, and my attempts to convince myself otherwise were the true deception? Between the hard, patient concrete of this grand and powerful house, and the soft grey matter of my own mind, is it really likely that the house would bend first?

I don't know why it's so funny, but as I cringe with laugher, my wide eyes staring at the grey padded ceiling of my bedroom, I realise I genuinely don't know if I was lying or not.

Late November

34

'It was horrifying!'

   'Julia—'

'It was mortifying!'

   'Honey, honestly—'

'Oh god, I'm going to throw up. Oh no! I'm so sorry, sir, I was joking, it's fine!'

You reach out instinctively in the direction of the cab driver who, upon hearing your intention to vomit in his taxi, has already begun a cautionary bearing towards the kerb. The rear-view mirror displays a flicker of wordless admonition, before the black cab drifts back to the centre of the empty London thoroughfare.

I look back from the driver to see you've already deposited your head in your hands, a groan escaping from between your fingers, a one-woman huddle of embarrassment and shame.

Comforting Julia Mason is an involved and multistage process. If something's gone wrong, and you feel it's your own fault, the first hour or so should be spent in silence. All attempts at reassurance will be immediately dismissed, and any efforts to fix the issue itself will be met with hostility and an outburst that quickly collapses into a wave of self-loathing.

In previous years, you have been known to appreciate a single comforting hand on the shoulder, but the benefits of such a manoeuvre are equally matched by its risks.

It's only recently, seven years on from our first meeting, with great pride and long-fought pedigree, that I have come to fully understand the intricacies of this process. A hard-won expertise has granted me and me alone with the knowledge of exactly when to speak.

'Honestly, Julia, it was fine.'

'How was it fine?!' You cut me off sharply, explosively, causing me to shrink back to my seat.

Maybe I'll be an expert next year.

'People don't remember this stuff.' I press forward as convincingly as possible. 'The next act came straight on stage, people probably moved right along.'

'Arthur! People remember that sort of thing! Sarah said it would be a small open mic! Small! And she brought all her friends; what part of low-key did she not understand?'

'No, I know,' I concede grimly. 'I don't actually think she's been there before.'

'Hah, oh, well, great. Ah, fuck *me*!' Memories of tonight's events stab through you once again, like a fresh but already regrettable tattoo sinking into raw skin.

I gingerly lift the ukulele case from the middle seat between us, tentatively shuffling towards you. Making no sudden movements, I slowly reach my arm around your shoulders and hold you in silence for a minute or two.

The rattles and rumbles of the taxi seem louder than usual, perhaps because they're all I have to listen to. I stare at the road ahead, as if my concentration might somehow truncate space-time and deliver us home sooner.

'I didn't really go on stage, did I?' you mutter wishfully, drawing my attention back around.

'Not that I remember, no.'

'And I definitely didn't choke halfway through my intro and then run out of the building in front of a hundred people?'

'It was only about eighty people … and no. Never happened.'

You breathe sharply through your nose, a short sardonic laugh, the anxious tragedy of the night's events slowly shifting into comedy. With relief, I begin to see your resilient, sarcastic spark ignite once again.

'I …' You hesitantly begin. 'I don't want to be dramatic but … do you think we could have them all killed?'

'No witnesses?'

'Exactly.'

'Way ahead of you,' I comment flatly. 'No one's getting out alive.'

A reluctant smirk forms on one side of your face, evening out into a heartfelt smile before you can possibly hope to suppress it. Pulling yourself closer against me, we stare out at the passing streets, the starless sky and the thousands of city lights that shine below it.

'This'll pass, hun, it's already started to, right?' I smile, you nod.

'I suppose so,' you comment, as if the realisation suddenly dropped from the aether. 'But I'm taking my ukelele to the farm on Monday.'

'Oh, don't say that,' I protest, dismayed to see your newfound enthusiasm dying on the vine. 'You're really good at it. Don't give up just because of one bad outing.'

'No, honestly. It'll be nice. The kids'll like it.'

'Oh, fuck the kids,' I jest dismissively, enduring the glare you're duty-bound to deliver. 'I'm kidding. I just … You loved the song-writing, right?'

'Yeah, but … I just … I thought I'd be able to perform them. Now I just …' You breathe in, rummaging through your feelings, before laying them out plainly. 'I'm embarrassed, and I'm worried that … maybe it's because the songs are just … embarrassing.'

I sit quietly in the face of a paradox, one that I've encountered repeatedly in our time together. One would think getting to know someone, loving them, dedicating your life to them, would give your reassurances greater weight. Instead, the opposite is true – the compliments of our loved ones sometimes feel the least valuable, the lack of objectivity robbing their words of effect.

If I was a stranger and I said your creations were beautiful, heartfelt and worthy of public audience, you'd take it immediately to heart. However, as your husband, I'm forced to find a different solution.

'Ok … well. How about we start small,' I begin. 'You and me, in the living room, same set list. We'll clear a stage, dim the lights, simulate the show, you know? Just until you have it down.'

I throw the idea out, half expecting a 'no'. But from the warm glow in your eyes, I can see that it's actually struck a chord. You look up at me, weighing the idea in your head, a wry smile betraying your inclination.

'And how do we simulate the crippling anxiety?'

'Well, *I'll* be in the audience. I still make you a bit nervous, right? You know, butterflies?'

Your lips part in a quiet, involuntary chuckle. As it dies away, with much more intention, you breathe sharply inwards through gritted teeth, your eyes scrunching in a wince of faux discomfort.

'Wow … I've got some really bad news for you.'

I feel the vaguest motions of a smile, while I stare at the moon and the myriad stars of a cold black sky. With calm confidence, I reach my hand out towards the lunar surface and, using a horse-hair brush, gently attempt to work in the grey.

Codelle sits quietly to my right, swaddled in a jacket of light grey down. Our seats are planted on the lawn of Prismall House, wooden easels propped up in front of us, a palette and brush pot resting on a shared table.

Villner stands behind us, guarding a small picnic hamper of hot beverages, as well as an optional meal of soup in a metal thermos.

Even a fleeting glance in Codelle's direction solidifies her as the greater artist; her perfectly steady hand dots stars with immense precision, her background a perfect blending of muted blacks and greys giving form and richness to the night. It's taken me three attempts to add moonlight to the waves, and the final product is more a matter of acceptance than satisfaction.

Still, the act of painting is entirely secondary to what it represents.

Firstly, it allows me to revisit my thoughts of you. Ticking through the increasingly strange collection which Codelle hasn't yet robbed of emotion: arguments, in-jokes, day trips, takeaway meals and the untangling of Christmas lights.

The second thing this painting session represents is a land-mark of the trust Codelle now has in me, allowing me to step out onto the grounds at night – under supervision, but with the understanding that I've earned my place through dedicated and increasingly enthusiastic compliance.

The last few weeks have been marked by tactical retreat, giving ground inch by inch. I'd surrendered moments, while acting as if I've lost entire eras of our life together, hoping that Codelle will call an early victory, unaware of the mental terri-tory she's failed to reach.

I tried to carry myself differently, to change for the better, compliance merging slowly into eager willingness, stoicism growing into the faintest flickers of actual happiness. The stretches of time I used to spend in quiet contemplation of your absence were now filled with reading, recreation, exercise and activity, visible evidence that I'm recapturing my life.

I put on this performance whenever Dr Codelle is watching and, for the sake of authenticity, whenever she isn't.

'I always loved night-time,' I comment, after an hour of silence.

'Really?' Codelle asks, interested.

'Work was non-stop all day,' I continue. 'Meetings, calls, emails. There was still work to be done in the evening too, of course; I was playing catch up until eleven, twelve, one in the morn-ing sometimes. But even though it was late, even though I had to work, it was at least quiet. No calls. Only a few emails. You could step out onto the balcony and just … I don't know … just breathe a moment.'

'Do you think you'll go back to your job?' Codelle asks. 'When you leave here?'

'I don't know,' I say quietly. 'I can't help but feel like I owe my mother something, for all she's … invested. I guess we'll talk about it when I'm home.'

A single green light breaks the pattern of pale white stars, a large, distant vessel forging its way through the midnight waves.

The water is so dark that it looks like it might be floating in mid-air. The *Flying Dutchman*. It brings me back to my first week here, signalling to boats with a dinky LED torch, so hopeful that someone would heed my call for help.

It feels like it happened a lifetime ago.

'Do you think you're ready to leave?'

'I mean ... I ... I don't know.' I consider. 'What do you think?'

'I think,' Codelle muses, 'I think that you seem dedicated to the process. I think you've displayed a renewed commitment to your physical and mental wellbeing. I think you seem to be sufficiently decoupled from the source of your addictive behaviours. But it's not my decision alone.'

Codelle turns casually in my direction, and the weight of the conversation begins to dawn on me.

'You're serious?'

Codelle doesn't move a muscle, never expressing more than she needs to.

I suddenly become aware of a hundred crawling insects in the pit of my stomach.

I'd thought so many times about this very moment, sitting up all night, playing out the correct approach in my head. I'd considered, as a thought experiment, if I were here for any other drug, any narcotic, any compulsion, what would be the most persuasive answer for her to hear? While a blanket 'no' would serve only to keep me on the island, too firm a 'yes' might seem artificial, the hollow affirmation of an eager addict, tipping their hand as soon as freedom appears within reach.

I thought about how I'd feel if everything had worked. If I were truly heading into the world as the changed man Codelle was working so hard to create.

I decided I'd probably be quite frightened. After all, nothing demonstrates that you're prepared to take a big step like fear of its consequences.

'I still feel a vague ... something for her,' I mumble, almost ashamed. 'A ... I don't know, a ...'

'A residual warmth?'

'Yes.'

'She was important to you, Arthur. She always will be.' Codelle smiles. 'The true enemy was destructive overattachment. That's what we've been trying to remedy. The real question isn't whether you still remember her fondly, it's about whether you're able to exist without her. If you placed her down right now, and you started to walk away, if you left her on this island, could you do it without looking back?'

I take the next few seconds in steps and stages. A moment to let the question hit me. A moment of contemplation. A moment of fear. A moment of reticence. A moment of quiet resolution.

'I …' I look up, with a weak but lasting smile. 'I think I could. I think I want to move on.'

Codelle nods almost unconsciously at my words. As objective as she seems, I can tell she wants to believe in my improvement. The easels are planted in unkempt grass, the potted plants of the atrium are wilting, and dust has collected on the Perspex casing of the varnished football table.

Prismall House has steadily declined around me, every fragment of Codelle and Villner's focus squared directly on my security and recovery. I'm willing to wager Codelle's status isn't too dissimilar to that of her beloved building: exhausted, fraying at the edges, silently yearning for rejuvenation and closure.

After an interminable moment, Codelle lowers her gaze and begins to shake her head. I watch the motion begin, my heart jumping into my throat, as I hang at the mercy of her decision.

Instead of saying anything, Codelle continues to shake her head, suddenly releasing the lightest burst of a chuckle.

'I just … I was so worried about whether we'd get here.' Codelle looks up at me. 'I know I should be professional, but in the interest of honesty, this has been difficult for both of us. The mistake with the phone records. My mistake. The *hatred* you had for me. You were well within your rights to resist the process.'

Codelle seems genuinely emotional, the lightest quiver in her voice, her eyes subdued and glassy. She continues with a muted tone of sorrow.

'It's the sole duty of my profession to reduce harm, or if it must be inflicted, that it must be incidental compared to the greater health of the subject. If I can do anything at all to ensure your future happiness, your future recovery, I want you to know I—'

'You kept me alive.' I interrupt firmly.

Codelle looks up, slightly taken aback.

'I'm not asking you to make me feel better, Arthur, it's my duty to apologise if I—'

'No. No. Honestly.' I meet her unsteady glance with firm eyes. 'Back in London, I was … I was living in a tomb. Not even a tomb to myself but … to her. I'd buried myself alive with her, just waiting for the air to run out, and if I'd been left there, I would've …' I shake my head at who I used to be. 'You wouldn't let me die, and maybe I didn't appreciate that before, but now I'm … now I'm here, now I can see this … light at the end of the tunnel for the first time in … I don't know what to say.'

Dr Codelle observes me, the lightest lift at the corner of her mouth; she's a logical woman, but also an intrinsic optimist. I can tell she wants to believe me, but she's unsure whether to let herself do so. She breathes in deeply, measuring my words in one final, all-important calculation.

I stare up at her, feeling like a dog simpering at its master's feet, shameless and entirely beholden to her whims. The act of playing along to this woman's ego, to her sense of beneficence, complimenting her, agreeing with her … it used to make me feel sick, like I was betraying my last few shreds of individuality.

Now, I'll say anything, do anything, believe anything, only caring whether my words have an effect.

'All right,' Codelle concludes. 'All right. We'll take the *De Anima* back in the morning.'

35

I feel the lightest breeze pass across the grass between us, the words falling upon me like the first raindrops of a cleansing downpour. I imagine if you were here, you'd be crying tears of happiness, like I would for you if our positions were reversed.

'I hope I can ... I don't know how I can repay you,' I stutter, keeping up the pretence, yet with genuine tears welling behind my eyes.

'Just live, Arthur, happily, healthily. Make the most of your time in this world.' Codelle smiles. 'That's all I ever hope for anyone.'

I watch the night pass with entirely open eyes, sleep keeping its distance, not even attempting to attend my room. All my Christmas mornings coalesce into a single anticipatory high, wrapped around the stomach-churning apprehension that I will not be fully free until my feet touch the ground in Porthcoll.

Once morning rolls in, I take the deepest breath that I can, wait for it to leave my body in its own steady time, and rise from my bed.

The shower bursts down around me, a wake-up call that travels through my nerve endings to my toes and fingertips. I clean myself thoroughly, as if there were an element of presentation to my return to the outside world. I pick a grey polo shirt out for myself, beige linen trousers and shoes, neatening up in the mirror before stepping outside.

Breakfast consists of tinned fruit, grains and long-life yoghurt, the last dregs of the Prismall House store cupboard.

I'm summoned to Codelle's office, a series of documents placed before me, declarations that the process has ended, a final invoice with a blank space remaining for my mother's signature.

After I've done my part, Codelle takes the papers from me, collates them with a short tap against the desk, and begins to sign what she needs to.

'You still haven't finished it?' I query, my eyes passing over the rough-hewn statue at the back of the room, the marble much smoother than my first visit, but still far from defined.

'Well, I've been busy.' Codelle grins. 'Excited to get back to it, though, it can really be anyone.'

'Yeah,' I comment. 'I'm not sure who I'd choose.'

Out the window, I can see Villner strolling to the *De Anima*, a large holdall in one hand, a slowly swinging jerry can in the other. He plods down the footpath and disappears into the darkness of the boathouse. After a few minutes, beams of light burst through the slats: the systems starting up for testing.

'What will you do with your first day home?' Codelle queries, fastening the paperwork together with a plastic spine clip.

'I don't know. Nothing probably. Visit my mother, have a long-overdue talk.'

Codelle nods in quiet approval, before falling into silence, the sudden overture of things left unsaid.

'Arthur,' Codelle begins. 'I'm under no illusions about the work we've done here. I'm happy that you're happy, of course, but that doesn't change everything that's passed between us. This was the most challenging process I've ever carried out – we're both aware of that. I want you to know that, regardless of your impressive and gratifying recovery, I don't harbour any resentment for what actions you may take upon your return.'

Codelle's blessing ignites a sudden rush of darkly pleasant notions, a smorgasbord of retaliatory actions. I picture the authorities making their way to the island, bleeding the institute dry in civil suits, the professional medical bodies of the United Kingdom tearing each title and qualification away from

Dr Elizabeth Codelle until she can never practise her twisted, manipulative style of medicine ever again.

'I think I just want to move on,' I comment. 'I want to remember the good that came out of all this, not jump straight into … Right now I just want to go home.'

Codelle nods. From her stoic expression, I suspect it's as good an answer as she could have possibly hoped for.

The ensuing silence is strangely comfortable, as I realise there's finally nothing more for either of us to talk about. Our business, our relationship, our time together mercifully concluded. I steel myself against a rush of optimism, aware that nothing is over until I'm back on the mainland.

Still, it's nice to entertain the idea that I'll never have to speak to Dr Elizabeth Codelle again.

'All right.' Codelle rises from her chair. 'Shall we?'

I smile nervously and rise to my feet in turn, collecting my crutch and slowly accompanying her into the corridor.

Instead of even, carpeted stone, I feel like I'm walking on a surface made up of countless taut threads, stretching their way down the second-floor hallway, threads which barely hold my weight, poised and positioned to snap at any moment, sending me tumbling back down into the depths of Prismall House. As we proceed to the iron stairway, every footstep's metallic ring reverberates with charged, jostling emotions: anticipation, dread, impatience, the faintest undertones of muted hope.

I stare up at the subtle smile, writ in black paint on the ceiling, as we pass beneath its gaze and across the chequerboard floor into the entrance hall.

'After you.' Codelle gestures to the double doors.

I nod, smile weakly in thanks, and finally pass through into the open air.

As soon as the doors open, my smile begins to waver.

Everything is bright and beautiful – even the untamed gardens and unkempt lawn look rich and verdant, a perfect clear blue sky hanging over a rich navy sea. The boathouse waits patiently for me at the end of the chalk footpath, a tantalising straight line interrupted by only one object.

Just beyond the gardens, an upright rectangle of matte black obstructs the pathway, the width of a refrigerator, rising just above navel height. It stands silently, unmoving, interrupting the idyllic scene like a dead pixel in the fabric of reality.

I maintain my smile and continue forwards, staring ahead at the boathouse, ignoring the object in my path. However, as I draw closer, I can't help but divine a few small details: a two-inch lid closed upon the object and a set of dials and buttons at the top left side.

Codelle brings herself to a stop beside it.

I stop next to her.

'What is this?' I ask, allowing an acceptable level of nervousness to bleed into my voice.

'The final step,' Codelle announces calmly as Villner appears at the entrance to the boathouse, holdall over his shoulder, walking at his own unhurried pace to meet us.

'I thought I was going home.'

'You are,' Codelle assures me. 'As I've always said, this treatment ends when you're better. You've assured me in no uncertain terms that you're ready to leave Julia on this island. That version of Arthur Mason will leave this island today.'

'You signed the release forms,' I respond, hoping feigned annoyance will cover my building dread. 'You've released me from your care; we decided I was going home.'

Codelle raises the stack of documents in one hand, before reaching out with the other towards the lid of the black, rectangular object. She lifts it and lets it fall back behind the machine, revealing a latticed grill of stainless steel, the metal tray below it dotted with evenly spaced puncture holes.

'We've done everything we can for you here.' Codelle speaks almost sadly. 'But we want you to escape this cycle of self-destruction for good. We've done our best to prepare you, curbed certain toxic relationships, built new habits ... but we have a duty to minimise the risk of relapse, slim as it may be, in every way we can.'

I feel my teeth clench together behind my quivering half-smile, afraid to ask, afraid to know, the entrance to the boathouse looming at the periphery of my vision as a constant reminder to stay calm.

'Look, I just want to get home.' I sigh impatiently. 'What do you need me to do?'

Codelle observes me, her gaze more piercing than it's been for the past few days. She nods to herself, and then once towards Villner. The man reaches to the side of the metal machine. Twisting a dial, the puncture holes below the metal grill release an unmistakable hiss of pressurised gas, a further click of an ignition bathing the grill in a white-hot blanket of steady flames.

'All addictions have their sources, Arthur. Methamphetamine, diacetylmorphine, alcohol.' Codelle holds her hand out to Villner, who passes her the holdall. She drops it onto her shoulder and draws the zip across the bag. 'But there's always more to it: secondary delivery systems, iconography ... the general term would be *paraphernalia*.'

Her thin hand reaches into the depths of the holdall, withdrawing a pale, dog-eared sketchbook, sealed with a cross of thick yellow tape.

She raises her arm delicately, reaching halfway across the space between us, lifting the book out for me to take. I know I should reach out and take it from her, but I just can't. The weathered scrapbook imprisons my focus with some stark medusan power, rendering me as cold and immobile as stone.

Everything in the background shrinks away until the pearl-white cover is all I can see.

'Where did you get that?'

'You know the answer to that,' Codelle comments. 'And you know what I need you to do.'

I take in every detail of the book, the faded outline of a craft shop price sticker still on the back, £6.99, picked up in the throes of a scrapbooking bug that bit you one day and never quite left. Alongside it, you'd purchased coloured card and a die-cutting machine, combining them to produce the patterned cover, the title embossed across the top: *Arthur & Julia – Adventures in Northern England.*

I can almost see the first page, pictures of a hilltop downpour, two drenched waterproofs huddled by an ordinance marker. Raindrops on the lens. Then pictures of tours around your childhood town, a picnic in a field, and then beyond the shores of England, as the book outgrows its stated purpose and begins to chart our first tentative holidays together. The campsite in France where we saw an eclipse. Your favourite picture that I ever took of you, smiling bright-eyed in the stained-glass light of a Budapest ruin bar.

Some of these moments have already been stolen from me, the memories held behind the unbreakable glass of Codelle's Detachment Therapy. I feel nothing for our hilltop excursion, except mild annoyance at the numbing, wet cold. The ruin bar was a beautiful night, but I might as well have been anywhere, with anyone. However, there's still enough in there, and enough left of my wounded, burning love for you, to lend the book a humbling weight.

'There are pictures,' I stammer, as I take our collected moments from Dr Codelle's hands. 'There are pictures of Julia and Lorraine in here … pictures she'd want of her daughter.'

'I thought you might worry about that.' Codelle nods at my generous consideration. 'They've been removed, they'll be sent to her separately. The only pictures in this book are the ones of you and Julia together.'

I nod in understanding, as if the matter were cleared up, buying myself scarcely five precious seconds as my mind scrambles for something else. The memories in this book can't be replaced – digital copies are on long-lost phones and overwritten memory cards. Losing them now means losing them forever, losing the aspects of a face I've already been manipulated to forget.

I would never be able to remember them as well as I'd want to, and the pictures that I no longer remember taking may never enter my mind again. But if I refuse, if I save them, then Codelle will know that I've been faking my indifference; I'll be brought back behind the walls of Prismall House and worked on until I no longer care at all.

I stand in this vacant, sorrowful twilight, choosing between keeping these memories alive, or escaping from this place with the precious final embers of my love for you.

'Are you all right?' Codelle prompts innocently, as my silence lasts a few seconds too long.

'Of course,' I answer nonchalantly as I drop the photo album onto the metal grill.

The effect is immediate, brutal and blindingly visible. As the book lands with a soft clatter, its edges burst instantly into charcoal-black cinder. I watch the flames eat away into the inner pages of the book, making slow, steady work of the cardboard cover.

I can feel Codelle's steady gaze, resting not on the book, but on me, testing for any reaction, any regret, any emotion at all.

I feel a sense of growing horror pulling at my cheekbones, at my smile, tears building like an irrepressible reflex that I have to battle relentlessly to keep down.

'It's a shame,' I comment, my voice a flat line.

'I know.' Codelle sympathises. 'But it's for the best.'

I watch the card cut-out letters of the scrapbook title. Our names, the ampersand between them, curling in at the edges like dying insects before shrivelling into ash.

The tears stay down, my brow unfurrows. I look up to the De Anima with clear eyes and back to Codelle, my insides hollow and aching as I keep everything inside.

Without another word, Codelle reaches into her still full holdall, collecting the remaining two scrapbooks that you made for us, one of them documenting eight years of our time together, the other, in leather-bound turquoise, containing the compiled photographs of a two-week span, starting in the cobbled courtyard of the Southwark Registry Office, ending with a picture of you asleep on the tube ride back from Heathrow airport. The final image of our honeymoon.

They hit the grill, burning like everything else.

Codelle keeps going, passing me the framed photos from around our apartment, your face obscured with black paint, ensuring no final glances of you before their destruction.

Finally, Codelle places a small plastic mood ring in my hand: a piece of jewellery we'd bought with arcade tickets on Brighton Pier at just fifteen years old. A ring that I'd presented to you as a mock-romantic gift, my heart in my throat as I tried to down-play its seriousness.

It was the first piece of jewellery I'd ever given anyone.

The ring topples through the grate, the photos bubble and tear, the wood of the frames petrify into charcoal.

I think about Lorraine, the albums she brought down from her attic. The pictures around her house. Not everything's lost, and as long as I still feel something for you, as long as I still care, I can find something to remember you by.

Villner reaches out with a telescopic metal prod, brushing the embers of the picture frames down through the grill. He pokes between the covers of the wedding album, its leather binding outliving the torched pages, and lifts the limp, smoking hide from the grill.

The square of flame burns, unspoiled, as if nothing had even touched its surface.

'Can we go home now?' I mutter, my eyes leaving the hungry flames and flickering to Codelle.

'You know, I think you might be ready.' Codelle gladly admits, an air of muted pride and warm finality to her tone. 'I was worried that, perhaps, you were just agreeing with me to end the process early; I had to be sure. If I discharged a patient with-out being confident of their recovery, I wouldn't be able to live with myself.'

I feel the heat of the sun on my back, the blaze of the incin-erator warming my side, the gaze of Elizabeth Codelle piercing through the lines of my face.

'I understand.' I affirm.

'Good.' Codelle smiles, a measure of peace in her voice. 'One last thing then.'

Codelle reaches into the seemingly empty holdall, retracting an object so small and slight that the canvas is unchanged by its removal.

The breath catches in my throat, my heart plummets, as I find myself staring at a square of yellow paper.

Razor-thin. Twelve inches on every edge. Opaque, textured crepe paper in the joyful hues of a cartoon sun. The central yellow label of the LP embellished with swirling black marker, and a title:

A Song for Arthur.

36

I can't even reach for it.

'Arthur?' Codelle queries. I fail to look up, despite knowing that every second of hesitation eats away at the careful façade I've constructed, despite knowing that everything I've destroyed so far will have burned in vain if I can't take this one final step.

They don't tell you how quickly your loved ones fade from your senses. Taste immediately becomes a mere memory, the last kiss before the unexpected tragedy. Touch leaves just as soon, abandoned after one last hand squeeze as I stepped away from the open casket. The smell of you faded from our sheets over months, sight graciously immortalised in the pictures that survived you.

Sound should have been the first thing to disappear, and it would have been, if you hadn't pressed it in vinyl and gifted it to me on my thirtieth birthday. In the weeks and months after you were gone, I'd savoured the melody, the music of your beautiful voice radiating from the record player. I'd played it so much that I started to resent it, exiling it to the mantle as I tried desperately to move on. Your lyrics were a promise that you'd always be there for me and, in the circling lines of this one black record, you always were.

The flame gently crackles beside me, and I feel tears forcing their way to my wide open eyes. My hands fight to stay steady as I stare, utterly empty, at your words on the label.

'Arthur.'

I collect myself, hoping to live forever in the moment before the next. After too short a time, I raise my head, look at the vicious, heartless face of Dr Elizabeth Codelle, and slowly reach out my hand.

'No problem.'

In a fluid set of actions, as if hesitation at any point were hesitation for the whole, I take the record from her, turn towards the waiting flame, lift my hand above the threshold and let go.

The record lands face up, the flames immediately wrapping around every edge. Hundreds of grasping claws, tearing away at the handmade sleeve, immediately exposing the black vinyl record within. As if cringing in pain, the vinyl warps and contracts inwards, curling up to the sky as throbbing blisters burst into gaping cavities of melting plastic.

And I feel everything, all of it, at the same time: the lyrics, the melody, the joy, the memory. A part of you, the last part, this precious, minuscule whisper of what we were, torched and eviscerated.

I feel white knuckles of a clenched fist, the juddering, jagged breath rising through my teetering body, as I watch everything melt away.

I stand firm, control myself, push everything down, my eyes staring up to the waiting boathouse, the *De Anima*, the sea, the distant shore. I need to just hold onto myself. Ten seconds more. Five seconds, and I can walk away from here with something left.

Like the banks of a flooding river, the first few tears spill out uncontrollably down my cheek. I fight with everything I have to bring it back but, once it's begun, it bursts forward, far beyond my capacity to control. My face retches into a mess of devastating, sobbing sorrow, my mouth opening in a rasping, breathless cry, the tears streaming down my face and pooling against my chin.

I feel the *De Anima* slip away, the distant shoreline withdrawing slowly behind the horizon.

'I can't help you if you refuse to help yourself, Arthur,' Codelle comments sadly. 'We both know what would have happened if you'd been allowed to carry all this back to shore.'

My eyes fall on the final dregs of black plastic, stretching like a Dali painting down through the flames. It feels like my mind is ringing, a deafening surge of all my sorrow mutating into a tidal wave of pure hatred and anger. My brain feels like it's expanding against the confines of my skull, the pressure building and building.

'Let's head inside, shall we?'

The wave breaks, a violent roar of blinding red fury that snaps in the doctor's direction.

I launch towards Codelle, my crutch toppling to the side as we both crash onto the lawn. I stare into the depths of her very soul, wide eyes chained to hers as my hands grasp for her throat, every finger straining to choke the life from every vein and artery. I scream in agony and devastation as the doctor gasps and wretches for air, my tears dropping freely onto the lapel of her white shirt.

I want to rip the life away from her. Defying every consequence, every ounce of my humanity, I grip even tighter, knowing that I would slit my own throat if I were promised she'd bleed the same amount.

A strong hand clenches the back of my neck, wrenching me from the ground and hurling me across the chalk footpath. I rag-doll through the dust and onto the lawn, the impact kicking the air from my lungs.

Villner steps over me, his head blocking the sun as he picks me up by the scruff of my neck. I see a flash of white light as a blunt freight train of a punch rattles my skull. I hit the floor again, head splitting in agony, choking on my own painful groans.

I have barely a moment to regain my vision, to watch a string of red saliva drop from my lips, before Villner raises me back up, the anger undiminished in his eyes, his fist raising again.

'Don't hurt him!' Codelle shouts desperately, a faint rasp to her voice. 'Villner! Put him down!'

Villner stops, staying his fist as her words carry across the lawn. His fingers reluctantly open and I thud back into the grass, my head swaying.

Unable to focus, I absorb the sounds around me. Villner stepping towards Dr Codelle, the doctor rising to her feet with his assistance, the turning of a dial as the flames die out, the closing of the heavy metal lid.

'I'm sorry, Arthur.' Codelle speaks solemnly. 'He should never have done that. It is against everything I stand for.'

'Just kill me. Please,' I mutter, the words flowing out of me, as blood drips from my mouth. 'Just let me be with her.'

'She isn't anywhere, Arthur.'

'Let me be nothing then,' I plead. 'I can't go back there, please don't take me back.'

I hear Codelle move closer, sensing her presence as she crouches down in front of me.

'I'm not going to ask any more of you, Arthur,' she states. 'And it's just as well. I can't operate on a patient who's fighting me from the table. It jeopardises my work and, most importantly, it endangers you.'

I hear, somewhere near me, the neat ripping sound of a sterile package being opened.

Codelle continues.

'I think this process would benefit from a more clinical approach,' she quietly resolves, her voice close to breaking beneath the surface of her calm, collected tone. 'As a trial, we're going to induce you into a medically controlled state of unconsciousness, allowing us to support your wellbeing and allowing our Detachment Sessions to proceed at a steady, mildly accelerated pace. We'll check in regularly, bring you out, see how you're feeling, but the lion's share of the work will sit with us from now on. You can rest.'

As Villner administers the grey solution, and I feel myself once again passing from this world, I try to think of you. I try to think of the moments we spent together, Edinburgh, Lisbon, home. But as my mind darts around to random recollections, I struggle to find the ones in which I still care for you. I slide off the glass walls of perfectly altered memories, as the barbiturate drags me further down into the pit of my own mind.

In the end, another figure imposes itself. As much as I search for you, as much as I try to keep you in the centre of my increasingly disparate final thoughts, visions of Dr Codelle flicker through my mind instead.

In a final, awful insult, on top of everything I've already been through, she's the last thing I think of before I fall away.

Winter

37

'*One. Two. Three. Four. Five. Six. Seven. Eight. Nine. Ten. One. Two. Three. Four. Five. Six. Seven. Eight. Nine. Ten.*'

I run. Closing the final hundred metres as fast as I possibly can, my feet throwing white powder into the air as I approach the waiting boathouse. I can hear Villner sprinting behind me, his steady gait easily keeping pace with my own, a distant pursuing shadow.

My legs burn from the effort, my eyes forward, forcing myself to tune everything out in a final, all-encompassing sprint.

I'd once measured this island as 1,872 metres in circumference. I'd judged that distance by painstakingly jogging the circular coastline. It had taken me thirteen minutes to make one pass around the island, even that fractional distance leaving me wheezing and gasping for breath.

Now? Now I can make the same journey in less than ten minutes, barely breaking a sweat as I complete my third full rotation. My pace remains constant and brisk, even in the midst of blistering cold, even with my footfalls cushioned by the compact layer of pearl-white snow.

It had fallen as a soft blanket the evening before, at the end of a cool, dry and perfectly still day. The night had been similarly calm, allowing the snow to settle, unblemished, across the garden and grounds, turned to grey slush by the lapping waves at the water's edge, but otherwise flawless.

I was just lucky to be around to see it.

I close in on the boathouse, arriving right back where I started after some five kilometres. I place my hand against the wooden wall and stretch my hamstrings, watching my breath rise as a cloud of ephemeral steam.

Soon after, Villner approaches, in a form-fitting grey T-shirt and black cargo trousers. He walks his exertion off, striding down to the edge of the shoreline and back, as his deep, controlled breaths grow level.

He looks to me, silently asking if we're ready to head to the house. I answer his question by turning my back on the water and proceeding up the gentle slope.

Under an overcast sky, surrounded by white snow and a grey seascape, the cement walls of Prismall House finally seem to fit in. It stands like a sturdy warden against the creeping winter, a warmth held within its insulated, stencil-shaped windows.

I almost feel happy for it, finally finding its niche. I suppose, why shouldn't I? It never had a choice in how it was used.

Back in the autumn, after my attack on Dr Codelle and my subsequent induction, I was carried to the third floor and placed in a far more involved medical environment. Monitoring was constant, with Codelle and Villner taking shifts to ensure my safety, check my vitals and minimise any potential complications.

The state I was lowered into was one of true nothingness but, mercifully – a nothingness so complete that I barely experienced it. The unconscious hours and days drifted on without my notice, not instant by any means, but so bereft of time and memory that it all seemed to fall away upon waking.

My brief moments of lucidity felt like surreal, guided visions, as I was brought to the minimum level of consciousness for the Detachment Sessions to take effect.

I was awoken with relative regularity, always for more days than I was under, given ample time for rest, recuperation and exercise under Villner's now unapologetically watchful guardianship.

This cycle of induction and recovery had continued inexorably, some of its effects gradual, some occurring in great leaps.

Every time I awoke, my ailing leg would feel a great deal better until, two weeks ago, I was able to abandon my crutches all together. My body has finally begun to fill out, the sharper outlines of my bones smoothed over by a healthy layer of fat and muscle. I'd seen clear improvements to my physical fitness, shorter lap times, heavier weights lifted. I'd even managed to cover five more laps in the pool.

Before I came here, I'd never been one to exercise for exercise's sake.

Warm air rushes past me as I open the double doors. Villner and I venture into the atrium together.

The potted plants at the corners of the room have lost their brown tinge, now as green and verdant as when I arrived. The entire house has recovered since I've been under, with freshly stocked food, polished surfaces and, before the snow fell, a newly mowed lawn.

It's almost like I never resisted this place at all.

A calm voice drifts down from the second floor. Looking up, I find Codelle waiting for us at the top of the iron balcony.

'If I might see you in my office, Arthur, when you have a moment?'

I look up to her, as she stands beneath the eyes of the atrium's great mural. She's a strange sight to behold. While my physicality and mindset have demonstrably improved over the last few weeks and months, Codelle, by contrast, seems undeniably diminished.

Her tone has become business like, yet it rings with an undercurrent of sadness and dispassion. Her posture feels shrunken, her shoulders slack, her confident smile now a flat, perfunctory line. Her usually brilliant, piercing gaze is now far less direct, prone to drifting towards the floor rather than holding my eyes.

I imagine she had once hoped for our reconciliation, that I would come around to her way of thinking in time and begin to approach my recovery with enthusiasm. Now, she spends her days whispering to a corpse, her precious doctor-patient relationship irreparably degraded, her dream of winning hearts and minds reduced to a brutal slog.

'Of course,' I reply.

'Thank you.' Codelle turns away, disappearing back into the second floor.

I turn to Villner, sharing a look of polite curiosity, before proceeding towards the spiral staircase.

Codelle stands by her office window, glancing out towards the south-east, a stretch of open sea that leads towards the shores of the Liverpool Bay. She appears acutely troubled, not looking in my direction as I slip through the doorway and take my seat. Even Codelle's office carries an air of dishevelment, the papers on her desk askew by half an inch, a layer of dust on the plastic sheet beneath the long-neglected marble statue, books not immediately returned to their shelves.

In the unfolding silence, I look to Villner, as if I might read the purpose of our meeting on his face. There's nothing there, just neutral, stoic loyalty: a refusal to give anything away.

'Over the past two months,' Codelle begins, still not looking in my direction, 'I've been engaged in a very difficult decision-making process, concerning the final stages of your treatment.'

'Oh,' I comment quietly. 'Well, I'm sorry about that.'

Codelle finally turns towards me. She pulls her chair neatly back and settles herself behind the large, wooden desk, interlocking her fingers and placing them under her chin.

'How was your run?'

'Good.'

'Villner says you're improving.'

'Apparently so. Though maybe I'm just trying harder nowadays.'

Codelle smiles fleetingly, before returning to the crux of the matter.

'The reason this decision has weighed upon me is because I believe it has the capacity for ... misinterpretation. I don't want you to view my motives as anything other than my commitment to your complete recovery.'

'Why would I see it as anything different?'

Codelle sighs.

'Because, from your perspective, perhaps even objectively speaking, I have the capacity to benefit.'

I don't think I've ever seen her so troubled. There's a rank discomfort in every inch of her posture, the words leaving her mouth clearly not to her taste.

'Go on,' I urge, increasingly curious.

'I believe you've experienced trauma in this place,' Codelle begins sadly. 'Some of it necessary, some of it born from your own opposition, from our clear inability to understand one another.'

'You mean my inability to understand you.'

Codelle doesn't answer.

'I believe you hate me.' She ploughs ahead. 'I believe you feel you've suffered here. I believe that if you carry that out into the world, it might invalidate your recovery.'

'How so?'

Codelle searches for the words.

'Given your opinion on the process, I can't assuage the fear that you'll reject it out of spite, or otherwise hold such a negative view of your recovery that it becomes a secondary trauma, if it isn't already.'

'So your treatment's had complications,' I clarify, slowly understanding. 'Like those surgeons who leave their car keys inside people. You're scared you fucked me up as much as you cured me.'

Codelle considers my statement, a gross oversimplification of the delicate point she's trying to make.

'Yes,' she confirms.

I can't disagree with her conclusion. I still feel everything from my time here – the horror of imprisonment, the violation, the anxiety of every escape attempt, the pain of every failure. I can still hear my leg snap, feel the bloody impact of Villner's fist, the combined cruelty of everything Codelle has forced me to endure.

'Well,' I mutter, nothing else to say. 'Comes with the territory, I suppose.'

Codelle accepts the blunt, dismissive barb, no expectation of being let off the hook.

'The previous induction was slated to be your last.' She reveals calmly. 'It's my opinion that the treatment has run its course.'

I stay quiet, allowing her to continue.

'But the trauma of the treatment itself is of great concern to me. Sending you out into the world with new trauma seems a direct violation of my oath.'

There are more than enough clues from Codelle's guilty preamble to infer what she's about to suggest. Still, I wait for her to say the words out loud, no intention of helping her across the finish line.

'It's my medical opinion that you be induced one more time, that we directly address the trauma through Detachment Therapy, targeting the memories of your time here, ensuring you head out into the world without any residual distress.'

'I see.' I weigh up the statement. 'And how do you benefit from …'

I stop dead, slower on the uptake than I'd like. When understanding arrives, however, it strikes with the force of a brick. I feel my teeth clench behind my closed mouth, my expression hardening.

'Because there's a chance I'll be grateful,' I surmise. 'That's how you benefit. If I'm cured, and I no longer feel anything towards the process itself, there's a chance that I'll thank you and just move on with my life.'

'An outcome which is infinitely better than the treatment not working at all, or a potential relapse or—'

'You're trying to save your fucking skin!' I find myself snarling the words. 'You want me to be like Monty Han, and all the rest of your patients. You want me to think it was all fucking worth it. How many of them did you do this to?'

'None,' Codelle comments flatly. 'I can say quite confidently they all underwent a much easier process.'

'Bullshit,' I retort. 'You're just trying to cover your own back. This isn't concern. It isn't your esteemed fucking medical opinion. You want to make me indifferent so I don't go to the police!'

'That is patently untrue,' Codelle replies sharply.

'Like fuck it is! You've just realised what's waiting for you if I—'

'You really believe I haven't considered it fully?' Codelle interrupts sharply. 'You think I don't understand that you might be the last patient I ever have? That you can make one phone call and raze this island to the ground as soon as you're home? Of course I do. There's no one to blame but myself. If I'd looked harder, if I hadn't missed that single weekend rendezvous in Edinburgh …' Codelle buries the regret, speaking her final words grimly. 'I am under no illusions, Arthur. I'm merely doing what I can to minimise trauma, as is my responsibility as a medical practitioner.'

I scoff, shaking my head in disbelief.

'You're lying to me. You've lied to me through this entire process.'

'I have only ever lied when it was required,' Codelle retorts. 'When it was needed to effect an outcome beneficial to your recovery. I can assure you I'm not lying now.'

'Why, because it's not *beneficial* to me? Too fucking right.'

'Because the outcome is the same either way,' Codelle argues sternly. 'My decision is made. One final induction, one more course of Detachment Therapy addressing the treatment's resultant trauma, and then we send you home, happier, healthier, ready to live your life. And yes, once I'm assured that you'll be ok, the rest is out of my hands. Call the police. Call the press. Call anyone you want. Yes, you'll doom my future patients to lives of pain and ineffectual treatment. Yes, it will be devastating to me and the life I've built here. However, until my last moment, my chief and preoccupying concern will always be to *make you well.*'

Those final three words land with the force of Codelle's conviction behind them. Her final rant convinces me of two things simultaneously. Firstly, that she's telling the truth. Secondly, that it doesn't matter either way.

'I'll still do it, you know,' I comment darkly. 'Purge away. I'll still tell people what you did here. I'll still get this place shut down.'

'If you're certain of that,' Codelle replies with an understanding shrug, 'then you have nothing to worry about.'

I stare quietly into the hazel eyes of Dr Elizabeth Codelle. She meets my gaze unapologetically, unwavering.

I doubt I'll ever meet anyone quite like her again.

'How long do I have?'

'We can move the procedure to tomorrow if you need some time to process—'

'No.' I interrupt. 'We'll do it today. When can you be ready?'

Codelle seems taken aback, but quickly recovers.

'I can have everything prepared in two hours, if that's what you want.'

I consider my options, consider how long I'm willing to live in the shadow of the inevitable, how best to leave this place with anything close to my humanity intact.

'What are we waiting for?'

I spend the entirety of my last two hours on a tour of Prismall House.

My footsteps echo as Villner walks just out of step behind me, silently supervising my final circuit through the eclectic rooms and corridors.

I pass through the colourful south-eastern corridor, past the swirling mural of interconnected mannequins' hands, my own fingers brushing over their bumps and valleys as I move beyond them. I visit the strange games room, countless taxidermy animals looking down on me, their sad eyes glinting in the artificial firelight. I pass the white marble pool and into the subterranean tennis court, the endless, zero-stakes game erupting into polite applause as I arrive, returning to a gentle rally upon my exit.

Finally, after walking quietly around the library, the sand garden, and most of the first and second floors, I step through the now familiar statuary corridor, moving beyond the blank-faced figures, turning down the hall of fractured marble and towards the grey door of my bedroom.

I walk to the bathroom door. Villner follows without hesitation, his remit to guard me without any concern about boundaries.

Resolved to ignore his presence entirely, I continue towards the shower, removing my tracksuit top and bottoms, stripping down as I step inside a storm of steaming hot water overtaking all sensation, sight and sound.

I tune everything out and, for the briefest moment, manage to escape inwards.

Codelle was right. There was no reason for me to worry about the coming session, not if I was confident that my convictions would survive it. If I'm certain that I will still want justice after all the pain of this place is removed from me, then I might as well stay silent, allow myself to go through the final treatment and tell the truth immediately upon my return home.

The problem is, I *am* worried. Frightened. Utterly and overwhelmingly terrified that Codelle will get away with all she's done. That I'll let her. I'm scared that, inexplicably, after all the trauma of this place is removed, I might actually be grateful for my time here.

Because it *has* worked.

I still remember Julia. I remember the warmth of her love and affection, I remember my own feelings towards her. But as Codelle described so long ago, they are now merely treasured memories, holding no particular sway.

Julia feels like an old friend, a friend who moved away a long time ago, a friend with whom I tried desperately to maintain a correspondence. But over time, as the letters have gotten further and further apart, and life placed other things in my way, the correspondence isn't the same, until I know that if I stopped writing, the relationship would quietly cease, leaving nothing but joyful memories in its wake.

I know that I loved her, but it's just knowledge, and the idea that those feelings drove me to the point of total self-destruction barely makes sense in retrospect.

When I leave this island, I'm going to go home and live my life, and, if I'm separated from my burning hatred of this place, the cruelty of Codelle's actions and the injustice of what was taken from me, I can see how I might instead thank her for what she's done, like everyone else who came to this place before me.

Even now, I wonder if that would be such a bad thing. Freedom from pain.

If I recall correctly, that's why I came here in the first place.

I turn the water off, hanging in silence for the briefest moment, before a towel appears within reach beside me.

I dry myself off and return to my bedroom, opening a drawer and selecting grey underwear, navy socks, a cream-coloured jumper and a pair of blue jeans.

'What do you think?' I ask Villner, as I hold the jumper up against my body.

I receive a calm, perfunctory nod for my troubles.

'Doesn't matter anyway,' I determine. 'I'll be in a gown in twenty minutes.'

I smile at Codelle's aide-de-camp as I move past him into the hall.

For a brief moment, my mind flashes back to our conversation on the lawns of Prismall House, as my hand reaches into my jeans pocket and grazes the medical syringe I had palmed from the gardens that night. It's remained in the sleeve of my least worn jumper ever since, stowed in my drawer until it might serve a use.

I have only the vaguest idea of how it possibly could.

'Home stretch, I suppose,' I comment to Villner, as he begins to follow me up to the third floor. 'Let's just get this over with, shall we?'

38

We ascend the spiral staircase, journeying through the second floor until we reach an unassuming wooden door. It opens straight onto a set of poured cement steps, which rise upward into almost total darkness.

The stairwell leads out near the northernmost wall of the building's third story, no railing or banister to hold onto, my head simply cresting through a rectangular opening in the floor.

My face is bathed in shadow as I take in this floor's barren architecture: the rows and columns of pillars, like lonely trees in a vast and open field. It feels exposed. A place without light, without warmth, without anywhere to effectively run or hide.

Villner arrives at the top of the stairs behind me and I shake the feeling of vulnerability off as best I can, pushing towards the middle of the room.

About twenty metres away, almost at the very centre, a long, opaque medical sheet drapes down from a temporary rail in the ceiling, separating a small theatre from the remainder of the empty floor. In the otherwise unlit space, harsh medical lights cast sharp, shadow puppet images from within the curtain. I can see the clear outline of a bed rail, a tower of monitors spitting wires from the back, and the figure of Dr Codelle, her shadow growing and shrinking intermittently as she patiently conducts her work.

With every step, my heart begins to thud more powerfully against my chest. I can almost feel the electric hum of the equipment, the antiseptic smell landing in my nose and throat. My mouth runs dry, my stomach groaning with a hollow pang of dread, the fingers of a clammy hand tapping against the syringe in my pocket.

These are my final moments of consciousness, before the doctor has me entirely at her mercy, before she can affect her irrevocable alterations upon me, and usher me to the state of happiness she had once guaranteed.

As I approach the curtained area, Villner pacing with quiet vigilance behind me, I extract the syringe from my pocket inch by painstaking inch, holding it against my stomach as I glance subtly down at the amber liquid in the chamber. The recovery, unlike the grey sedative Codelle employs, had been useless as a weapon against Villner. Knowing my luck, it would simply make him even more alert, scouring any sluggishness from his already superior physique.

Timing the action with a loud footstep, I click open the injection port on my arm, slowly slide the needle into the minute cavity, and depress the plunger until it can't be pushed any further.

In the fleeting few moments I have left, I close the port and stow the empty syringe back in my pocket.

'Mr Mason.' Dr Codelle looks up as I part the long sweeping curtain. 'Are you ready?'

I pass from hollow darkness into light and activity. Illuminated by the circular glare of an operating lamp, Codelle is a creature entirely in her element, attending to her final preparations in a set of immaculate white medical scrubs, hat and surgical mask.

'Yes,' I respond, looking towards the ivory hospital bed, a pale blue gown folded and wrapped in polyethene on the duvet. 'Yes, I think so.'

'Well,' Codelle continues, an air of suppressed melancholy to her tone, 'we'll make this as easy as possible. I promise.'

I proceed towards the gown, tearing the plastic open, dropping my jeans and jumper to the floor. I feel the cool ambient air on my skin as I fasten the delicate straps of the gown around my back and, without another word, sit on the edge of the bed.

I wait in silence as Codelle moves to and fro, laying out the items on the trolley in her own good time. My eyes flicker to Villner, now changed into medical scrubs, washing his hands thoroughly at a stainless steel basin. Despite my dread, I'm suddenly overcome by a restless, impatient energy, an itch at the base of my skull willing them to move faster.

In the past, the effects of the recovery had been somewhat immediate, an overpowering rush of alertness and adrenaline. The cocktail of drugs was created to easily neutralise the effects of Codelle's sedative – however, it had always been introduced to my system *after* the anaesthetic had been injected.

I have no idea of the recovery's potency when administered prior to the anaesthetic. I hang onto the barest glimmer of hope that the amber liquid will linger in my bloodstream long enough for the two treatments to interfere with one other, for some measure of counteraction to diminish the sedative's effect.

One thing seems clear to me, even as a layman: the more time I allow to pass between the two injections, the less effect any counteraction is likely to have.

'We're going to move as we did previously,' Codelle comments. 'The strongest memories first, then continuing on to lower-level experiences and emotions. We'll wake you up for consultation and, if there's anything we need to go over again, we'll follow up, but I'm sure we'll give things their proper due the first time around.'

'Fine,' I mutter, attempting to evoke a sense of resigned impatience. 'I just want to be done.'

'On my way,' Codelle says, absorbed in her work. 'No one wants a doctor who rushes.'

Feeling my chances ebb away with each passing second, I swing my legs up onto the bed and assume a restful position. I watch from the corner of my eye as Codelle delicately lifts the tray from her workbench, carrying it over to my bedside.

I observe Codelle lifting a syringe, the medical lights shining through its translucent grey contents. The doctor brings it to my arm, before pausing mere inches from the injection port. I find myself growing incensed, silently begging for the needle to slip underneath my skin before it's all too late.

'Before we begin, I want to say …' Codelle ponders, earnestly searching for the right words as I feel every muscle in my body tense up. 'I want to say, however you may feel about me after this, even if we never saw eye to eye, I hope that you—'

'– Can we just get the fuck on with it?' I remark sharply.

Codelle pauses, taken aback, crestfallen by my pointed disinterest, by the fact that I would rather retreat into unconsciousness than bear one more word between us.

'Of course,' she continues, collecting herself. 'See you on the other side.'

I hear the port open with a soft click and watch the sedative pass into my already polluted veins.

Of the two drugs, the effect of the sedative hits far more powerfully. I'm pitched immediately backward, lowered into the cushioned depths of the medical bed as the bright lamplight fades to black. A rolling fog of mindless slumber consumes me, dragging me through the darkest recesses of my mind and out the other side, towards a place of true, unthinking oblivion.

As I drift through this space, my last thought is one of solemn realisation. It dawns on me that, upon waking, I'll have no idea how long I've remained in this state. With my grasp of time jettisoned into the opaque miasma of unconscious thought, I could be waking five minutes from now, or five days in the future, on the cusp of potential escape, or far beyond it.

The lights finally go out, with no sense of when they might ignite once again.

When they finally do, it begins with a spark.

A jolt of sensation shimmers through my body, followed by a second, third and a fourth. A building electricity that runs, tingling through my nervous system in sudden rushing waves. I feel a lifting in my abdomen, travelling outwards before exploding in a cascade of sparkling grey matter.

I immediately conduct a full and thorough inventory of my every thought and feeling.

It's all still there. My fury and indignation at Codelle's lies, the slow dawning horror of my captivity, the trauma of post-mortems, cruel goodbyes, Polaroid ghosts, burning plastic and singed yellow paper. I feel the inhumanity of having a once great love gradually and painfully stripped from me until I barely remember how it had felt.

I have everything I need for one last chance.

Yet I still keep my eyes closed, my body relaxed, my breath steady, as I hang on the threshold of what I know will be a desperate, painful struggle – certainly dangerous, potentially futile. I consider what I'm really fighting for. The chance to carry my trauma back to an empty house? The chance to escape with my pain intact?

Part of me could simply wait right here, wait for the recovery to fade from my veins, for a renewed influx of intravenous sedative to slowly overpower me. I could simply allow this opportunity to slip past me, abandoning the stress and pain of opposition, accepting a simpler, happier life, truly free from damage and struggle and guilt.

After all, if I wake up from a successful, painless treatment and no longer believe Codelle has wronged me, then who's to say she has?

'Are you frightened?'

The three words catch me entirely off guard. I hear them as clear as day, spoken to me in a voice full of anxiety.

The memory's not what it once was. I'm not even sure what brought it to the forefront of my mind at a time like this.

I entertain it nevertheless; nowhere else I have to be.

I'm back in me and Julia's first rented flat, lying in bed, staring at the ceiling with wide open eyes.

We'd finished moving all the boxes barely an hour ago, a day of packing, lifting and ferrying, leaving us utterly drained of energy. Our new bed had called to us and we'd gladly answered, yet, once I climbed inside, I felt wide awake.

I bored two perfect holes in the ceiling for almost half an hour, thinking the same thoughts over and over again: that I was now living with another human being. That, from now on, I'd be going back to my bed to find someone waiting there always, that all the bad habits of my sheltered youth would now be fully on display to the person I love most in this world.

I'd known it was a big step, but I hadn't realised how big it really was until I was lying under that ceiling. I remember a swell of anxiety rushing through me. What if I make mistakes? What if I screw it all up? What if she learns that I'm not the person she thought I was at all?

'Are you frightened?'

I hear the voice coming from beside me, as if its owner were staring up at the very same ceiling, a relatable quiver of nerves in every syllable.

'I just … Sarah said to me that once you move in together, you can't … *de-escalate.*'The voice quietly continues. 'There's no cooling off, there's no breaks, you live together and that's reality, and you either get married or you break up. I just … now we're here, I … Are you frightened?'

A hand journeys through the covers, inch by inch, until it passes to the midpoint of the space between us. I slowly move my own to meet it, our fingers interlocking.

'I'm …' I nod slightly, to no one in particular. 'Yeah. I'm terrified.'

'Good,' the voice replies, a smile suddenly audible. 'That actually makes me feel much better.'

'Hah yeah,' I reply. 'Yeah, me too.'

In that moment, I remember exhaling a sigh of utter relief, feeling perfectly at ease in a way I never thought possible, in a way I had perhaps never achieved in my life before then. I remember closing my eyes right after, smiling, effortlessly falling into a deep and peaceful slumber, happier, safer, and braver than I'd ever been.

And then I wake up.

39

I open my eyes carefully, just wide enough to observe the blurred movements of Villner and Codelle. The doctor is over at the workbenches, her back towards me. Villner is by my side, towering above the bed as he checks the calibration on the monitors.

Neither seem to have noticed me.

I wait with impatience for any hint of an opening. The effects of the sedative seem genuinely suppressed, potentially even eradicated by the pre-emptive injection of the reversal, but I'll need to act under the assumption that this newfound wakefulness won't last for long.

I watch as Villner pauses, turning away from the monitors and stepping silently towards Codelle. In this brief window, I lift my groggy head, craning my neck towards the metal tray at my side.

A set of medical tools rest on the trolley: transparent suction tubing, a grey-tipped cannula and, on the furthest edge of the tray, three packs of grey anaesthetic syringes. I raise a silent, arcing hand up and over towards the tray, my fingers searching for the syringe packet, getting closer inch by inch until I can almost reach the nearest one.

'No, it should present around fifty right now.' Codelle responds to an unknown query. 'Why? What are you seeing?'

I whip my arm back down to my side, hiding the packaged syringe in my downturned palm as the pair turn immediately to my bedside. Their shadowed figures drift back across the room towards me, leaning to examine the monitors.

'Yes, definitely tachycardic,' Codelle comments, a sudden concern colouring her voice. 'Doesn't make sense. I'll draw up a smaller dose, we can supplement it.'

Codelle picks up one of the remaining two syringes from the metal trolley and begins to peel the sterile packet open. At the same time, I press my own packaged syringe into the bed and work the seal open with my fingers.

'I'll get some of this out,' Codelle says, returning to the stainless-steel basin as Villner looms quietly by my side.

I slowly work to extract the plastic syringe from the small opening. I get a quarter of it free, half, three quarters.

'Wait.' Codelle turns in sudden alarm towards Villner. 'How many syringes are left on that tray?'

As soon as the words hit my ears, I shake the syringe free of the packaging, swing it in a violent arc into Villner's arm and force the plunger down to the bottom of the barrel.

Villner knocks the patient trolley to the side in shock, his eyes widening in utter bewilderment as he stares at the empty syringe sticking out of his forearm.

The pristine theatre bursts into chaos.

His bewilderment snapping into burning anger, Villner reaches his thick hands towards my arms, forcing my wrists together and pressing them down against my sternum. I feel the heat of his sharp, furious breath as it snarls through gritted teeth above me, his weight pushing down as I yell and struggle.

Straining to shift my position, I manage to turn myself ninety degrees, my head and shoulders hanging off the bed, my feet pressing against Villner's chest as I fight to push free of his grasp. Codelle immediately comes to join him, doing everything she can to help hold me down as I writhe, like a caged animal, against them both.

'Arthur! Arthur!' Codelle pleads for calm as I glare at Villner with hate in my eyes, watching with immense and cruel satisfaction as his breathing slows in his chest, as he suddenly grows sluggish, unbalanced, his grip becoming steadily limp.

With a final push, I tumble free, falling backwards from the bed and landing with a thud on the cement floor. I hear clattering from the other side, see Villner's legs buckling beneath him, medical tools clattering to the floor.

I burst up to my feet and take the man in. He's struggling for mobility, his head swaying, his breath heavy, yet he still clings firmly to his duty, placing his body impassibly between me and Codelle.

Codelle fixes me with a look of betrayal and anguish. She has one arm around Villner, her free hand already clutching a syringe of amber recovery. She says nothing. Instead, she goes about her work efficiently, opening the packaging, looking for a vein.

At most, I've earned myself a three-minute head start.

I take a final look at the devastated face of Dr Elizabeth Codelle, before turning my back and bursting through the medical curtain.

Cement pillars whip past me as I cross the third floor, plunging down the stairwell that descends into Prismall House. I collapse through the door at the bottom, slamming into the opposite wall before righting myself and vaulting along a hall of thick glass windows. Stars, circles, triangles, moons and hearts rush by as I see the second-floor balcony emerge around the corner.

I sprint from carpet to marble to cool, wrought iron, a breakneck helter-skelter descent down the tight spiral stairs and across the first-floor atrium. The ceiling mural smiles down on me, bemused, watching me leave, listening to the hurried approach of my pursuers two floors up.

The double doors fly open, an arctic barrage of biting winter air stealing the breath from my lungs. My half-naked body feels like it's on fire, a token sheet of cloth against the merciless elements. Controlling my breathing, I fix my sights on the distant shoreline and hammer my bare feet into the snow.

I launch myself down the path towards the edge of the gardens, passing onto the lawn and immediately veering to a point just along the shore, some twenty metres west from the boathouse. Frosted grass crunches underfoot as I sprint away from Prismall House and into the frigid, moonless night.

I reach the lapping shoreline in sixty-seven seconds.

Personal best.

Collecting my breath, taking one final look towards the distant, grey titan of Prismall House, I pass through the slush at the water's edge. My legs screaming at the eviscerating cold, I unfasten my medical gown, allowing it to drift down to the snowy ground behind me, until I'm wading through the ocean in nothing but my underwear.

On the cusp of unspeakable pain and struggle, aware that I've perhaps entered the final hour of my life, I take a deep breath, fix my steady eyes towards the invisible mainland, and dive into the freezing black sea.

40

My senses are plunged into darkness. No feeling but the biting cold, no sound but the muffled rush of water. I raise my head to a cacophony of violent waves, my arms battling the surf in thrashing, draining strokes.

I duck below the water again, kicking my legs furiously as I surge blindly towards my destination. Raising my head one final time, my lungs fill with a sudden swell of hope as I find my effort has carried me where I need to go, my outstretched hands now a mere five metres from the wall of the boathouse.

I look back as Prismall House opens its doors once again, expelling Villner and Dr Codelle into the frosty air.

I thrash against the final few metres, my numb fingers wrapping onto the underside of the boathouse wall, allowing me to dip down and emerge on the other side.

I watch the pair through the narrow wooden slats, barely noticing the effects of the Irish Sea as it strips the warmth from my bones. Codelle and Villner rush through the garden, heads swivelling, the situation spun out of their control. They notice my deep footprints in the snow, following them across the white lawn to the very edge of the water.

I watch Villner, his sense of movement renewed, crouching down to the slush-covered ground, lifting the now sodden medical gown in a closed fist. Codelle raises a hand to her mouth, scanning the empty sea ahead of her.

I can imagine her heart breaking at the thought of my being out there, her logical brain profiling whether I would actually attempt to reach the mainland amid these terminally cold waves.

I only hope I've given her enough reasons to believe it.

Wasting no time, Codelle sprints through the wind and snow, yelling for Villner to follow her.

I shrink back into the unlit recesses of the boathouse, bones rattling from the cold, my back bumping softly against the fibreglass bow of the *De Anima*.

I move myself to the port side, the wooden gangway some two metres above my head. I hear two sets of feet hammer on the boards above me, passing onto the deck, a door wrenched open before slamming shut.

My heart in my throat, I swim as quietly as possible towards the boat's stern, making my way back around the starboard side, where the recessed rungs of the permanent ladder stretch upward from the water's edge. I reach for the first rung and haul my quivering body out of the water, scaling a few more and clinging to the boat's hull.

An interminable stretch of time later, the *De Anima* finally hums into life, the turbines roaring into a hard reverse. Holding tightly to the boat's ladder, I watch the walls of the boathouse gradually slip away as the *De Anima* pulls back, pivots in a steady circle, and launches into a desperate search.

The *De Anima* spends almost a minute at the shoreline, before venturing out further in the direction of the mainland, attempting to follow my imagined trajectory towards the opposite shore. I grip the ladder, limbs frozen, teeth gritted against the icy spray as I'm carried further and further out to sea. I force every ounce of determination into my shuddering limbs, the wind and waves lashing against my skin.

The bright beam of a searchlight ignites across the water, the smaller light of handheld torch moving freely across the decks, passing erratically from bow to the stern.

Someone is making their way around the boat, peering out over the side, searching for me in the water. Unbeknownst to them, they're destined to find me if they look over the starboard rail. Heart in my throat, I haul myself up the rungs until my hand grasps the rail that spans the deck.

I haul myself, shivering, onto the starboard deck, hoping the engines, wind and sea will mask my footsteps. I glimpse the figure of Dr Codelle, leaning over the stern railing, her high-powered torchlight dancing desperately along the waves. Needing to get off the deck, I step as deftly as possible towards *De Anima*'s external door, softly testing the handle.

Warm light glows through the decadent lounge, reflecting off the central glass coffee table, glinting on the lacquered wood of the corner bar. My shivering feet sink into the carpet as I step inside, closing the door delicately behind me.

As soon as it's closed, the exquisite lounge starts to swim, a familiar vertigo rolling through my limbs. The recovery is starting to lose its battle inside my body, the sedative pulling me back towards oblivion.

I doubt I have five minutes before it succeeds.

The faintest drag in my heels, I walk gingerly through the room. Glancing up the steps towards the ship's bow, I can see Villner's legs standing at the *De Anima*'s controls.

Torchlight suddenly streams in from outside as Dr Codelle makes her way back across the starboard side of the *De Anima*. I shrink away as she passes by the windows, quickly descending into the grey walled corridors leading towards the back of the boat.

The sleek, executive 4x4 still sits at the centre of the onboard garage, unmoved since it carried me here a lifetime ago. Its bodywork matches the light grey of the walls, a uniform hue that covers the pipes, wire boxes and a set of large latched cabinets built into the wall.

I approach the cabinets and clumsily throw the latches open, my fingers numb from the cold and the creeping anaesthesia. I work my way across the room, opening and closing compartments as I go, searching for anything that might help.

Cleaning supplies. Life jackets. Board games. Mechanics' tools.

It's only when I make it to the other side of the room, to the first high cabinet, that I find what I'm looking for.

The latch gives way above my head, revealing a set of three dark green jerry cans, secured in place by a lattice of bungie cords, presumably held as spare fuel for the *De Anima*'s engine. It's more than enough.

I reach up and pull at the bungie cord, attempting to lift the petrol out of its position. My aching fingers push at the underside of the can, lifting it from the high shelf and carrying its considerable weight as I work to bring it down gently.

With a lurching jolt, the *De Anima* swerves, turning at the worst possible moment and throwing my precarious stance off. I'm thrown backward towards the car, my shoulders slamming against it as the jerry can leaves my grip, bouncing off of the car's boot at an erratic angle, sliding to the very back wall of the garage.

A deafening sound rings in my ears.

I whip around, eyes widening in horror at the sudden blinking of the car's lights, the blare of its alarm ringing through the otherwise silent vessel, screaming for its masters in a cacophonous, unending cry.

I reach up to the cupboards, forcing them closed, fumbling desperately to reset the latch. Then I turn my attention to the stern, making my way behind the car towards the fallen jerry can.

The car alarm cuts out.

The jerry can is still three metres away as I duck down in the now resounding silence. Crouching behind the boot, I lower myself onto my hands and knees, staring through the undercarriage for any sign of movement.

It doesn't take long before I spot the heavy boots of William Villner, stepping purposefully into the garage.

My blood runs cold, my muscles tensing. Every step tonight had passed unnoticed by the *De Anima*'s two occupants, each move bringing me closer and closer to the mainland, only for me to become trapped once again, cowering in the face of overwhelming force.

With a sense of calm, Villner slips his car fob back into his pocket, and steps with unhurried curiosity around the garage.

I watch his feet journey down the right side of the car, as I crawl slowly and silently towards the left. I edge along the passenger side, my head peeking through the windows as I see Villner study the right-hand side of the room.

I edge further towards the front of the car, the corridor ahead mere feet away from me, a tantalising chance to make a break for it, to slip back into the *De Anima*.

'Arthur? You're not onboard, are you?' Villner speaks almost playfully, entertaining the possibility with a certain dark glee. I can tell it's merely a suspicion, and yet I know from his voice that he so wants to be right. 'I hope you are. It's my hour, you know. We can talk, man to man, ay?'

41

I hold my breath, staring at the open corridor.

Without warning, as if catching me out were the object of some twisted game, Villner's footsteps start to lazily tip backward, his pace quickening as he heads back around the front of the car.

In the scant few seconds I have, unable to retreat to the back of the room, I drop onto my stomach and shift my way beneath the undercarriage.

I watch Villner's feet arrive at the passenger side, staring down the now empty aisle.

'Mmm, fair play, maybe I'm wrong.' I hear him muse.

I watch his steps carry him down the passenger side, coming to a stop part-way, his boots resting inches from my face. I edge slowly along to the opposite side of the car, my back brushing against the 4x4's underside, my stomach pressed into the cold linoleum floor.

'You could've really hurt me, you know,' Villner comments. 'Sticking people with syringes, it's a nasty business.'

I slowly emerge on the right side of the car, clambering quietly to my knees just as I see Villner stoop onto his.

I shift anxiously forwards, concealing my legs behind the front wheel as I watch Villner crouch down and peer through the undercarriage, still suspecting my presence, and with all the time in the world to find me.

I step outside of myself, looking down on the horror of my situation: trapped in a room, on a boat, in the middle of the sea. Weak, half-naked, shivering, the effects of sedation slowly lapping at the corners of my brain. In this moment, I'm nothing more to Villner than a rodent, scampering through the bowels of his ship, ready to be picked by its tail and thrown back into the cage of Prismall House.

I stare out towards the corridor, considering a futile attempt at escape. Instead, I'm suddenly struck by every violation this man has laid against me, all the polite brutality, all the pain that I've endured in his shadow. Somewhere, in the crucible of my anger, I begin to consider something new, reaching my hand for the car's front door and gently pulling against the handle.

The door gives way, the keyless entry fob in Villner's pocket held right beside the car.

Anywhere in this room would be range enough.

Villner slowly brings himself up onto one knee.

'You over at the back?' he asks conversationally. 'I'm not being funny, mate, you're fucking this up for everyone … and to think she's still goin' to treat you. World doesn't deserve 'er.'

Villner rises up and begins to make his way to the back of the car. I can hear a noise of quiet surprise as he approaches the stern, finally noticing the lone jerry can.

'There we go,' Villner comments, observing the fallen object and the locked cupboard it inexplicably came from, his theory of my presence confirmed. 'Well, that's enough of that now.'

As Villner crosses to the back of the room, I slowly work the car door open, clambering into the driver's side as silently as I can. I steady my breath, place a hand on the wheel and, with a quivering thumb, press the ignition.

The car bursts into life. For the briefest moment I see Villner spin in the rear-view mirror, his eyes startled, his mouth opening as if to speak.

I throw the car into reverse and stamp the accelerator down.

The collision detector screams as the wheels screech backwards, the overwhelming force of the car slamming into Villner with an audible crunch, pinning him against the back wall as his forehead slams into the rear windscreen. Even with nowhere to go, I force the car into an even harder reverse, Villner crying in bewildered agony.

I put the car in drive and roll forwards, Villner falling to his knees behind me as the bumper taps the front of the room.

I see Villner slowly attempt to climb to his feet, only for them to give way beneath him. Instead, he raises his arm up, his pleading eyes visible in the rear-view mirror.

'Please—'

I throw the car into reverse once again, forcing my foot down as the 4x4 launches towards Villner's now crumpled form. A dull thud and a wet crunch echoes from behind me, falling immediately into silence, until there's nothing but the sound of the *De Anima*'s idling engines.

In the charged silence, every suppressed protest, every swallowed injustice and buried cry of rage rushes through my throat into a guttural, cathartic scream. A volcanic outburst of unhinged emotion roars outwards before leaving me to collapse against the steering wheel.

I clamber out of the driver's side door, my legs weak. I turn with a sickly stomach towards the jerry can, lying half a metre from Villner's limp fingers.

I stumble over to it, righting it as the petrol sloshes inside. I slowly unscrew the cap, turning away from the pungent kerosene odour before letting it fall back onto its side.

Thick, pearlescent liquid laps across the floor, spreading slowly out beneath the 4x4, soaking into Villner's clothes.

I remember what the man before me had once said, during our midnight conversation on the lawn of Prismall House. He said that I couldn't imagine the freedom of acting without guilt. I think he's right. I could never live without guilt, even for the things I've done tonight. I don't think I'd ever want to.

Though, I don't feel particularly bad about this next part.

Losing the feeling in my hands, I hook my arm through a set of life vests and hoist them onto my shoulder. Fumbling with the car's glovebox, I manage to draw out a book of Chatsworth-blue matches before climbing back out, stumbling on unsteady feet towards the exit corridor. In the doorway, I place a match between my teeth, gripping the book in my quivering palm. It takes three tries and all my coordination to bring them sharply together. I light a single match, ignite the entire book with it, and cast it, almost lazily, across the room.

The fumes ignite immediately, a pillar of flame bursting from the floor and snatching at the ceiling of the *De Anima*'s garage.

I push myself up the stairs, the effect of the sedative dragging upon my limbs, the heat of the crackling fire pushing me forwards.

When I reach the carpeted lounge, Codelle is standing in front of me. She's still holding the torch in her hand, a look of shock when she sees me. Though the fire seems contained to the garage for now, a column of black smoke is beginning to peel through the corridor, rising up into the lounge behind me.

'What have you done?' She speaks in stunned horror. 'Where's Villner?'

I stumble towards one of the plush leather sofas, dropping down as the strength drains from my body.

Codelle stares towards the burning garage, taking a few steps in Villner's presumed direction.

'Don't ... don't ...' I mutter sluggishly. 'There's nothing you can do.'

I watch Codelle's face fall, a hollow anguish echoing from beneath her silent exterior. Her breath catches in her throat, released as a soft, desolate whimper. I observe the doctor, feeling neither joy nor guilt as I see her composure fall away.

Eventually, my head becomes harder to support, my gaze dropping to the glass coffee table.

'What have you done? What have you done?!' Codelle screams against a crescendo of crackling flames.

'I didn't know how long I had,' I mutter, already feeling the shadows creeping in. 'If I passed out now, on a working boat ... I'd just wake up back on the island. And even with Villner gone, you'd still treat me. You'd treat me if it was the last thing you did.'

'We were trying to save you!' Codelle yells. 'Everything! We gave everything to save you! You monstrous fool! And we were done! We were finished! We gave your life back and now you—'

She falls into silence, unable to vocalise the reality of Villner's death, the faintest touch of denial on her lips.

'It doesn't matter now; we're not making it back,' I continue. 'Call the coastguard, get them out here, let them take us both back to the mainland.'

Codelle fixes me with a look of pure, fathomless hatred, not even flinching as the electric battery of the 4x4 finally explodes downstairs, rocking the *De Anima*, sending a new swell of heat through the vessel.

'And what if I don't?' she retorts defiantly, as I begin to feel myself truly slip away.

'Then we die ...' I reason with my last, whispered breaths, '... here, together, in the name of principle. How romantic.'

I don't see her reaction as I push her up against the mirror of her own inflexible philosophy. I finally drift to the very edge of consciousness, still not knowing what she'll choose, realising that I'm suddenly scared. Scared that this is truly the end, that I won't get to see the sun rise tomorrow.

I tumble into darkness, listening as Dr Elizabeth Codelle steps up to the bridge, the passing sounds of defeated conversation, and the distant crackle of the radio.

'Thank you,' I whisper, as I pass from this world, to the sound of her pleas and crackling flame.

7th February

42

I wake up in a cold and familiar place.

I stare at a grid of ceiling tiles, an intrusive light shining directly into my bleary eyes. My body lies reclined on a hospital bed, dressed in a medical gown, surrounded by blurred monitors and a floor-to-ceiling curtain.

My head like a lead weight, I use all my remaining strength to lift it and briefly look around.

The curtain is still out of focus, a swimming abstract blur of colour, pale blue and pearl-white slowly coalescing.

Slowly, unexpectedly, blobs of orange appear across the curtain's unfocussed tapestry. As everything draws together, the orange objects begin to take shape, the white rising up to form clouds, the blue forming the waves of a simple ocean vista. The orange objects become bright cartoon ships, the bridge windows replaced by two oval eyes, a cheery dimpled smile across the bow.

I turn to the monitors: boxy plastic with fading labels, decades out of date.

I fall back against my pillow, the faintest smile at the corners of my mouth.

My hand brushes against a thick, plastic-covered wire. My fingers work their way along it, locating a single call button at the end.

I press it a few times, listening as a group of orderlies make their way towards me.

'Why did you just laugh?'

I look up, surprised at the figure behind the desk, as I sit myself up in the middle of a throw-covered sofa.

'Did I? I didn't notice.'

Dr Dunn nods. She waits, curious to see whether I have an answer. I look briefly out the window of her Belgravia office, then back, my eyes coming to rest on her face.

'Well, it wasn't *funny*, but the nurse told me that my *friend* was ok, meaning Codelle, of course. They said that they were looking after her. I asked what happened and apparently the coast-guard found us both in the water. I was unconscious. They told me people die all the time from passing out in their life vest. They can't right themselves; they turn over in the water without knowing.'

Dr Dunn watches as I shake my head, still bewildered by the nurse's final comment.

'Turns out, Dr Codelle kept me upright for twenty minutes before the boat came.' I almost laugh again out of sheer disbelief. 'She held onto me, made sure I didn't drown. Right up to the end, she was trying to save my life.'

'And what did you say to the nurse?'

'I think …' I search my memories, a journey into anti-climax. '… I think I asked them to call the police.'

A fortnight had passed since I was pulled from the water and spirited away to a hospital in Bangor, the authorities arriving within the first hour of my requesting them.

I'd put all my energy into recounting the events at Prismall House. The two officers listened dutifully, slowly recognising they were woefully unequipped. More officers arrived to support the enormity of my confession, a final set arriving in plain clothes, stoic faces taking in all the pertinent details. I heard them making plans for the recording of my official statement, suggesting a protected ward in case Codelle still threatened my wellbeing.

My mother arrived on the second day, a company solicitor in in tow, who advised me of my liability for the death of William Villner. By that point, a police boat had already reached Prismall

House, evidence of my captivity building a case for reasonable force.

I hadn't seen Dr Codelle since the *De Anima*, though the upcoming criminal and civil suits would inevitably reunite us someday. I did ponder, once or twice, if she now feels as trapped as I had; her precious freedom stripped away, the moral framework of her captors so utterly divergent to her own that it must feel like madness.

My recovery was quick, impressively so: a brief period of observation, reaching the bizarre conclusion that, despite the harrowing nature of my ordeal, I had left Prismall House in better physical health than when I'd arrived. There were still many questions concerning my mental state, some frankly bordering on the philosophical, but none of them justified keeping me in place. My mother went back to London four days after I woke up and, less than a week later, I followed her.

My apartment was neat, bed made, perishable foods removed from the fridge, the walls totally bare. Standing in the calming silence of my home, I found myself returning to the hallway, collecting the towering pile of correspondence on the hall side table.

It took me two hours to sort through it, collecting the important letters and placing them into my folders.

I'll admit, it felt good to get it done.

'Are you worried?'

'I'm sorry?'

'Going back to the office,' Dunn comments. 'You were terrified about heading back after your bereavement leave.'

'I was, wasn't I?' I chuckle at the anxieties of my past self. 'No, I'm not worried at all.'

'No?'

'No.'

'But you scheduled a therapy session for the morning of?' she queries, prodding gently at my motives.

'This isn't a therapy session.' I calmly set the record straight. 'This was just an overdue apology.'

'You apologised half an hour ago.' Dunn checks the clock at her side. 'You're certain there's nothing further on your mind?'

I search my feelings under Dunn's patient gaze.

'Honestly … no. I really appreciated your guidance, but I just don't feel I need it anymore. I feel fine.'

I can tell Dr Dunn believes me, or at least believes that's the truth I'm telling myself.

'You're still carrying your time on the island with you,' she continues. 'You're sure you want to carry that alone?'

'I can handle it,' I reply, a confidence in my voice that I haven't heard in a long time. 'Anyway, who do you even see for a crippling fear of psychiatrists?'

Dunn doesn't laugh.

'What happened on that island wasn't psychiatry, Arthur,' she begins. 'It was a human rights violation. I know why Codelle's offer seemed alluring at the time. I know she painted modern psychiatry as flawed, and slow-moving and ineffectual, but … you can't just fix something of such infinite complexity. Healing the mind requires respect and compromise and care, and I care about you a lot, Arthur, I really do.'

'Well, I appreciate the offer. I'll genuinely think about it.'

'All right …' Dunn concedes, another thought clearly occurring to her. 'Do you still think about her much?'

'Dr Codelle?'

'Julia.'

A moment of silence passes between us. I realise I haven't said that name in almost five days, and never outside the context of my official statement.

'No. I wouldn't say so,' I admit casually. 'But I still have the memories. I can think about them whenever I want.'

I grab breakfast at Victoria station, taking the District Line to Westminster, before changing for Canary Wharf.

The elevator ticks up to the thirty-first floor, its doors opening out to a chaotic smattering of applause.

I step out into the glass-walled reception of my company, met by a throng of almost fifty people clapping, cheering and whooping at my return to the fold. Surprised, embarrassed, with no idea where to look, I keep the crowd's benevolent intentions in mind, smiling at the vague semi-circle with gratitude.

My mother stands in the very middle of the group, a beaming smile on her face.

Five minutes of handshakes and well-wishes follow, kind words ranging from genuine to performative. I arrive at Myra Stewart-Mill, acting head of Operations in my long-augmented absence. I'm surprised to see a look of genuine warmth on her face as she shakes my hand, even in the shared understanding that, upon my return, her title reverts to me.

Eventually the crowd disperses, and I step into the CEO's office. I bask in front of the wall-spanning window, drinking in the cold blue sky and painted white clouds that drift across the city.

'Did you see how happy everyone was?' My mother smiles as she joins me. 'You really inspire something in them.'

I accept the unfounded compliment with all the grace I can muster.

'I inspire something all right,' I comment glibly. 'I'm sure they put two and two together when they read the papers.'

My mother ignores the notion entirely.

Since the details of Codelle's practice had leaked, the doctor's face had been plastered unceremoniously across every national tabloid. She'd been portrayed as part cult leader, part angel of death. Though disavowed by her former colleagues, she'd been defended by many of her patients, with none more vocal than my old school friend Monty Han.

My name had been kept out of the press, at least for the moment, allowing me some measure of breathing room. But most of my department knew that I'd gone there and that I'd returned just before the story broke. In the eyes of my colleagues, I might as well have spent five months in Dracula's castle. I could see them in the lobby, nodding and smiling, wondering if I'd left as a free man or a mind-addled thrall.

'How's the *Ardour*?' I ask.

'Ongoing,' she comments. 'We lost a few key consignments, which is a shame, but it won't be on your docket anymore – other people can handle it.'

I feel the weight of the subject about to be broached, my mother's inhalation like a receding wave.

'Have you given any thought as to when you'll be coming back in earnest?' she asks. 'I know you're easing in.'

I sigh as a cloud passes silently across the sun.

'I still think about my time over there. The things she did.'

Mum places a hand on my shoulder, a sweet sadness in her eyes at the mention of Codelle's institute.

'I know.'

'She wanted me to think that Julia had been unfaithful. That was her original plan, at least. She called it Conceptual Immortality, trying to destroy my image of her, make me accept the Detachment Sessions willingly.' I suddenly smile. 'You know what fucked it up? Julia snuck up to visit me when I was at a conference. It was just a snap decision on her part. A random idea. But if she hadn't done that, if she hadn't missed me as much as I missed her back then … I would have believed Codelle, hook, line and sinker.'

'She was a monster,' my mother mutters. 'You know I'll never forgive myself for sending you to her. Sick woman.'

'Yeah,' I agree quietly. 'The thing is … Codelle said she got the call records from you, from a private investigator you hired.'

'Hah! The nerve on her.' Mum laughs derisively, shaking her head.

I fix her with an unwavering look, not laughing, not smiling. The unamused lines of my face tell a story of patient accusation. It takes her a while before she notices, and when she finally does, she looks almost offended.

'Wait, you're … I don't understand.' My mother scoffs incredulously. 'There never *was* any investigator; it wasn't even a real document, Arthur, it was all a lie. You just said so yourself.'

'Of course it was a lie,' I concede calmly. 'But she thought I'd be going back to the mainland believing it. She wanted me to

believe it for the rest of my life. Why would she implicate someone who I work with every day, someone who I could simply
check with when I got back home? How long would that lie
really last?'

'Well, insane people aren't exactly detail-oriented,' my mother
points out scornfully.

'Dr Codelle was,' I state bluntly, watching her squirm in place.
'I can't help but think someone that meticulous would never
have involved you in such a big lie, not unless she knew you'd
corroborate it. Not unless you'd agreed to be part of it ahead
of time.'

My mother looks at me, on the cusp of some flippant denial,
the truth of the matter held in her wide, dread-filled eyes.

'You knew what I was going into,' I conclude calmly. 'At least
in part. You knew.'

I see a shock of emotion pass across my mother's face. I sense
each option passing through her mind: denial, deception, mini-
misation, escape. I can feel her trying to clamber out of this
confrontation until every strategy gives way beneath her and she
tumbles back down into its depths.

Her face contorts into a look of guilt and sorrow, tears brimming in her eyes as she speaks.

'You don't ... you don't understand, sweetie, please. I was
scared. I mean, you almost ...' She holds a quivering hand up to
her mouth. 'I was frightened of losing you. I ... I just wanted you
to be well and she ... she made it sound like it wouldn't be ...'

'I know. I know.'

I put my arms around my mother, pulling her into a rare and
sincere hug. After everything that's happened, even knowing her
complicity, I also know the state that she'd seen me in. Her only
son suffering so immensely – Codelle's dark promises must have
seemed like salvation.

I hug her close, trying to balance the wildly swinging scales
of her benevolent intentions and the harrowing consequences.

'I couldn't let you go on like that!' my mother cries into my
shoulder.

'I know.'

'I just couldn't do it, darling! You know how much we need you!'

My arms stiffen, any semblance of colour draining from the moment.

'*We* need you?'

I pull slowly, dispassionately away. Noticing the deer-in-headlights stare that my mother fixes me with, it's immediately clear who she was referring to.

'I meant everyone, you're important to everyone!' She tries wildly to explain, scanning my face, pleading for me to take her words onboard.

'You didn't want Codelle to save your son, did you?' My voice is low with bleak understanding. 'You wanted her to save the Director of Operations.'

'They're both ...' Mum begins, unable to help herself. 'I was trying to save *you*, so you can live, so you can lead this place! I want you to be happy and healthy and productive!'

'I understand,' I reply, a heavy sadness in my tone. 'But I think it's time I gave my notice.'

'No, sweetheart—'

'I'm sure you'll be considering Myra Stewart-Mill; she has my endorsement.'

'Don't do this,' my mother pleads. 'Take some time, take as much time as you need.'

'I think I'm out of annual leave, actually.'

'You can't do this, Arthur! This place, it needs you. We need you!'

'That's not true.' I half laugh, my tone utterly incredulous. 'You always said that. You always made it seem like this place would crumble without me. And I was good at this job, before Julia died, but I wasn't irreplaceable. You just wanted me here. It's what you wanted.'

My mother stares up at me, shocked, as everything I've held back streams forward, not out of anger, but simply in respect of the long-avoided truth.

'I'm so grateful for everything you've given me,' I continue. 'And I know passing this place down is an act of love in your eyes, but the love our family has, it's material and it's transactional and it's cold. I used to think love just *had* conditions, I didn't know any better. I think that's why you hated Julia, that's really why ... because she gave away so *freely* something that you thought I had to earn.'

My mother says nothing, her eyes brimming, a mix of denial and indignation across her face.

'Codelle's got into your head,' she mutters. 'You never thought this before. You never felt this way before.'

In the face of her justifications, I find myself releasing a long, calm sigh.

'You know, Mum,' I comment, with a steady tone. 'I honestly wish you the best.'

I return to my apartment by twelve thirty. The rest of the day to myself.

Enjoying the liminal space between my liberating decision and the inevitable consequences of leaving my employer, I find a record for the turntable and sit quietly on the sofa, drinking in the sudden, prevailing calm.

I sink backwards, a sensation of quiet contentment washing through me. Dr Dunn's question returns, hovering politely at the edge of my consciousness. She'd asked if I ever thought of Julia – one of the first people to ask me that since I returned to London.

She really is a good psychiatrist.

I wonder whether I should feel more distressed by my answer, by the lack of feeling engendered by my time with Dr Codelle. However, the more I consider the question, the more it feels decidedly moot. Whether I simply stopped loving Julia, or forcibly had that love torn away from me, the end result is the same. My memories of her no longer hold any strong emotion, and that emotion can no longer collapse in on me, no longer threaten me with grief and sadness and pain.

My eyes cross the room, falling upon the landline phone.

No messages.

I haven't called yet today, but as with my efforts for the past week, part of me suspects it's fruitless. My relationship with Julia's mother seems irreparably tarnished by my time at the institute, so much so that she's letting my calls ring into silence. Perhaps she's respecting my wishes, perhaps she's angry, perhaps she's trying to get over her own pain in a similar way, avoiding someone who reminds her only of her own anguish.

After a moment's contemplation, I pull myself to my feet, desperately hoping that it's not the latter.

43

I pay for the train on the bus ride over, sprinting the final few minutes through King's Cross and passing through the barriers at Platform 4. In less than three hours, I'm carried through the midlands to the north of England, a second, shorter train dropping me off at a small town station.

As the winter sun shrinks below the horizon, I briskly navigate the winding streets towards my mother-in-law's house. When I find it, I hurry up the small garden path and knock sharply on the door.

Silence.

I knock once again.

Nothing. No movement inside. No lights in the hall or living room.

Worry begins to worm its way through my chest; I raise my hand once again.

'Arthur?'

I look to my left to see Lorraine emerging from the path to her back garden, a blue crate of empty bottles in her hands. A wave of relief washes over me, a smile spreading across my face as I exhale heavily.

'I've been calling for a week, I thought ... I thought something might've happened.'

'Oh,' Lorraine comments softly. 'Oh no, I was in the Lake District. Peter and Bridey had the camping club so I went with them.'

'Right,' I utter, my worst-case scenarios crumbling around me. 'No, that's … it's just, I left messages, I was worried—'

'Oh … I don't know how to check for that sort of thing.'

The pair of us stand in silence for a moment.

'I don't want to …' Lorraine begins cautiously. 'I know you said you were, um … uh, recovering or—'

'Can I come in?' I intercede, hoping beyond hope that we're not too far gone. 'Please?'

Lorraine considers it, attempting to parse my prior demands with the self-effacing figure in front of her. In the end, a warm smile rises on her face, hospitality shining through.

'Of course. I'll just drop this by the gate and I'll make us some tea. You need to tell me how your trip was.'

It's well into the evening by the time I've told Lorraine everything. I watch tears fall from her eyes on three occasions throughout the story, and I almost join her as I apologise profusely for our phone call.

Lorraine bears my apology with a boundless understanding that I've come to expect but wasn't sure I'd deserve. When I'm done talking, two long-empty teacups resting on the table between us, Lorraine collects her thoughts, a look of sadness in her eyes.

'So you don't feel anything? All that love you had for her, it's just … gone?'

'I still have the memories,' I reply. 'I can still remember everything, but just … She's like a good friend. I still have all the lessons she taught me, the confidence—'

'But you don't' – Lorraine's face falls in dismay – 'you don't love her at all? I mean … Arthur, you loved her more than anyone I know. You loved her as much as I—'

'I know,' I say.

'And you …' She prods hesitantly. 'And you're all right with that?'

I see a sense of horror in Lorraine's eyes. If I was speaking to anyone else in the world, I might feel judged. However, I can understand how shocking, how incomprehensible it must seem.

332

'Is it wrong to say I feel fine?' I speak tentatively. 'I mean, I know that's how I *would* feel, I literally had the *care* taken out of me, so by definition I can't care as much as I did before but …' I search for the words, before pressing forwards. 'It's gone, and that should make me sad, but that same sadness is gone as well and, I mean, that sadness almost killed me. I just couldn't live with it. She was everything to me back then, you know? It tore my soul apart, every minute of every day. Now I'm on the other side of it and, even knowing what it cost me, it's … I don't know, maybe it's for the best.'

As Lorraine listens quietly, I find myself pushing onward, hoping to hear that she agrees.

'I mean,' I continue, searching her eyes for understanding, 'I mean, you know how it feels, right? You know what it's like.'

Lorraine nods, and I feel something within me stop pushing. I see reflected in her the person I once was: tears never far away from her eyes, her smile a feat of strength and perseverance, an air of wounded dignity and quiet understanding that nothing will ever be quite what it once was.

'Yes, Arthur, I do,' she replies, smiling sadly. 'And I feel so sorry for you.'

I feel myself grow still, the words landing softly against me and sinking deeply into my soul. I can see in Lorraine's eyes that she means every word of what she's just said. As she senses the weight of her statement upon me, leaning across to hug my still body, I feel a single thought emerge from the darkness, staking its place in the centre of my mind.

'Do you have any pictures of me and Julia at our wedding?'

Lorraine, momentarily caught off guard, chuckles at the answer. 'Hah, oh goodness, hundreds.'

'Could I have one?'

Lorraine pulls away, a little confused, before shrugging offhandedly.

'No problem at all.' Lorraine picks herself up, collecting the teacups as she goes. 'Do you mind which one?'

'No,' I answer. 'Any will be fine.'

44

Every time I see it, I think the same thing: that one wooden gate will outlive us all.

It just has the attitude for it.

The dark brown timber is warped and weathered, the hinges rusted, the throw-over latch jamming so often that most people don't bother to fasten it at all. Yet still, after all its years of service, subjected to wind and rain and scrapes and slams, it performs its function with unending persistence. It does what it does, perhaps not beautifully, but with undeniable consistency, even when so much else breaks around it.

I force the latch open with more difficulty than I'd care to admit, pushing at the creaking timber and closing it once I've slipped through. Woodchip crunches under my feet as I step along a narrow footpath, drinking in the sights and sounds around me. A row of wooden buildings draws steadily closer.

The air smells earthy and not entirely pleasant, a rich fog of fertiliser and animal feed hanging thick around me. To my left, rows of muddy allotment plots lie dormant, only a scattering of greenery from the hardy winter vegetables: savoy cabbages, brussels sprouts, celeriac and beetroot. To the left, a large network of pathways wind around wooden pens, home to braying grey donkeys, pottering goats and sheep. In the far distance, a man-made pond lies empty beside a small apiary painted in yellow and white.

It's been a long time since I last visited this place. Not that I didn't like it, but I spent most of my weekends with Julia and, as much as she loved her work here, she never quite wanted to visit as a guest.

'Excuse me.' I raise my hand to the lone visible staff member, a fresh-faced twenty-something covering some outdoor chairs with a tarpaulin.

'Yes, darlin'?' she replies.

'Sorry,' I begin, a pre-apology for the odd request I've brought with me. 'I know you're closing in half an hour.'

'No problem at all, how can I help?'

'I know this is …' I begin, already starting to feel awkward. 'My name's Arthur Mason, I was … I was Julia Mason's husband; I don't know if you worked here at the same time or—'

I sense her answer in the sudden change of tone. A look of gentle shock overcomes the woman before me, her mouth slightly open in a soft 'Oh'. I feel a cloud of shared sadness drift between us both, connecting us immediately, lingering as it always does.

'I, um …' I fumble in my jacket pocket. 'Just so you know that I'm telling the truth.'

I withdraw the single photograph and hold it out between us. Julia and I on the cobbles outside the Southwark Registry Office, a bright blue suit and sleek white evening gown, my arm hugging her close towards me.

'No, it's ok.' She nods, grinning slightly. 'We used to share holiday photos. I remember you now.'

'Oh, well, that's good.' I smile, collecting myself and replacing the picture.

'I'm really sorry for your loss,' she states earnestly. 'Julia was … We loved her.'

'She was a really special person,' I agree. 'I was wondering. I've just been looking for examples of Julia in her daily life. I don't know if you have any pictures of her, and no worries if not … I'm just trying to find some more memories of her, I suppose.'

I see a familiar sad smile appear on her face, a look of pure sympathy. I might once have mistaken it as pity, but I realise now that's rarely the case. Pity is one-sided, detecting a sorrow in someone that doesn't exist in yourself. There's perhaps nothing quite as mutual as the pain of human loss, of grief. I'm starting to feel as if my severance from those feelings is, in turn, a severance from one of the few collective forces in this vast, disparate world.

'I actually think I have something.' She smiles in cheerful revelation. 'Come inside.'

I follow this stranger into the warm interior of the farm's activity room. Animal masks made from paper plates line the walls: owls, foxes, a lone and displaced panda. Drawers of coloured paper, pencils, glue, safety scissors and countless other materials run along the yellow walls.

The staff member unlocks a set of filing cabinets and skitters through the myriad contents, before lifting an entire folder out and shutting the drawer.

'One second, ok?'

I nod as she disappears into the back room.

Looking around, I notice a familiar smiling face on the wall. I draw steadily closer, making out staff photographs hanging on the individual branches of a painted tree.

I see Julia in winter, standing out by the animal pens in her favourite fleece, the fleece she never forgave herself for losing. I know she's only smiling for the photograph, but even so, there's a genuine light in her eyes, that easy, kind smile that I could never hope to replicate.

Dr Codelle's work had been undeniably successful. She had taken every memory I held of Julia and robbed it of feeling. Even now, when I think back to those memories, to the entirety of our life together, I can't retrieve an ounce of the love that once filled my waking hours.

But I wasn't the entirety of Julia's life, I was just lucky enough to be there for most of it. There are other memories out in the world, new memories of the person I loved, entirely untouched by Codelle's process. Moments that I could actually feel something for, if I'm not too far gone already.

'Ok, bear with me!'

My new acquaintance backs into the room, easing a tall trolley through the narrow door. The trolley carries an old television, a shelf below it sporting a DVD player. I thank her as she plugs the electronics into the wall, turns the television on and thumbs through a series of blank channels.

'We have this activity day every spring,' she explains as she finds the correct channel. 'The kids do a presentation, like a play, about things waking up, the life cycle. It's nice. Everyone who works here has a go at running it.'

She reaches into the folder and pulls out a translucent CD case, clicking out the disc inside and pressing it into the player.

'I forgot about this,' she says, almost sheepishly. 'Sorry about that.'

The screen bursts into life.

'Ok, guys! So, there are four parts of the room split between spring, summer, autumn and … ?'

The room of energetic children yell the word 'winter' boldly into the air. The staff member onscreen is smiling at their answer, speaking once again with unbridled, infectious enthusiasm.

'That's right! Ok! So, I'm going to say something that happens at some time in the year, and I want you to run to the part of the room when it takes place – so if I said "Bears hibernate in …"'

The children stream past you, crossing the floor to the side of the room with the giant paper snowflake on the wall. You stoop over the few kids who didn't run, guiding them with a gentle hand towards their friends.

'That's right, it's winter! Great job! Ok, what's next …'

I watch the rush of feet as the simple game continues, as the woman with the unbeaten, brilliant smile guides them on their way. The sound of your voice, the sight of you dancing through the room as it lights up around you. It all shines in glorious technicolour from the screen, enriching the very fabric of my soul.

The tears arrive quickly, expected and welcome, flowing freely down my cheeks as the breath catches in my throat.

338

It's not like it was and maybe it will never be that way again, but it's something, a swell of effortless and intoxicating love that rises in my chest and across my body.

It's glorious, it's beautiful and it hurts terribly.

Acknowledgements

To Steve Anderson, Sharon Fitzpatrick and Kirsty Anderson. You've listened to more ideas than any of us can count. You've been my biggest supporters and the inspiration behind my most noble characters. I hope I can someday encourage others half as much as you've encouraged me.

To Jane Flint, who stood among several incredible English teachers at King Ecgbert School, but who made it a personal point to encourage me to pursue writing. I always hoped I'd get the chance to acknowledge you in my first book.

To the NoSleep community, whose gracious reaction to my story the Left/Right Game is the only reason I ever got noticed. I genuinely owe you a debt I can never repay, for your enthusiasm to read my work and your patience in waiting for ten (frankly, indulgently long) instalments to be posted. Perhaps the most exciting period of my life was the time we were discovering that story together.

To Kate Prentice and everyone at 42 Management, thank you for believing in me, and for making this all possible. You were the first people in the industry to invest in me and I'll do everything I can to prove you right.

To Dan Erlij and Orly Greenburg at UTA, thank you for representing me and for advocating for this story.

To Joely Day, the copy editor who gave this book so much of her attention. I promise I've since learned to correctly spell 'guarantee'.

To Alexandra Cliff at Rachel Mills Literary, for representing the language rights of this book and taking this story beyond the shores of Great Britain.

To Josh Prime, who read through the story and gave me incredible insight. In your feedback, you asked me for a co-writing credit, and I want to answer from the bottom of my heart. No.

To my literary agent, Marilia Savvides, who has been my greatest ally in the writing of this book. You were patient when I needed patience, pushed me when I needed pushing and remained utterly gracious throughout. I don't know anyone who understands my writing better, and I will never underestimate my good fortune in getting to work with you.

To my editor, Alison Hennessey, whose every note served to elevate this work. Thank you for taking a chance on me. Without your insights, *The Grief Doctor* would have just been a story; it was through your guidance that it became a book.

To Emily Jones, Grace Nzita-Kiki, Faye Robinson and all the amazing people at Raven Books, I admired your publishing house before I ever got a chance to work with you, and I've only come to admire you more. Thank you for taking a chance on me.

To Ye-Sung, the most inspirational person I have ever known. Any of the authenticity of Arthur and Julia's relationship; the friendship, the mutual support, the admiration, it all came from the time we've spent together. I couldn't have written this story without your ideas, your insight and your encouragement, and I will never understand how I got so lucky.

A Note on the Author

JACK ANDERSON lives with his wife in Sheffield. He is the author of the viral internet serial 'Has Anyone Heard of the Left/ Right Game?', which has since been adapted into a hit QCode podcast. *The Grief Doctor* is his debut novel.

A Note on the Type

The text of this book is set in Bembo, which was first used in 1495 by the Venetian printer Aldus Manutius for Cardinal Bembo's *De Aetna*. The original types were cut for Manutius by Francesco Griffo. Bembo was one of the types used by Claude Garamond (1480–1561) as a model for his Romain de l'Université, and so it was a forerunner of what became the standard European type for the following two centuries. Its modern form follows the original types and was designed for Monotype in 1929.